Sisterhood of Hermia

A Collection of Six Women's Studies

JMC North

ISBN: 979-8-5478-7137-5

Dedication

This collection is dedicated
to my husband and son who partnered my shenanigans,
to my father who instilled the thirst for knowledge,
to my family for their inspiration and support,
to my friends and colleagues for their encouragement,
to my many students, and
to all women.

Introduction

William Shakespeare in *A Midsummer Night's Dream* portrays the complexity of women's lives. A major female character in that play is Hermia. The comedy reveals that romance and love can be chaotic and misconstrued. Lysander says, "The course of true love never did run smooth" (Act 1, Scene 1). In addition, the fairies play havoc while Bottom says, "To say the truth; reason and love keep little company together nowadays" (Act 3, Scene 1).

The studies in this book are based on the female characters found in the three books of the *Battle Axe Ranch Trilogy* and present events from the female viewpoint. Each woman is a true member of the sisterhood of Hermia. Their lives are not simple. Like Hermia, they struggle against society's expectations of women.

The statuary in Vigeland's Park in Oslo, Norway documents the stages of life from the very young to the old. In the *Sisterhood of Hermia,* mirroring Vigeland's work, the reader will find stories of women at different stages and situations of life, confronting the challenges of their lives.

Torri's Path

In the small western mountain town of Riverside nestled against the Rockies, a tiny baby girl was born to Bobby and Doris McClure. As the sleeping baby yawned, her two brothers BJ (Bobby Jr) and Ronnie stood beside the bed. They were five and two. They looked at each other, rolling their eyes at the doll-like baby. *What was this bundle doing in their mom's arms? How did she get there?*

Their dad Bobby quietly said, "I can't believe it's a girl. We'll have to call her 'Victoria' instead of 'Victor'." He lifted her delicate, tiny pink hand with one of his rough, oil stained fingers, playfully feeling her soft skin. Baby Victoria spread out her miniature-sized fingers and folded them around her dad's finger. "My, my. She does have a grip," he proudly said, smiling at his wife and then, at his sons.

The McClure family had added a daughter. They had been residents of the town operating their gas station, garage, and renting a couple of small houses. The town folks were glad to hear the news of a new baby added to their family. They watched the three children grow up and become an important part of their community and were shocked by the tragedy that hit the family years later.

Victoria became "Torri" shortly after her birth. Her mom would take her to the garage in a little bassinet and nurse her between customers. In their early years of starting their business, it took both parents to run the gas station and garage. While her mom took care of the cash register in the office, her dad pumped the gas in between working on vehicles in the garage. When a vehicle would pull up to their gas pump, the tires crossed a buzzer that let Bobby know in the back that a customer wanted gas. He would sprint out to pump the gas and return back to the garage.

Even though Torri appeared to be a perfect baby, she was fussy. She had colic at all hours of the night. Her mom couldn't understand why her two sons had been such good babies while her daughter had become so much trouble. Torri cried and fussed while her two brothers in their bedrooms lay listening to their loud bawling sister. *Why couldn't she just go to sleep?*

When Torri began to crawl, her mom brought a small cardboard box of toys with her to the station. She put down an old blanket with the box in the corner for her daughter to play which kept her busy while her mom worked.

Later when she grew older, her mom bought a big yellow storybook that had beautiful pictures and little poems and stories. When business would slow down during the day, her mom would read to her. Torri would listen to the fantastic stories that her mom read: stories of trolls under a bridge, of twinkling stars, of mermaids in the sea, and of goblins at night. The little reddish-brown headed girl never got enough of those stories, for customers would always show up and interrupt her mom. That's when Torri's little temper would grow to a scream, crying. Finally, her mom had to stop reading at the station and only read to her at home before bedtime.

Most of her young years were uneventful. Being the youngest, she became independent and created her own little world. Her brothers had little to do with her when she was a young baby. She would toddle towards the back of the garage where there was an alley. In a small stretch of ground, her dad had built her a little dirt box where she had a few toys—wooden blocks, a toy shovel and bucket, and a couple of rag dolls—that she would play with until her mom came to get her.

Gradually, her world expanded when she would ride her tricycle down the alley, playing with her imaginary friends. Being the only girl gave her freedom that she dearly loved more than anything. Plus her dad spoiled her, calling her "sunshine." When she wanted something, her dad would give in to her with just a sweet smile and a blink or two of her hazel green eyes and a "Please daddy." Her two brothers noticed how different their parents treated her than when they had grown up. They were raised in a disciplined world. But not Torri. Her parents would let her carry out her temper tantrums without any words.

As Torri grew up, her brothers put up with having a young sister around. When they were home from school or were off in the summer, the two followed their dad around, learning about being a mechanic. As the oldest brother, BJ had to take on the responsibility of her when her parents were busy. He became a caring, thoughtful, and considerate brother.

7

However, growing up with her second brother Ronnie had been a different experience than with BJ. Torri's relationship with him gave her a delightful thrill, but yet, he bothered, irritated, and aggravated her. Even though she loved him, Ronnie could set her temper on fire. He loved to tease her and get her mad which he did about every day when they were young: tugging her pigtails, having water fights, or tickling her. It had never been serious, just child's play. He called her "freckles," taunting and teasing her about them. She had never even noticed her freckles. When she cried about his teasing, her mom had reassured her that the freckles would fade when she grew up. Despite those comforting words, those freckles bothered her the rest of her life. They never faded away enough for her. When she grew older, she covered them up with make-up.

One summer around the 4th of July, Ronnie began teasing her with the fireworks that he had purchased. They were a sorted package of small firecrackers, a few bottle rockets, a Roman candle, the long sparklers, and the round cherry bombs. While holding a little firecracker, he would strike a match and tell her that she'd better run because he was going to throw it at her. All of the fireworks scared her at that young age, so she would run away screaming from the fizzling firecracker. He would laugh and call her "chicken."

At night, he would lite his collection of fireworks. He lit the bright sparklers for Torri, but she didn't care for them. She preferred the bottle rockets and the Roman candle the best and watched them shoot off into the dark night sky. When she was older, Torri would lite off a couple of her own firecrackers and threatened Ronnie to run. He looked at her and laughed, daring her to throw them. Knowing the danger of fireworks, her parents finally put a stop to the two of them threatening each other every 4th of July.

One Saturday afternoon, she found another way to get back at her brother. Since he was always in the garage working on cars, she started calling him a "grease monkey." While he worked on a car, she danced around like a monkey, teasing him. Suddenly, he came after her, smearing his greasy hands on her little freckled face. He told her that she was really the grease monkey. Screaming and crying her dad rescued her, giving Ronnie a reprimand and making him sweep and clean the station and garage for the next two weeks. Torri delighted in the fact that her brother had gotten into trouble that afternoon.

Sometime later, Torri found out what being in trouble meant. A week after school started, she decided to climb the old tree in the backyard. This wasn't her first time up there even though her parents had told her never to climb that tree. She had ignored her parents warning, unlike her brothers, for she loved the challenge.

That day, she had climbed all the way up the old tree, feeling good about her climb. Up in the tree, she could see all around her neighborhood, feeling the fresh air whip through her hair and against her face. When she was on her way down, her hands slipped on the last branch, and she fell about ten feet. As her bottom hit the ground, she tried to brace herself with her left arm, but it broke and collapsed. When she felt it snap, her painful scream split the air clear throughout the neighborhood.

BJ had been at home; he carefully scooped her up and rushed her to the gas station with Torri sobbing loudly. Her mom immediately took her down to the doctor's office. While they waited, any little movement around her sent her crying. Her mom had been looking at a magazine; every time she turned a page, Torri would whimper, telling her not to turn the page. Her mom looked at her and said, "Nonsense." Finally, the nurse called them back to the doctor's office. After a few torturous x-rays, the doctor placed a big, plastered cast on her lower left arm and told her she was lucky that she didn't break her elbow.

The incident imposed all kinds of changes to her life at home and at school. At home, her mom was furious with her, for she had told her daughter over and over to stay out of that old tree. Her mom had to cut open the seams of the left sleeves of all her school dresses and blouses. Torri also had to wear an irritating sling around her neck.

Her dad took another extreme step; he decided to chop down the old tree. A few days later with some of his friends, the tree came down. With the sound of the chainsaws buzzing in her ears, Torri stood at her window inside her bedroom with tears sliding down her cheeks as she saw her beloved tree being cut down. Her parents had a frightening experience and had reacted the only way they knew how. Her disobedience disappointed her parent's trust in her.

At school with her cast on, her classmates were told to be careful and not to bump her arm. Her teacher gave her special attention on all their lessons until she just wanted to disappear under her desk. At first, her classmates felt sorry for her, but later, they resented her.

But their school recesses had been the worst time for Torri. She would be left out, sitting lonely by herself watching all her classmates play. Sadly, Torri couldn't play on the swings, the slide, or the monkey bars. Before her broken arm, her favorite game had been tetherball. She loved hitting that white ball and watch it wind itself around the pole. That's when two girls name Doreen Retter and Patty Hauklind became her friends. The two of them would sit with her and talk for a few minutes outside.

After six weeks, the cast came off. Her left arm appeared thin, pale, and strange to behold, appearing so different than her right arm. The doctor gave her a special exercise to strengthen her emaciated arm. She had to stand in front of a wall, place her hands on it, and push, back and forth, to strengthen it. When she would exercise against the wall, sharp pains shot through her skinny arm, bringing tears to her eyes.

While she was still young, another event happened that changed their home life. A young Dave Knox had come to live with the McClure's. After his parents had lost their ranch to the bank in Hadley, Dave had run away, relieving his parents the burden of raising a child. The rumors said that his folks kicked him out, but that had not been the truth.

Coming to Riverside, he had been hitch-hiking and homeless when he stopped in at the McClure's Garage one winter night looking for work. Her dad couldn't give him a job but brought him home for a good meal and a bed for one evening. Dave slept on the couch that night, but in the morning, her mom wouldn't hear of putting him out on the street. Thus, he stayed and lived at their home for a few years.

Her brother Ronnie and Dave bunked together and became like brothers. Her mom insisted that if he went to school, Dave could stay as long as he wanted. He enrolled and finished high school with her brother. In the summers, he worked the ranches wherever or whenever he could, saving his money. He also developed into a close friend to Torri who was still a young, skinny kid. Eventually, he moved out on his own.

One year during her childhood, her dad fixed and painted a used bike. Her brother BJ would keep her bike tires repaired when they would go flat. And flats would happen all the time, for none of the streets in the town were paved. Only main street was paved since it was a state highway. However, her bike let her go farther around town and the surrounding area. She rode her bike everywhere but avoided the alleys since all of them had barrels of burning or smoldering garbage.

After checking with her mom, she liked to ride over to her friend Doreen's house and play. Most of the time, they played with her paper dolls. She had a book of cardboard dolls and their paper wardrobes. The book was title *Terry May and her Friends*. The two of them had fun changing the dolls' outfits from going to the beach to a fancy party. They would fold the tabs on top of the outfits to the cardboard doll. Each time Torri went over, the hour playing past quickly.

Another time when she came over, Doreen introduced Torri to the game of jacks. From her dresser bureau, she took out a bag that held ten six-pronged metal pieces with a tiny, red ball. Her friend would push her bedroom rug back to clear a place where they could play. Doreen was really good at jacks, picking up the jacks and the ball with swift motions with her hand. Torri loved watching her more than playing. Doing well at the beginning, she often couldn't get past three jacks at a time and catch the ball. But Doreen was fast, going through the game with lightning speed. It was obvious to Torri that she must have practiced quite a bit to get that good.

One place that Torri like to ride her bike was down by the big Rock River which snaked around the town. There was a big eddy along the river that had become a swimming hole for the young kids. During the run-offs, no one swam there, but later in the summer the whirlpool slowed its spin to allow them to swim. When they did, they would emerge blue-lipped from the cold water since the river was fed by the icy glaciers high in the mountains. The river never warmed up even in the warm summer months.

When Torri went down to the swimming hole, she would just wade around near the banks, too afraid to go into the deep part.

One warm summer day, she had ridden her bike down to the river and saw several of her friends swimming around. A few had their inner tubes.

"Come join us," they hollered. "It's fun."

"I will. I'll be back," Torri replied. She pedaled quickly back home. Coming into the house, she asked her mom if she could go down to the whirlpool and swim with her friends.

Her mom replied, "You don't know how to swim."

"I know, but BJ fixed me up an old inner tube and I just want to float around. My friends are all down there swimming with their inner tubes. Please mom. Can I? I'll be careful," begged Torri.

"All right but keep your tennis shoes on. That pool has all kinds of junk in it. You could cut your foot and get an infection," cautioned her mom.

"Can I take one pair of my old jeans and cut them off?" she asked.

"Yes, there's a worn out pair in your bottom drawer. Take one of the old bath towels with you. Please remember to keep your tennis shoes on," replied her mom.

"I promise. Thanks, mom," said Torri, excited to go floating on the old inner tube that BJ had fixed up for her. Quickly, she got ready and left.

When she returned to the whirlpool, some of her friends were warming up on the shore with bath towels wrapped around them. When she walked to the edge of the pool, she threw her inner tube onto the water.

One of her friends came over, and said, "Get in. I'll push you out."

She squatted down and positioned herself into the tube. When her bottom hit the water, it took her breath away—shockingly cold. As soon as she was in, her friend shoved her out into the slow moving pond. After she floated, two girls brought over one of their inner tubes and sat in it together, laughing and splashing around. Torri joined them as the eddy moved them around and around. Then, the girls stepped out of the water, wrapping their towels around themselves, shivering.

One of them hollered at Torri, "We're too cold. We're leaving." The others left with them and waved goodbye. Disappointed that they were leaving, she waved back.

By herself, Torri leaned back and relaxed as the inner tube circled the pool for a while. She enjoyed the feel of the eddy when, unexpectedly, the air changed, and she gazed up at the once blue sky. In the distance, she heard the rumble of thunder. Knowing she would have to leave soon, she paddled around one more time.

Suddenly, she saw the bright flash of lightning and heard the crack of thunder above her. All of a sudden from the darkened clouds above, the rain came down in sheets. Soon, the river outside the pond became muddy. While she paddled back towards shore, the eddy's water turned murky.

A swift undercurrent caught her inner tube and pulled her out into the wide muddy river. She frantically paddled trying to get back to shore. Torri thought about jumping off, but fear gripped her body. She didn't know what she should do. Not knowing how to swim, she feared the cold river water more than her inner tube, so she stayed on.

Frantically looking around for an overhanging branch to grab, she saw the town slowly pass her by: the barn and the corrals, the town park with wooden picnic tables, and the thick willows lining the river. She saw a few people walking away from the river, and she waved frantically. Only a little toddler saw her and waved at her. But her mom picked the child up and headed away. She hollered "Help me" several times, but her voice was drowned out by the thunder every time.

After passing the town and coming around a bend, she saw a fisherman standing on shore, getting ready to leave. She hollered and waved. Shocked at seeing her, he waved back. Torri paddled hard and fast, and slowly, she moved towards him. When she came closer, she could tell it was Dave standing there. Waving at him, she hollered, "Dave. Help me."

He suddenly recognized her and moved closer to the edge of the river. Seeing that she was floating nearer, he stepped into the river and started walking towards her. Holding on to a low hanging tree branch, he moved out into the water. She could tell that the river swiftly moved around his waist while he struggled to keep his balance. Outstretching his arm, he reached for her as she twirled towards him.

Fortunately, he grabbed her outstretched hand just before she passed him. With their hands clasped together, he fought the current, bringing her in towards him. The inner tube almost knocked him over, but he snatched her into his arms. The tube kept going on down the river. Torri cried out for it, but he ignored her and slowly dragged her through the raging water towards the shore.

Breathing heavily, Dave stood on the shore, chilled and dripping wet. He looked at her, shocked, and said, "What in the hell are you doin' Torri?" He glared at her, upset at seeing her floating down the river.

"It happened so quickly. I was in the swimming hole going around and around. Then, an undercurrent took me out into the muddy river," she responded with her body quivering.

"Why didn't you jump off of the inner tube," he asked.

"I can't swim," she replied, shaking.

"Come on. Your lips are blue," replied Dave. He picked up his pole and his fishing bag and said, "You're cold and wet. Let's get you home."

"No. I can't go home yet. Take me back to the pool; I need to get my bath towel," said Torri.

Dave nodded his head, "Let's go," as he pointed to the direction out of the stand of trees. They walked through and around the thick willows, jumping over a small stream, until they reached the dirt road where his old black pickup was parked. He grabbed a blanket from behind his seat and wrapped it around her, holding her tightly against him and rubbing her back and arms to warm her up. Stepping into the pickup, he started up the engine and turned the heater on full blast.

As they drove away, Dave said, "That whirlpool is no place to swim. You should not go there. Listen, one kid nearly drowned there several years ago." She sat silently listening, shivering while she warmed up. "Promise me you won't ever go there again."

"Don't tell my parents. Please," said Torri, worried.

"I won't tell them *if* you promise not to go there again. I'm serious Torri," warned Dave, frowning and waiting for her to respond.

"I promise," she replied, sadly. Satisfied, he nodded.

After parking near the eddy, she stepped out of his pickup. He waited for a few minutes and just shook his head. She walked over and picked up her old towel near the shore.

Wrapping it around her waist, she said, "I'll walk home. I'm fine."

Dave didn't like leaving her, but he backed up his pickup and left.

The rainstorm had past but the cloudy sky still drizzled with a light rain. After Dave had left, Torri stood looking at the eddy and the whirling dark, murky water that seemed so peaceful, but in reality was a treacherous monster in disguise. She had been lucky. When she got home, she told BJ that one of the patches came off the inner tube and it sank. She never said a word about her frightening experience. That was the first time that Dave rescued her.

* * *

A few years later, BJ graduated high school. Seeking his own way, he left their family and the town to attend a trade school in Denver. Torri's life changed and she missed her big brother who had been always around her.

While he had been attending school, he met a girl named Sally Kordell and married her. After a short wedding, BJ stayed in Denver near her folks, found a job working at a garage, and started a family. Within a few years, they had two children, Roger and Pamela. After each of the grandchildren was born, her dad bought Doris and Torri bus tickets to Denver to see the babies.

In Denver, BJ and his family lived in a small apartment in a five-story building in a dirty, run-down part of the city. Torri liked Aunt Sally, for she seemed like a sister that she never had. They were a happy family, but her mom complained that an apartment was no place to raise their children. But BJ said they took the kids to the park whenever they could on the week-ends. When they returned to Riverside, her dad sat and listened intently about BJ and his family. Even though her parents didn't visit them, they called regularly to talk and keep up with their lives.

After her brother Ronnie grew older and could drive, he acquired his '58 black Impala with a huge 409 engine and started drag racing it with his friends—Dave Knox and George Weaver.

His focus was not on teasing Torri as much as before which was fine with her, but she had missed the interaction with her brother.

About that time, he had also purchased a used guitar and taught himself to play and sing. Even though he had worked at their family's gas station and garage, Ronnie began to play and sing at the bars on Friday or Saturday evenings. He told our parents that he had liked the money in his pocket to help pay for his car, but he had loved the music. When he performed, Ronnie had the warm Irish charm that made him liked by all. With his deep, strong voice, he had a passionate way to express the words in the songs. The town had loved to hear him perform.

Torri loved to hear her brother practice and sing at home in his bedroom. That's when she became interested in music; she would listen to the radio at night to the rock n' roll hits across the country. Even though she liked the new hit tunes, she also enjoyed the country sound that her brother had played on his guitar.

In addition, Torri and her girlfriends watched the television show that had been the rage across the country with young teens dancing to all the hit songs. After school, her girlfriends would come over to her home to watch the popular television show and dance to the songs. They'd learn all the dances—the pony, the twist, the watusi, the mashed potato and the different kinds of line dancing. Torri, Doreen, and Patty practiced all the different dances until they were exhausted.

During the school year, there had been several scheduled dances. Once in a while during the lunch period in the gymnasium, the students would have sock hops. While all the hit songs played, the young students would kick off their shoes and would dance in their socks to keep from scratching the pristine gym floor.

Torri's high school years passed quickly by. She took her required classes and had a narrow metal locker with a combination lock for her coat, books, and notebooks. In the scheduled study halls, she finished most of her homework. Once in a while, she would bring assignments home to finish. Mostly, her time at home was free to be with her friends, to listen and dance to music, and to do a few chores around the house. Her parents were busy with the station, the garage, and their rentals. Sometimes, Torri would help her mom if a renter moved out and the place needed repairs or paint. Her mom had a loving, care-free nature about her. Nothing rattled her, and she took problems in stride and did her best to solve them. The two had a comfortable relationship.

Her dad worked long hours and seldom stayed at home. If Torri wanted to see or talk to her dad, she would go down to the garage where he would be working on a customer's vehicle. He wouldn't stop working but would listen while his head was stuck under the hood or while he laid underneath a vehicle. Once in a while, he'd ask for a wrench, or a socket, or some tool from the bench. Torri became good at identifying the different tools around the garage. They had a close, quiet relationship where he said little, but when he did have advice, she listened. Her dad seemed to strike right into the heart of her teenage problems, making them seem smaller than she had thought.

Her boyfriends in high school had been one of her biggest problems. One boy named Darin whom she liked in her class was too immature to have any kind of relationship. He was a popular, loud, smart-alecky guy who played basketball and went out for track. He turned out to be her biggest competition in every class, claiming that he was smarter than she was. Torri didn't care about being smart, or popular, but she did like him and wished he'd ask her out. But he never did, just teased, joked, and laughed at her in school every day. He knew how to set off her Irish temper. She didn't even know why she had been attracted to him, but she mooned over him despite his unruly personality.

When she mentioned Darin to her dad, he told her that she could do better (he knew the family). Her dad said, "Don't chase a guy if he doesn't like you. You can't force a relationship. Now, when I met your mom in high school, we were drawn together. Torri, it was like two magnets coming together by an unknown force. When we were apart, we were always thinking of the other person. A relationship should be a natural attraction, not forced. Does that make any sense?"

"Yes dad. I'll keep that in mind," replied Torri who kept that advice close to her heart, hoping to meet someone like that someday.

During her high school years, her dates were with guys whom she didn't particularly like, but she went out with them. She never became serious with any of them; most of them disappeared out of her life. But that didn't stop the many tears coming from her eyes at night.

Torri felt left out and lonely. Many of the other girls at school had steady boyfriends. Those girls flaunted their boyfriends' class rings on long, chained necklaces, held hands going to class, and went to all the dances together. Torri kept her head held high at school and didn't let anyone know the hurt that she felt. She finally thought that she had to leave Riverside to ever find happiness.

* * *

After graduating high school, Torri decided to make a big change to her life. She applied to attend the junior college in Midler along with her two girlfriends, Doreen and Patty. During their senior year, the three of them talked often about what to do after graduation. Doreen recalled that her brother had gone to Midler's junior college. Patty had an aunt and uncle who lived in Midler, so her parents would allow her to go there, and her relatives in Midler could help them find a place to stay. Thus, the three started making plans. When she asked what they planned to study, her friends said, "We're going for our MRS degree." She thought they were serious about their studies until she realized that they were going to college to find a guy to marry.

Torri had her own goal: to get out of that small town of Riverside. She wanted to be on her own and to do what she wanted without depending on her parents. Torri did not have any desires to get married, but her friends gave her the reason to leave.

Under the belief that Torri would be attending the junior college, her parents were surprised, but delighted with her decision to go to college. Her dad sat down with pencil and paper, figuring out how they could afford to send her. Her parents were glad to support her and ended up giving her enough money for the tuition, but she needed to work part-time to pay for her part of the rent. Unlike her situation, her girlfriends' parents paid for their college and their rent with a small monthly allowance. They would not have to work while going to college.

The fall after they had graduated, the girls all moved down to Midler together, living in a partly furnished basement apartment. Even though Torri's family were surrounded by vehicles, she never had her own car. Doreen was the only one who had wheels, and it was a grey jeep with a canvas top. The three girls drove down to Midler in Doreen's jeep while Patty's parents drove down with their belongings loaded in the back of their car and trunk. Patty's aunt and uncle also showed up and helped them get settled into their apartment. All three were excited to be finally on their own.

For Torri, living on her own was fraught with disappointments. She became homesick within a week away from her family. The cost of a long distance call was too much for her. She missed hearing their voices. However, after a time, she began to love the feeling of being on her own.

One drawback was that her girlfriends were hard to live with; they lived like slobs. Torri tried not to be so particular, but the apartment became so messy in a short time. The kitchen sink filled up with dirty dishes, the bathtub had a grey ring around the sides, and the garbage can was spilling over. Here in this basement apartment, they needed to change the way they lived.

Finally, one day, Torri told them that they should divide the cleaning up among them. Her two friends didn't want to do anything, complaining that they were too busy. However, she insisted that if they ever wanted to have guys over, or maybe have a party, they'd better keep the apartment cleaner. Somehow that struck a chord with them, so they agreed to divide up the chores. She made a little chart, showing how they could rotate the chores without always doing the same thing every week. For the most part, the dishes did get washed, the bathtub looked cleaner, and the garbage can was emptied every week.

When registration day came, Patty wanted all of them to take the same classes so that they could study together. However, Torri suspected that Patty wasn't above copying or cheating to get her grade. Doreen wouldn't do that, but Torri decided she definitely did not want to be with her girlfriends in the same classes.

While Torri sat with a college counselor, she realized she didn't know what she wanted to take. She signed up for three courses: a math class, a government class, and the community choir. In her mind, she couldn't justify spending the money as a full-time student. However, when her parents phoned to find out how she was doing, Torri never told them that she was only a part-time student.

When they went to the bookstore to purchase their textbooks for their classes, Torri couldn't believe the prices. But she discovered the used textbooks and purchased those instead of the brand-new ones. That helped save the meager money she had left. Within a few days, she found herself a part-time job as a waitress at a local diner to pay for the rent and to have some spending money.

Doreen and Patty soon became friends with some college guys who knew where all the keggers were on the week-ends. Fixing her up with blind dates, Torri went along just to be part of the college scene, but every guy that she met never impressed her. Most of the college crowd were there just to get "shit-faced" drunk, as her brothers would say. Doreen and Patty were there to catch a guy, so they shamelessly flirted and encouraged the guys to kiss and make out at the parties. Sometimes, they left, leaving her to find her own ride back to the apartment. Torri drank a little too much at her first parties, but the hangovers in the morning made her wish she hadn't. Sometimes, she had to work on the weekends at the diner. When she drank too much, she had been miserable trying to work. As time went on, she learned to limit her drinking.

At one of those keggers, Torri met a guy named Floyd Tratone. Quickly, he latched onto her, as they stood around and drank beer. Floyd seemed nervous at first. He was medium height with short brown hair and a pocked face from acne as a teenager. But he was friendly, so Torri drank and talked with him. Wearing a black leather jacket, he drove a motorcycle and tried to give her a ride home on it. But she refused, saying she didn't feel safe on one. He asked her for her phone number and said he'd like to call her.

After that evening, Floyd did call her for a date the next week; she refused, saying she was busy studying. But he would not leave her alone and would call the next day and the next. She recalled what her dad told her about chasing someone. He was doing that to her. Finally, she asked Doreen and Patty what to do.

Patty said, "Go out with the guy. Give him 'a break.' He didn't seem that bad to me."

"He's friendly, but I don't like him that much," Torri replied.

"Go out with him and let him down gradually," said Patty.

Doreen piped up and said, "I would rather be dating than stuck in this basement apartment."

Nodding, she said, "I guess I will," as she decided to go out with him.

When Floyd called to take her out, and she said "Yes."

They double-dated with one of his friends and they went to a drive-in movie. Floyd and Torri sat in the back seat, and he told her how much he liked her. He complimented her on how she looked and loved the color of her hair. To deflect the focus on her, she asked about him. That opened up the flood gates and he grumbled about how unhappy he felt.

He was in his second year at college, and admitted, "I'm on probation. My life is miserable. Meeting you has given me hope."

She knew right away that she didn't want anything to do with this guy. She recognized the "pity me" line. His victim's view meant that he had no ambition in life and seemed a loser to her.

While the couple in the front seat were kissing and making out, Floyd glanced at them and then back at her. He moved towards her and held her in his arms, kissing her lips a couple of times. His tongue attempted to open her lips, but she turned away quickly, shaking her head. He hesitated for a second, then moved to kiss her neck. Chills went down her spine, but she had no real feelings towards him and felt no attraction to him. His hands slipped underneath her coat, and he caressed her breast a couple of times. He pulled her tighter towards him, breathing heavily. She could tell his desires were stirred. As she kissed him, she still didn't feel any emotions as she went on making out. Finally, she leaned back and told him she needed to catch her breath. That gave her a chance to talk.

"Listen. You're a nice guy, and I like you as a friend. But I want to date around. This is my first year at college. I hope you understand," Torri whispered to him. In the darkness of the back seat, he still held her tightly against his body.

"Sure, that's fine with me. We can date around. But I like you," he whispered back, obviously ignoring her point. "I've got you in my arms right now. Come on and kiss me."

He moved towards her again and continued to kiss her lips and her neck. They made out until the movie had ended. She didn't want to hurt his feelings; he seemed so sensitive and lonely. His sadness had worked on her that evening, but never again.

21

After that date, he would call and ask her out again and again. She would refuse him, making excuses. A few times, he would drive to their apartment at night and stop. She could hear his motorcycle's engine idling outside. He seemed to be waiting for her, for he hadn't gotten the hint that she didn't want to go out with him.

When Floyd wasn't calling or harassing her, her three classes during the week and her waitress job kept her busy. She found herself enjoying the community choir, for they sang all kinds of music. Scheduled on Wednesday evenings, her music class became her favorite one. The music director told them that there would be no exams, but they had a final performance at the end of the semester. In addition, their attendance and participation would also decide their grade. She kept that night free so that she could attend. Her other two classes were in the morning. She worked afternoons at the diner and sometimes, a few week-ends. The three friends posted their class schedule on the fridge, but they seldom saw each other during the day.

Torri made a real effort at focusing on her courses for the first weeks. With chalk in hand, her math professor worked problems on the board all hour, his back to them as he talked to the board. The room had three chalk boards, so he went from the front board to the two side boards on either side of the room. At first, the math problems that he had worked were those that she had done in high school. However, her math professor said that the first two weeks of class were a review before they started on the new material. Finally, after the review, the new material lost her quickly as she glared at his back while he worked the complicated problems on the three boards each class meeting.

When the students filed out of the classroom one day, Torri overheard another girl say she couldn't understand the problems and that she was going to drop the class. Torri caught up with her and introduced herself. After talking with her, they went together to the main office and dropped the math class. Torri was relieved, for she knew that she would certainly fail that class with the professor talking to the board all semester.

Her other course that she had taken was a government class. Her government professor droned on and on in a voice which nearly put everyone to sleep. She tried to read the assignments before class, but sometimes the chapters were so long that she hadn't finished them by class time. She often fell asleep reading that textbook. However, with pencil in hand, she took notes in class to keep focused.

Unfortunately, Floyd pestered her and continued to call. He wanted to know what she was doing and wanted to go out. Each time, she told him that she had to study or had other dates. And then he finally showed up at the diner where she worked. He'd sit in a booth and order coffee. Once in a while, he'd order a piece of pie or a dish of ice cream. When she served him, he wanted to talk. Not wanting to be rude, she would make small talk with him for a while. But her work at the diner kept her busy, so it irritated her to think that he came just to speak to her. If she spent too much time with him, she could get fired. However, Floyd always left a big tip when he left. He pursued her all semester, calling or showing up at the diner or driving by the apartment.

During the semester, she saved up her extra wages and purchased a record player which could play both 45's and 78's records. Doreen and Patty started buying a few hit records and albums, and together, they had quite a large collection. The girls continued to play music and dance in the late afternoons. Plus, Patty had a radio that would play the hits every week from an Oklahoma station. Late at night, they would listen to the countdown. Her two friends had their favorite artists—Brenda Lee, Connie Francis, and Elvis Presley. Torri didn't have a favorite, for she liked them all even some of the early hits by Ritchie Valens, David Seville, the Kingston Trio with their folk songs. The songs were of love—the sadness and the heartbreak or the deep devotion. The words and music stirred their hearts as they listened and dreamed of their own situations, hoping to find love.

Finally, during the week of the Thanksgiving holiday, Doreen and Patty wanted to put on a party with all the college friends that they had met. Doreen had been dating a basketball player named Reese Votmer and he had several friends who wanted a party. Patty asked the owner of the apartment and for some reason, they agreed as long as they kept the noise level down. Excited, they cleaned up their messy apartment, taking them two days of hard work. Patty planned the snacks and punch while Doreen planned the music.

During the evening of the party, the apartment soon filled up with all their friends. The word got out, and others showed up as well—so much for keeping the noise down. As expected, the punch bowl got spiked right away. Liquor stirred up everyone. Doreen went around and told students to keep it down, but the party had escalated with everyone dancing, making out, and drinking.

Unfortunately for Torri, Floyd showed up. He cornered her in the kitchen; he talked while he drank, but he got bolder as the party went on. She listened to his sad story again; his parents wanted him to sell his motorcycle. He didn't wear a helmet and the insurance wouldn't pay if he didn't. He had argued with his parents about their demands. His classes weren't going well, and he figured he'd be kicked out at the end of this semester. He was an angry man: mad at his parents and mad at the college. He couldn't live his life the way he wanted to. As the party progressed, Floyd got louder, feeling that nothing was going his way. He kept drinking and soon became so drunk that he slurred his words.

With other people coming in and out of the kitchen, Torri tried to shake him off and move with the others into the living room. But Floyd kept her trapped, stepping in front of her and putting his arm around her. Eventually, he moved forward, pushing her up against the fridge with his body. His hands shifted around to hold her tighter against him as he kissed her despite her telling him to stop. He ground his hips into her body, grabbing her ponytail and forcefully, kissing her. As he sucked on her neck, she knew she would have hickies from his aggressiveness. Then, his tongue pushed over her lips and down her throat so fast that she gagged. In his drunken state, he kept telling her how much he liked her, mumbling in her ear as his wet tongue covered it. Torri had been struggling to keep her balance and tried to turn her head from his slobbering kisses, whispering "Stop...please, stop it."

Finally, her Irish temper took hold of her; she had had enough. She brought her hands down to his chest, shoved him away, and shouted, "Will you stop? I don't want to see you again. Get lost Floyd." Her fiery, harsh words shocked him, and he loudly cussed at her and called her a couple of nasty names.

Those standing around the kitchen heard him, shocked at his outburst. Doreen and her boyfriend Reese had been nearby. Reese stepped over and took hold of Floyd by his black leather jacket and said, "Hey, buster. It's time for you to leave."

Floyd struggled against Reese's hold, but he was too drunk to do anything. Shoving Reese's hands off his jacket, he stepped back. Angrily cussing, he stormed out of the basement, knocking couples out of his way, slammed the door, and stumbled up the stairs out to his motorcycle. Revving his motor, he screeched away.

Concerned about her friend, Doreen looked at Torri and asked, "Are you all right?"

"Yeah, what a jerk. Sorry, everyone," she replied apologizing to all those who stood around.

"No problem. It happens. Here, have a drink," answered Reese, handing her his pint of whiskey. Torri glanced at him, grabbed the pint, and took a deep drink from it. After that encounter, she needed a drink, cleaning out the nasty taste of Floyd in her mouth.

Reese had brought a university friend with him to the party. He motioned to his friend who had stood in the background to come over. When he did, Reese spoke to him quietly for a few minutes. His friend nodded. Torri stood taking another drink from the pint as the two came over to her.

"Torri, I'd like to introduce you to Joel Hanson. He's one of my friends I met at the university basketball camp last summer. Joel, this is Torri McClure, a friend of Doreen's," he said.

She looked up at the tall, blonde-haired, brown-eyed young friend of Reese's. Hesitating, she felt vulnerable after the incident, but Joel smiled at her, giving her a wink, and said "Hi, Torri. Would you like to dance?"

Despite the recent encounter, he thought she was beautiful. Joel gazed down her shapely figure and up to her bright hazel eyes. He took the pint of whiskey from her, swallowed a sip, and held his hand out for her to join him. Torri nodded. With the liquor coursing through her veins, she took his hand. *Yes, anything to get her out of the center of attention and the embarrassing moment.*

Together, they moved into the living room where another record had been playing. Lightheaded, Torri leaned into Joel as he took her into his warm arms. They danced slowly. Her emotions were shaking inside of her. She clung to him as if he were an anchor to keep her from losing herself in an emotional sea of hurt. She felt something drawing her to him. He held her carefully as if she would break into a thousand pieces.

After they danced, Joel moved over to the couch and suggested they sit. She apologized again for the incident in the kitchen. Nodding, he understood. But he wanted to get something straight, right from the beginning. He became serious and said, "I don't mind dating and being friends, but I don't want to get involved with anyone." She understood perfectly since she also just wanted to date around. He further explained, "I have responsibilities to my family who live in the Midwest."

He went on to tell her about his family. "My parents agreed that I could attend the university so far from home if I promised not to get caught up with a girl." She glanced at him curiously. He continued, "You see, for several generations, my family has had a dedicated military tradition. My parents expect me to follow in that tradition. Even though I play basketball at the university, my main focus has been the ROTC (Reserve Officers' Training Corps). After my bachelor's degree, I will go on into the Air Force and become a pilot."

His life seemed all mapped out; his father had made him swear on a Bible to promise to stay true to their military tradition, no matter what. She listened and thought: What a difference between Floyd's failing life and Joel's.

Torri told him she appreciated his honesty and agreed that they could be just friends. He relaxed after that and the two of them enjoyed the rest of the evening. They danced a few more times, closely. She had to keep reminding herself that he was off limits, but he certainly took her breath away with his quiet, gentle manners. Plus, he was a handsome guy.

Around midnight, everyone started to leave. Joel said "goodbye." He left without ever asking for her phone number. *Would she ever see him again?* Torri felt let down, but she shook her head. He had other commitments that kept him from getting close.

A day later, Doreen drove Patty and Torri home for Thanksgiving. They stayed for the short time, enjoying being back with their families. For Torri, it had been a typical holiday. Her mom fixed the usual turkey dinner, and her dad kept the gas station opened. After closing for an hour, he came home, ate quickly, and went back. He also had worked most of the other days at the station and in the garage, he had been repairing a rancher's pickup.

On Sunday, Doreen picked Patty and Torri up and they drove back to Midler and their basement apartment. While the semester continued on, Doreen managed to drag Patty to their classes. They studied together, worked on their assignments, and wrote their papers. Their portable typewriters would be tapping away during Thursday evenings, for their papers were due the next day.

Torri's government class was not going well. Not only did she receive a low grade at midterm, but also many of the other students did. The professor then gave them the option to read an assigned book from his special reading list and write a report. Torri debated with herself whether it would be worth it or not, but she had written book reports before. She decided to do the extra credit, walked to the library, and selected a book from his list. The book looked dry and uninteresting, but she would read it over the Christmas holiday.

Since her girlfriend had been dating Reese, Doreen would attend the college basketball games throughout the rest of the semester. She talked Torri into going a couple of times. They sat in the bleachers and watched the team play. While she watched, she thought about Joel and their one evening together. She could easily get serious with such a great guy like him, but he had been so focused on his military plans. She held her tender feelings for him tightly in her heart. Doreen gushed over Reese and thought that Torri liked Joel. But after she explained, Doreen thought that she should not give up on Joel. But Torri knew differently.

Despite everything, the two of them did get together another time. This time Joel had come up with the university team to play against Reese's college team. It was an exposition game to recruit potential players from the junior college. Through Reese, she found out that Joel would be at another party after the game and that he wanted to be with her. Doreen insisted that she attend the exposition game between the two teams. She reluctantly went. They watched as the university team eviscerated the college team. But it was all done in fun. Reese and Joel loved the competition.

Torri came with Doreen and Reese to the party. Joel met her at the door and took her coat. This was another typical kegger with drinking and dancing. The basketball teams had dressed up with each wearing a sports coat, white shirt and tie, and a pair of dark slacks. Joel had on a rich, brown corduroy jacket and a brown tie to match. Most of the players at the party had taken off their jackets, pocketed their ties, and rolled up their sleeves. But Joel didn't; he only loosened his tie. He looked even more handsome than Torri recalled.

The two of them spent the evening drinking beer from the keg and dancing. He talked about his basketball and his studies. She asked about ROTC, and he laughed and said that he was still in the basic course with morning fitness runs and a military class. He explained that he had a ROTC scholarship which put a lot of pressure on him. Even though she admired him more than before, she kept her feelings buried. They danced several times, drank, and quietly talked.

But on the last dance, Joel became more attentive to her. When they danced closely together, he relaxed more and caressed her lower back as they moved to the music. His head leaned down against hers with his breath on her neck. She felt his tenderness and her knees weakened as her body leaned into his body with her heart beating hard. For the first time in her life, she felt her desires rise within her, while her mind said: *he's off limits*. At the end of the song, he gave her a slow kiss to her temple. He paused and held her while he breathed in her scent. Obviously, he had been controlling his desires. Then, he stepped back, and the warmth and tenderness disappeared. *How could he control himself? How could he stop?* She wanted more from him.

Sadly, the party ended. Joel helped her with her coat and said he'd ride back with her to the apartment. In the back seat of Reese's car, he held her hand in his, saying that he enjoyed being with her. She glanced at him, so handsome and dressed up. She glanced into his eyes as he spoke in the darkness of the car. He turned his head quickly avoiding her questioning eyes. *Why deny his feelings?* She felt so confused and perplexed with this whole situation with him.

As they pulled up to the house and parked, Torri looked longingly at his soft lips and realized that Joel had never kissed her directly on the lips. Keeping herself together the best she could, she quickly said "goodbye," afraid that her Irish tongue and anger would destroy their evening or their friendship. She knew that his feelings were just below the surface; he again closed her off, restrained. He helped her out of the back seat and said that he hoped if he came up again that they could see each other. She nodded, huddled in her coat, and headed to the basement apartment while they drove away.

Tears started streaming down her cheeks as she raced down the stairs and unlocked the door, running to her bedroom and throwing herself on the bed, crying and sobbing. She had let herself fall for him; he had been able to keep his distance. *Why?* What a fool she had been.

Before her girlfriends came home that evening, she soaked in the bathtub for a while, resolving never to let herself get emotionally involved with a guy again. She then crawled into bed, exhausted physically and mentally, closed her sore, puffy eyes, and fell into a restless sleep.

* * *

When the Christmas holiday came, the three friends rode home in Doreen's jeep. Torri was happy to be home. Still stinging from the evening with Joel, she slept in every morning. Her library book sat on the table next to her bed, reminding her that she had to read it. Excited that her daughter was home, her mom had cooked all her favorites: chocolate chip cookies and brownies. Relaxing at home meant healing for Torri. She smiled and put on a good face for her family, not letting them know of her disappointed entanglements at college.

With the business being her parents' income, her dad took off only Christmas day. Bobby had a tradition that he had started years ago. On the 24th, the day before Christmas, he would mix up a punch bowl of eggnog and mom would make sugar cookies for the customers who stopped by that day. For those who wanted it, he would add a little brandy to the eggnog. The whole town got into the spirit by doing the same at some of their stores, only offering different drinks or sacks of peanuts or candy.

Torri enjoyed being around her family again, but after a few days, she started to feel guilty about lying to them. They thought that she had been going full-time. Eventually, her mom had asked her about her college classes and Torri told her it was really different than going to high school. She explained that she enjoyed her community choir, what songs they were learning, and about their final performance and concert that was planned. Her mom asked about her other classes, so Torri told her about the government class, the professor, and the midterm exam. She showed her mom the book that she had to read and write a report.

To change the topic, Torri went on about her work as a waitress at the diner and about all the tips that she had collected and saved. In fact, she needed to get some coin wrappers so she could change them into dollars. She had brought the coffee can of tips home with her. One day, she spent a couple of hours in her room wrapping up the pennies, the nickels, the dimes, and the quarters. Later that day, she walked to the bank and exchanged them.

While at home, she felt delighted to be with brothers. BJ and his family came for a couple of days, driving up from Denver on icy roads. Her parents worried all day until they arrived safely. Torri had a chance to visit with her Aunt Sally and her nephew Roger and niece Pamela. The children were well-behaved. They left after a short visit.

After BJ had left, her parents were having a serious conversation one evening in the kitchen. She overheard that her dad was going to have some medical tests after the new year. Dr. Carter had arranged for them at the hospital in Winston, so her parents were going to drive down and spend a few days there.

A day later, concerned about her dad, Torri decided to confront her mom about what she had heard. Her mom shook her head and told her that the doctor suspected that her dad had a condition with his heart, but without a few tests, he couldn't be certain. She looked at her mom in disbelief, stunned. *His heart? Would he die?* Her thoughts whirled around in her head, thinking about the worst possible outcome.

"What are you and dad going to do?" asked Torri, concerned.

Her mom explained that until they knew more, they weren't going to do anything.

Then Torri suggested that they let Ronnie take over the gas station and garage, but her mom replied, "No. Your brother has his head in the clouds with his racing cars and music. He just doesn't have a business sense about him."

"Racing? Why is he still racing?" she asked. She recalled that her brother drove a black Impala and that his friend George had a two-tone Fairlane. They talked intensively about their engines and tuning them up. *But racing?* She feared for her brother's safety.

"I guess he loves the thrill. I don't know. I have asked him to be careful, but his car is everything to him right now, along with his music, which I don't mind," replied her mom. Her dad thought that maybe BJ would be better taking over, but that seemed an unreasonable request at the time. Her mom asked her not to tell Ronnie about her dad until they knew more. She agreed but felt terrified about her dad's heart.

Her brother Ronnie continued working at the gas station and garage and practicing his guitar at home. One day, he curiously asked about how college had been for her. She told him that it was different than anything she had experienced. He particularly wanted to know about what parties she had been to. She laughed and said that she had been to several. During this time of the year, Ronnie focused on playing at the bars over the holidays. The town partied late into the evenings, so he had a chance to make some extra money playing and singing with his guitar.

His friends Dave and George came over to the house and talked Torri into going out with them one evening. She called her girlfriends Doreen and Patty to come with her, but they were busy with family get-togethers. While they were down at the bar, Dave and George wanted to hear about her college experience; she told them the simple version as they proceeded to drink. She didn't stay long since no other girls were with them. She listened to her brother sing and play for nearly an hour and then, slipped out and walked home.

Later that evening, Ronnie returned home with his buddies Dave and George. They were in high spirits after a night of drinking. His friends left, making sure that he had gotten home okay. Earlier, Torri had gone to bed but had been reading her government book, unable to sleep. When she heard her brother, she got up, put on her robe, and walked down the hall to the kitchen. He was sitting at the kitchen table, having another beer.

"Hi, sis. Why are you still up?" asked Ronnie, looking bleary-eyed at her.

"Couldn't sleep. Do you want a sandwich?" she asked as she went over to the fridge.

"Sure, I could eat," he replied. While she worked at making them a sandwich, the two made small talk. She poured herself a glass of milk. Sitting down at the table, they both munched on the sandwiches.

"Thanks. Why didn't you stay with us tonight?" he asked.

Shrugging her shoulders, she replied, "I don't know. There weren't any girls with us. You sounded good tonight. "

He said, "Thanks. I love playin' and singin'. So, tell me really how college is. I heard there is little studyin' and lots of partyin'." Smiling, his head was swimming as he ate. He was glad to get something to eat after a busy evening at the bar.

"I already told you before. The students manage to have keggers almost every week-end. I've gone to a few. But I am working and going to class. It isn't much different than here. You guys go down to the bar or up to Skyline and drink," replied Torri, taking a sip of her milk. The two sat silently for a few minutes. She recalled a few Skyline parties with a campfire and a case of beer.

"Sounds like you're really busy," responded her brother.

"Yes. Tonight, I was working on a government assignment," she said.

"Have you met any guys?" asked Ronnie. He wanted to know if she had been dating.

Torri took another sip before answering. She looked down at her glass of milk, keeping her true feelings to herself. "Sure. I have met lots of guys."

"Anyone interestin'?" he asked.

"No, no one interesting. How about you? Are you seeing anyone?" she asked.

"Oh, we've hooked up with some high school girls. They're all cheerleaders. I've been goin' with a girl named Deirdre, but it's nothin' serious," he replied. "You know that mom and dad are sure proud of you goin' on to college. They also worry about you being down there by yourself. Are you being careful?"

"Oh, really? They shouldn't worry. I can take care of myself. Besides my roommates and I stick together. They're good friends. I'm doing fine," she replied, finishing her sandwich and milk.

"Well, I'm tired. Thanks for the sandwich, freckles," said Ronnie, laughing. He rose but stumbled. "Gee, I drank too much tonight."

She stood and quickly grabbed her brother by the waist to steady him. "Don't call me that. Here let me help you," she said. Together, they walked down the hall to his room.

Coming to his bedroom, he whispered, "I've got this. Luv you sis." Nodding, she let him go and stepped quietly down to her bedroom.

Ronnie sat on his bed, undressing and thinking about his sister. He loved her and hoped that she would do all right at college. He noticed that she seemed sad and out of sorts, but he knew that she had always been a difficult person to be around.

In her bedroom, Torri slipped under her covers, thinking about her brother and how much she missed being around him. But his conversation had brought up some bad memories. Sadly, she thought of her unfortunate dating situations with Floyd and then of her disappointments with Joel. After avoiding her brother's question about dating, she didn't want him to know how sad and dismayed that she had been. Dating seemed hopeless. She felt like she was on that inner tube floating around in the murky eddy, a whirlpool of heartbreaking dates. When she thought about her future, darkness surrounded her. *What did her future hold for her?* She feared that she would drift around and around with no control. Hopeless thoughts of finding someone to love kept her worried throughout that dark night.

* * *

After Christmas, she decided to finish reading her book, spend a day or two writing the report. On a handout, her professor had indicated the requirements for the report: typed, three-five pages, three important quotes from the book (with page references), and a bibliography page listing the book's title, the author, and such. She wrote up a rough draft of her report, knowing she'd have to type it when she returned to their apartment. She would have to use one of her girlfriends' typewriters. To her, this seemed like a lot of work for just extra-credit, but if this would help her pass the class, she'd finish it and turn it in.

A few days after the first of January, Doreen called and said she was headed back to Midler earlier than planned. Her boyfriend Reese had called and said he had started basketball practice on campus. He wanted her to come down so they could spend time together. After Doreen called Patty, they all three agreed to go back. Torri thought she could make some extra money at the diner before classes started again.

One wintery day, they drove to Midler in Doreen's jeep. It was a long, cold drive, but the roads were clear. They all shared and talked about their holidays with their families.

After arriving at their apartment, Torri received a phone call from one of Floyd's friends, saying that he had been in an accident and was in the hospital. His friend hoped that she would go see him. Torri debated about going when Patty said she'd go with her, just to cheer the guy up. Doreen dropped them off and they went into the hospital, got his room number, and walked down the long hall to his room. Floyd had a bandage around his bruised head, his leg was in a cast, and ugly scratches were on his face. He looked battered up and weak but grinned when he saw the girls come into his room. Obviously, he was in pain and low spirits.

Torri asked if he needed anything; he asked for more water. When she left the room, Patty stayed and talked to him. He told her how his motorcycle had hit a patch of ice, had slid out from under him, and had crashed. He had ended up with a concussion, a punctured lung, and a broken leg. His college was over since he wouldn't be able to finish. When Torri came back, Patty had him smiling and almost laughing. She was sitting on his bed, flirting with him, as she held his hand. Torri smiled and just handed the glass of water to Patty so that she could help him drink it.

During the next two days, her friend went to see Floyd again until he got out of the hospital. One day Patty asked Torri if it was okay to date him. Undeniably, she had no desires to go with him and told her that she was free to date him if she wanted. On the third day, Floyd's parents came and took him home. Even though he was on crutches for six weeks, he called Patty, talked nightly to her, and eventually, they went out together with his friends.

Patty was thrilled to finally meet someone who called her and took her out on a date. They continued to date and seemed to be seriously interested in each other. Patty couldn't talk about anything else but Floyd. Torri was ecstatic to have him out of her life. One evening when he came to pick up Patty, he came down into their apartment. Torri had been in her bedroom, resting after a day of working when Patty called her out to the living room. Floyd cautiously glanced at the fiery Torri and apologized for that night at the kegger. She told them that she was happy for both of them, but deep down, she hated the creep who had stalked her.

They started to leave when he turned to her and said, "Sorry, it didn't work out for us. No hard feelings. But Patty and I have hit it off. I hope you find someone. Bye." And they left, leaving Torri glad for his honest apology and words. She felt that Patty had helped him.

While still on the semester break, Torri had called the diner and the owner scheduled her for a couple of days. One evening, she wanted to borrow Doreen's typewriter but needed a new ribbon. The next day she purchased one. Doreen felt bad, but Torri didn't mind since it was a way to pay her for letting her use the typewriter. She struggled to get her report typed and finished before classes started up again.

After classes went on for a week, final exams followed. The library was filled with students cramming for their exams. No keggers, just a tense feeling on campus that here was the end. The final grades would be coming soon. In their basement apartment, her girlfriends studied together for their exams.

For her, the community choir had an evening concert before exam week, so Torri had completed that class with no problem. She then had to study for the government class, reading over her notes, skimming through the textbook at different chapters, and hoping for the best. Walking down the hall to her government exam, she started to get anxious. She had no idea what the exam would be like but found out that it was an objective exam—multiple-choice test. The exam questions seem to come from the textbook and not from her notes; she didn't feel that she did very well. She now felt glad that she had written the report for extra-credit.

After a week, her grade report was sent to her. She had passed both of her classes, a meager four credits. Her girlfriends had both good and bad news, passing three of their five classes. However, they signed up for another semester while Torri signed up again for just two classes: the math class and a science with a lab.

Within the first week of both classes, Torri felt overwhelmed. The science lab conflicted with her afternoon hours working at the diner. Finally, she stopped attending both classes and just went to work, collecting tips and wages for her rent. Both Doreen and Patty were also skipping classes. They were heavy into their boyfriends---Reese and Floyd. Her girlfriends continued going to keggers on the week-ends; Torri avoided going to them. She had no more interest in meeting another guy who would disappoint her.

* * *

Then, unexpectantly, the ground underneath her dropped away. The shocking news came with a late night phone call from her dad. Torri had come home after a long shift at the diner. Exhausted, she had listened to her dad's words but could not comprehend what he was telling her. What? *Her brother Ronnie was dead.* She couldn't believe it. When the words finally sunk into her mind, her world tilted. She grasped the meaning and dropped the phone as she slid to the floor. Torri's world changed forever in that second, turning ugly when her dad's words hit her. Bright spots danced around her vision, her mind whirled, her insides shook, and she shut her eyes against the cold reality of death.

Fortunately, Doreen had been in the kitchen, picked up the dropped phone, and spoke to Torri's dad. She listened in disbelief while she heard the news that Ronnie had died in a car accident. The funeral would be that Saturday. On the phone, she agreed to drive Torri home.

Tears flooded her cheeks as Torri sat on the floor with her back against the wall. Hanging up the phone, her friend helped her up. Sobbing uncontrollable, she stumbled into her bedroom and collapsed on the bed. Later, exhaustion took over, and she fell asleep.

The next morning, she rose and took a bath, crying as she sat in the warm water. Torri thought of her last evening with her brother when he had performed at the local bar during the holidays. After he had come home drunk, they had sat together in the kitchen, eating and talking. But what bothered her the most was Ronnie's last words to her, *"Luv you sis."* She had responded but with only a nod. She never said the words that were in her heart—she loved him, too. It had been a lost moment in her life that she wished that she had back. That night—that moment—haunted her.

After her bath, she packed a bag and called the diner to cancel her scheduled work for a couple of days, saying that she had an emergency. In Doreen's jeep, they drove to Riverside, both in a sadden mood. Her friend dropped her off at her home and said she'd stay until after the funeral. If Torri needed anything, she'd be there to help. Torri thanked her and said "goodbye."

Returning home, she discovered that her parents were shocked beyond belief. Her dad had to phone Dr. Carter, for her mom had collapsed when the news came. The doctor had prescribed some pills to settle her down and to sleep. When Torri saw her mom, they huddled together and cried.

Her dad's pale appearance scared her, and turning to him, she asked, "What's wrong, dad? You look sick." She recalled the medical tests that he was to have.

In a daze, he explained, "I have heart condition that is more serious than we thought. Along with medication and orders from the doctor, I have to stop workin' so hard and long if I want to avoid a heart attack."

"Oh dad. What are you going to do?" she asked. She hadn't heard, so this came as a surprise. *Would he die?*

"We've called BJ and he is movin' back and takin' over the gas station and the garage. This had happened all before now." His voice trailed off. Pulling his daughter in his arms, "I'm so glad to see you. I wish it were under different circumstances. We'll have to get through this together, sunshine. Your mom's havin' a rough time."

That murky eddy had spun her life out of control again. Her happy family life had disappeared with her brother's death, her dad's heart condition, and her mom's grief.

* * *

On that Saturday, the day of the funeral, most everyone in the town attended her brother's funeral. Inside, the little church was packed; outside, the people filled the lawn and the parking lot in the front and on the side of the church. The tragedy hit everyone hard. As the family grappled with the death of Ronnie, they went through the lifeless motions of the church ceremonies and the burial at the cemetery.

In the church, her mom could barely manage. Flowers of all colors of blue, yellow, white, and red surrounded his polished, closed black casket as it stood at the front of the altar. The heavy air smelled of the flowers and the burning candles, stifling those sitting in the closed church. Torri never saw her brother's body; her dad had identified him but refused to let anyone else in the family see him. He wanted them to remember his son alive, not dead.

Weak and in shock, her dad and BJ had to tightly hold her mom from collapsing throughout the ceremony. Mournful songs resonated throughout the small church. Prayers were chanted. In the front pew, Ronnie's friend Dave had sat and stood with the family. When Dave hugged Torri, she felt his sorrow as he leaned sadly against her. Along with others, he had stepped in and helped comfort them throughout the day.

At the cemetery, her mom clung to Dave and her dad when they walked together to the grave site. The family and the town gathered around his black casket and the dark deep grave. It was a cold day even though the sun shone bleakly through the thin clouds above. The deep forested mountains surrounded the family, the people, the cemetery, and the town, standing as sentinels of that agonizing day.

The rest of the sorrowful day went on with the town's people bringing food and drink over to their house. Torri stepped into the kitchen to keep her hands busy and her mind empty. The ladies of the town had brought food. Someone had baked a large ham; another lady had baked a beef roast. Torri sliced the ham and the beef, fixing platters filled with the meat. While someone had brought paper plates and plastic forks and spoons, another had brought a large coffee maker, making a pot of brewed coffee. The men of the town brought bottles of beer and several bottles of whiskey, scotch, and vodka. One counter in the kitchen held the liquor bottles with plastic cups. Many drank, drowning out the sad feelings. Such a young and loved man to die, they thought.

As people came and left, they ate and drank, quietly giving their sympathies to the family. Her grieving mom sat on the couch in the living room, medicated. Doreen came over to their house after the funeral. Her friend quietly told her that she had planned to return to Midler the next day. She wondered if Torri wanted a ride back or what she planned to do. Torri didn't know what to say but told her that she'd call her. Before Doreen left, she hugged Torri and said she couldn't believe that Ronnie was gone.

After her friend had left, Torri sat in the living room with a plate of food in her lap. *What should she do? Return to college? Stay at home?* She had to talk to her dad and get his advice. The guilt of lying about college felt heavier on her shoulders now. Her future seemed even more dismal than it had ever felt before. Even though she felt numb and empty inside, she managed to move through the day. Finally, everyone left, leaving the house deathly quiet, filled with cigarette smoke and empty plates and cups.

Torri went into the kitchen to clean up. She opened the window over the kitchen sink, to air out the house. Most of the food had been devoured, leaving enough for a few days. She put everything away as the fridge filled up quickly with the leftovers. Tired and exhausted, her parents went to bed. Going into her own bedroom, Torri followed her parents to bed with images of the day in her head. She cried again with tears that soaked into her pillow. Finally, she fell to sleep, knowing that without Ronnie, her life would never be the same again.

When the sun came up the next day on Sunday, the McClure family rose like hollowed out beings, dulled by the death. Her family had been nearly destroyed with this death. But somehow, each got up and moved on through the motions of living. Her dad had closed the station for a few days. Waking up this morning, he had been eager to get the business opened again which had been his livelihood.

As he got dressed, he felt worse knowing that he had encouraged Ronnie to work on cars, to be the mechanic like he had done. Bobby never dreamed that his son would drive that Corvette so fast that he would wreck it. He felt a heaviness in his heart for his role in Ronnie's death. But he knew that he couldn't have stopped his son from loving his cars. He too had driven fast when he was young. Accidents happened; however, he never thought that he would be faced with his youngest son's death. Burying those guilty thoughts for now, he knew he had to run the station until BJ could move back. He had to be strong for his wife and keep going.

The emptiness in the house struck Torri as a stark reality of Ronnie's death. When she passed his bedroom that morning, she realized that his shadow would never pass through his door ever again. He would never occupy his room. Before, Torri usually had heard her brother humming, the musical chords coming from his guitar, or the opening of drawers in his room. Now, his bedroom remained empty with a deadly silence while his death still hung heavy in the air. His smiling face and sparkling hazel eyes were gone forever. His never-ending teasing had disappeared from her life. His word "freckles" echoed in her heart, bringing tears again.

At breakfast that morning, Torri cooked eggs and made toast, for they needed to eat. But food could never fill the emptiness that they felt. They were just going through the motions that the living did, the mundane events of the day. Her dad and Torri sat at the kitchen table, eating and drinking coffee.

Since they were alone, she asked her dad what she should do. After breaking down and talking to him, her dad sat quietly listening to her confession about college. Apologizing, she felt bad spending all that money on something that hadn't worked out. His face remained blank, and he seemed unaffected with what she had revealed to him.

Finally, he reached over and took her hands in his, and said, "You're a big girl now, sunshine. You have to make your own choices. I don't care about the money. I'm glad you went to college and tried." He glanced kindly into her troubled eyes.

"But dad, I feel so bad. I'm a failure. Maybe, I should come home. Mom's going to need help," she replied. Even though she felt relieved, her future still felt dark and doubtful.

"That's true about your mom. I am worried about her. You're welcome to come home. If you want, I'll drive down and move you back here. But, Torri, it's up to you," said her dad.

"I'm not sure," she said, frowning and concerned.

"I can't tell you what to do. Give yourself time. Just remember that we love you," said her dad.

"Doreen is headed back today. I best go with her. Later, after I figure it out, I'll call you," she replied.

"That's fine. BJ will be movin' back. Your mom will have the grandkids here soon. You do what's best for you," he said, understanding her dilemma and trusting her to decide.

About this time, her mom came into the kitchen, shuffling along in a daze. Her dad stood up and took her into his arms, giving her a hug. They stood together. Torri got up and the three of them stood clasped together in a desperate attempt to comfort each other. While they stood there, the anguish flowed through all their hearts.

Her mom moved over to the kitchen sink while she took out a bottle of pills from the pocket of her robe. Her dad walked over, putting his hand out to stop her from taking a pill. He whispered to her, "Doris, don't take those. They're strong pills."

She looked at him, "Bobby, I need to get through this. The doc gave me only a few days' worth of pills. Give me some time, please."

He nodded, "Okay, but just a few days. Listen, I have to go to the station. Will you be all right?"

She replied, "Yes. Did you take your medication?" With her reminder, he moved to the cupboard next to the sink, took down his bottle of heart medication, and with a glass of water, swallowed a pill. Handing her the glass, she took her pill.

After giving her another hug and a long kiss on her forehead, whispering to her, "We'll get through this. Torri's leavin' today. Call me if you need me." Turning, he left the kitchen and went to work.

After her dad left, she asked her mom if she wanted breakfast. Her mom handed her the bottle of pills and asked if she wanted one. Torri shook her head "no," thinking that she needed to keep a clear head today. If those pills were so strong, she didn't want one. Even though the thought had occurred to her the day before, she had resisted, despite the agonizing feelings of grief in her heart. She shook off her thoughts and fixed her mom breakfast. She then called Doreen.

After her mom finished eating, she suggested that she take a warm bath. Helping her mom, she bathed her, shampooed her hair, and dried her off. Her mom was like a baby in her arms, numbed by her sorrow. Her mom's hair was permed so she asked Torri to put it up in curlers. The pills had taken over, so her mom sat relaxed in a kitchen chair while she rolled up her mom's hair in curlers. The fridge was stuffed full of yesterday's food and her mom started to worry about that.

Torri said she'd take care of it and suggested that her mom go into the living room and rest on the couch. She brought a blanket to cover her mom. Their living room had a big picture window, so she opened up the curtains. The sunshine beamed down, filling the room with warmth. The beautiful, blue mountains filled the picture window. She hoped that the sun and the view would give her mom some peace.

While her mom rested and gazed out the window, Torri went to work in the kitchen and swept and mopped the floor. She then went down to the bedrooms and made their beds. She stopped for a heartbreaking moment to open up her brother's bedroom door. She glanced around his empty room, seeing his clothes hanging on a chair, some odds and ends on the top of his dresser, and his guitar leaning against the wall. Tears filled her eyes as she brushed them off her cheeks. Quietly closing the door, she walked back down the hall into the kitchen, knowing that someday they would have to remove his belongings, but not today.

Opening the fridge, she took out the left-over food, emptying out the casserole dishes and bowls. Her parents would have enough food to last a few more days. Washing the dirty dishes, she knew that the ladies would be by their house to check on her mom and pick up their dishes. The town's people were very supported of families who faced tragedy. In fact, one of her mom's closest friends came by that morning, just to sit and be with her mom. Torri felt good that she could leave, knowing that her parents would be all right with friends around.

Before Doreen came by after lunch, Torri had taken a quick bath and had packed her bag. She had fixed her mom a sandwich with a cup of hot tea. She carefully pulled the curlers out and brushed her mom's hair. Again, her mom stayed on the couch, medicated. Giving her mom a long hug and a promise to call, she left.

* * *

The drive back to Midler was cold and miserable. The shock of Ronnie's death had kept Torri's nerves raw and edgy; Doreen didn't talk much either. She anxiously wanted to get back to see Reese. During their drive, Torri did mention that she might have to return home. She wondered about her part of the rent. Doreen said she'd talk to her folks. Getting back to normal would take time for Torri.

When they arrived at their apartment, they walked down the stairs to the basement. Opening the door, they saw Patty and Floyd making out on the couch. They quickly stopped. Rising, Floyd said he was sorry to hear of her brother's death. Patty hugged her. She had known Ronnie and felt sorry about his death. The moment was awkward. Floyd finally, left, saying he'd call Patty later.

For the first time, Torri glanced closely at their basement apartment and realized how dismal the place looked. The furniture was old, faded out, and worn, the apartment smelled damp, stale and moldy, and the kitchen sink was filled with dirty dishes and glasses. There was no sunshine. The small basement windows were curtained and had a few cob webs hanging around them.

Going into her bedroom, she noticed there were no windows. The room was like a tomb, dark and unwelcoming. After turning on the overhead light, she dropped her bag on her bed and sat down. After a long day, she was exhausted. She leaned back, looking up at the low ceiling. Her hopes and dreams of being on her own fell like discarded trash, piled on the floor. Tears again pooled into her eyes as she recalled her brother's shocking death, the funeral, his black casket sitting next to that opened grave. *How cruel this world had become.* His absence sent her sobbing again. Not bothering to fully undress, she slipped off her jeans and crawled under her covers. Wrapping herself up, she cried again into her pillow. She fell asleep while her roommates worried about her.

In the morning, she woke up hearing her roommates moving around the apartment. Rising from her bed, she walked down to the bathroom to wash and clean up. Glancing in the mirror, she saw the dark circles under her red eyes. *What a wreck she had become.*

But she woke up knowing that she had to move back home. She couldn't go on living here; working at the diner didn't appeal to her. Her depressing situation left her cold. If she moved back home, she could help her mom and dad, and she also could find a job in one of the cafes. Putting on some make-up under her eyes and over her freckles across her nose, she prepared to talk to her roommates. She combed her long reddish-brown hair into a ponytail.

In the living room, her roommates had already been up and had been talking about Torri's situation. After a short conversation, both friends concluded that their parents would understand and pick up the difference. Even though they had skipped a few of their classes, they wanted to stay, both having steady boyfriends. By the end of the semester, Patty had hoped that Floyd would ask her to get married. He had been hinting that he wanted her to move in, but she didn't want to do that without a ring on her finger.

In Doreen's situation, she just didn't know how things would work out with Reese. He wanted to transfer to the university next year with dreams of playing basketball there. But she had to wait and see. He didn't seem to want a serious relationship. Doreen thought that she may have to look around for someone else.

Torri listened to her girlfriends and their thoughts about settling down and marrying. After her misfortunes here at college, she didn't want to get involved with a guy. She knew that she would never marry until she found the right one. And her prospects at home gave her no hope either.

The next day, Torri made all the arrangements to move back home. She called the diner and gave them her notice. After talking to the owner about her brother's death, he told her to stop by and pick up her last week's paycheck. She then called her dad, and he said he'd come and get her. After picking up her final check at the diner, she sold her two textbooks back to the bookstore. The next few days went by fast as she cleaned her bedroom out, emptying the drawers and the closet. She also cleaned up the apartment for the last time.

Before her dad came, she thanked her two friends and hoped that they would write and let her know how things were going. They both had a few tears, seeing her leave. But Torri felt relieved to be going home. Her dad came down the stairs, packed her belongings into his pickup, and they drove back to Riverside.

After returning, she moved her belongings into her bedroom. Both her mom and dad were happy to have her back home and never asked about her college. She helped her mom with the housework since she had been medicated for days, not being able to get past Ronnie's death. Day by day, week by week, the hurt became buried in their hearts.

Soon after the funeral, her oldest brother BJ and Sally and their two children Roger and Pamela moved back to run the business. BJ had never liked the city, so when his dad had phoned about taking over the station and garage in Riverside, he convinced Sally that it would be the best for them. His wife had attended beauty school and had a job as a stylist at a beauty salon. She had worried that she wouldn't be able to find work in Riverside, but BJ had persuaded her that they would work something out.

So after years away from Riverside, BJ had returned to run the McClure's Garage. Working those long years of building up his business, Bobby halfheartedly turned the business over to her brother who had been the most level-headed. Due to his heart condition, her dad only worked in the garage on a part-time basis, cutting back on the hours he worked. He continued to repair people's vehicles in the garage, letting BJ run the gas station. However, BJ kept a watch on the repair jobs and would help his dad from time to time.

In a small way, her mom shook off her grief when BJ and his family moved back. She now had grandchildren to focus on. Her grandson Roger attended school, but her granddaughter Pamela still had another year before she went to school. With the McClure's help, Aunt Sally started her own beauty shop, opening a small salon name Sally's Beauty Salon. The town had depended on the McClure's skill as mechanics to keep their vehicles repaired and running. And now, the women had a place to get their hair cut, styled, and fixed.

Coming back to Riverside changed Torri's life. This move back took away the freedom that she had so desperately had sought when she left. That independence had been only a short time of her life, only seven months on her own. Even though her brother's death shocked her, her failure at college bothered her deeply. She could not see her future. Balancing her college classes and working had been overwhelming for her. She didn't like the taste of failure, but she focused on helping her parents get through the loss. Her parents were glad to have her home; they said the house felt empty without Ronnie. After coming home, she put on a smiling face while she buried the hurt deep inside. She felt like a shadow, moving through the motions of living.

After a week at home, Torri succeeded in obtaining a waitress job at Bert's Café. The owners Bert and Kay were pleased to hire her. Spring had arrived with summer close to follow. Summer meant the tourists would be coming through the small mountain town heading towards the national parks. With her past experience at the diner, she stepped right into the job, knowing how to handle the customers. The full-time job kept her busy. She met the town's people who all knew her and her family. The wages and tips gave her money into her pocket. She also felt that this was a temporary stopping point in her life. Torri didn't know her future, but this would do for the time being while she gave emotional support to her parents.

When at home, her parents never talked about the details of the accident. In fact, Torri did not know how the accident had happened. She had to piece it together gradually from different sources—from hearing conversations by the people in the café. She also noted that her dad planned to sell Ronnie's Impala; she had assumed that he had been killed driving his own car. However, she discovered that Ronnie had driven a Corvette owned by Matt Fletcher who lived on the Battle Axe Ranch. His name kept coming up until her Irish anger slowly grew.

One day, her dad's best friend Victor Dickerson and his son Bill drove over from Scottsville and stayed at their house. During their stay, Torri connected with her namesake. Vic said that she had certainly grown up from the skinny kid he remembered. Her dad wanted the Impala sold to someone across the state. Thus, Vic had found a buyer for the Impala, and they came with a big flatbed truck, loaded with an old Chevy. One of the other reasons that they came was Bill and his dad wanted to take the engine out of Matt's wrecked Corvette and put it into that older car. The men talked about cars and engines for days. All this talk went over Torri's head. She just shook her head and went to work each day.

However, one day at the café, Bill and his friend Matt had come in and sat at one of their tables. It shocked her to see Matt as her heart thumped in her breast. Bill teased and flirted with her, but she ignored him. While serving them, she noticed that despite Matt's good looks, she hated him for owning the Corvette that had killed her brother.

One evening, Dave asked her to join his group of friends at a Skyline party. He encouraged her to come with him, saying that she needed to get out. She really didn't feel like partying, but after he kept pressuring her, she agreed to go. When they drove up to the party, the campfire was roaring hot with sparks flying into the night sky. As they joined the group around the fire, everyone was introduced. She knew George Weaver and Bill Dickerson. A new face Craig Webster, an ex-military guy, had joined the group. The girls were all new to her—Deirdre, Rebecca, Suzie, and Melanie. They were still in high school, so she felt her full nineteen years among them. But what really shocked her was meeting Matt again and his younger brother Tom Fletcher who stood on the other side of the campfire. They were imposing figures, standing taller than the other guys.

Dave gave Torri a can of beer from the case. The conversations among them continued through the evening with all kinds of stories. Torri drank a couple of cold beers, but slowly, she simmered hot as she watched Matt. Finally, the alcohol loosened her tongue. She wanted to give him a taste of her Irish temper. Stepping around, she threw her beer can into the campfire. She confronted Matt with her pointing finger. Filled with anger, she lashed out at him with words that accused him of killing her brother.

While the alcohol coursed through her body, her emotional hurt swirled inside of her. Deirdre stepped in front of Matt and defended him, telling Torri that she was being unfair that Matt had lost his mom the same day. Torri didn't hear those words right away and just kept calling him nasty names until she had worked herself up into a frenzy. Then, suddenly, the news hit her hard. She hadn't known the whole terrible tragedy of that day. She didn't know anything about Matt's mom dying. No one had told her.

After her hot tempered was spent, her knees buckled under her as Matt grabbed and kept her from falling. His touch sent electric shocks into her. Struggling to get away, she didn't want him to touch her. Her Irish tongue lashed out at him again like a bull whip cutting into him. She had expected him to call her nasty names like Floyd had done. But he didn't. At first he pushed back with his own words, but then finally, Matt's kind words rang in her ears: *"I know what you're goin' through."* In her mind, his compassionate words echoed in her head as she pounded on his chest, crying. She sobbed while tears flowed from her eyes, wetting her freckled cheeks.

Finally, Dave stepped in and took her in his arms like a brother comforting her. While she turned and wept against Dave's warm chest, he quietly told her to go ahead and cry. Everyone around the campfire felt bad for both Torri and Matt. Dave guided her around the campfire over to the wooden picnic table. Sitting down, he continue to hold and comfort her. She finally dried her tears and quieted her angry thoughts. Then, the embarrassment of the situation descended on her.

With her dried eyes, she now felt sorry at what she had said. Dave asked if she wanted to go home and she nodded, whispering, "Yes, please take me home." He walked her over to his old black pickup, letting her step up into his cab. He then drove her back home, rescuing her for the second time from a terrible situation.

When Torri came home, her dad was sitting at the kitchen table. He noticed that she looked upset and had been crying. "Come here sunshine. Sit and talk with me," said her dad Bobby.

Like so many times in the past, Torri sat down at the kitchen table and began to talk. He listened quietly, waiting as she explained her role in accusing Matt. She hadn't known about his mom's death that night. A quiet moment descended on the two of them. Her dad then explained that her brother and Matt had become close friends, loving their cars and music. He briefly explained the two tragic deaths shocked everyone in both families. Shaking her head, Torri regretted her words.

"What should I do dad?" she asked, worried.

"You should apologize," replied her dad.

"How? I don't even know him," she said.

"I can't tell you how or when. You're a smart girl. You'll figure it out. Listen, it's late. Time for bed," commented her dad. Standing, he walked over and gave her a quick kiss on her forehead, placing his warm rough hand on her shoulder, and squeezed. She felt her dad's comforting touch.

She responded by replying "Thanks, dad. Good night."

Torri walked down the hall to her bedroom. Getting ready for bed, she had much to think about. While her head rested on her soft pillow, her eyes burned from her tears. Her heartbreaking thoughts churned around through her mind, recalling her horrible words. The dark images of the evening kept her awake —the red, hot campfire, the taste of the cold beer, Ronnie, her anger, her striking Matt, his mom's death, and the stares of those standing around. *She didn't know about his mom.* Even though she could never completely forgive him, she vowed to apologize for her words

48

somehow. In her bed, the dark shadows of the night surrounded her, and she finally fell asleep.

The next days swiftly went by as she worked at Bert's Café. In the back of her mind, she continued to consider finding a way to apologize to Matt. One day, Chet, Matt's oldest brother, met a young woman in the café. After serving the two of them, Torri came up with the idea of writing Matt a note. She quickly scribbled her apology and added her phone number. She hoped that he would call, and they could talk on the phone. This would smooth over that terrible night. After giving Chet the note, he agreed to give it to Matt; the apologetic note lifted part of her guilt and anxiety.

Torri waited to hear from Matt. Days went by. He never called. Then, she heard through the rumors around town that he had joined the Army. Her dad mentioned that he had offered to store Matt's car in the old shed next to the house. One day, the '51 light blue Chevy (the Blue Demon) was dropped off by one of the Fletchers.

Torri's dad checked on the coupe every week, turning the engine on, keeping it tuned and running. Her dad seemed obsessed with the car. One time finally she asked him why he kept such careful care of the old car. He looked at her and said, "Come with me."

Grabbing the car keys from a kitchen drawer, they walked out to the shed. He popped opened the hood and lifted it up. "Look at that engine. I helped mount it in this ol' car," he whispered, admiring it. She looked at the Chevy orange engine. It did look impressive, colorful, but to her, it was just an engine.

"Let me start it up," her dad said. Walking to the driver's side, he crawled in and started it up. The devil engine roared to life as he revved it several times. He let it idle and stepped out from behind the steering wheel. "Now, that's an engine," he said smiling. She nodded and understood her dad's love of engines. Every fiber of his body thrived as a mechanic. Smiling, he turned off the engine, lowered the hood, and left.

Standing beside the light blue coupe, her hand traveled down the long hood to the door. She opened the door and sat behind the steering wheel, smelling the old car. Never having her own car, she wondered what it would feel like. She imagined the freedom she would have to drive beyond the town limits and go anywhere. She had her driver's license and her dad had taken time to teach her how to drive. But to have her own car had never occurred to her. Getting out of the coupe, she went back into the house, thinking that she'd never own a car—too much trouble and too expensive on her waitress' salary.

* * *

Spring turned to summer with Riverside becoming alive with tourists and visitors to the dude ranches. The mountains turned greener with the meadows blossoming spring flowers. The cottonwoods by Rock River leafed out, and bits of cotton floated on the light breezes coming down through the canyons. The white barked aspens brightened up with their green leaves, shaking in the breeze. Birds were nest-building and robins hopped around on the ground for worms. Daylight became longer and temperatures warmed the cool mountain night air.

At Bert's café, visitors and tourists streamed in sitting down for breakfast, lunch, or dinner. During her shifts, Torri had been kept busy with few breaks. She met many people from different towns, cities, and states. She went to work and saved her wages. At home, she helped her mom around the house. Gradually, her mom became herself again—taking care of Pamela while Aunt Sally fixed ladies' hair at her salon downtown. There were times when Torri felt sadness descend on her, but she learned to shake off those thoughts, focusing on the here and now. Her dad enjoyed working with BJ at the gas station and garage. His eyes again had the sparkle in them.

After working one day, Torri came home, exhausted. She called out for her mom but read the note on the fridge that she was over at BJ's house. While she drank a cool glass of water, the phone rang, echoing through the empty house. *RING. RING.* Answering the phone, she heard a voice that she didn't recognize. The caller was Matt Fletcher. *Why is he calling me?* She never imagined that he would call. After he told her that he needed a ride home, he explained that no one was at their ranch. He wanted her to come and get him at the bus depot in Hadley. His desperate voice sounded in her ear. After he explained further that he had been discharged from the Army, she finally understood and agreed to come and get him.

Torri hustled and changed out of her work clothes, putting on a pair of jeans and a white sweater. Brushing out her hair, she gathered it into a ponytail. Grabbing a jacket and the keys from the drawer, she wrote a quick note to her parents. Excited about driving the blue coupe, she headed to the old shed, got in, and headed out of town. The Blue Demon sprang to life as the devil engine roared. Torri heard the powerful engine under the hood as she drove it out of the shed.

Driving down main street, she crossed the bridge over Sheep Creek which had reached its banks with the melting snow from the mountains. While she drove, the car gave her a sense of liberation with the open road sitting in front of her. The highway north of town went along the many ranches which lined the valleys. Their fenced pastures were turning green with their livestock grazing.

The two-hour trip took her through the most beautiful mountains that she had ever seen. Deep forests covered the mountains with dark green. Glancing once in a while into those tall pine trees, she saw columns of sunshine streaming between the dark outlines of the trunks. Driving over Tepee Pass, she drove down the other side to more forested mountains and deep canyons. The Blue Demon drove like a dream. Now, she knew what her dad meant by having a good engine.

When she arrived in Hadley, she couldn't belief the crowded streets. Stopping at a gas station, she obtained directions to the bus depot. A few blocks off of the main street, she located it. Parking across the street, she sat for a few minutes, wondering where Matt would be. A big bus had pulled up in front. Cars were dropping travelers off, carrying their luggage. For a while, she waited in the car.

Finally, she stepped out and walked across the street and into the crowded bus depot. People were everywhere; some were sitting, some were lined up, buying their tickets. The noisy place was filled with sounds of the travelers talking and a baby crying, excitement filled the air. Glancing around, she looked for Matt. No Matt.

At the door of the bus depot, a uniformed guy waved at her. He carried a big, green duffle bag slung over his shoulder. At first she didn't recognize him, but then her heart skipped a beat as she gazed at his handsome face in an Army uniform. Walking closer, she saw

Matt's serious look. His eyes showed that he was glad to see her. A little smile crossed her face when she recognized him.

She nodded, handed him the car keys, and said, "Hello, Matt."

Taking the keys, he replied, "Hi, thanks for comin'. I was over at the diner down the street. Have you eaten?"

"No. That's quite a car you have," she said, as her stomach growled at the thought of food.

"Yes, I saw my Blue Demon out there. Listen, there's a drive-in at the edge of town. We'll stop there and get you somethin' to eat," he replied. As he stood looking at Torri, he finally said, "Let's get out of here."

While he lifted the Army duffle bag over his shoulder again, he recalled everything that had gone on between them before he had left—her brother's death, her harsh words, her striking him, and her note that apologized. That *note* had saved him today. Without a phone number, he thought that he would have to stay in Hadley tonight.

Torri looked different than he had remembered, more grown-up and more gorgeous. When her hazel eyes glanced up at him, he noticed her attractive face with its faint freckles spattered across her cheeks and her full lips. Glancing at her ponytail, he saw her slender, white neck. His desires stirred. He looked down and felt embarrassed at staring at her. He'd been too long among men.

Torri felt his dark brown eyes scrutinizing her as if he saw her for the first time. She glanced at his dark green military uniform with its shining, gold brass buttons, the shirt with a narrow tie, and his tall broad figure filling out the jacket. Inside, something fluttered, she felt herself tumbling towards him. *No, not him, anyone else, but not Matt.* Suddenly, she felt uncomfortable, standing in the middle of this loud crowd. Nervous, she glanced around, ready to leave and get back home.

Turning, together they moved through the crowd to the door of the bus depot and walked over to his car, parked across the street. He opened the door for her. After putting his Army duffle bag in the trunk, he took off his military hat, revealing his short crew cut. Loosening his tie, he unbuttoned the top button. He smiled at his Blue Demon and mumbled something under his breath while he unbuttoned his military green jacket. Crawling into his beloved car, she noticed his opened shirt and his broad shoulders. She noticed his firm jaw, shadowed with his dark beard. His handsome profile sent wild thoughts about him. *Stop Torri.*

Matt drove to the drive-in, ordered a meal, and paid for it. While they sat waiting, an awkward silence fell upon them. Both were wondering what to say and how to go forward. Their past had been fraught with mayhem, anger, and sorrow.

When the car hop brought out the meal, she hooked the tray on Matt's rolled-down window and smiled at him. Flirting with him, she asked where he was stationed. Matt said he had flown in from California. She gushed more. Torri interrupted and asked for her food.

Finally, the car hop left, and Torri smiled and said, "Wow, you can sure turn on the charm."

Smiling to himself, he replied, "She just liked the uniform. I've gotten that all the way here. It means nothing." Quietly to herself she thought *Yes, a handsome guy in a military uniform would impress any girl, even her.*

Sharing a few fries with him, Torri ate the hamburger and fries. In the driver's seat, Matt leaned back, closed his eyes, and relaxed. He said that he had a long trip that day, flying into Billings and then riding the bus to Hadley. Pulling out a bottle of aspirins, he shook out four and swallowed them. She asked if he wanted a sip of her soda. He nodded and took a long sip, telling her he had a bad headache. She understood, but she never took four pills—only for a hangover.

Their small talk still felt awkward to Torri. Her feelings were mixed and confused about driving here and meeting Matt again. Her heart pounded as her nerves felt jittery. She couldn't forget her past bitterness, her nasty words at the Skyline party, and her embarrassment. Her written note apologizing hadn't accomplished anything, for he never called—until now.

After she had finished the meal, he tapped the horn, and the girl came and took the tray. When he handed her the tip, she held his hand a little longer than necessary, giving him a big smile and telling him to come again. Torri thought *What a flirt. Was that jealousy she just felt?* Her eyes sent daggers at the flirting car hop. Matt was here with her, but he really wasn't *with* her.

"Let's go. I can't wait to get back to the ranch," he admitted. Smiling at the car hop, he backed up and waved "goodbye." Torri knew that the car hop would be dreaming of this soldier tonight.

While he drove through the crowded streets, Matt noticed that he needed to get gas and wanted to also check the oil. Torri then told him that her dad had taken care of his car. He was surprised but pleased. So when the gas attendant asked if he wanted the oil checked, he replied, "No."

Then, they drove out of town towards Riverside, leaving behind the busy resort town. The two of them sat quietly, listening to the radio. Matt hummed along with some of the songs. With a full stomach, Torri started to nod off. She finally scooted up against the door, leaned back, and closed her eyes. Her ponytail bothered her head, so she took out the band, letting her hair flow down her back and around her shoulders. Her day also had been long: starting early that morning, working her shift, and then driving over to Hadley.

Matt drove, glancing several times at her. He turned the radio down a little. His heart quickened in his chest as he gazed at her long hair, her full bosom rising and falling, and her slender body lying against the door. Even though she came with a complicated past, his feelings towards her surprised him; he felt a deep attraction to her. He had to be careful, for he had had his fill of bad relationships. She wouldn't exactly be receptive to any advances. She could be still grieving and if her previous words meant anything, she hated him. Between them, Ronnie's death would always be there. His own guilty feelings had eased up, knowing that he couldn't have prevented the accident. Somehow, he could feel her hesitation. Maybe, it was that Irish temper. Shaking off his thoughts of her, he focused on driving and getting back home.

Closing her eyes, Torri slept a little, but stay curled up against the door. Her thoughts were swirling around her head about Matt. She didn't want to get involved with him, not him. She still had raw, angry feelings towards him. But she felt herself being drawn to him despite the past. While he drove through the canyons and around the curves, she kept her eyes closed and let the car rock her gently as she dozed.

Matt drove through the forested mountains towards Tepee Pass. He could tell that Torri had been asleep for a period but now, had been just resting. He turned off the radio and cleared his throat.

"Torri, are you awake? Can we talk?" he asked. He wanted to talk to her and find out more about her. Besides chatting with the car hop, he hadn't talked to a girl in a long while. On his long trip, he had listened to a dozen conversations among people. They were all strangers; he had felt isolated and alone. Now, he needed to connect with someone.

Torri straightened up when he said her name and replied, "Yes, I'm awake," rubbing her eyes and yawning. Much to Matt's disappointment, she gathered her hair up into a ponytail again.

They talked about nothing important. He wanted to know about her college experience and about her family, particularly about her dad. She told him about her dad and mom, about BJ who had taken over the business, and about her family. She glossed over her time in college which hadn't been that great. He seemed interested in her college, but she cut him off. She wanted to know more about him.

Torri asked, "How was the Army?"

Shrugging his shoulders, he replied, "It was just Basic."

"Oh. Tell me about it," she said.

"I'd rather not. Nothin' happened," he answered, ending their conversation for a few tense moments. She felt his hesitation.

The two of them sat quietly as he drove. Dropping down to the other side of Tepee Pass, they watched the sun drop behind the tall peaks, bringing bright colors of reddish orange and painting the disappearing blue sky. Twilight encircled the car while its yellow headlights shown the highway ahead of them.

Since the sun had gone down, Matt had to closely scan the forests and the roadside for wild game crossing the highway. While the dark forests passed by, he drove down into the valleys with the ranches, dotting the pastured land. The glow of yellow lights shone out of several ranch house windows. An occasional light could be seen in a barn or stable.

Matt's heart beat fast in his chest with the excitement of coming home. He had missed these beautiful mountains and their Battle Axe Ranch more than he could ever explain in words; he had missed his big horse Diablo, riding him along the pastures, through the forests, and up into the mountains; he had missed his brothers, his dad, and his uncle; he had missed his life at the ranch. His brief stint in the military had changed his view of Riverside and his ranch life.

So far, the trip to Hadley and back had piqued Torri's interest in Matt. Here he sat, a returning soldier. He seemed so different than she remembered, more confident. The drive had given her a chance to bury a little of her dislike of him. Her curiosity had been aroused. She wanted to know more about him.

But as they approach his turnoff to their ranch, everything didn't seem normal. There were a line of cars and pickups parked along the road. Grey and white smoke filled the dark night, surrounding the ranch and hanging low in the big valley. When he drove down the dirt road to their log ranch house, she recognized one of the pickups as her dad's. There must have been emergency—a fire. She became worried and anxious to get out of the car.

Parking, they both jumped out, smelling the acid burning smoke in the air. Tom came rushing up to his brother Matt, shocked at seeing him. They hugged each other. Torri watched as Tom glanced at her and nodded, recognizing her. She glanced at the line of people, passing the buckets of water. Her dad came from behind the big log house. He recognized Matt, shook his hand, and said they saved the house. Torri sensed the devastation in front of them and was saddened at the news of the fire damage.

She moved closer to her dad who had been talking to Matt. Thankful that the house had been saved, the Fletchers were shaking the men's hands as they finished up. After the men rolled up the hose, the firetruck pulled around to leave and others walked to their vehicles parked along the lane. The line of cars and vehicles drove into the ranch to turn around and then, headed away into town or to their own ranches.

Standing beside her dad, Torri waited as they finished. Finally, she turned to Matt and said, "I'll catch a ride with my dad." Before she turned to leave, Matt stepped towards her and reached out to her. His hand moved down her arm as he clutched her hand.

"Just a minute, Torri. Thanks for comin' and gettin' me. Can I call you?" He looked into her hazel eyes, questioning her. Her insides fluttered at his touch. His hand squeezed hers, sending shocks through her. *This can't be.* He would be the last person that she had expected to have any feelings for. But here he was, in his military uniform, a changed man, and handsome. Taking a deep breath, she gazed into his dark brown eyes.

"Yes. I'd like that. Call me," smiling, she replied and turned. Torri walked with her dad to his pickup. Getting in, she glanced back quickly at the tall, broad-shouldered guy who had caught her attention. Her life didn't look so dark anymore. She would anxiously wait for him to call her. Only Fate could tell how it would work out. But she went home, dreaming of the soldier who sent her heart ricocheting in her bosom.

* * *

After Matt had returned from the Army, their first contacts were filled with disappointments. After the fire, Matt had been very busy with the ranch. She heard that the whole town had come together to help them repair the damaged log home. Torri continued to work at the café, saving her wages and tips. Matt didn't call right away and when he did, he just wanted to talk to her. He phoned her at night when she was tired. She didn't have much to say; nothing exciting happened to her at the café.

Finally, Matt asked her out on a date. They went to a movie, shared a box of popcorn, and held hands. While he drove her home, he kept his hands on the steering wheel. Stopping in front of her house, he walked her to the front door. In an awkward moment, he stood, hesitating. She wondered if he would kiss her as he leaned slowly down and kissed her lips gently. It was a chaste kiss that left her empty and frustrated. However, he smiled and said he'd like to see her again. After he left, she walked into her bedroom and threw herself on her bed. She couldn't wait to see him again.

The rumors buzzed around town about them. The town watched as the young couple dated. They talked about Matt returning from the Army.

One evening, Matt drove her up to Skyline and they sat watching the twinkling lights of the town below the mesa. He brought a pint of vodka that he shared with her. She cautiously drank a little, afraid to get drunk. She held back. Matt had a gentle, caring nature about him that reminded her of Joel. When he kissed her a few times, she controlled and guarded her emotions. She wasn't ready to lose herself with him.

During that summer, Matt took her to the Saturday night dances at the community hall with live bands coming to play. They double dated with his brother Tom and his date Melanie Carter. Matt only danced the slow dances. She loved their time together with his arms around her and their bodies leaning into each other. He would gently kiss her on the temple or her neck as they danced. His tenderness sent warm feelings down her body.

There were other times during the summer days when they wouldn't see each other. The ranch work had kept him busy. He would call when he had time and they would talk on the phone in the evenings. She had kept her expectations up, but he was taking it slow, hesitating and uncertain.

In September, Matt's brother Chet and Sophia were married at the Battle Axe Ranch in a private ceremony. Matt had called Torri and had invited her to the wedding reception at the Dark Horse Tavern. He said he'd pick her up. Excited about going out with him, she had purchased a new light green dress to wear and a pair of tan heels. When she bought the dress, she had made sure that it had sleeves to cover her lightly freckled arms. Aunt Sally had styled her hair, cutting it just above her shoulders. She wanted to change her look for this reception. She again had warm feelings about seeing him.

Matt picked her up and then drove down to the tavern, where they met many of their friends and family. The reception was in full swing by the time they walked into the crowded room. Everyone was in high spirits. His brother and bride were cutting the wedding cake, followed by a special dance for the new married couple. Torri looked on with hope in her heart that she too would someday be a bride.

Torri and Matt sat together at a table with his friends George and Dave along with their dates. They all had a piece of the wedding cake. With the open bar, the draft beer flowed freely as the guests drank. Matt with his friends drank heavily. As she glanced around to see if any of her friends were there, she saw Doreen with Craig Webster. The two girls made eye contact and Doreen nodded to the restroom. Torri excused herself and met her there.

Smiling at Torri, Doreen asked, "I love your dress and what did you do with your hair? It looks great. How are things going with you and Matt?"

"My Aunt Sally did my hair. She's really good. About Matt, I just don't know where I sit with him. We haven't gotten serious yet. How about you and Craig?" asked Torri.

"Well, I do like him, but he told me he's just dating around, like Joel did with you," answered her friend.

"Oh, great. Is there anyone else you're dating?" she asked.

"Yes. I've been out with a couple of the wranglers. And then, there's the truck driver who comes to the motel to fill the soda machines. He's been making eyes and flirting with me. I might go out with him if he ever asks," commented Doreen.

Finally, she said, "Good luck. I better get back. Call me sometime, maybe we could go to a movie or something just for old times' sake," laughing as she left.

When Torri came out of the restroom, Matt had been standing near the door, waiting for her. That summer, she had noticed that his military look had disappeared. Today, he wore a bolo tie with a white western shirt, a brown leather vest and jeans; he now looked like a rancher. His dark brown hair had grown out. She wasn't disappointed, for he had an astounding presence with his tall build, his broad shoulders, and his handsome face.

Glancing at her, he said, "I've missed you. Let's dance."

He walked her out to the dance floor as a slow song came up on the jukebox. He pulled her close to him. She felt his strong arm around her waist. Glancing into her hazel eyes, he whispered quietly to her that she looked lovely with her hair down. Moving closer to him, she slipped her hand around his neck, fingering his thick dark hair. She put her head against his cheek and felt his smooth shaved skin and smelled his pine-scented cologne. They felt each other's warm bodies as they moved slowly around the dance floor. He stumbled a couple of times and apologized, saying that he had too much to drink. She held him tighter, and he leaned in closer. As the song ended, he moved his lips down to hers and gave her a passionate kiss. They stayed together while others around them left. Realizing that they were alone, he broke off the kiss. Wrapped in each other's arms, they walked off the dance floor. As they approached the table, he whispered in her ear, "Do you want to leave?" She smiled and said "Yes." His affectionate touches and kisses had become more intense, and her emotions were swirling with anticipation.

They drove up to Skyline, parking on the mesa road above the town. Torri had never been up there in the afternoon, so the view of the huge mountains, their sharp peaks, and the small town below amazed her. The fall colors of yellow and orange were brilliant against the dark green of the forests. Reflecting the sharp blue sky, the river below flowed through the valley, looking like a shiny blue ribbon enveloping the town and the ranches. The view stunned her; she felt small against this vast wilderness.

Matt slid out from behind the steering wheel towards her, taking her into his arms. He looked down at her pink lips, leaned down and kissed her. Torri felt her insides warm while his hands embraced her, his lips moved down and kissed her just below the ear. She tried to relax and let herself go, but she held back, just a little. They kissed for some time and then, he leaned back with a frown on his face. He moved away from her, threading her hand into his. While he sat breathing heavily, he shook his head.

She didn't understand why he had stopped, and asked, "What's wrong?"

He didn't speak for a few moments, just looked out at the scenic mountains in front of them. Finally, turning his head towards her, he spoke, "Torri, you know I like you a lot… really, it's more than that. I'm serious about you. When I am away from you, you're always in my thoughts. I was hopin' that you felt the same way. I've been takin' this slow because I'm unsure about how you feel about me. But tonight, when I hold and kiss you, I'm not feelin' it. Are you serious about me?"

"What do you mean?" she asked.

"Let's be honest with each other. It seems you're stringin' me along. You're holdin' back for some reason. What is it?"

She sat shocked that he had felt her hesitation. While he held her hand, she slowly drew it away from him into her lap and lowered her head and closed her eyes. *How could she tell him? Could she be honest and admit her reluctance with him had been Ronnie?*

With his finger on her chin, he lifted her face, and he gazed into her hazel eyes and at her lips, searching and waiting for an answer.

She nodded slowly. He had been right. Matt's involvement with her brother still had her simmering, ever so slightly. She had tried to hide it, but he had known.

Matt finally broke the silence with a quiet, calm voice, "You know that I'm sensitive to the horses when they are hurtin'. My dad and brothers can't believe it. We've spoken about that several times. Like the horses, I can tell you're hurtin' or holdin' back from me. I've been with several girls before who have betrayed me. I have an empty feeling inside of me. Torri, for god's sake, just be honest. Tell me what you feel."

She let her guard down and whispered quietly, "I'm not playing you. I've tried to let the sorrow go, but it's still there." She paused sadly, "Yes, it's Ronnie."

Her words confirmed what he had known. It hurt him to think that she had let her brother come between them. The air became tense for a minute. He thoughtfully replied, "You know that your brother and I became very close. Our music and our cars brought us together. I'd felt guilty for a long time after the accident. But I knew somethin' that most of you didn't know. He had fallin' in love with a girl in Scottsville." Matt paused, thinking of his friend Ronnie and the black silk panties. "Her name was Gail Gibson and he met her when we drove together to Scottsville. They spent a night together. When we came home, he repeatedly phoned her for days—morning, noon, and night, never getting in touch with her. He had been so frustrated that he planned on drivin' over to see her that week. Yes, Ronnie had it bad; he wanted to marry her. With her in his head, he wasn't thinkin' clearly. I don't know for sure, but it was a rotten time for him."

Thinking about what he had revealed, she replied, "Oh, I didn't know anything about a girl. But why did he have to die?" This story about him loving a girl gave her a clearer picture of how frustrated her brother must have felt. Maybe, the girl had him all messed up that he couldn't think. She knew how frustrating a guy could make her feel.

Pulling her into his arms, he asked, "There are no answers to that question. But Death is part of life, and we have no control over that. We all live with the dead surroundin' us. I have mine, dealing with my mom's death and others." He looked at her closely, "You don't have to forget him, just don't let him come between us. I thought we had somethin' here. What do you want? Do you want to break it off ?" He paused, "I know what I want. I'm serious about you and I know that I love you." He waited for her to answer.

She cradled his face with her hands. Gazing into his warm eyes, she said, "No, I don't want to break up. I'm serious about you. Since I came and met you at the bus depot, I have thought about you. I want to be with you. I love you." She moved towards him and kissed his soft lips. Her tongue sought out his mouth and she felt her emotions soar. He mumbled, "Oh, Torri. I was so afraid."

His strong arms pulled her onto his lap. He slipped off her tan heels, moving his hands up her silky legs. While she straddled him, his warm hands moved to push up her green dress. He gently touched her thighs sending her heart beating fast.

As he caressed her, she quickly slipped off the bolo tie, unbuttoned his shirt under his opened vest, and pulled the white shirt up from his jeans. Moving her hands under his t-shirt, she felt his broad muscled chest. Kissing his neck, she moved her hands down his bare chest. She loved the feel of his warm naked body as she dug her nails into him. They breathed hard together while they drew closer to each other, kissing.

Leaning into his chest, she felt her body pressed against him. While he called out her name, he sought out her breasts as he fumbled with her buttons on the front of her dress. He then kissed the tops of her round breasts, moving from one to the other. In the late afternoon light, he gazed at her bosom. He whispered, "Are those freckles?" kissing them across her bare skin and smiling.

"Don't tease me," she gasped, feeling nervous. She put her hand to cover them, but he pushed it gently away.

Glancing at her, "Don't cover them. They're beautiful. When I was a kid, my mom told me that freckles were nothing but fairy dust," he whispered more sweetly to her. She complained that they embarrassed her. He murmured, "Nonsense. They're lovely, just fairy dust. I love them." Ignoring her, he tenderly continued to kiss her breasts, sending warm bolts of desire throughout her body.

Their pent-up longing created a momentum within them. He whispered in a husky voice filled with emotion, "How far do you want me to go?"

Whispering quietly, she admitted something that took him by surprise, "I've never been with anyone." She blushed, admitting her virginity.

"What about college? Didn't you date there?" he pushed her further, for he couldn't believe it. He knew what went on at colleges.

"Yes, I dated, but no, there was no one," she replied quietly while she thought of her bad dating experiences. *Was he disappointed in her?*

Glancing at her, he kissed her gently, closing his eyes while he thought of her purity and innocence for a silent moment. Making an easy decision, he whispered, "We should wait. I want to be with you but for now, let me touch you. I won't go any further than that. Let's keep that special moment for another time. Will you trust me?" She nodded, and he slipped his hands up her thighs. "You're all I want. I love you," he murmured into her ear as he kissed her. She relaxed and filled her mind and heart with Matt's offer of love.

While his hands pressed against her and caressed her body, she lost herself, drowning in his fiery kisses and his tender touches. The ecstasy of that moment made her gasp and call out his name while his lips covered her mouth in an impassioned kiss. For each of them, their burning desires had become much deeper and more meaningful. From that afternoon forward, they had moved into a romantic relationship. Both were drawn to each other, dizzy, dazzled, and in love.

* * *

Over a year had passed since Chet's wedding reception and their afternoon up at Skyline. Much had happened over that period of time. Torri sat in her bedroom, putting on her make-up and getting ready for her wedding at the small church in Riverside. Matt would be waiting for her at the altar along with their families, their friends, and other guests. Dressed in a dark brown western jacket, he would be wearing her wedding gift of a special bolo tie—a turquoise inlay of a horseshoe. He loved the bolo tie, reminding him of his beloved horses.

Early that morning, Aunt Sally had styled her hair on top of her head. Her friend and bridesmaid Doreen had come over to help her get ready. She had helped Torri cover all her freckles with make-up across her cheeks and on her upper chest. Her long, white wedding dress with a scooped neckline lay on her bed next to her bouquet. She had chosen white roses adorned with baby breaths, all surrounded with green leaves. Two wide, white satin bows tied the bouquet together.

Doreen had been so excited for Torri but admitted that she had been envious. Since she had finished that one year at college, she had come home to Riverside. While she looked for a better job, she worked at a motel cleaning rooms, hoping to meet a guy, marry, and settle down.

Her friend Patty was Torri's other bridesmaid, and she waited at the church with everyone else. Last summer, Patty had married Floyd by the justice of the peace at the courthouse in Midler. She had invited Doreen and Torri, and they had attended a short reception at the River Bend Supper Club. Patty and Floyd were now a happy couple.

Today, Doreen had been fretting about the veil, trying to decide where it should be placed on Torri's head. While her friend fussed, her mind whirled around with an emotional excitement that seemed to grow each moment inside of her. She was anxious about finally getting married.

She reached for the black box that held the elegant pendant necklace that Matt had ordered for her wedding gift. The triangular pendant was an Irish Celtic knot, representing eternal love. Slipping it around her neck, Doreen helped her with the clasp, saying it looked gorgeous on her. Glancing at the special necklace in the mirror, she saw the small diamond in the center of the knot sparkling brightly, sending warm feelings through her body about being Matt's wife.

Even though she now loved Matt, getting to this day had not been easy. She didn't know if she would ever find someone whom she could love. She recalled all of her dating experiences at college. However, after meeting Matt, dating him, and being with him, she knew that she loved him.

She glanced at her engagement ring, recalling the months before. They had spent the past year getting acquainted with each other. Matt would regularly call every week. They'd drove up to Skyline, drank vodka, and made out. Each time they were together, they became closer to each other. They had shared their past experiences, good and bad. She told him of her failure at college. Finally, she had asked him about his Army days, and he had told her what the military x-rays showed—a malformed vertebrae. She discovered that his headaches had continued nearly every day, causing him much pain. Hoping that he would go and see a doctor, she worried about him.

That fall, Torri had left her waitress job at Bert's Café. The rush of customers had finished after the summer and the business had dropped off. Bert's daughter Eveline had returned to work at the café, so they had to let her go. Torri had gladly stuffed her aprons in the bottom of her dresser—finished with waiting on tables. She helped BJ at the gas station, working the cash register while he pumped gas and worked on the vehicles in the garage.

During the Christmas holiday, Matt had asked her to marry him, surprising her with a sparkling diamond engagement ring. Their holiday had been filled with making plans for their future. They announced their engagement in the newspaper and decided on the wedding date—April 21st, waiting until after Easter. And here she was today, going to the church to marry him.

Torri carefully slipped on her white wedding gown, letting Doreen fix her veil on her head with a few bobby pins. Stepping into her heels, she was ready to meet Matt at the altar. In the Irish tradition, her dad had given her a small coin to put in her shoe which felt odd at first, but soon warmed and she forgot it was there. For their honeymoon, they were driving over to the resort town of Hadley for a few days, where it had all started. They planned to visit the bus depot and stop at the drive-in.

When they returned home, she would be moving to the Battle Axe Ranch into one of the large upper bedrooms. The Fletcher family looked forward to Torri joining them. They saw their family expanding in their big, log ranch house.

At the little church, she slowly moved down the aisle, holding her dad's arm and carrying her beautiful bouquet. Her parents had sent her wedding announcements to their distant relatives in Boston. Surprising her, their Irish relatives had sent her a laced handkerchief with a couple of green embroidered shamrocks. Their initials of *V* and *M* with their wedding date had been eloquently embroidered onto the handkerchief. This would become a cherished heirloom that she would pass down in her family. She carried it in her hand with her floral bouquet.

Stepping towards the altar, Torri thought of her brother Ronnie and said a silent prayer. She knew that he would be happy for her. She smiled, for she recalled her brother's playful voice in her head calling her "freckles." *She missed her brother.* Her mind shifted to Matt. *He loved her fairy dust.*

She didn't know what her future held with Matt, but they would be happy together. Her dad squeezed her hand and gave her a gentle hug as they stopped in front of Matt, smiling with a knowing glint in his eyes. Matt's hand reached out to her. She felt his warm hand take hers as he squeezed her hand gently, sending her a meaningful message of love. His eyes moved up her stunning wedding gown to her lovely face and into her amazing hazel eyes. Here's the girl who had dominated his mind and had captured his heart. Their thoughts were of tonight when they would become husband and wife. They had decided to wait, so their desirous emotions waited just below the surface. He stood tall next to his two brothers Chet and Tom. Matt's breast filled with love, and Torri felt the magical, magnetic tug that her dad had described about meeting the love of one's life when she became Victoria Fletcher.

Eveline's Path

Eveline Merther tried to stand as the bus bounced her around in this small compartment of a bathroom. She heaved into the small metal sink as she rocked back and forth. Her knees threatened to collapse and send her tumbling against the door. This was the second time she had been in this small cubicle. Her stomach had been emptied the first time. Her queasiness left her gagging. She pulled out a paper towel, wetted it, and wiped her mouth. With the water running, she rinsed out the metal sink. Then she cupped her hand under the water to rinse out the acid taste in her mouth. Spitting the water out, she would get some gum from her purse to freshen her breath. Glancing at the mirror, her skin looked pale, and her curly black hair needed to be combed. What a mess and what a disaster her life had become.

From her brown purse, she took out a comb and began to untangle her messy hair. While she comb it, the bus swayed this way and that. Reaching into her purse, she found a band to gather her hair behind her head and away from her face. Again, the rocking made her dizzy and her stomach lurched. She found the pack of gum, took out a piece, and unwrapped it. She recalled the time she had given her phone number to Matt Fletcher when they first met one evening at a Skyline party. She had written it on a gum wrapper. Even though it seemed like eternity, it was only a few weeks ago. But she had to forget about him and focus on the present—the here and now.

Her life had become a catastrophe. Her parents were sending her away to have the baby. Before leaving home this morning, she had begged her mom to come with her. But they had a business to run, and it took both of her parents to run the café. No—she would have to go alone.

The week before, Dr. Carter had examined Eveline and she had discovered that she was pregnant. In his private office, he had spoken to her mom about the options, which were few. She had fainted in the waiting room and caused a great deal of fuss. From that moment on, her life had changed. The doctor had sent them home with all of the information. Finally, her parents had decided to send her to St. Magdalen's, a charity home in Colorado, where she would stay until the baby came. Her parents would tell the town's people that she had gone to help her sick aunt for a period of time. Before Dr. Carter returned to his main practice in Winston, he kindly offered to drive her to the bus depot. Everything had happened so fast. Eveline's head couldn't grasp why she suddenly had to leave so quickly.

During the week following her doctor's visit, her parents went to the café and worked every day. Her mom made her stay home from school, phoning them with an excuse that she had an upset stomach. At the evening dinners, the tension with her parents had swelled. Her dad had avoided looking at his shamed daughter and wouldn't talk to her. She had waited for his usual lecture that would condemn her, but it didn't come, just a cruel silence. Her mom did not have a sympathetic feeling towards her either. Whenever she'd glanced at her daughter, she'd just shake her head in disgust. While Eveline nibbled on her food at meal times, her nausea would spread through her. She would have to dash for the bathroom, slamming the door on her parents and their uncaring attitudes. Crying and gagging, she'd slipped to the bathroom floor with a bad acid taste in her mouth. She felt miserable every day.

Finally, she had to think about getting ready to leave. She needed to pack her clothes into one of their suitcases. Looking for some support, she asked her mom to help her. Her mom shook her head and said, "Eveline, none of your clothes will fit you within a month or two. I have my old maternity clothes in a box downstairs. We'll see if there's anything you can wear."

They went down the stairs and her mom found the cardboard box that contained her old clothes. None of them looked good, for they were old, worn out, and faded. All of the skirts and slacks had an expandable panel in the front. Eveline glanced at these and noticed how odd they looked. She didn't want any of them. However with her mom pressuring her, Eveline picked out a sleeveless white blouse, a skirt, and a pair of slacks. Her mom selected two of her faded nightgowns and a few pairs of underwear.

"Now, take these. You're going to be uncomfortable in your own underwear. How about a few more tops? Do you want any of these?" asked her mom, holding up more tops. Eveline just shook her head; to her, they looked too old for her, out of style. She didn't like them, and she wouldn't wear them. No way. They were grotesque looking.

Closing the box, her mom said, "Okay. We need to wash these tonight, so that you can take them with you." Carrying the few items of clothes, Eveline and her mom went back upstairs. She asked her mom to tell her what it was like having a baby. But her mom cut her off and said she'd have to find out by herself, for every woman's pregnancy was different.

Her mom Kay had been so appalled and angry at her daughter that she couldn't talk to her. She simply had no advice, and she couldn't tolerate her daughter's condition and being unwed. She wanted no part of it. By midnight, a small brown suitcase sat packed next to her dresser in her small bedroom.

Crawling under her covers exhausted and tired, Eveline thought about leaving. While thinking of her parent's dreadful looks and cold manners, her shame and guilt felt heavy in her heart. Even though they had said they loved her, she felt their anger, their displeasure, and their disgust towards her. In addition, her mom ignored her and pushed her questions away. She had no one to talk to. Her parents hadn't allowed her to phone her girlfriends and even tell them "Goodbye." Her pregnancy had to be kept a secret from her classmates and the town. For Eveline, she realized that her leaving home would be the best solution. Her situation at home became impossible for her to deal with. Her dad left her with only these words: "You have to go away. No discussion."

* * *

This morning before dawn, Dr. Carter had picked her up. He had assured her parents that she would be taken good care of and that he would get her to the bus depot. While they drove down to Winston, the doctor had spoken to her, trying to comfort her. Being a doctor, he had reassured her that as a young woman, having a baby was a natural process and there was nothing for her to fear. He had told her that there would be other girls like her; she wouldn't be alone. Emphasizing the importance of keeping herself healthy, physically and mentally, he told her to eat well and to get plenty of rest. He felt bad for Eveline. An unmarried pregnant girl always worried him. Her plight would not be easy.

Concerned about the baby, Eveline asked about the adoption procedures. He further explained that married couples who couldn't have babies turned to adoption. A caring couple would raise the baby as their own. The adoption process would take time, but everything would be handled for her. After the baby was born, the adoption would be final. He informed her that all of the records would be sealed for the protection of her, the new parents, and the baby. The doctor gently reminded her that after the baby that she could return home and start her life again.

While the doctor talked, Eveline quietly listened to his advice, recognizing that she had so much to think about. Even though these plans all sounded good, somehow Eveline felt that there had to be more to it. This couldn't be that simple. She knew that she had six months in front of her before the baby would be born. *What would the next months be like?* The time seemed to stretch out in front of her like a dark tunnel, not knowing what to expect. Her future seemed dark and terrifying.

The thought of living at the charity home frightened her. Where would she sleep, eat, and bathe? What would the other girls be like? Her body had slowly been changing, but she didn't feel different. The odd knowledge of being pregnant made her mind swirl around and around. But as the extreme pressure and stress descended on her, her eyes watered up as she tried to control her fearful feelings.

Turning her head, she brushed away the single tear that slid down her cheek. She listened to the doctor, thinking that her life had turned itself upside down. Dr. Carter's sympathetic voice spoke to her without disgust and without condemning her. She wanted more time with him, so she could find out more about having a baby. But the time slipped by fast before she had a chance to ask any more questions.

After arriving in Winston, Dr. Carter told her that he wanted to stop at his office and give her some non-prescription medication for the nausea that she had been experiencing. While he was there, he also phoned St. Magdalen's to let them know that Eveline would be coming that day. To his amazement, he discovered that the charity home was filled and did not have a room for her. But knowing that she was coming, the Mother Superior had called around and found another nearby charity home for her. She had contacted and arranged for Eveline to go to the Samuel Wickerson Home in a small town in eastern Colorado. They had an opening and would accept her. The doctor took down the information, asked a few questions, and hung up the phone.

Dr. Carter had been disappointed in hearing about the change, but at least she had somewhere to go and stay; that had been the main focus. He quietly explained the situation to Eveline, wrote down the new address for her, and told her that he would contact her parents and let them know. She sat shocked at the news with no words. *A change in her destination? She was not going to St. Magdalen's.* As he then drove her down to the bus depot, she tensed up, worried about the Wickerson Home. Nervously, she bought her bus ticket to Flat Rock. Before stepping up into the big bus, she turned and thanked Dr. Carter for driving her here. She knew that he didn't have to. He was such a kind and understanding doctor. Giving her a fatherly hug, he smiled, told her to take care of herself. He then said "goodbye." Nodding sadly, she stepped up into the bus, found a seat near the back, and sat down.

* * *

The long bus ride from Winston to Flat Rock allowed Eveline to get her mind set to what she faced. She had to gather strength and courage in confronting her situation. She didn't know what the future held, but every mile, every turn, and every hill rocked her in her seat. She couldn't stop her mind from wondering through the last few months, replaying her ugly past. *How did she get here?*

Long before this all happened, her dad's lectures had warned her about guys and drinking liquor at parties. He had told her there were good and bad guys. His long, tortuous rants would go on and on. She had endured the duration of them while she blocked out most of his words and nodded her head in agreement. When she had started high school, he had set down strict rules about her after-school activities, her dating, and giving her curfews. She could go to the school-sponsored activities, but no other parties without their approval.

Eveline had been a quiet, shy girl in high school. For years, she had sat at the back of the classrooms and had done her homework. All her classmates had liked her, for she had been friendly and courteous. Several of her girlfriends had encouraged her at the end of her junior year to try out for cheerleading. She had never thought that she would be chosen. But she had. Everyone had liked her. She had a beautiful look with her long, curly black hair, her sweet smile, and her caring nature.

After she had become a cheerleader, she started down the path of popularity. Before her senior year, she had spent that summer practicing with the other cheerleaders, ordering their outfits, and learning the cheers. For Eveline, this had been a fun and exciting time. Her friends also had encouraged her to go to their late-night parties, despite her parent's rule—no parties, no drinking. They had covered for her always getting her home before curfew.

However, that one stormy evening in January after a basketball game with Hadley High School had changed everything. She had gone along to the party, ignoring her dad's warnings about good and evil in the world. Tears started to fill her eyes as she thought of that horrendous night and of the basketball player. She wiped the tears away quickly with her hand. She knew that he had taken advantage of her and the situation—the snow storm, the motel room, and the liquor. She had asked him to stop, but he had ignored her. It had happened so quickly. His smug face had smiled at her, saying that he knew that she liked it and that this wasn't her first time. She had been shocked that he could tell. That evening, her tears had streamed down her face as she tried to stop his kisses and caresses.

Yes, at twelve, she had been with a boy—an awkward moment at the big swimming hole down by the river one summer. Curiosity about her body had driven her towards that never-talked about subject—sex. Not many parents talked about it to their children, openly; only a few told their daughters and sons. Among the young, they spoke about it in hushed whispers and curious laughs. The inquisitiveness of it caught her, and she lost her innocence. Now, she realized that she had been stupid to experiment with such a serious act. But this pregnancy had not been totally her fault. That one night had been all wrong.

Even though she had buried that horrifying experience, she sometimes would have a reoccurring nightmare about it. Dark images kept replaying that evening in her dreams. His smug face never failed to scare her awake, cold, sweating, and frightened. She had faced the devil and she had lost. She knew that this had been her biggest mistake of her life.

The anger grew every time she had dreamed of it. How foolish she had been. Why couldn't it had been with someone she liked. She then would have gotten married, had the baby, and made a life for herself. But no, it had to be that conceited, arrogant stranger Devin Banes, the tall, blonde star basketball player. When her parents found out about her pregnancy, her dad had forced her to reveal the guy's name. But after that, she never mention his name again. After weeks of crying at night, Eveline eventually buried everything deep inside. She cleared the memory of him. Now, she had to face this pregnancy, alone. She was on her own.

* * *

While the bus rocked back and forth, she sat with her eyes closed, not wanting to engage in conversation with anyone on the bus. The other passengers watched her make a quick beeline to the back bathroom, twice. When she came back down the aisle, she told them that she had eaten something that had made her sick. They just smiled and nodded; one woman suspected her condition. The bus driver made several stops at the towns along the highway, picking up and dropping off people. The stops allowed her to stretch her legs. One time she bought an orange soda, needing something in her stomach.

She carried her purse close to her body. Her dad had warned her not to trust anyone on the bus and to keep her purse with her at all times. Her purse had been stuffed full of important items. Her wallet carried money for spending. Since she thought that someone could steal her wallet, she hid half of the money in her bra. She had a small address book with all the important phone numbers and addresses. She had her comb and hair brush with a small make-up bag. Her mom had given her a small bottle of aspirin, telling her to not take them too often. The doctor had given her the pills for the nausea.

After the last time to the bathroom, she took one of the doctor's pills from the bottle. With a little water cupped in her palm, she had swallowed one, hoping that the medication would help. Before leaving this morning, she had slipped a few saltine crackers wrapped in wax paper into her purse for her nausea. Hunger wracked her stomach, empty of food. She took out a cracker from her purse and nibbled on it. Closing her eyes, she let the bus rock her, taking her farther and farther away from her home in the mountains.

Her Aunt Vera and Uncle Max Hench were to meet her at the bus depot in Flat Rock, Colorado and to drive her to St. Magdalen's charity home, only she wasn't going there now. A sudden change in plans. Now, she was headed to the Wickerson Home. She hoped that her aunt and uncle would be able to make the switch and take her to an eastern Colorado town called Stockford.

Eveline had met her relatives only once before when she had been a little girl. But they would be an important part of the fabricated story which her dad and mom used to explain her absence from home. Undeniably, her aunt had not been sick, but that's the story they would tell. Her parents also had insisted that any letters from her friends were to be addressed to her aunt and uncle's home address in Flat Rock. Her parents didn't want anyone to know her true address. These lies all seemed so complicated to Eveline. She did not want to be away from home for months. But this had been her parent's decision. She definitely could not stay at home, go to school, and have the baby. It simply wouldn't do. She had lost control of her life and she was on her own.

When the bus finally stopped at her destination in Flat Rock, Eveline looked out of her window to see if she recognized anyone. But she didn't. She rose, slipped her coat on, and grabbed her purse. Walking slowly down the aisle with the others on the bus, they all moved towards the opened doors. The driver had stepped off the bus and had been unloading the suitcases and other gear. After stepping off the bus, the travelers pushed and moved around her. She stepped back from the crowd who were picking up their luggage. Finally, the crowd dispersed, and she saw her lone brown suitcase sitting by the bus. With it in hand, she looked up and down the sidewalk. No one was there, so she moved into the bus depot, thinking her aunt and uncle would be waiting for her in there. She saw a middle-aged couple sitting on a row of chairs. When she came through the doors, a dark-haired woman rose and walked towards her,

"Eveline? I'd recognized that curly black hair anywhere. My you've grown into such a beautiful girl," said her aunt. She reached out and hugged her. "My poor dear child. What did you get yourself into?"

Her tall, thin uncle rose and stood beside them, "Now, Vera. Keep quiet."

Eveline took in the sweet smell of her full-figured Aunt Vera. The comfortable hug that she felt made her love her aunt immediately. "Hi, Aunt Vera and Uncle Max. Thanks for coming and picking me up. We have a change of plans."

Uncle Max's face showed his confusion and surprise. Looking around, her uncle nervously replied, "Let's go to the car and we can talk there. Not in here." The three of them left the bus depot, walked down the street, and stepped into their car. Eveline sat in the back seat. Her uncle turned to her and said, "Okay. Tell us what's going on. Aren't we going to St. Magdalen's?"

Eveline quietly explained why the change and where they would be going now. She handed her uncle the address written down by Dr. Carter. After looking at the address and town, he asked Aunt Vera to get the state map out of the glovebox. Silence fell on them while he looked over the road map.

Finally, Eveline asked, "Will you be able to drive me to Stockford? I'm sorry about the change." Her uncle folded up the road map, handed it back to Vera, and turned back to her.

"It'll be fine. We will just be going eastward instead of westward. It's about a two-hour drive," he replied. Eveline nodded and her aunt turned to her.

"Oh, my dear. How was your bus ride? How are you feeling?" asked her aunt, concerned.

"It's been a long trip down here from Winston to Flat Rock. I did get sick a couple of times. I'm doing okay now," replied Eveline.

"Have you had lunch?" asked her aunt. Eveline shook her head "no" as she felt her empty stomach take a roll at the thought of food. Aunt Vera continued, "Well, on the floor back there, I packed a little cooler with some sandwiches, a couple of pickles, a little bag of potato chips, and some homemade cookies. I also have a thermos of coffee. We can eat while we drive. Can you get them out for us?"

Eveline opened the little cooler on the floor next to her and passed the food and thermos to her aunt. They sat quietly eating their lunch. Even though Eveline's appetite had returned, she ate slowly, hoping that her food would stay down. Her aunt talked the whole time, never stopping. She asked her about her mom and dad, about the café, and about her school. Eveline answered her, keeping her answers short. Aunt Vera recalled the time that her sister Kay had come down with Eveline when she was just a little girl with her curly black hair. She went on and on about that visit. Not surprisingly, Eveline didn't remember any of it, except meeting her aunt and uncle.

Her uncle drove, eating and listening. Every once in a while, he would glance up at the rearview mirror and see Eveline in the back seat. He thought that she looked too young to be pregnant. How old was she? Seventeen? Maybe eighteen. She didn't look a day older than fourteen. What an unfortunate situation. He knew that Vera would want to drive and visit her niece every chance that they could. He didn't know anything about these homes for unwed girls. But he knew that they might not be able to see her as much as his wife wanted to. From the beginning, he didn't want to get mixed up in this mess. A dark past creeped back into his thoughts every time he thought of his niece.

Max remembered that when he and Vera were first married, she had experienced a difficult first pregnancy. He bitterly recalled that her pregnancy had ended with the death of their newborn—a stillborn. The poor baby girl never drew a breath. On her second pregnancy, his wife had miscarried and had to have an operation in order to save her life. He had become more concerned and worried about his wife Vera than having children after those two devastating experiences. He had loved her dearly and feared losing her. And he never wanted to adopt, so they had stayed childless. They had a good relationship and a solid marriage, becoming very close. Hearing and seeing Eveline had brought all those dreadful memories back to him, making him feel uncomfortable with this situation.

Naturally, Vera would want to pamper her niece as much as she could. Max thought that as a parent, he would not want to deal with an unwed pregnant daughter. He had gotten to know a little about Bert Merther who probably would have come unglued when he had found out about his daughter. It must have been disheartening. Even though he didn't know her, Eveline seemed genuinely nice. He speculated that she would have been an easy target for a scheming guy. He had known quite a few in his lifetime. Shaking off his thoughts, he focused on driving, drinking his coffee, and dropping off his poor niece. *The sooner the better.*

While they drove on, Eveline became sleepy, and she leaned her head back on the seat. Her aunt noticed her niece's closed eyes and finally stopped talking to her. Vera quietly turned towards her husband. As the car rocked her, she fell asleep.

"Max, what are we going to do? She's so young. Why can't she stay with us?" whispered Aunt Vera.

"No, we've talked about this. We can't interfere with their plans," he replied.

"Well, I don't know anything about this Wickerson Home. At least, I have heard of St. Magdalen's. I am going in with her. To get a good look at this place," she whispered.

"Now, now. We can visit her, but we can't interfere," he replied.

"I don't know what Kay was thinking sending her down here," she whispered back.

"Listen, Vera. Stop it. This is not our daughter. Like I said, we can visit her and make sure she's doing all right. But beyond that, we can't meddle. Your sister is doing what she thinks is best. Kay told us that she could have sent her to California, but she chose Colorado because we're here. We'll come and visit her," he quietly said.

"It just doesn't seem right," she responded.

"She'll be taking care of. I am more worried about you. Don't get too involved," he whispered back to his wife. He loved her too much to watch her go through the emotional trauma of Eveline's situation. Even though it had been years ago, the past memories were fresh to both of them. And this situation would stress her daily. For the next months, he had to be strong and protect her against getting embroiled with Eveline.

"Oh, well. None of it is going to be easy," replied Vera. He reached over and squeezed his wife's hand. She scooted nearer to him, and he put his arm around her shoulders, comforting his wife.

By now, Eveline in the back seat had heard her name. She woke up slowly, listening but keeping her eyes closed. At least, her aunt and uncle cared about her and planned to visit. That gave a little hope in her heart to know that they would be nearby.

Yawning, she sat up and looked around, noticing they were driving towards the horizon with telephone poles lining the highway for miles and miles in front of them. She turned around and squinted out the back window. The sun had been shining on her while it had moved towards the western horizon. The dark blue Rockies stood behind them on the far distant horizon and they were slowly disappearing until they were gone. She glanced at the places along the highway—the farmland, the farmhouses, the big barns, the grain silos, and the small towns. The land became flat as the sky grew like a giant above them. Rows and rows of farmland, with dark soil turned up, planted, and irrigated. While they passed different farms, Aunt Vera talked about seeing a chicken farm, then, a pig farm, and finally, a dairy. Drifting into the car's vent, the heavy smells of those farms reached Eveline in the back seat and sent her stomach in a lurch.

She quickly tapped Aunt Vera on the shoulder, "I'm going to throw up."

"Max, pull over," said her aunt to her husband. She glanced back at Eveline. "If you can't hold it, use the cooler." Nodding, Eveline swallowed and held her hand over her mouth. The car slowed and Max pulled over and stopped. She grabbed the door handle and threw it opened. Stepping out of the car, she heaved her lunch out on the side of the road. Aunt Vera came to her side, giving her a handkerchief.

"I'll get you something to drink," she said. Getting the thermos, she poured her a little coffee. Eveline took it. Rinsing and spitting it out, she gasped, "Thanks. Sorry, I couldn't hold it down."

"Don't worry. It's fine. We'll stop somewhere and get some water," her aunt replied, trying to comfort her niece.

Uncle Max hollered at them, "If you're done, get in the car. We'll stop in the next town and find a bathroom." The two got back into the car. Her uncle had been worried about being parked along the highway. He relaxed after they headed on towards the next town.

"I have some nausea pills I can take," said Eveline, feeling bad about the trouble she had caused.

"Good. We'll stop at a gas station," replied Uncle Max. They drove on in silence for some time. Finally, a small town emerged in front of them. He pulled into the first station, stopped, and waited while the two got out and went in to ask about using the restroom. The gas attendant gave them a key, indicating that it was around to the side.

Inside the restroom, Eveline rinsed her mouth out several times. She splashed water on her face and mouth, refreshing her pale face. In her purse, she took out the bottle of pills and swallowed one with some water.

Her aunt stood beside her with her purse. "You know that this nausea will disappear after your third month. You should be close to that now. Aren't you?" she asked.

"I don't know. Were you ever pregnant?" asked Eveline, looking pale and weak.

"Yes, but that's not important. How many times have you thrown up? Can you keep anything down?" she asked.

"Twice on the bus and now. No, food comes right up after a while. I can keep crackers down. But I thought you didn't have any children," she replied, curious to hear her aunt's story.

"No, I don't, but that's all in the past. Listen, I want to give you some money. How much did your parents give you?" said her aunt, avoiding her niece's questioning eyes.

"About $30," she answered. Nodding, her aunt gave her a $20 bill from her wallet. Eveline shook her head, but her aunt shoved it into her hand.

"You never know what you may need. Keep it," explained her aunt.

"Okay," and she stuck it in her bra under her blouse.

"If you need more, let me know when we visit. Now, we have to go. Drink a little more water," said her aunt. Eveline drank some from the faucet using her palm. She did feel better. Her aunt embraced her into a long, caring hug. She leaned into her affectionate aunt, wishing she could stay with her. Her aunt patted her back, "Let's go."

They came out, stepped into the car, and her uncle drove them out of the small town. He looked back at Eveline, and said, "We're almost there. The next town is Stockford."

* * *

As they drove into the small town, Eveline glanced around with renewed interest. On the north side, Stockford had a co-op with three silos and a gas pump out front. Surrounding the town were farms with long, plowed fields. There were four streets of four or five houses—two on either side of main street. The highway ran down main street which had a café, a grocery store, a post office, a bar and liquor store. An elementary school building with a little playground sat one block from main street. A tall, white round water tower stood on the south side of town with the town's name written across the front in black letters. The "t" and the top of "o's" had disappeared off the town's name so that it read "S uckfurd." All three of them in the car snickered at the ridiculous name. Eveline held her hand over her mouth to keep from laughing out loud.

"Someone should get up there and fix that," commented Uncle Max, disgusted.

"Yes. I wonder about the missing letter," replied Aunt Vera, chuckling under her breath and shaking her head.

Sitting by itself and facing west, the Samuel R. Wickerson Home sat at the edge of town, just twenty miles from the Kansas state border. Uncle Max found the place within a few minutes. Pulling up and stopping in front of the two-story wooden house with a long front porch, Eveline's eyes roamed over her new home, a plain white house. A wooden sign with ornate lettering stood in front of the home.

The Samuel R. Wickerson Home had a small front yard, a large turned-up garden on one side, and a drive way and garage on the other side. A concrete ashpit sat next to the garage where the garbage would be burned in the evenings. A long clothesline stretched along the backyard. Nearby, a sizable root cellar could be seen with long grass growing on top.

Two girls were in the garden, hoeing the ground. Two were out back, taking the washing off the clotheslines. One girl had finished sweeping the porch. Upstairs, curtains moved while another girl gazed down at the car.

As the director for twenty years, Miss Blanche Drost, a slim, middle-aged woman, stood inside, waiting to greet the new girl and the parents of the fallen girl. Her greying black hair had been pulled into a bun at the back of her head. With long deep wrinkles across her forehead, her youthful looks had long ago faded, but she wore bright, red lipstick on her big lips with matching red fingernails. Today, Miss Drost had dressed-up and had worn her grey suit with a pencil skirt and her white and black Mary Jane low heels which had been her dancing shoes. Taking a deep breath, Miss Drost prepared herself.

Eveline, her aunt, and her uncle carrying her suitcase walked up to the long porch. Uncle Max set the brown suitcase down on the porch, put his hand on Eveline's shoulder, and said "goodbye." Heading back to the car to wait, he had no reason to go inside. He cringed at the thought of a house full of pregnant girls. Aunt Vera stepped towards the front door and pushed the doorbell, waiting with Eveline who had picked up her suitcase. Smiling, Miss Drost opened the door, welcoming them to come in. They made their introductions. Miss Drost wondered where the girl's parents were.

Aunt Vera's curious eyes took in everything, noting that it was a plain, stark house inside with a brown and white decor, no warm colors. The director showed them into the small sitting room next to the front door. The two women made small talk about their trip while Eveline sat and glanced at a large portrait of a distinguished man with a stern face. A brass nameplate with "*Samuel R. Wickerson*" hung on one wall. Next to it, a framed written document hung next to the portrait. The top heading read "*The Four Guiding Principles.*"

Miss Drost gave her the prepared introduction about the wealthy man in the portrait and how he had established the home and provided the funds to build the two-story home. She covered all aspects of the charity home: the six bedrooms upstairs, the small non-denominational chapel, the medical office, the kitchen, the dining room, and the laundry room. Miss Drost emphasized that they were here to help provide a healthy environment for the girls. She said that they had on staff a nurse, a cook, and her assistant who had just walked into the room to be introduced. Miss Flossie

Everill was a young, brown haired, big-busted woman. She shook Aunt Vera's hand and looked over at Eveline with shaded eyes, scrutinizing the young girl who looked no more than fourteen. To Flossie, the girl looked pale and tired with dark circles under her eyes.

Miss Drost continued, "We have a visiting doctor that comes monthly and checks each girl and their progress. We do expect adoption for the newborn babies. Within a few hours of birth, we arrange for an adoption agency to take the newborn."

"Do the babies go directly to a family?" asked Eveline, quietly speaking for the first time. She had started to think more about the baby than herself. *Who would take care of her child if she didn't?*

"No, they go to an orphanage until the adoption is completed," answered Miss Drost. Eveline lowered her eyes to avoid letting anyone see her reaction of horror. *An orphanage?* Dr. Carter didn't mention that. In her English class at school last semester, she had read two horrendous novels about orphans and their abandonment. She cleared her mind and focused again on the ongoing conversation.

Aunt Vera spoke up and asked, "I didn't see a hospital. Where do the girls deliver their babies?"

"Right here at the Wickerson Home. We have a nurse who lives here in town, and we call our doctor to deliver the babies," replied Miss Everill, speaking up for the first time. She seemed friendly and smiled.

"What happens if there are complications?" asked Aunt Vera, knowing full well what she had experienced during her pregnancies.

"The closest hospital is in Bender, only thirty-minutes away. We would send a girl there if something would occur. We have clear procedures for all deliveries," responded Miss Drost, being very officious. Glancing at Eveline, she asked, "Have you visited with your doctor? Are you taking any medications?"

"Yes. I've been to see my doctor. He's given me some pills for my nausea. I have them in my purse. Would you like to see them?" asked Eveline.

"No, my dear. The nurse will want to make a note of them when you see her," replied Miss Drost.

"Oh, what about her education? Eveline hasn't finished high school," commented her aunt. She knew that her sister Kay would want her to finish.

"We provide classes. We have a local teacher who will teach her along with the others," replied Miss Drost. "Are there any more questions? We must get busy here. Thank you for dropping off your niece, Mrs. Hench. Be assured that we will take good care of her." Miss Drost avoided directly answering the educational question. They weren't set up to award diplomas since their main goal here was to care for these unwed girls.

Standing, the director extended her hand toward her Aunt Vera, ending her visit. After shaking hands, her aunt looked over at Eveline, walked over, and gave her final hug and said "Goodbye dear. Call if you need anything. We'll come and visit you. Take care of yourself." Tears pooled in both of their eyes as they both brushed them aside quickly. Then, she left. Eveline felt the loneliness descend upon her as she watched her aunt leave.

Outside, Uncle Max saw his wife coming out of the door and he started the car. After getting in, Vera waved to Eveline who stood at the front door with Miss Drost and Miss Everill standing behind her, watching. Vera felt awful, leaving her niece there.

While they drove away, Max said, "I need to stop and fill up."

"Oh, Max. I didn't like the place," said Vera.

"Why not?" he asked.

"There were no decorations in the house. I didn't like that Miss Drost with her big mouth and red lipstick. She seemed so cold. Her welcome came off memorized and so official," replied Vera, critical about the home and the director.

"Now, don't prejudge. You've just met her. You're making a snap judgement without really knowing her. She has a difficult job, dealing with a house full of pregnant girls," he said.

"And that's another thing. She seems so disciplined," she added.

"Now, that's not a bad thing. It takes a strong hand to keep order. I think Eveline will be all right. I found out in the Army that a little discipline doesn't hurt anyone. Creates a strong character. Let's get home. We have a long drive back," replied Max.

He stopped at the co-op to fill up. After Max stepped out of the car, an elderly man greeted him. As they filled the car, Max asked, "What happened to the town's name on the water tower?"

"Those darn farm kids. They paint over the 't' and the tops of the 'o's.' This is the third time. I'm not fixing that name again," complained the co-op guy. Max shook his head, paid for the gas, and left. While they drove out of town, Max explained to Vera about the water tower. They both laughed, thinking of how mischievous the young can be.

* * *

Back at the Wickerson Home, Eveline turned her attention to Miss Drost and Miss Everill as they led her down the hall to an office with a desk and chairs. The friendly Miss Drost all of a sudden turned cold and severe. Eveline couldn't believe the changed expression on the director's face. When they walked down the hall, Miss Everill stopped at one of the doors and came back out carrying something.

"Sit down. We have an hour to go over some important things. First, hand me your purse," said Miss Drost who picked up a glass case and slipped on a pair of wireframed glasses which sat at the end of her long, aquiline nose.

"But... but, why?" asked Eveline, trying to be polite. Her dad told her to protect her purse from others.

"Listen. I don't like to say things twice. Hand over your purse," insisted Miss Drost.

Without realizing it, Miss Everill gently took the purse from her hands, handing it over to the director who quickly opened it and emptied the contents on the desk. Her personal items all scattered out on top of the desk. Picking through the items, the director picked up Eveline's wallet, opened it, and pulled out the money.

"Is this all the money you brought? Just $15?" she asked.

Eveline just nodded, knowing that she had more, but decided not to say anything.

"Okay. This is how it goes. I'm going to write out a receipt for the money and keep it for you. By the way, Miss Everill has a smock for you to wear. You will need to change into it before dinner tonight," she said, taking out a receipt book. "And let see, the smock will cost you $2. And you will need other incidentals, such as bath soap, deodorant, and shampoo, for the time you're here. So, you'll have $10 left. Any long distant phone calls will be deducted from this amount of $10. You don't have much left, so be careful. And by the way, that long hair will have to be cut and shortened. You won't have time around here to fuss with it," said Miss Drost as she finished writing out the receipt and handed Eveline the paper with the figures deducted and the director's signature and date.

Miss Everill carefully picked up the scattered items on the desk, putting them back into Eveline's purse. She left out the bottles of aspirin and of pills. Miss Drost indicated that the nurse would keep her aspirins for her. She could keep her pills for nausea. Before handing back the wallet, Miss Drost took out Eveline's driver's license and remarked, "You certainly won't be needing this. I will keep it with your money deposit. Miss Everill, go through her suitcase. We will hold most of your belongings until you leave here."

Miss Everill picked up Eveline's suitcase, put it on a side table, and opened it. She went through her clothes, holding up each item for Miss Drost's approval who flicked her hand quickly if she approved and she shook her head for those to be removed. A chair next to the table filled up with those she removed. Her mom's maternity clothes, nightgowns, and underwear were left in the suitcase. Her favorite pink sweater Miss Everill had set aside on the chair.

Eveline got her nerve up to speak, and said, "I'd like to keep my pink sweater. I tend to get chilly." She glanced quickly down after the sharp black eyes of Miss Drost looked at her over her spectacles. The paused tension made Eveline nervous and afraid.

"Sure. Why not? Give the girl her sweater, Flossie," responded Miss Drost. "Put in the smock. That will be all. See to the other girls while I finish up here." Nodding, the assistant slipped the smock into her suitcase and snapped it shut, setting it next to Eveline's chair.

After she left, Miss Drost set back in her chair, glaring at her. She slowly took out some paper work from her desk drawer, arranging them, as she looked them over. She picked up a ball point pen and filled out the information on a form, using Eveline's driver's license.

While she wrote, she spoke her name, "Eveline Maria Merther. You'll be called 'Eve.' I need more information. What is your father's name and occupation?" As the director fired questions at her, she answered quietly.

"Is this the correct home address? What's your mother's name? Occupation? What's your home phone number? I will be notifying your father about his donation to the Wickerson Home. Now. Your aunt's name is Vera Hench? What's your aunt's phone number?" Eveline had to stop and take out her address book from her purse in order to give her that number. "Give me your aunt's address. What's your uncle's name and occupation? What is his phone number?" From the book, she gave her the information. But Eveline stalled out and said, "I'm not sure about my uncle. I know he works, but I don't know where."

Miss Drost glared back at her, "You don't know? Listen, they are your closest contact. We need this information. So, the next time you talk to them, find out. Understand?" She nodded, shaking inside at being put on the spot. *Was this woman the Grand Inquisitor? What would she say next, "Off with her head"?* Right now that didn't sound so bad to Eveline. She started to feel sick again.

"Now, there is this other form which will be your health information. The medical record will be kept, noting the doctor's visits and the notes that he makes about your progress, such as your weight. Dr. Robert Smith, who will come once a month to see you, will want more information about your pregnancy. Let me say, most girls can give the month and date that they got pregnant. From the call from St. Magdalen's, you're about three months along. Right?" asked the director.

Eveline just nodded. "I didn't hear your answer," remarked Miss Drost.

Quickly, she spoke up, "Yes. I'm sorry, but I'm going to throw up," as she held her hand over her mouth, feeling nauseated.

Miss Drost looked disgusted at her, and pointed, "Out the door to the left is a bathroom."

Eveline jumped up, ran out the door and to the left. Opening the door without knocking, she headed for the toilet, just making it in time to empty her stomach.

Another shocked pregnant girl stood at the sink washing her hands and said, "Excuse me," as Eveline retched into the toilet again.

"Wow, you've got it bad," said the pregnant girl, taking down a clean washcloth from a shelf. She rinsed the cloth with water and handed it to Eveline. "Hi, I'm Mona. You must be the new girl."

She took the washcloth and wiped her mouth, "Thanks. I'm so sorry."

Miss Drost had followed her. Standing in the hall, she said, "Go back to work Mona. This is Eve, our new girl."

"Yes, ma'am," said Mona who quickly left the bathroom and headed down the hall.

Eveline stepped to the sink and turned the faucet on and rinsed out her mouth. She held the washcloth, wondering what to do with it. "Drape it over the bathtub to dry out." Miss Drost, pointed back to her office, indicating that she should return.

Eveline quickly left the bathroom while Miss Drost followed her, going behind her desk again and putting on her wireframed glasses on her hooked nose. Selecting another document from the pile, she glanced at it.

"As you noted, in the sitting room is the portrait of our illustrious founder Samuel R. Wickerson. He not only funded and built this home but required a set of Four Guiding Principles. We are here to provide not only a home to care for you and to have your baby adopted but also to develop you as a person. These four principles are posted throughout this home: in the bedrooms, the medical office, the dining room, the kitchen, the laundry room, and the chapel. I expect you to learn them, memorize them, and recite them without hesitation. While you are here, those principles will benefit you. And when you leave, they will help provide a new life for you." She paused, letting Eveline think about her words. Handing her the document, she continued, "Now, here are the Four Guiding Principles. Read along as I go over them with you."

Anonymity: "We need to safeguard and protect you and your family. Keep your family's surname a secret. Your full identity is known only to me and my assistant. Thus, your name here at the Wickerson Home will be 'Eve' with no last name."

Educational Improvement – "We provide classes that will continue your education. The general goal is to improve your mind. We will teach you skills that will help you when you return to society."

Develop Work Ethics – " Our general goal is to build a hardworking attitude. We are all part of a group, working together with efficient results. The girls are assigned regular work details to maintain our home."

Humility & Self-control – "We have chapel weekly. We read, reflect, and recite appropriate Bible verses. We are nondenominational, so there is no preaching. We intend to develop uplifting thoughts and feelings to control the immodest impulses that you have experienced. We want to help you control your defiant attitudes and become humble and proper individuals."

Miss Drost ended with a proud sigh. Those principles had inspired her all these years. Her work here never ended. New girls were always showing up, needing her help with these four principles.

For Eveline, she had stopped listening after the director told her that her name was to be 'Eve.' *Why take away my name?* That didn't make sense to her. When her dad had lectured her, she used to block out his words. Now, with Miss Drost's lecture, she did the same. Eveline had gotten good at ignoring adults. Rules, rules, rules. At the end, Miss Drost had added something that caught her attention again.

"If for any reason that you intentionally violate these Guiding Principles, you will be disciplined. And if you continue to violate our principles, you will be sent home. I need you to sign this document on the bottom line," said the director, handing the ball point pen to Eveline who scribbled her name with a shaking hand.

"We have one more document for you to sign. Here's the adoption paper," she said handing her another document. Eveline's insides started to shake, and her mind started to spin. This felt like a huge decision to make without a discussion. She wanted to ask a few questions, such as how did the adoption work. But there was no discussion. Just silence with Miss Drost's glaring black eyes looking at her, daring Eveline to question her authoritative manner. No options were left to this young pregnant girl. She again, scribbled her name with a trembling hand.

Miss Drost took off her glasses, arranged all of the documents into a folder, and put them into a desk drawer. "Let's get you settled upstairs in your room. I'll put you with Stella who has been here for quite some time. She can help you get acquainted with our schedule."

Rising, the two left the office with Eveline carrying her suitcase and purse. Upstairs, Miss Drost told Eveline to unpack, get dressed into the smock, and come downstairs for dinner. She said, "Tonight, you can start by setting the table." Then, she left.

Eveline walked over to the curtained window and looked out over the backyard where some of the girls were finishing up in the garden and others were at the clothesline. Tears streamed down her cheeks, and she sobbed. The recent experience in Miss Drost's office left her feeling overwhelmed with raw emotions. Throwing up had left her mouth dry.

Turning, she looked around the small bedroom through blurred eyes. Two metal beds with one long dresser. That was it. On the wall between the beds, the framed Four Guiding Principles hung. Wiping her cheeks and eyes, she lifted her suitcase and began to unpack. She found two drawers empty on one side of the dresser. She separated the clothes: underwear and outfits. The faded blue smock looked too big for her, but she undressed and slipped it on over her head. It hung shapelessly from her shoulders. Eveline had always prided herself in her appearance and had worn good-looking outfits, but this smock took away that pride. The smock hung like a sack, making her feel unattractive.

The money in her bra had to be hidden somewhere. She looked around. But where? The mattress—no. Her purse—no. The dresser drawer—no. Nothing seemed safe to her. She kept them where they were, tucked under her arm in her bra. She had to be careful not to let Miss Drost or Miss Everill find her money. Later that evening, Eveline hid her money in her make-up bag. At the end of the zipper, a little opening in the liner allowed her to slip her bills through the little hole. Having the money gave her some small comfort. The thought of running away hung in the back of her mind.

She glanced at the small closet on the other side of the room. Taking her suitcase over, she opened the closet which was packed with colorful clothes. There was no room for her suitcase or her slippers. As she closed the closet door, a very pregnant girl walked into her bedroom.

"So, you're already snooping around my things ?" she said with a sarcastic voice.

"No, I'm sorry. I wanted to put my suitcase and slippers in there," replied Eveline.

"Well, stay out of my things. You're the new girl. I don't envy you. I'm almost out of this place. I'm Stella," she said with a harden voice.

She nodded, and replied, "I'm Eveline...no, I mean Eve." She quickly remembered her shortened name. Then, she walked back to her side of the room and slipped the suitcase under her bed, leaving her slippers beside her bed on the floor.

"I need to change. I'm dirty from the garden. So, where are you from?" asked Stella as she quickly changed out of her orange smock and put on a green one from the closet.

"I'm not supposed to tell anyone," replied Eveline quietly and courteously.

Laughing, she said, "You passed. That was a trick question. Did you swallow all of Miss Drost's BS? If you're going to survive, you follow the rules. But among ourselves, we don't respect those four ridiculous principles. I'm nearly out of here. No one intimidates me."

She stood studying Stella's big stomach as she undressed and dressed. "Oh, I see. You look big. I mean, sorry," she said.

"I've got another month here and I'm out of this god-forsaken-place. I've got to wash up. Let's go to dinner. Be on your guard for a while. Miss Witch of Wickerson will be watching you. Just keep your mouth shut tonight," commented Stella. Even though she seemed hard, Stella had a soft spot. She wanted to help the new girl Eve.

They walked to the upstairs bathroom down the hall. While Stella scrubbed her dirty face, arms, hands, and fingers, Eveline waited her turn in the hall. Several others were coming up stairs to get ready for dinner. They just glanced at her and went into their bedrooms. One girl—Mona—waved her hand but said nothing.

When she came out of the bathroom, Stella asked, "Did the witch give you an assignment for tonight?"

"Yes, I have to set the table for dinner," she replied.

"Okay. Hurry and wash up. We'll talk more tonight," said Stella.

She waited in the hall for Eveline. Together they walked down the stairs and into the kitchen. Smells of cooked cabbage filled the air, giving Eveline a queasy feeling in her stomach. But she had nothing in her stomach, so she felt all right. Stella showed her the cupboard where the dishes, glasses, and cups were stored and the drawer where the silverware were placed. The kitchen was soon a buzz with a few of the girls helping the cook get ready for dinner.

"How many are there for dinner?" asked Eveline.

"There are six of us girls, Miss Drost and Miss Everill. Nurse Litton doesn't eat dinner but eats lunch with us. The nurse lives in town and walks home. Set a place over on that small table for Mrs. Farnway our cook. Come I'll help carry the plates. You get the cups and saucers. Use the serving tray over there. You can come back for the silverware. Fill the small glasses with water for everyone. I have to help with the dessert," said Stella, carrying the plates through the door and into the dining room off the kitchen. She left Eveline to set each place on the long dining room table covered in a lace table cloth. Miss Drost walked into the dining room as Eveline began setting the plates around the table.

"Oh, Eve. Take off the table cloth before you set the table. Fold it and put it in the top drawer of the sideboard. We don't want to get it dirty. After dinner, you will put it back on the table," instructed Miss Drost.

"Yes," she said.

"The proper way to reply is 'Yes, ma'am," she added. "Say it."

"Yes, ma'am," replied Eveline, looking down at the floor.

"Get busy. You don't have much time before we sit down for dinner. Hurry up," she said as she left the dining room, walking back to her office.

Eveline hurriedly followed her directions, went back to the kitchen, filled the glasses with water, and counted the silverware out from the drawer. She wondered if there were any napkins. Looking around, she didn't see any. Mona stood by and told her where everything else that she needed to put on the table—the napkins, the butter dish, the salt and pepper shakers, and the sugar bowl and pitcher of cream. Finally, after four trips to the kitchen with the tray, the dining room table looked set for dinner. Eveline worried that she might have forgotten something. But she knew that if she did, that the director would reprimand her.

Miss Drost came down the hall to the dining room. Glancing at the table, she rang a little bell to announce that dinner was to be served. She moved to the head of the table and waited for the girls and her assistant to come. Slowly, they all appeared and stood behind their chairs. Miss Drost rang the bell again and everyone sat down. Soon the cook brought out the pot of ham stew and cabbage and set it down on the sideboard. Stella had brought out the small dessert dishes filled with gelatin and fruit which Eveline discovered was the standard dessert at dinner. Mona had brought out a loaf of homemade bread, already sliced.

Miss Drost and Miss Everill picked up their plates and walked over to the sideboard and filled their plates, picked up a piece of bread, and took a dessert dish. Sitting down, Miss Drost rang the bell, and one side of the table went over to fill their plates. No one spoke. The sound of the ladle in the pot, the shuffling of the feet, the scooting of the chairs, and the plates being set down were heard in the dining room. When those girls had returned, Miss Drost rang the bell again for the other side to fill their plates. Eventually, everyone sat with their dinner in front of them.

Miss Drost, cleared her throat, and said, "Let's all say a quiet prayer before dinner." Heads bent and eyes closed as they all had a silent moment. Eveline's mind just wanted to get through dinner without throwing up. The heavy smell of cabbage hung in the air.

The director then rang the bell, and everyone began eating their dinner. Again, no words were spoken. Eveline had taken only a couple of pieces of potato and carrots with the juice. The butter dish was being passed around. She sliced off a small piece to spread over her homemade slice of bread which tasted delicious. She ate slowly what she could, stopping to drink some of her water. The other girls' eyes glanced at her once in a while. They were curious about who she was. Only a few kind words had been spoken to her since her aunt had left. The ominous silence of no voices felt odd sitting with five girls. *How was she going to survive this place?*

When they were almost done with their meal, Miss Drost said, "Girls, you noticed that we have a new girl. Her name is 'Eve.' Let's all help her get settled in here in the next few days. Miss Everill, after the dishes are washed and put away, Eve needs her hair cut. A proper girl needs to keep her hair trimmed. Would you take care of that for me?"

Suddenly, Eveline noticed that all the girls had shortened hair. She remembered that Miss Drost told her that she would have to have no time to fuss with her hair. She didn't like this place; it seemed so unfriendly.

"Yes, ma'am," replied Miss Everill looking down the table at Miss Drost and then over to Eveline who sat turning red. Eveline didn't like the attention. The assistant felt sorry for the young girl.

"Thank you," said the director. "By the way, Eve, check the activity board in the kitchen for your individual duties. Your roommate Stella will help you. Let's eat our dessert." She rang the little bell again. Everyone ate the cherry gelatin with fruit. Just then, the cook came in with a pot of tea which she poured into our cups. Eveline waited for the sugar bowl, but it didn't move. The cook had moved the sugar and the cream nearer to Miss Drost's place. She took her spoon and added two teaspoons of sugar and a little cream into her tea and stirred it smiling. The sugar bowl was passed down on the other side of the table to Miss Everill who spooned a teaspoon of sugar into her tea. No one else took any sugar.

"While we have our tea, please introduce yourselves like proper girls. Let's go around the table," said the director, taking a sip of her tea. Each girl said her name: Lucy, Mona, Stella, Liz, and Meg. Eveline wanted to say hello to each, but remembered what Stella told her—*don't talk*. Each of the girls slightly grinned at her. She figured that all of their names had been shorten like hers, so their names were probably Lucinda, Monique, Estelle, Elizabeth, and Margaret. Shortening their first names and no last names felt wrong to her. They all sat quietly finishing their tea which tasted bitter to Eveline. She would have liked some sugar, but that didn't seem possible.

Eveline again noticed that each girl wore a smock like hers. However, their smocks were of different colors with rickrack or ribbon trimming the neckline or at the sleeves. She wondered about her faded blue smock. It did not have any trimmings and she had only one, recalling that Stella had a closet full of smocks. Her clothes were in the two dresser drawers. *Would she wear this old worn out smock every day?* She hoped not.

The little bell rang, and the girls piled their plates with their silverware, the glasses, the cups and saucers, and their napkins. Standing, they picked up their plates and headed towards the kitchen. Two girls picked up Miss Drost's and Miss Everill's plates and silverware, leaving their cups of tea. The cook came out and filled the director and her assistant with another cup. In the kitchen, each girl scraped her plate and threw her napkin away. They stacked the plates, the silverware, the glasses, the dessert cups, and tea cups next to the kitchen sink. Eveline followed and imitated them.

Standing next to the sink, Stella said, "Let's look over the board and see what your duties are." They walked over to a bulletin board with the girls' names and duties. Eveline glanced at the board, trying to figure how to decipher her duties, but it all seemed to be a jumbled mess of colored name squares with tacks through each name. The duties were listed across the board: set table, do dishes, clean floors, vacuum rugs and dust, clean bathrooms, do laundry, take out garbage, and plant garden. There was no organization of the details or times. The girls' names were tacked under each of the duties. To Eveline, the board looked like a muddle mess of details.

"What a hodgepodge. How do we know our duties?" asked Eveline.

"You just look each day at the board and find your name. See there; your name is under 'set table' and 'do dishes.' What's not on this board is our classes at ten in the morning every day. On Monday, Wednesday, and Friday, we have Home Ec. (economics). On Tuesday and Thursday, we have a class called Studies. I'll fill you in on them later. The point is that you keep busy. Don't let Miss Drost find you doing nothing," replied Stella.

She continued to explain how each of the duties were to be completed. Eveline listened closely but so many little details that she feared that she would forget them all. Stella assured her that she should just ask one of the girls since they always worked in pairs. She emphasized again the fact that Eveline should not be caught talking or standing around.

"You've set the table, and now, you are to help with dishes. Mona has already started. You're to dry them. Be sure to put the lace tablecloth back on the dining room table after Miss Drost and Miss Everill are finished with their tea. We'll talk tonight," said Stella.

After she left, Eveline shook her head. She couldn't believe that this morning she had left her home and ended up here in this place so far away. The water tower with 'Suckfurd' written across it fit not only the town but also this place. This house definitely sucked. But what frightened Eveline the most was Miss Drost—the witch of Wickerson. She had them all under her thumb and demanded them to jump with her little bell. *Ugh. She already hated that bell.*

Eveline walked over to the kitchen sink, opened a drawer, and found a kitchen towel to dry the stack of dishes which Mona had washed and rinsed. She mindlessly wiped the dishes, stacking them on the countertop. The two of them worked for a while.

Suddenly, she heard the little bell ring with her name being called out—*RING. RING.* "Eve. Eve come here." She jumped and nearly dropped a cup but caught it before it fell to the floor. Mona looked at her and whispered "Go." She hurried through the door to the dining room. Miss Everill had left, but the director stood waiting for her.

"Eve, we are done with our tea. Take our cups. Clear the table and wipe it down after dinner. You forgot to put the placemats down before setting the table. A proper girl knows how to set a table. Didn't you see them in the sideboard when you put the lace tablecloth in there?" asked the director glaring at her.

"No. I'm sorry," she answered with a quick glance at the dining room table.

"Eve that's 'No, ma'am.' Again, a proper girl knows how to respond to her elders. Oh, and polish the table. The furniture oil and a cloth are in the bottom drawer. Make sure you rub out those little marks and scratches. You will be setting the table for all our meals and doing the dishes for the rest of the week," explained Miss Drost.

"Yes... ah ma'am," replied Eveline. She picked up their cups and saucers, took them into the kitchen, and gave them to Mona to wash. Picking up the tray, she brought back the butter, the salt and pepper shakers, and the sugar and cream. After putting them away, she moved back to the dining room, found the furniture oil and a rag and began polishing the table. She had never polished furniture before, so she did the best she could. She poured a little oil on the marks and scratches and rubbed in the oil. After she finished, the table shined.

Eventually though, the heavy smell of the oil made her nauseous. Quickly, she slipped on the lace tablecloth and put everything back into the bottom drawer. Heading down the hall to the bathroom, she held her hand over her mouth. This time she tapped on the door, hoping no one was in there. It was empty. She swung open the door and retched into the toilet. Her dinner in her stomach hadn't lasted very long. Exhaustion took over her body as she retched the last remnants in her stomach. After rinsing her mouth, her pale face stared back at her as she looked into the mirror. The drab smock looked awful on her. *What had she become?* A pitiful looking person.

After leaving the bathroom, she went back to the kitchen to finish up the dishes. Mona had stepped in and had been drying the rest of them. Eveline thanked her quietly. Mona nodded, not speaking a word. Together, they put all the dishes, cups, and glasses back into the cupboard and separated the silverware into the drawer. Miss Everill came into the kitchen with a towel and a pair of scissors.

"Let's get your hair cut Eve. We'll do it on the back porch. Grab a chair," she said, pointing to a chair with the small kitchen table. Eveline picked up one and moved to the back porch. Sitting down, Miss Everill covered her shoulders with a towel.

"My word... you certainly have thick, curly black hair," she said undoing the band at the back of Eveline's head. She combed it and separated the back from the front. As Miss Everill snipped and cut her hair, Eveline sat quietly recalling all the compliments that she had received about her hair. During her childhood, her mom had pampered her hair, fixing it several different ways. Later in high school, her cheerleading friends had adored her hair.

Sadly, she also recalled that Matt Fletcher had liked her curls the evening that they had first met. After a few dates, she had really gotten to like him. Before she left home, he had called her, and her mom had let her talk to him. She told him to forget about her. And now, she knew that he wouldn't want anything to do with her after all this. Even though her mom had made her stay home from school, she had called her friends secretly and found out that the students knew about her pregnancy. In fact, the whole town knew about her. Shame filled her heart as she thought of all the gossip that would be going around about her pregnancy.

And then, the rush of that horrible night came to her again. Her girlfriends had abandoned her that night in the motel. Many times before, they had stuck together at the parties, taking care of each other. But that night, her friends had wanted to stay at the motel partying and making out with the basketball players. Eveline knew that she had to leave. Her dad's words and her curfew had kept ringing in her ears. However, that one basketball player had talked her into taking her for a ride. What a mistake. She hated his guts after what he had done to her. All of her trouble had started that evening after the basketball game.

Today, on one of their bus stops, Eveline had called her friend Rebecca Klency on a pay phone late in the afternoon. She had felt so lonely on the bus that she just wanted to hear a friendly voice. They had talked for a few minutes. Her friend had wondered how she was doing. Eveline had told her that she felt fine, but she wasn't. She didn't tell Rebecca anything else except that she wanted her to write. She had told her friend that her mom would send a letter down to her. As she sat thinking of her friends, she hoped that they would write.

Eveline buried her past memories as Miss Everill had finished with cutting her hair. When she stood, she looked down at her black curls lying on the tiled floor. Her hand felt her bare neck and her long hair gone. Her fingers tried to pull her hair over her ears. All the girls had short hair and wore different colored smocks like hers. She was now one of them—short hair and pregnant.

Miss Everill handed her a broom, "Your hair looks beautiful. Here's a broom. Sweep up and shake the towel outside the porch."

"Yes, ma'am," she replied.

"Listen this is your first day. Don't worry. You'll be fine. I'm here if you have any concerns. I sleep upstairs in the bedroom at the top of the stairs," said Miss Everill with compassion in her voice. She picked up the chair and left Eveline with the broom.

She just nodded as she finished sweeping the floor. Stepping outside, she shook out the towel. Gazing up into the inky dark sky, she saw all the twinkling stars. She recalled that those sparkling stars used to offer her hope and dreams of a happy future. Her world had been filled with beauty. Now, the world had lost its glitter and her dreams had turned into a terrible nightmare.

She felt a slight cool breeze on her face and wondered if her friends were up at Skyline, huddled around a campfire, drinking and laughing. Her past life had disappeared within a week. Tears started to cloud her eyes as they spilled down her cheeks. She sat down on the steps and sobbed into the towel; her voice muffled. This had been too much for her to deal with in one day. Sadness and loneliness filled her heart as she cried.

She heard a movement on the back porch. Standing up, she brushed aside her tears, stepped back onto the porch, and faced the cold witch, watching her.

"It's time for you to go upstairs. You have until ten when it's bedtime and the lights are turned off," she instructed Eveline.

"Yes, ma'am," she replied, keeping her puffy eyes lowered. Walking into the kitchen, she headed upstairs to her bedroom.

Glancing down the upstairs hallway, she saw at the end a half-way opened door with girls' voices coming from there. As she came down the hall, Stella stepped out and motioned for her to come in. Eveline wanted to go to bed, but she came through the door. At the end of the hall, the room had a small table and chairs with a small couch and a few comfortable chairs. Four of the girls were at the table playing cards and quietly talking among themselves. Turning towards her, everyone said "Hi, Eve."

Mona asked, "Did you learn how a 'proper' girl sets a table?" Sarcasm laced her words.

And it continued with, "Did you learn to say 'yes, ma'am' and 'no, ma'am' like a proper girl?" added Stella.

Meg piped up and said, "You'll be hearing what a 'proper' girl does until you leave here." They were all joking and kidding around.

Liz responded, "Eve I see you have had your hair cut like a 'proper' girl. Your cut looks good on you. But look at those curls. They are beautiful."

Stella pointed to one of the chairs, "Sit down and relax before bed time. This is our activity room at the end of the day. We play cards or a board game once in a while. Sometimes we just sit and talk. We let off steam after a long day of work, ending with that little bell." Everyone could tell that Eveline had been crying so they all turned and focused on playing cards while Stella sat down beside her. "Listen, tomorrow, you will be sewing a new smock during our Home Ec. class."

Shocked, Eveline said, "But I don't know how to sew."

"Don't worry. Who can help Eve with sewing?" she asked, looking over at the girls.

"I can," responded Meg. "I have to make me another one. I'll show you how to cut the pattern and use the sewing machine. A local women's quilting club donates the material and sewing items so we can make our smocks. We also use the scraps to make our own quilts."

"Thanks. Do we have to wear these smocks every day?" asked Eveline.

"Yes. Besides, they are comfortable when you get big like me," she replied.

"How many months along are all of you?" asked Eveline quietly. Each took turns to answer—Meg four, Lucy and Lizzie five, Mona seven, and Stella eight.

"So, you're just about three? Have you had any nausea?" asked Meg. Everyone noticed that Eveline was a soft-spoken girl while she nodded, and whispered, "Yes. I'm doing okay." But she really wasn't okay, not since getting pregnant.

"Do you have any questions?" asked Stella.

Thinking for a minute, Eveline said, "Yes. Tell me about the classes—Home Ec. and Studies." Nodding, Stella started by explaining that in Home Ec., they learn to cook and sew. After she sewed herself a few smocks, she would have to either embroider, crochet, or quilt. A few of them made embroidered kitchen towels or crocheted doilies; a couple of them sewed on a quilt. When they were finished, these sewing projects were taken down to a local store and sold. The money went to the home for expenses.

In Studies, Stella described the different subjects that they studied—such as shorthand, letter writing, and etiquette. Meg spoke up and said that the father of a past girl had donated typewriters to the home this month. The girls were all excited about learning how to type.

"Where do we go for the classes?" asked Eveline.

"We go to the big room next to the stairs. The room serves as our classroom and on Sunday becomes our chapel. Oh, we have to memorize certain verses from the Bible. That's the most unnerving thing that we have to do. I can't memorize anything, so I'm always given laundry to do. That's our discipline," said Stella. All the girls voiced their dislike of memorizing verses.

Meg mentioned, "Miss Drost thinks that she is saving us from public ridicule. We are unwed, soiled girls. She seems to want to make us dignified individuals."

"Are you all giving up your babies for adoption?" asked Eveline quietly.

"Listen Eve. We don't have any other choice," replied Stella. All of them nodded.

"But the babies are sent to an orphanage before they are adopted," replied Eveline.

"Who told you that?" asked Meg, now concerned and worried.

"Hey, girls. It doesn't matter. We can't raise the babies. They force us to sign those adoption papers. That's the way it's done," replied Stella, strongly disliking the conversation and all the questions about the babies. "We have to do what's best. Afterwards, we can begin our lives again." The girls nodded their heads, knowing that each of their situations left them no options. At least they had a place like Wickerson Home to come to, even though it had been miserable to live here. The girls talked for a little while. Stella said that she was headed to bed. As each girl got ready for bed, they took turns in the bathroom.

Eveline asked, "When can I take a bath?" Stella told her tomorrow would be better since she and Lucy needed one after working in the garden. Stella said that the girls made up their own schedule for baths. Miss Everill let them bathe as much as they needed. That night, she could wash up before going to bed.

Eveline hurried down to their bedroom and grabbed her purse which had her brush and comb and a toothbrush. After stepping into the bathroom, she looked into the mirror for the first time with her short hair. Just like Liz had noticed, her short black hair had wavy curls. She brushed it, trying not to get upset. She knew it would grow back, but her image shocked her for the second time today. She had never had her hair cut so short and she looked pale with circles under her eyes. Pieces of cut hair tickled her neck and underneath her smock. Brushing her teeth, she thought of how many times she had thrown up today. Maybe, she should take her nausea pills before the meals. Finally, she finished and went down the hall to her bedroom.

Stella had been waiting for her to finish before taking her bath. Eveline changed out of her smock, giving it a good shake to get the hair out of it. She slipped on her nightgown, leaving on her bra with the hidden money. Crawling into her bed, she stretched her exhausted body out under the covers. She closed her eyes against the overhead light in the center of the room. Her exhausted mind whirled with all the images of this long day. She felt beaten down but somehow thinking about the other girls gave her a little hope to this unreal situation. Her roommate seemed to be the leader; the others she would get to know later.

Soon, Stella came in and went to bed, turning off the overhead light. In the darkness, Eveline whispered "Good night." Stella said, "Nite." Down the hall, she heard the little bell. *RING, RING.* Ten o'clock and time for bed. She heard Miss Drost's heels click down the hall as she opened each of their bedroom doors to check that they were all in their beds. Afterwards, she heard her heels click down the wooden stairs and fade into the night.

Eveline breathed a sigh of relief. Homesickness swept over her, and she cried into her pillow. Today, she had landed in another state, in a strange house with a witch of a director, and with a group of unwedded pregnant girls. What her future held here in this house made her tremble in fear. She didn't feel safe nor protected. Feeling exposed and vulnerable, she had reached the bottom. Defeated and drained of energy, she fell into a restless sleep.

* * *

Eveline's miserable stay at the Wickerson Home passed slowly, day by day. Stella woke her up before dawn to start each day. After waiting her turn in the bathroom and dressing, Eveline stood at the window and watched the sun's fire ball rise above the distant horizon. The land all around her appeared as flat as the dining room table downstairs.

As time moved on into the hot summer months, the farmland had slowly turned into green crops—tall corn stalks, swaying wheat and oats. She missed seeing the dark forested mountains of her home town of Riverside. She missed the cool days and nights of the mountains. But nothing around here rose tall above the flatland and except for the three silos and the water tower in this town.

Eveline followed the girls and worked physically at her duties, but mentally, she moved mindlessly through the days. She swept floors, mopped them, and did her duties again and again, week after week. Every day at ten, she sewed. Her smocks came out all right, but her fingers were pricked by the sharp pins so many times that they hurt for a day after sewing. Afterwards, she ended up embroidering kitchen towels for her long term project. Whenever she had time, she would embroider her towels. In the evenings upstairs, she sewed, keeping her hands busy while her mind ran on nothing. The girls chatted all around her. Eveline said little as had been her nature.

On the cooking days, she learned to put together various casseroles, tossed green salads with curled carrots and radishes, and baked sweet cupcakes for their lunches.

During Studies, the donated typewriters were a godsend to all of the girls. They liked typing far better than learning etiquette or shorthand. Eveline started on the electric typewriter that buzzed when she turned it on. Those typing exercises in learning the keyboard were mindless, but she enjoyed the activity. She liked seeing the words form under the little arms of the typewriter. Often she would jam them, have to stop, and finger the arms loose, getting the tips of her fingers black. After they had learned the keyboard fairly well, the local teacher taught them about writing business letters, giving them assignments to type. Again, Eveline worked at finishing them, but nothing excited her. She just wanted to get through each day and go to bed at night.

The first week, the Nurse Litton met with Eveline about her nausea and made a note about her pills. The nurse came each day, sat in the medical office, ate lunch with them, and went home.

A week after she arrived, Eveline's queasiness suddenly quit. That night in bed she said a little prayer, thankful that her meals had stayed down that day.

One evening, Eveline asked the girls if they ever had any visitors, calls, or letters. All of them shook their heads. Stella spoke up, "No. They discourage any visitors coming here or any contact with the outside. They are keeping our parents, our friends, especially our boyfriends from calling or writing. If they do call, Miss Drost doesn't tell us. Any letters are destroyed. Tell them Meg." She looked sadly at Meg.

"Yeah. One time I had to clean out the ashes in the incinerator. I found a fragment of an envelope that had an address on it. I recognized it as my boyfriend's address. It was just plain cruel." She wiped a tear from her eye, shaking her head at the harsh rules that had been put into place by the director. She had wanted to hear from her boyfriend.

Shocked, Eveline couldn't believe it, and responded, "But she told my aunt that she could visit. I thought I would hear from her by now."

"No, Eve. You won't hear a word from your aunt or see her while you're here. Get used to it. You're here with us. We'll get through this together and return to our lives again," replied Stella.

* * *

Eveline discovered that the medical office and room sat next to the chapel room and was nothing more than a big closet. No windows. Nothing on the light green walls but the framed document—the Four Guiding Principles. A long examining table with stirrups occupied most of the room. A small, locked medical cabinet sat along one wall. Several medical instruments could be seen through the glass doors, covered with just the silver ends sticking out. A pile of sheets were stacked on the bottom shelf. Eveline didn't like the windowless room with a huge, bright overhead light above. *Is this where we deliver our babies in this stuffy room?*

Every week, she read the kitchen board and got her duties. Stella told her that the director somehow each week found two girls who didn't measure up to the Four Guiding Principles and assigned them the dreaded laundry duty. An old wringer washing machine sat in the dark basement with two big tubs. A large laundry basket with a bag of clothespins sat on the floor next to the outdated washing machine.

The first time Eveline had laundry duty came in her third week. She couldn't recite the Four Guiding Principles when asked at dinner time one evening. She had been embarrassed and insulted when Miss Drost implied that she needed to know these to be a "proper" girl.

The other girl Meg had been caught sleeping in one of the chairs in the sitting room after she had vacuumed the carpet. Meg and Eveline had to be disciplined and assigned laundry duty for the next day. Naturally, the director thought that she was shaping these young, unwed girls to become better.

That night upstairs, the girls all talked about what they called the Blue Sheet incident. Stella told the story. Miss Drost, the witch of Wickerson, had purposely slipped in some blue dye capsules in one of the pockets. The two girls, Liz and Mona, who had laundry duty were told to check all pockets, but they missed one. All of the washing came out blue. The laughter filled the room as they recalled the blue sheets and the blue panties and bras hanging on the clotheslines. The next week, the girls had to bleach out the blue sheets. Their underwear remained blue until they faded out in the washings each week. Liz and Mona laughed along with the girls for they all understood how one pocket could be missed. Stella told Eveline and Meg to check *all* the pockets in the clothes when they did the washing.

The next day, down in the basement, Meg and Eveline faced the mountains of sheets and clothes that had to be washed that day. They decided that both of them would check the pockets in case one of them missed one. They came up with the oily furniture rag from the dining room and a couple of nickels in the pockets. Meg told Eveline that Miss Everill was known to leave change for the girls. They each took a nickel.

The two of them washed the clothes, ran them through the wringer, rinsed them in the tubs of water, ran them again through the wringer, and put them into the laundry basket which took both of them to carry up the basement stairs to the clothesline outside. After six loads, they had managed to finish and hang them up to dry on the lines. That afternoon, they had to take down all the sheets, fold them and take them upstairs to the girls' bedrooms. The underwear and smocks were folded and left in the laundry basket. That evening the girls went through the clothes, taking out theirs to be put away in their dresser drawers. The girls had to make their own beds with the cleaned sheets. By the end of the day, both Meg and Eveline were exhausted and worn out, going up and down the stairs. Doing the laundry had to be the worse duty that Eveline could imagine. No matter what she did right or wrong, she ended up having laundry duty once a month during her stay. The witch of Wickerson made sure that every girl had laundry duty.

* * *

After a month at the Wickerson Home, Eveline had her first check up with Dr. Robert Smith who drove from Bender to the home. He seemed to be a quiet, caring doctor. A middle-aged man with sharp brown eyes and short blond hair. He had large, smooth hands. Eveline felt nervous in front of this stranger. Dr. Smith weighed her, carefully examined her on the table, and told her everything looked fine. Previously, Nurse Litton had pricked her finger and had her blood typed. He commented, looking at her file—"no Rh factor, good." Cautiously, he asked her a few uncomfortable questions. He wanted to know the month that she got pregnant which would help him figure her due date. Frightened and scared, Eveline hid all the ugly details and told him the end of January. He also asked her if that was her first time. *Yes*. She lied about that. He didn't need to know that, for her parents didn't even know. After he probed her about the date, he asked for the name of the guy. She didn't want to reveal that, so she said she didn't know his name. He found that hard to believe; he insisted that he needed it for the record. Eveline then told him that she didn't know him, that it was a blind date, and that she had been drunk. He nodded and wrote down *Unknown*. The doctor asked her more questions about her family—her mother and her aunt and their pregnancies. She knew little and had nothing to add about them.

The days that followed when the doctor finished with the monthly exams, he would stay for dinner, sitting next to Miss Everill who sweetly talked to him throughout their meals. The assistant had put him on a pedestal, being a doctor and all important. The doctor would smile at her and enjoyed the attention, time and time again. When the girls would leave the dinner table, he would stay for a second cup of tea, chatting quietly with Miss Everill. They were very friendly with each other. Miss Drost would

105

sit at the opposite end of the dining table, glaring at them through lowered eyelids, time and time again.

Finally one evening after dinner and the doctor had left, Miss Drost asked Miss Everill into her office. Even though her office door was closed, her loud, harsh voice traveled down the hall. The girls stood around and heard her say that Miss Everill shouldn't act like that especially in front of the young girls. The director went on and on, telling her that she had been a bad example to the girls, flirting with the doctor.

Miss Everill left the office angry with a red face. She had only been respectful and friendly to an important person like Dr. Smith. The tension between the two remained, for Miss Everill never forgave the director for accusing her of flirting. The girls upstairs that night speculated that she would probably be leaving. The next month when the doctor came to examine the girls, Miss Everill ate in the kitchen with the cook.

And sure enough, Miss Everill left soon after that with her three suitcases one summer day. The cook told the girls that Miss Drost couldn't keep an assistant director very long—maybe a year or two at the most. Miss Everill had lasted two years. Her bedroom remained empty for a couple of months. All of us girls felt the chill settle in without the friendly, kind Miss Everill. Her coins would be missed in the washing and her kindness would be missed during the long, hot summer days. She would let the girls have small breaks during their daily chores, letting them have a drink of cold, ice water. They would definitely miss her.

A month later, a new assistant moved in upstairs—a Miss Vozenich, an older woman with a round figure. She asked us to call her Miss V since we would have trouble saying her name. Surrounded by short, grey hair, she had a wrinkled face with light hazel eyes. Her posture was bent a little and she wobbled when she walked. The girls thought her comical.

The director spoke to Miss V and told her that the home provided the girls with a controlled environment. Under no circumstance were they allowed to have visitors, phone calls, or letters. Miss Drost felt that the outside people would only upset the girls. She gave Miss V the Four Guiding Principles and their focus on taking care of the unwed girls. Even though the girls thought her amusing, Eveline knew that Miss V carried authority in her voice and manners towards them. She reined them in with a firm hand. Later, the girls learned something interesting about Miss V that they didn't know.

When Miss V moved upstairs into Miss Everill's bedroom, she kept her door closed at night, never checking on the girls like Miss Everill often did. Only a few changes came with Miss V that the girls had to adjust to. Otherwise, the same tiring duties and grueling schedule continued on through the long, hot summer months.

* * *

More importantly than anything else to Eveline had to be her pregnancy. She feared what she did not know. While her body changed, she paid attention to the girls who were further along who complained of being uncomfortable, of having indigestion, and of being kicked by their babies. So far, Eveline felt that being pregnant meant being tired. She never had much energy working at her duties. Even after a night of sleep, Eveline's tired body never left her. With only a few hours of sleep in the hot, upstairs bedroom, she desperately desired to take a nap in the afternoons, but her duties never allowed her to do so. During those first weeks, she thought of home, of her own bedroom, and of her own bed. She cried often. Finally, Stella had enough one night, told her that she had to "get a backbone" and to quit being a "weeping Wickerson girl." She said that crying didn't make the situation change one bit except make herself miserable and kept her awake. Stella was near her last month and wretched all evening with little sleep. She had slept sitting up most of the nights. And she couldn't sleep with Eveline crying.

One month later, at the end of dinner, Stella's water broke, right there on the dining room floor. Miss Drost immediately rang her little bell, and the cook came in with the tea. Seeing what had happened, the cook rushed back and brought out a mop and bucket. The director went to her office and called Nurse Litton who came. Stella was taken into the medical office and placed on the hard examining table. Her feet were slipped into the stirrups.

After dinner, the dishes were washed and dried. The girls went upstairs and occupied the time with playing cards. Eveline continued to embroider her kitchen towels. Meg told them that her mom had explained how the labor pains started far apart, got closer and harder as the delivery came closer. Eveline made note of the time and thought how uncomfortable that table must feel to Stella in labor.

The summer nights had been getting hotter and hotter upstairs, so the girls had opened all the windows to catch any breeze from outside. That evening, they all went to bed sweating, wondering how Stella was doing. Early the next morning, they all came down to breakfast to hear a few moans and muffled groans coming from the medical office. Stella's voice sounded more desperate; Miss Drost called Dr. Smith in Bender who drove to the home for the delivery.

While the girls were in Studies, they were typing when they heard more frantic screams coming from the room next to them. They all stopped and listened. Eveline couldn't believe her ears. She couldn't imagine what kind of pain that her roommate must be having.

A half hour later, Stella delivered the baby. The news rippled through the Wickerson Home with a sigh of relief for Stella. Within an hour or two, a car with an unidentified man and woman came and took the tiny, wrapped bundle away, driving it to the orphanage to be adopted. From the window, Eveline sadly watched the car back up. On the side of the car were the words High Street Orphanage. All the girls took a quick look as the car drove away down the block.

After the delivery, Stella stayed upstairs in bed for a week. Miss V brought up her meals to her. We heard that Stella had gotten up on the third day and walked around upstairs. At night, Eveline tried to talk to her and to find out how she felt. She also wanted to know if the baby was a girl or a boy. But Stella told her to "shut up" and leave her alone. Harshness laced her words while Eveline noticed that she looked worn out and tired. Then late in the next evening, she heard her roommate cry quietly into her pillow. Even though Stella had been a strong person, going through painful labor had traumatized her. Sadness filled Eveline while she listened to her friend, crying, but she said nothing.

The next evening, all of the girls wanted to talk and see how Stella was doing. But she still didn't want to talk with them, saying that she wanted to forget about the whole incident. Nurse Litton checked on her each day. At the end of a week, Stella received a bus ticket home from her parents. She packed her suitcase, leaving all her smocks in the closet which were divided up among the girls. The director took a few. Miss V drove Stella to Bender to catch the bus that took her home.

After Stella left Wickerson Home, we never heard from her again. The spirit of the girls diminished with her gone. She had kept them alive in their night-time talks, joking and poking fun at their situation. Eveline felt the loss deeper than the others, for now she had an empty bed in her bedroom. The deafening silence hung in the hot, dark nights, making her feel the loneliness settle in around her.

Stella's long hours of labor remained stuck in Eveline's mind—nearly twelve hours. She worried about the traumatic experience that she would definitely have to face herself. But then, she looked forward to the day when she could leave.

A week after Stella left, a new unwed pregnant girl named Rose came to Wickerson Home who became Eveline's roommate. Rose was younger than all of them—only fifteen years old. Eveline tried her best to acquaint the new girl to the duties and rules, but Rose was more delicate and vulnerable than any of the other girls. She cried and made herself miserable every night. Eveline finally gave her the "get tough" speech, but she didn't have Stella's harshness or hardness to make any difference. Her message fell flat, and Rose continue to cry and be wretched. She never got her backbone.

* * *

The dry, hot summer months continued. Miss Drost's next main emphasis at the home had become the large vegetable garden. At dinner on several occasions, she spoke about the necessary vegetables to feed them and about the root cellar that needed to be stocked for the winter months. In the cooking class, the girls were to learn how to put up the garden vegetables.

When Eveline first came in the spring, the girls were just preparing the rows and planting the seeds. With such a large garden, Miss Drost assigned four girls to weed and thin in the early months of the growing season. Soon, the seeds had sprouted, and the garden sprung into life. In this dry, hot climate, the vegetable plants had to be watered every day. Eveline spent many weeks in the garden; she burned at first and then, turned brown.

As her baby grew inside of her, bending over became more difficult for Eveline. She had to use the hoe to cut down weeds when months before she had been able to reach down and pull them out. Her breathing became more difficult, and fatigue yet plagued her. At nights, she laid on top of her covers—too hot to sleep. When she did sleep, she sometimes woke hearing Miss Drost's bell ringing in her dreams or hearing Stella's groans.

When the harvest came, all of the girls spent hours in the hot kitchen preparing the vegetables and watching the pressure cooker process the quart jars. They canned green beans, tomatoes, beets, and creamed corn. They made dill pickles, bread n' butter pickles, and pickled beets.

Once during the last summer months, a fruit truck drove to town to sell their produce of blueberries, peaches, and pears. The girls learned how to put up fruit and to make jams with the jars submerged in the big kettle filled with hot steaming water. Jars of vegetables, pickles, fruit, and jam filled the root cellar. Miss Drost smiled and knew that she had helped these unwed girls learn the importance of hard work—one of the Four Guiding Principles.

Finally, Eveline and the girls had finished their sewing projects. A beautiful quilt had been completed by Meg, Lucy, and Liz. Eveline had finished embroidering her kitchen towels. Mona had crocheted several dainty doilies. Miss Drost announced at dinner one evening that they should take their finished sewing projects to the local store to sell. Eveline and Rose were to take them down to the store where they were displayed and sold.

The evening before they went, the girls all wanted them to buy something—mostly candy which they never had. Rose particularly craved bubble gum. Eveline told the girls that she would buy them all some candy. The girls all had to pledge secrecy since Miss Drost would certainly disapprove—candy would not be 'proper.' They all laughed. The next day, Eveline took out her hidden money and with Rose walked down to the local store. At the store, she bought a small paper bag of one cent candy and six candy bars. Carrying the contraband in her purse, she managed to get the candy upstairs without the director or the assistant knowing.

That evening, they all thoroughly enjoyed the candy, devouring the candy bars and sucking on the hard one cent candies. The bubble gum became the activity of the evening. The girls all challenged each other in blowing the largest bubble. One after another, they popped their gum, laughing and enjoying the fun of it. When it came close to ten, Meg mentioned that they needed to hide all the wrappers and make sure they were burned in the garbage that week. They didn't want any evidence of their improper activities.

However, one of the girls left a chewed piece of bubble gum stuck under the dining room table one evening. Miss Drost discovered it a few days later and called Eveline and Rose into her office. Sitting behind her desk, she had her slender hands clasped in front of her. The long red fingernails looked ready to strike them. Fear rose inside of Eveline.

"Did you buy bubble gum at the store the other day?" asked Miss Drost, glaring at the two girls who had been to the local store. Both girls denied the accusation. Finally, the director drilled down as her anger rose. Her hand came slamming down on the desk. The sudden noise made both of the girls jump. Then, she pointed her red nail at each of them.

"I guess I'm going to have to send you both away. I will not tolerate liars living here in our respectable Wickerson Home. You both have purposely violated my trust in you," she continued.

Rose burst into tears, wailing and weeping. "I can't go home. Please, I am sorry. Eve did it. She bought the candy and the bubble gum," she replied through her sobs.

Miss Drost turned her attention to Eveline, and sarcastically said, "So, it's not just bubble gum, but candy, too. You must have hidden some of your money from me. There's another lie. I definitely disapprove of such deceit. I'm going to have to call your aunt and send you away."

"No, please, ma'am. Rose craved bubble gum. I didn't think that a little candy and some bubble gum would hurt. I am terribly sorry. I'll give you all the rest of my money. And I'll do the laundry," pleaded Eveline.

A tense silence filled the air while Miss Drost stared at her and Rose who still cried quietly behind her hands. Slowly, the director softened her glare. "I want *all* of your money plus *all* of the candy or bubble gum left. And you both will be doing the laundry for the next four weeks. Let's go upstairs right now," replied Miss Drost.

When they all came out of the office, Miss V met them. The director filled her in quickly and they all went upstairs. Eveline handed over the money and her bag of one cent candy. Rose relinquished her precious bubble gum. They went through the dresser drawers to make sure nothing had been left of the candy or bubble gum. The director threatened them both that they were considered on notice that if anything like this occurred again, she would be sending us both away immediately. No exceptions.

That evening with all the girls, Rose and Eveline told them of the Bubble Gum incident. One girl asked who stuck the bubble gum under the dining room table. Liz admitted it quickly. Eveline asked her, "Why did you stick it under the dining room table?"

Quietly, she replied, "I've always stuck my gum under a table. My mom's been after me to stop. I never thought that anyone would find it."

All of the girls laughed, leave it to the witch to inspect every inch of this house. Clearly, their actions were being watched more than they thought. This Bubble Gum incident gave all of them a warning to be on their guard and not overstep their actions or behaviors. That evening in bed, Eveline cringed at the thought of doing laundry for a month, but she also hated Miss Drost for taking her money. It left her with an uncomfortable feeling and no backup plan of running away if she got a chance.

* * *

Along with the hot summer days came the sudden rainstorms that swept across the plains. The dust clouds proceeded the storm with thunder and lightning, sending everyone into the house with thin dust clouding their eyesight. The town had a loud, warning siren that rang out when word came of a severe rainstorm. Glancing across the wide-opened plains, one could see an approaching storm. Several thunderstorms came and went, drenching the flat countryside and fields. In addition, the cook told the girls about the dangerous tornadoes that sometimes came with the rainstorms and about the town's warning signal. She instructed them to head for the root cellar in the backyard if they heard the siren.

One sweltering afternoon while Eveline had her body bent slightly down hoeing and weeding the garden, she heard the warning siren split the hot air. Looking around, she saw the large, dust cloud coming towards her. Behind it came an enormous black bank of storm clouds. They were tinged with an odd dark green hue. Out of this black cloud came a huge spinning tornado. Eveline watched it descend from the cloud. When this spinning dark funnel touched the earth, all havoc came loose. A distant red barn exploded and disappeared into the twister. The girls were all hollering for her to get to the root cellar.

Eveline stood captivated by the sight of the chaos all around her. The roar of the tornado had deafened the girls' voices. She never heard them. She had been mesmerized by the dangerous storm as the twister roared and wailed towards the town. Finally, Meg came running up to her, grabbed her hand, and pulled her towards the root cellar. Into the dark cellar, they stumbled down, dragging the cellar door closed. In the black crowded musty space, they huddled down. The only light came from the cracks in the rattling cellar door. Rose, Lucy, and Mona were crying, terrified and frightened while the deafening roar continued for an hour. Rain with hail finally came as the storm clouds dumped its small icy projectiles to the ground. They loudly peppered the root cellar door, creating a splitting sound that made the girls cover their ears. A few of the girls cried even louder, horrified of the sounds.

When the dangerous storm had passed, the girls slowly opened the cellar door to find that the tornado had missed the town but had torn up the cemetery on the edge of town. Word came that the heavy tombstones were overturned, a tall statue of an angel had been tipped over face down into the muddy ground; crosses and tombstones were tossed across the cemetery. The branches of trees had been stripped off and tossed all around. An old pine tree had been uprooted and deposited miles away. The path through the farmlands left a swath of destruction, laying low the tall corn, wheat, and oats. No lives were lost, but Eveline never forgot that destructive storm.

* * *

In the middle of summer, Mona went into labor. After eight hours, she had her baby. The same unidentified man and woman from the orphanage came and took the baby away. Mona laid upstairs for seven days, depressed while she recovered. Her parents arrived and took her away.

Watching Mona's baby being whisked away hurt Eveline's sense of motherhood. Now that she could feel her baby move, the thought of being a mother came sweeping over her like the ocean waves hitting the beach. The loving feelings came and went, over and over. Waves of emotions sent her mind whirling at the possibilities of motherhood. In her dad's café, she recalled that mothers would carry their babies in and set them in a highchair. Some would hold and coddle their babies. Touching images of a baby in her arms brought another wave crashing in on Eveline. But Stella's words echoed in her head: *"we have no choice," "we have to give them up,"* and *"that's the way it's done."* Miss Drost's temerity about adoption further pushed the matter to a close. Eveline had signed away her precious baby as did all of the other girls who had come to the home.

Every miserable day. Duties, duties, duties. The grueling work became more difficult for Eveline to handle as the months passed. Physically, she continued to be tired, fatigued, and worn out. She couldn't get her breath, and the sweltering heat made the sweat drip off her body heavy with child, around her neck and down her back, between her swollen breasts, and down her forehead into her eyes, stinging them with the salt.

The heat laid all the girls low in the late afternoons and into the sleepless nights. Too hot to sleep. Without Stella, Eveline brooded about her future. The new girl Rose looked to her, but she didn't respond. She was not a leader like Stella who had been able to jar a girl back to reality. No more laughter came out of Eveline's dry, hot mouth. She became more despondent and depressed.

Another two deliveries came about a week apart. After going through labor, Lucy and Liz had their babies shuttled away to the orphanage. While the two girls lay in their bedrooms recovering, another girl named Stacy arrived to take Mona's place. She became another weeping unwed pregnant girl traumatized by Miss Drost's Four Guiding Principles. The new girl's smock and hair cut seemed uneventful to Eveline after the months at the Wickerson Home. Eveline's callousness surprised the other girls. When Lucy and Liz were sent away, only Meg was left of the original girls whom Eveline had met months ago.

Within a week, two new unwed pregnant girls showed up to replace Lucy and Liz. They were Mary and Jane who arrived, both early in their pregnancies. The same drill—the Four Guiding Principles, the smocks, and the haircuts. When she heard the new girl Mary crying, Eveline recalled that Stella would have called her a "weeping Wickerson girl." Eveline had gotten past that early stage of despair and had been harden by the long months of being reprimanded.

Miss Drost and Miss V continue to hover over the girls and monitored all their duties. Small incidents happened every day to raise the girls' concern over the "proper" way to behave—the 'yes ma'am and no ma'am' and the little bell during their meals and at bedtime. The abusive control never ended. The threat of being sent home hung over every girl's head. We marched to their commands, slaved at our duties, and slept at the ten o'clock bell. The intense heat of the late summer months plague them constantly. No escape.

However, one new girl arrived that week that changed their views at Wickerson. Jane emerged as a rebel ready to fight. First, the required hair cut started her battle against Miss Drost and Miss V. One particular principle became her downfall—humility and self-control. Jane's anger spilled out in her manners, her voice, and her mean-looking eyes. She bulked at the rules, and she hated the duties. She felt that they had no right to treat the unwed girls with such contempt, pushing them around with their commands and making them feel ashamed and unworthy. She wanted no part of becoming a victim.

At evening, upstairs, the girls' get-togethers became nothing more than a complaining session among them. Eveline kept quiet and listened. She hated how Jane had soured all of the other girls. At least with Stella, they had poked fun at their situations, sarcastically mimicking the witch's words. They had laughed at the red lipstick and the painted red fingernails. They joked about the Blue Sheets and the Bubble Gum incidents. But Jane had come from a rough neighborhood of gang fighters. She had a fighting spirit that put her deep into trouble. Every other word she spoke was a four-letter word. Eveline sat shocked at her audacity and her rebellious attitude.

115

Finally, it all came to a head the first week during chapel when they all were waiting to read their assigned verses. Jane simply refused to read the biblical verses which were all focused on immorality and promiscuity. Over the past months, the girls had been assigned the verses to read, memorize, and recite. Most of the girls could memorize without much effort. Eveline just memorized the words, but the meanings never entered her soul. She didn't feel that the verses spoke about her directly; the biblical people were of a distant place and time from her.

Perhaps, it was a survival attitude that put Eveline's mind at ease. She didn't take the verses personally as a criticism of her. Even though she felt like a fool to get pregnant, she felt innocent of the forced rape. But when the other girls talked about getting pregnant, they had been complicit in the sexual act. Most liked their boyfriends and looked forward to getting back home. That had not been the situation with Eveline. Her experience had been opposite of theirs. Most of the girls were affected by the biblical verses, making them feel guilty and unworthy.

Naturally, the new girl Jane riled against just reading the verses. "I refuse to read such bull shit that attack me and my boyfriend. It's none of your damn business what we do. You can go to hell," she spewed out her protest loudly in the quiet chapel hall. The other girls were stunned, gasping at how Jane dared to speak her mind. No one had ever done this during chapel. Eveline shivered at the anger and hatred laced through Jane's harsh four-letter words.

"Why you little Miss Jezebel. We'll just see how far you will take this. Let's go to my office and talk about your refusal to accept the fourth Guiding Principle," said the director through her gnashing teeth as her face turned as red as her lips. Together, they left the chapel. Jane's anger matched Miss Drost's. They were in full battle mode.

When they left, Miss V took charge of the chapel hour. She said that she needed to get something and would be back in a few minutes. During that time, we sat quietly waiting. Our minds were focused on Jane and what would be the consequences of her words and actions. She would probably be doing laundry, no doubt about it. No one had ever stood up to the witch of Wickerson like that. What would Stella have told Jane? Could she have stopped her?

Stella would be offended by Jane's words. At the very least, we had to respect our elders whether we agreed with them or not.

Later, Miss Vozenich stood in front at the podium. Clearing her throat and in a soothing voice, she started, "Listen, let's focus on something a little different than your verses for today. Many people of the world look to not only the biblical verses, but also some look to Buddhism to inspire them. I would like us to read these quotes or sutras as they are called. They give us a unique approach to our lives. I'll read a few to get us started. Then, each of you come up, select one, and read it from this book. I think you'll find them very soothing and comforting in nature."

Miss Vozenich read a few. And we followed, one by one we read the quotes. The readings were more uplifting—more of a wider, accepting attitude. The time went quickly by for the girls who enjoyed reading the Buddha sutras. The calm respite from the usual derogatory verses of condemnation came to an end when Miss Drost came back into the chapel room.

"What is going on here, Miss Vozenich? Why are they not reading their verses?" she inquired, surprised that her assistant had stepped in and changed their verse reading. She grabbed the book from the podium, gazing at the quotes as she thumbed through it, page after page.

"I thought that I would introduce the girls to a unique view through quotes and principles of Buddhism. It's just a different approach," replied Miss V, hoping that her director would not be to upset. She realized, however, that she had overstepped her place.

"What were you thinking? We have a Christian founder who has required us to teach Christian values. We can't allow these Buddhistic views of openness and tolerance. These unwed girls need the biblical verses to remind them of their transgressions. They have to become humbler and more contrite. We have restrictions and regimentation to reshape them into 'proper' and noble individuals," said Miss Drost, frothing at the mouth.

"I agree to a large degree, but certainly, a little break from the usual couldn't harm. I thought that they would gain a wider view of the world by reading these," replied the assistant. She felt her valid reasoning slipping away.

"You thought wrong, Miss Vozenich. We will have to discuss this further in my office." Turning towards the girls, she announced, "You will recite your biblical verses for next week—the ones that you had memorized for today. You're dismissed."

The girls all rose and filed out of the chapel. The air filled with tension as the two headed to the director's office to talk further about the chapel incident. When the girls came upstairs, Jane had packed her suitcases which stood inside her bedroom door. They were all stunned and realized that she was being sent away.

Looking at the girls, she exclaimed, "I'm leaving this hell-hole. Just as soon as my mom can arrange it, I'm out of this fucking place."

"Where will you go?" asked Stacy.

"It doesn't matter to me. I just want out of this damn house. I don't know how all of you can stand staying here. It's like a jailhouse—certainly not a place of comfort or of compassion. There are other places out there." replied Jane.

Eveline quickly glanced at her, wondering if she would do better at another place. With her rebellious attitude and her bad mouth, she doubted that she would stay long anywhere. Then, the conversation turned to the chapel and Miss Vozenich. Meg thought that this might be the end of the assistant director, but Mary thought that Miss Drost wouldn't let her go. The assistant director had been here for such a short time; it would look bad on Miss Drost if she didn't keep her longer. Besides, the assistant would certainly step in line and never read them any more sutras.

That evening after everyone was in bed, Eveline thought about the different verses that she had heard. Something inside of her changed when she heard them. The sutras had been about peace and joy, and they had a calming effect on her. Suddenly, she felt different about herself. As she lay there in the hot night air with the full moon outside, she felt her baby move. A little foot or elbow traced her belly inside. Her motherly instincts rose again within her, overtaking her emotions. She wondered if she had a girl or a boy. Tears filled her eyes, for she would like to hold her baby before she gave it up to that unidentified man and woman who came. Sadly, she knew that she did not have the means to raise a child on her own. Being unwed had put her here with no options.

The next morning the fiery fierce ball of the sun rose up from the eastern horizon. Another scorching day of heat and sweating for everyone living on these flatlands. The green fields were nearly ready for the harvest. The town council had paid someone to repaint the water tower, so now it read "Stockton."

Today, Eveline had garden duty along with Stacy, Meg, and Mary. They were to bring in some of the vegetables, picking the peas and beans from the vines held up by sticks and string and pulling up some of the carrots and beets. The work would be difficult for Eveline and Meg, but not for Stacy and Mary. After a few hours, the sun had risen, slowly heating the long day ahead. The girls washed the carrots and beets with the garden hose before putting the water on the long rows. Heading into the house, they all were talking about getting inside for lunch.

As Eveline wobbled up to the back porch steps, she tripped at the top and sailed down the steps, falling on her side and scraping her elbow and arm. The air rushed out of her lungs as her body heavy with child hit the ground hard. Her legs and arms thrashed around her, trying to catch herself. Pain shot through her body while the awkward fall started her labor. When she struggled to stand, she felt another sharp pain, and then her water broke and ran down her legs. Her water quickly soaked into the dry ground. At least, no one would have to mop it up, thought Eveline as a pain went across her back, taking away her breath. Meg stayed and held onto her while Mary ran into the house to get help.

Everything became a blur to Eveline. With Meg helping her, she moved into the house, into the small medical office, and onto the hard, flat examining table. Voices were talking to her and all around her; excited voices filled the small room. Next, she heard Miss Drost tell her that she was too early to have the baby here. They were sending her to Bender to the hospital where Dr. Smith would meet her.

Nurse Litton came with her in the car as Eveline laid down in the back seat. The nurse told her to lift her legs and not to push. Exhausted after working in the garden all morning, Eveline did as she was told. Every once in a while, an all-consuming pain gripped her back and abdomen. Yes, she was in labor, and she was too early. This thought panicked Eveline and she started to cry. Nurse Litton told her to calm down but to breathe deeply. Nothing could stop the labor once it started. With tears streaming down her temples and into her black hair, her mind closed out everything.

Time was suspended as she felt her tired body move periodically into the labor pains.

After the ride in the car, she felt herself being taken through the hospital doors where she sat in a wheelchair which was being pushed down a long hall with bright overhead lights. Through a door and into another room. They lifted her body onto the hospital bed. The nurses took off the dirty smock and slipped on a clean, smelling hospital gown. Dr. Smith in a green scrub came to ask her a few questions; he wanted to know what happened, how far did she fall, and when did her water break. She mumbled the answers the best she could. He then examined her, touched her shoulder, and told her that they were going to take care of her. The labor pains shot through her body. Mother Nature had taken hold of her. She had no control.

The nurses comforted her with words. Many hours slipped by in a daze. The masked doctor examined her from time to time; the nurses would come and check on her. The room around her blurred as the labor pains increased. Time had been suspended in her mind while she rested between the labor pains.

After the masked doctor examined her another time, excitement filled the air while she felt herself lifted and taken to another room with brighter lights. Her legs were lifted, and her feet were placed in the stirrups. She felt naked and exposed, but she forgot about modesty. Hands were taking care of her with more encouraging phrases, and then, the words came "to push." She did. The nurse told her that she did great. She was given an anesthetic while she relax and dozed. When the afterbirth pains came and hit her, she woke, gasping. A nurse checked in on her and informed her that those pains were normal after a birth. Finally, she closed her eyes and the room disappeared.

* * *

When Eveline awoke, her Aunt Vera sat next to her hospital bed with a concerned look on her face. Her Uncle Max sat in another chair next to her. Aunt Vera spoke softly to her, telling her that she would be all right. Tears streamed down her aunt's face. Her uncle stood and came over to her bedside and took her hand in his.

"I'm going to drive over and get your belongings at the Wickerson Home. I'll be back soon. You rest, Eveline," he said quietly to her. His voice was filled with emotion as he squeezed her limp hand. His comforting touch sent a warm wave through her. She had not felt compassion for many months.

Aunt Vera squeezed her hand on the other side of the bed, and said, "You are coming home with us for a few days." Eveline sighed and nodded. She looked into the face of her dear aunt with loving eyes. Thank goodness. She was free of that awful place. *But what happened?*

She wanted to know, afraid to ask, but knew the awful truth. She felt her usual exhausted self, but there was something different. Her stomach was flat under the covers. An overhead tube ran down and into her arm. Her aunt held a glass of water for Eveline to swallow and refresh her dry mouth. Her loving aunt leaned down and kissed her on the forehead, touching her matted hair and caressing her head. The loving touches gave her comfort, warming her heart.

"You know that the baby was born too early. Dr. Smith said you'll be all right after a week or so of rest. Are you hungry? They will be bringing in lunch soon," said Aunt Vera, sitting back down.

Eveline closed her eyes and nodded. She had no words for a few minutes, trying to catch reality in her situation. She asked, "How long have you been here?"

"We came today. They have let you sleep so that you can rest and recover, dear," responded her aunt quietly. "We'll take care of you. Then, Max and I will drive you back to Riverside."

A nurse came in and took out the tube in her arm. Dr. Smith then came in, looked over her chart, and stood beside the bed. He asked her a few questions while he nodded writing on the chart with a pen.

"After you have eaten your lunch, I am releasing you to your aunt and uncle. I want you to rest, eat, and take your medication for a while. Your fall caused the baby to be born too early to survive. I am sorry. He didn't make it. You're a healthy young girl and fortunate to recover so well as you have. Give yourself time to rest and heal," explained Dr. Smith. "Do you have any questions?"

Eveline asked quietly, "What about the baby?"

"Your aunt and uncle have taken care of the arrangements. I have to issue a birth and a death certificate. Do you have a name we can give the baby?" asked the doctor.

As she took in the shocking information, she could not think of a name. Certainly not Devin, the father's nor Bert, her father's. "What is your first name?"

"Robert," he responded.

"Let's name him 'Robert'," she whispered with sadness filling her heart and her eyes flooded with tears as the doctor disappeared into a smeared image. She brushed aside her tears and turned her head away, embarrassed of her emotional response. Dr. Smith moved away to the end of the bed and talked with her aunt quietly, giving her some final directions. He left and Aunt Vera came to sit down beside her.

Later, an orderly brought in a tray with her lunch on it. Her aunt fretted around the bed and helped her sit up so that she could eat. Eveline ate a little of everything—the soup felt warm on her throat. She nibbled on half of a sandwich, ate some strawberry gelatin, and drank a half pint of milk. Resting back on her pillows, she closed her eyes as the food filled her empty stomach. A nurse came in and gave her a pill to take.

Two nurse came in and announced that she needed to take a shower. As the two helped her out of the hospital bed, her weak legs and sore body could barely stand. She saw the room spin around her. The two nurses held her up as she grasped their arms. Together, they slowly walked her into a bathroom with a warm shower running. They gently washed her sore body with the warm water and sudsy soap. They shampooed her flat dirty hair, making it spring back to life. Slowly, she shuffled back to her hospital bed, putting on a clean hospital gown and laid down. Dizzy and sore, her aunt carefully covered her up.

After an afternoon nap, Uncle Max showed up with her suitcase and left. After fussing with the clothes in the suitcase, Eveline dressed slowly, putting on her own skirt, a blouse, and her pink sweater. With her breasts full of milk, she wanted to cover them up. They tingled and felt full. Feeling her own clothes made Eveline remember the smocks that she had worn for nearly four months. Brushing her curly hair reminded her that her hair had grown below her ear. Her aunt said she looked a little like herself again. But her clothes hung loosely on her.

Coming into her room with some papers for her to sign, Dr. Smith smiled and told her to take care of herself. A nurse came back and wheeled her down the hall to the two doors that led to her Uncle Max and his car, waiting for her. The heat and the fierce sunlight hit her blinking eyes and her weak body as they emerged from the hospital. With slow motions, she rose out of the wheelchair, crawled into the backseat of the car, and laid down, resting her head on a pillow. The medication had relaxed her with no feelings to what was going on around her. She went through the motions without any reaction, doing as she was told.

They drove out of Bender and headed toward Flat Rock. Time stood suspended for Eveline. She fell asleep and before she realized it, they were at her aunt and uncle's small little home two hours later. Her aunt took care of her for the next two days, feeding and pampering her. On the third day, Uncle Max loaded their suitcases, and they started on the long trip to Riverside.

Even though she was medicated, Eveline felt better. She sat up in the backseat and watched the countryside pass by. The flat green farmland and grassy prairies slowly changed as they headed toward the dark blue mountains in the distance. Uncle Max drove and Aunt Vera talked. Miles and miles of sagebrush passed by with a few small towns dotted along the way. The farmland turned into ranching with its livestock and pastures. The temperature dropped as they moved away from the flatland and into the canyons with mountain walls rising above them. Eveline recalled her long bus ride months ago and how sick she had been.

The car now rocked her as her eyes closed and she tried to forget Miss Drost, Miss V, and all the girls. However, the memories of those dreadful times at Wickerson Home wouldn't go away, nor the memory of her hospital stay. While the car rocked her into a deep sleep, she dreamed.

She imagined that she was trapped in a fiercely hot room. Sweat dripped down her back. When she opened the door, she saw a dark swirling twister outside, moving towards her, going around and around, making her dizzy. Mixed within the swirling mass was the face of Miss Drost, pointing with her finger with a long red nail. She panicked and wanted to scream *STOP, let me go.* The dream seemed so real and clouded her mind, filling her with fear. Through the darkness, she heard that bell, *RING. RING.* It was ringing for her to stand, to sit, or to go to bed. She heard the loud clatter of voices rehearsing the verses with words swimming in her mind—immoral, soiled, wicked, and improper.

Suddenly waking, she gasped, breathing heavily. She put her hands over her face, shaking off the horrible images of that dream. Her heart beat fast within her breast. Listening, she heard the car horn, *HONK. HONK.* Her uncle cried out, "Did you see that guy? He turned without signaling."

Her aunt said to her uncle, "Be careful, Max." After a pause, she continued, "I never liked that place. Something wasn't right."

"Now stop that," replied Uncle Max.

"Did you see her? She looks like a scarecrow. Who loses weight when you're having a baby. No wonder they wouldn't let us come and visit her," commented Aunt Vera. Eveline thought: *they were denied a visit.* Stella had been right.

"They had their reasons. Let's focus on getting her home. She'll be all right," he replied, trying to keep his wife from getting upset.

"I think that Wickerson Home mistreated those young girls," her aunt stated in a final comment. "The place reminded me of a gothic nightmare."

Eveline couldn't help but agree with her aunt's assessment. Those horrific memories of *that place* were etched in her mind for several years. She would struggle continually to keep her mind from taking her down, down into that depressed dream-like state. She would wake, soaked from a cold sweat of those nightmares.

* * *

After the long drive to the mountain town of Riverside, Uncle Max, Aunt Vera, and she arrived at home. That evening, her aunt and her mom stayed up late, talking and catching up on each other's lives. The next morning, her uncle and aunt took off. Eveline hugged her aunt tightly and thanked her. Uncle Max gave her a quick hug. They both wished her well and told her to come visit. Eveline promised to write them.

When they left, she felt a deep loss. She would forever remember how they had comforted her at time when no one else was there. Her parents seemed oblivious to her traumatic experience, not asking her anything about the Wickerson Home or the childbirth. Not asking about the miserable days she spent there.

Not asking how she felt about losing the baby. Not asking how empty and lonely she felt. They asked her nothing.

The day that her aunt and uncle left, her mom and dad went to work at the café, telling her to get some rest for the next few days. Her mom had handed her the town's old newspapers for her to read. She read through the headlines and only a few sentences, tired and depressed. But then she read about her friend Dave Knox who had been injured and about the terrible fire at the Battle Axe Ranch. Those few articles brought her up-to-date. However, she didn't want to face anyone, feeling weak and vulnerable

As the days slipped by, her mom and her dad avoided speaking about her four months' absence. They still had their bitter view of her past circumstances. And her dad knew about his daughter's earlier promiscuity that kept him angry deep inside. He never had told his wife about it, but that knowledge clouded his view of his innocent daughter. He would never trust her again.

While she had been gone, her parents had to face the town's gossip. A few town's people stopped coming to their café, upset that Bert had an unwed pregnant daughter. But he and his wife ignored the gossip and continued to work at their café. Their business suffered a little, and like most gossip, it faded with time. Bert's Café continued to thrive.

The tense atmosphere at home didn't help her feel welcomed. She took her pills that medicated her into a lull and allowed her to get through each day. She waited for her breastmilk to dry up which took the full two weeks to completely stop. After her fall off the back porch days ago, she had a bruised hip that continued to be sore when she rested on it. Unpacking her suitcase, she put her mom's old maternity clothes back into the downstairs' cardboard box. She also checked her purse and found her driver's license and money had been returned. At least, Miss Drost had been honest enough to replace them.

Staying home as long as she could, she slept in her comfortable bed and listened to the radio. She avoided calling any of her friends, but one afternoon, her friend Rebecca called who wanted to know all about what happened. She didn't tell her much, except that she was home recovering. Her friend kept pressing her for more details, but Eveline finally said that she rather not talk about it—that she wanted to forget about it, just like Stella had told her. Rebecca finally gave up, and they both said their goodbyes.

The traumatic experience had darkened her soul and she slipped into depression for several days and nights. The Wickerson Home haunted her memories in the day and at night. One evening, she relived another nightmare, waking up shivering and frightened.

She remembered all the girls that she had lived with from the first girls to the last ones. Her roommate Stella emerged with fond thoughts. But Jane's short stay dominated her mind. So many things had happened that one week to change the way she looked at her stay there.

The harsh, disturbing words that Jane had spoken came rushing back to her. Eveline had never cussed in her life, but now she said a few to herself. *Those bull-shit verses and they should all go to hell.* Somehow Jane's words rang with truth—life at the Wickerson Home had been intolerable. A rising anger filled her inside as she recalled all of her terrible experiences there, and her depression disappeared. Now, she developed a rebellious attitude like Jane who had spewed out at Miss Drost and at her "proper" lady edicts.

* * *

One evening at dinner after days resting, her dad had enough of his daughter's staying at home. He had given her plenty of time to recover.

"Eveline it's time for you to come back to the café and work. I'm letting Torri McClure go so that you can step in and help us with the café. You and your mom can split waiting tables and working the cash register," said her dad, glancing at his daughter. She lowered her head and nodded.

Her mom agreed and added, "Yes. You can't stay home any longer. You'll feel better if you're up about doing something." They seemed insensible to what she had gone through. *Get up and go to work*—those words sounded so familiar. She desperately wanted to talk to her mom about the loss of her baby, but she recalled what had happened before she left. Her dad's words of *No discussion* rang in her mind.

Early the next morning, Eveline rose from her bed, dressed, and left the house with her parents. The café would keep her busy.

After the days of rest, she knew that she should help her parents. Even though she feared public scrutiny, she knew that she had to face them someday. Working in the café gave her a safe place to begin. She could hide in the kitchen if things got bad. Nonetheless, her body felt weak and stiff, and her mom told her to pace herself throughout the day.

During that busy Friday, customers came, and she served them, taking their orders, and slipping their tips into her pocket. The only thing that caught her unexpected was her dad's little bell that he tapped when a meal was ready to pick up. A little chill went through her the first time that she heard it. But she braced herself and shook the memory away.

Toward the dinner hour, two of her friends, Dave Knox and George Weaver, came in to eat. Sitting at one of the tables, the two guys smiled when she came over to take their order. They both welcomed her back. Dave smiled at her, thinking how different she looked. Taking a closer look, he noticed that she was thinner and had shorter hair. They ordered their meals and waited while she served them their coffee. After she left, the two men made small talk about their ranch work.

Their meal came and they ate. After they finished, Dave left a tip on the table for her. At the cash register, she took George's money and gave him back his change. George left while Dave hung back to talk to her.

Her dad watched as his daughter served and talked to the two cowboys. He frowned while his anger grew in his gut. Bert couldn't trust Eveline ever again. She had deceived them.

Smiling kindly at her, Dave tipped his hat with his scarred hand and left. As her sad mouth turned into a smile, he remembered that she was easy to talk to as he glanced into her gentle brown eyes. He'd be back.

After Dave had joined George outside the cafe, she watched them drive away. Turning back to work, she cleared away their dishes and carried them back to the kitchen. Her dad looked up at her and growled, "You stay away from those damn cowboys. Don't you get friendly with them. Don't even think about goin' out. You're grounded. Do you hear me?"

Her eyes opened wide at the restrictions. How dare her dad start ruling her life again. Those were her friends. Her dad didn't know how nice a friend Dave had been. He had spoken softly and politely with a caring, respectful, and considerate attitude towards her. She had never looked closely at Dave before tonight since he often had been in the background at their parties. Standing tall with broad shoulders and a narrow waist, he had a long, handsome face with soft blue eyes. He was a quiet, confident man.

That evening after dinner and a warm bath, Eveline lay under her covers, stretching out her tired, aching body. Somehow, she had to get her tattered life back together. Being only eighteen, she had the rest of her life in front of her. She recalled that the Buddha's sutra had mentioned living in the present and forgetting the past. Bracing her mind against all the emotions of her pregnancy and of losing the baby, she had to bury the past.

Tonight at the café, her dad had started to put down rules, criticizing her, and telling her what she could and couldn't do. Feeling rebellious, she recalled Dave's kind words, his smile, and his respectful tip of the hat. Closing her tired sleepy eyes, her exhausted body dozed off.

* * *

The fall weather in Riverside started to cool off with warm days and cold nights. The moon went through its phrases each month. Each day, Eveline loved seeing the dark, heavy forested mountains again surrounding the town. Against the green pines, the yellow and orange of fall colored the mountains. A little snow came early but melted during the Indian summer days.

Eveline worked six days a week, slept in on her day off, and counted her tips from the customers. Around town, the coming wedding and reception of Chet Fletcher had been the recent gossip. The wedding would be held at the Battle Axe Ranch with a catered lunch for the family at the Dark Horse Tavern. Bert and Kay were asked to cater their well-known barbeque beef dinner. The evening before, Eveline's parents were busy preparing the meal. She had been expected to help serve the family.

That Saturday morning had been busy for Bert, Kay, and Eveline. When the wedding party came to the tavern, a long table had been set and the dinner had been ready to serve. Eveline busied herself, helping. Her friend Dave was among the wedding party.

He sat at the end of the long table. They hadn't seen or talked with each other since he came into the café with George that one evening. She was glad to see him, and he smiled at her.

When the wedding party had finished eating, the tavern opened up to the public for the reception. The married couple cut the beautifully decorated wedding cake, danced their first dance together as husband and wife, and said their goodbyes. Chet and his wife had planned to leave early and ride up to their summer camp in the mountains for a short honeymoon.

Eveline enjoyed seeing the Fletchers, particularly Matt whom she had dated a couple of times before she left. However, he ignored her when she served him. He definitely didn't want to talk to her. Shaking off the hurt, she busied herself in helping her parents clear the luncheon table. Her parents loaded everything in their car and left for the café. Eveline took off her apron and stayed behind.

Her friends had invited her to join them at their table. The usual group of girls were Rebecca, Deirdre, and Suzie and the guys were Dave, George, and Craig. Dave particularly wanted to be with her and stood up, sliding out a chair for her to sit next to him. The tavern was serving draft beer for an hour, so Dave and George came back to their table with a pitcher of beer and mugs. The girls eyed Eveline, but Rebecca had told them not to ask her anything about the pregnancy. They talked all around her. When the two guys came back with the beer, they all sipped their cold drinks. Someone had punched in a few hit songs on the jukebox. Everyone at the table left to dance, leaving Dave and Eveline sitting and drinking.

Dave wanted to talk. He moved his chair closer to hers and asked her how she had been. He wanted to know more about her four months away. Relaxed, Eveline found it easy to talk to him and opened-up. She side-stepped her pregnancy which he already knew. She told him about Wickerson Home and generally about the exhausting duties and the silly rules. She told him how they had cut her hair and how hard the girls had to work. She kept her lost baby to herself, a secret that she still couldn't grasp. Naturally, she told him how fiercely hot it had been and about the tornado that she had seen and experienced. Dave was shocked to hear her bizarre story. He realized that she had been through a horrific situation and came out as a strong, self-reliant, and confident woman.

When she finished, she asked him how he was doing. Shaking his head, he took a deep breath, drank a sip of his beer, and glanced into her gentle brown eyes. She waited. Dave looked around at the Fletchers who were still partying, even though the married couple had left.

"You already know about my injuries. But things have gotten a little uneasy at the ranch. It's gettin' too crowded out there. I mean, I'm gettin' along okay, but I'm just not happy with the situation," he said quietly.

"What do you mean?" she asked.

"Clyde has been givin' me light duty around the ranch since my injury. I'm a wrangler and I like workin' with the cattle," he replied, rubbing his scarred hand. "He's sidelined me, thinkin' he knows what's best for me. I disagree." Dave finished his mug of beer and poured himself another one. All of their friends were still dancing. He glanced at Eveline, "Do you want to dance?"

"No, thank you. I am too tired after serving the meal," she replied. He nodded and took another long drink. She continued, "I'm not happy at home either. My parents are putting down rules, treating me like a little kid. I resent it."

"That's too bad. I understand that you've had it rough," he paused, wondering how she had managed. But he had his own demons to fight. "I just received a letter from my ol' man in Montana. He has a foreman's job waitin' for me if I want to come. He works for a big ranch called the Circle R which manages several ranches. The owners just took over another one and they need a foreman."

"Do you want to go?" asked Eveline. That seemed so far away, but he would be with his family. She could tell that he had a lot on his mind.

"I don't know yet. Haven't decided," he replied. They sat looking at each other, thinking about their miserable situations and sipping their beer.

Suddenly, Eveline saw her dad come into the tavern through the back door, glancing around for her. He looked towards their table. Dave had his back to him, so she rose up from her chair and said, "I better go now. Thanks for the beer. Can I see you again?"

Dave nodded, looked up at her, and replied, "Yes. I'll come see you at the café again." He kept drinking his beer, never turning around to see her dad coming towards them.

But everyone else in the tavern saw the big, bald man come in, and her friends watched as he came and took her arm. They knew all about how Bert had ruled her life, grounding her when she had been at school. Even though she had been gone for four months, they realized nothing had changed for her now that she had returned.

She managed to meet her dad before he came to their table or before Dave saw him. Her dad had a frown as he took her arm. He whispered quietly through his teeth, "Let's go. We have *work* to do at the café. I don't want you hangin' around that cowboy."

"I'm coming. Don't make a scene. Let's go," she whispered as they headed out the back of the tavern. She angrily stepped outside and into his car. How dare he tell her that she can't be with Dave. She felt stuck again, trapped by her dad's demands, annoyed, and upset.

A week past. Eveline worked at the café, collecting her tips. She avoided talking to her dad who yet monitored her every move and rang his annoying bell in the kitchen. But thinking about Dave at the wedding reception had given her something to ponder. She wanted to see him again and find out if he would be going to Montana as his dad suggested. Her mind fixated on his quiet, serious nature and she liked his deep commitment and his intense focus on his work as a wrangler. She recognized the rebel in him that recently had emerged within herself.

On Friday evening, Dave walked into the café to have dinner. After he ordered his meal, he considered his disagreement with Clyde who yet had insisted that he take it easy at the ranch. The doctor had informed Clyde that Dave could have a relapse with his spinal injury. The two had heated words over his recent light duty.

Dave finally had come to a point of knowing what he wanted. He told Clyde that he was quitting, telling him that he was moving on to Montana and joining his dad. He had enjoyed his work at the Battle Axe Ranch and had no regrets. But for him, it was time to leave.

While he packed his belongings in the bunk house, the Fletchers came over and Clyde handed him his final paycheck, shaking his hand. Chet and Matt helped him load his brown stallion Bullet and his rodeo horse, the red gelding Flame, his saddles, and his gear into his old horse trailer. They were sorry to see him go, but they understood. Dave stepped into his pickup and drove into town.

When Eveline brought out his dinner, Dave smiled at her, happy to see her again. Even though he kindly spoke to her, his mind was preoccupied. He hadn't seen his mom and dad for nearly six years. Quickly, he ate his meal and then, eased back in his chair, considering his plans and the new challenge that awaited him in Montana. After finishing his meal, Eveline asked him if he wanted any dessert. No. He only wanted another cup of coffee. She filled his cup, gave him his ticket, and waited on another table.

While Dave sipped his second cup of coffee, he closely watched Eveline as she worked, recalling how comfortable he had felt around her. Ever since the wedding reception. she had been on his mind. His desires stirred as he thought of her gentle brown eyes, her beautiful face, and her quiet manners. He would love to have her by his side and in his arms. He felt the need to protect her and to make her happy. Together, they could settle down and make a future for the two of them. Everybody needed a second chance, and he knew that Eveline certainly deserved one.

Rising out of his chair, he walked up to the counter to pay. Smiling, she took his money and then, gave him his change. Seriously glancing into those beaming, brown eyes, he smiled at her, "I've made up my mind."

"What about?" she asked.

"I'm headin' to Montana." He paused for a thought-provoking moment. "Would you want to marry me?" He paused again, "If you say 'yes,' I'm leavin' tonight." His intense eyes stared at her, waiting for her answer.

Stunned at first, she suddenly realized what he meant from their conversation last week. Eveline's heart quickened at the thought of leaving with Dave, a man she had known and liked, and she realized this was her chance to start again.

Gazing up into this man's serious blue eyes, she nodded and whispered, "Yes. I will. I can be ready in a half an hour."

While she slipped off her apron, took out her pink sweater from under the counter, and slipped it on, he raised his scarred hand and tipped his hat respectfully at her, nodding. "Well then, let's get out of here." They walked out of the café, determined to make a new life for themselves.

Betsy's Path

In the small mountain town of Riverside, a dark grey pickup with an out-of-state license plate pulled up in front of the Mercantile. The driver sat, staring into the store.

* * *

Four Years Earlier

Over the last few months of her senior year, Elizabeth (Betsy) Crocket heard her folks discuss their plans of moving to Ohio. Her mom's brother, Jeb, owned and ran a Ford dealership in Crayton. A job opportunity had opened up there for her dad. He vacillated back and forth about making the move.

Throughout the many years, her dad had eked out a small living by working for the lumber mill. As a lumberjack, he would saw down huge lodge pole pine trees in the summer but would have to spend a couple months laid off until spring came each year. In addition, due to the recent recession, the lumber mill had been cutting back on their operations in Riverside, and her dad didn't know if he would have a job here or not. The indecisive future kept him in a constant uncertainty.

But after a few months of calling her mom's brother Jeb, he realized that the pay would be more, and they would be close to family. After discussing this new possibility, her dad decided that he would try selling cars. At least that job would be year around. He needed the security of an income to take care of his family.

Her parents decision to leave Riverside surprised Betsy. Even though she had been born in Crayton, she had grown up here in Riverside. Her parents, Gordan and Clara, moved here a few years after they were married. Her dad had been lured by the stunning Rocky Mountains and the outdoor activities of hunting and fishing.

During the years living in Riverside, her mom had to work, cleaning rooms at the local motels. When Betsy was old enough, she would help her mom, working beside her to make the beds, to clean the bathrooms, and to dump the trash. And then when she turned sixteen, she hired on cleaning the rooms like her mom. They would have to quit during the winter months when the tourist season ended.

Her mom's health became another key reason to move. The year before Betsy graduated, her mom had suffered from terrible pains, dizziness, and eventually, had collapsed at work. After seeing the doctor, Clara found out that she had experienced a mild heart attack. The doctor recommended rest and prescribed medication, but eventually, her mom had to quit working. That year Betsy had to help her mom whenever she came home from school. Her mom recovered but looked frail and weak. That year had been a meager time for the family. The money was tight. Furthermore, her dad worried about her mom's health and decided that she should be near her family.

Her parents decided to wait until after Betsy had finished school. At the end of May '57, she graduated. The day after, her dad left to find a place for them to live in Crayton. He would then return to move them.

Her mom Clara looked forward to moving away from Riverside. Not only was she tired of living in the small town with the cold, snow-filled winters, but she wanted more than ever to move back home to Ohio. She had always missed her family and constantly harped about living here in a small town. Her dad had enjoyed living here, but her mom's unhappy face and her tired and frail body finally won out their constant battle.

* * *

While her dad drove back to Ohio to find them a place to live, Betsy and her mom spent the time packing up their belongings. Her mom talked about how happy it would be to move out of this old log house and move into a proper one. Until now, Betsy had paid little attention to their home. Growing up here from a young child, she knew nothing else.

Glancing around, she realized that this old house had its problems. All of the narrow windows were low on the walls. They could not see much from them even though there were stunning mountains surrounding the town. She saw that the ceilings were low and that the floors buckled in places in the living room. During the winter months, the house never warmed up with only a standing propane heater in the living room. The bedrooms and the bathroom remained unheated and cold.

Everything in the kitchen spoke old. A large, stained sink with a dripping faucet, an outdated gas stove, and a small fridge stood in their kitchen. Their metal table with four chairs sat against one wall. She recalled that her mom had scrubbed and cleaned those old appliances, making them shine. Several times over the years, her mom had painted the walls to brighten the old log house.

Before packing, her mom wanted to sort through much of their belongings. Both of them went through their clothes in their closets, getting rid of old clothes, donating them to the church. They went through the kitchen cupboards and the other closets, sorting out belongings they didn't want. Her mom's face shone brightly with her eyes sparkling even though her frail body had worn out quickly each day. Betsy had finished most of the boxing, marking and stacking them in one corner of their living room. They washed all their bedding, hanging them on the clothesline. With excited anticipation, the two of them waited for her dad Gordan to return and move them to Ohio.

All of Betsy's friends had heard that her family was moving. A few of her girlfriends wished her well. Her closest friend Valerie Fayler wanted her to write and tell her about the exciting city life. Betsy promised that she would write. All of her friends were hiring on for their summer jobs. A few planned to leave Riverside, excitedly looking forward to their futures.

During that week of packing, her mom spoke about Crayton—a big city with more to do. Betsy started to think of how thrilling it would be to move to a big city. The lure of a new experience stirred her imagination. She eagerly thought of it as a new adventure.

When her dad returned, they loaded up a large trailer that he had borrowed from Jeb. The drive to Ohio took three long days. Betsy noticed that the dynamic Rockies disappeared as they headed east. They crossed the wide-opened plains with miles and miles of sagebrush. They drove past the farmlands with miles and miles of fields. They crossed rivers, passed through small towns and by-passed large cities. They travelled through the states of Nebraska, Iowa, Illinois, and Indiana. Her dad stopped only for gas or for a quick bite to eat. He drove on and on each day. They slept two nights in small motel rooms, resting their tired bodies.

Finally, they reached Ohio and the city of Crayton. Her dad drove them to a small box house which he had rented. The neighborhood had rows and rows of these same box houses with matching porches but painted differently. Their yellow house trimmed in white had a big tree in the front yard. A garage sat towards the back yard with a long driveway alongside the house. A trellis adorned the sides of the front porch.

Inside, her mom Clara walked around their new home, sighed a thankful breath, and said a little prayer. This Ohio house would be a great improvement over their old log house in Riverside. The house had two small bedrooms, a large kitchen with modern appliances, one bathroom, and a living room with a curtained picture window.

Jeb, Clara's younger brother, along with his wife Alisa, met them at their house. Their teenage daughter Amy trailed behind them. Clara hugged her brother Jeb whom she had not seen for many years. Alisa stood by smiling at the reunion. Betsy felt the warmth coming from them. Her dad and Jeb slowly unloaded all their belongings into the small house. At the end of the day, their beds had been set up ready to sleep.

The next day, they awoke to boxes scattered throughout the rooms. In the neighborhood, they could hear outside the sounds of children playing. Her aunt and uncle lived only a few blocks away from them. They had driven over that morning bringing food for breakfast. Her mom and aunt cooked their first meal in their new home. While they ate and drank coffee, Betsy found out that Jeb and Alisa both worked at the car dealership. Her aunt worked in the office, taking calls and keeping the books while her uncle sold the cars. The two of them were happy. They looked forward to her dad working for them.

Their daughter Amy sat quietly, listening to everyone. When asked about her summer plans, she said she would be babysitting and getting together with her girlfriends on the week-ends. The two cousins for the first time became acquainted with each other. Amy stared at Betsy who seemed so grown-up. Betsy had a large bustline and a small waistline with a slender, shapely body. Her long, thick auburn hair reached below her shoulders, and her shining hazel eyes looked at Amy who glanced down at her own flat chest and her straight figure. A little envy rose up into Amy's heart. Her cousin Betsy seemed to have it all together. But her bubbly personality made Amy forget about her undeveloped body.

As an energetic, positive girl, Betsy adapted easily to their move to Crayton. Her aunt asked her to come work at the dealership in the office. After a few days of unpacking the boxes and getting settled, Betsy went with her dad to work at the dealership. That year, Jeb had expanded his business to include a repair shop. Repairs on the vehicles brought in additional customers year around. The place was very busy from the first day that she walked into the door. Alisa spent time showing her the books and how to maintain their records. She learned quickly.

Working at the dealership had kept Betsy busy for a week. Aunt Alisa enjoyed having the company, telling her that she had gotten behind and that she had been a great help. Each night in bed, Betsy began to consider what she really wanted to do. Sitting at a desk all day, doing errands for her aunt was starting to wear on her. She would rather be up and about doing something else. But what? The only other type of work she knew had been cleaning motel rooms. Could she be a housekeeper again?

Naturally one evening, Betsy scanned the newspaper want ads. She found several listings for housekeepers. "Look mom. There are all these jobs," she said pointing to the ads.

"I don't understand. Why would you want to clean rooms and scrub toilets when you have a nice, clean job at the dealership, sitting at a desk?" asked her mom.

"It's obvious that Aunt Alisa is just being kind, and she won't need me after a week of working the books," replied Betsy.

"Well, it's up to you. Do what you think best," said her mom.

When she went into work, Betsy had told her Aunt Alisa that she wanted to look around for a permanent job. Naturally, her aunt understood. Before leaving that day, Betsy looked for her dad and wanted to talk to him. He had just finished with a potential customer, hoping he would be back for a test drive. Her dad walked into his office, drinking a cup of coffee. He smiled seeing his daughter come in. They sat down.

After they had talked for a while, her dad said, "I like having you around here. Are you happy living here in the big city?"

"Yes, I am. It's new and exciting," she replied.

Her dad than received a phone call and she left and walked back over to her aunt's office. Pulling the newspaper out of her purse, she asked her for some help. The two of them read over the ads. Aunt Alisa told her about the historic hotels which would be good places to work. Looking at the ads, her aunt circled the ones that would be best for her to apply. With her past work experience, her aunt told her that she would certainly get interviews. After that, it would be up to Betsy to sell herself as a capable worker.

As they sat talking, her aunt offered to take her downtown and to show her around. Betsy said she couldn't wait to see the city. Since they had moved here, she had only been to the dealership and to a grocery store. A few days ago she had gone with her mom to buy groceries at a nearby store which turned out to be the biggest store she had ever seen. Everywhere, fresh produce and canned goods were in large supplies. Displayed in tall stacks, the canned goods amazed her. Before they left, her mom asked the clerk for a few savings books. As they loaded the groceries, her mom told her about the green stamps, about the books, and about a catalogue of free items in exchange for saving the green stamps. Her mom laughed at her daughter's amazement. Shopping for groceries in the big city had been a new experience for her.

Today, Aunt Alisa walked over to Uncle Jeb's office and told him that she was taking Betsy downtown to show her the city. The two left the dealership and caught one of the yellow trolleys a couple of blocks over. It was car No. 22. Betsy realized that she would have to know how to get around the city if she did get a job. Without a car, she would have to depend on the street cars.

Her aunt started telling her about Crayton as they rode. Betsy's eyes opened wide when she gazed toward the downtown area, as she listened to the ticking of the wheels on the rail. Being from a small mountain town of 1,000, the sprawling city stunned her. As they rode towards downtown, tall and short buildings rose above the horizon. The streets were wide with cars parked up and down each side. She glanced down the side streets when the trolley came to an intersection. Miles and miles of avenues stretched out in all directions. They passed a block-long park with wide-sidewalks, trimmed lawns, shade trees, and a small blue pond. People were all through the park, strolling and enjoying this warm summer day.

Betsy saw a fountain with a large grey statue of a winged angel in the center of the park. The gorgeous fountain fascinated her with its artistic imagery. Crystal-clear streams of water poured out of the base of the statue, splashing into the fountain below. Grey city pigeons fluttered and strutted around the ground. Children ran around the fountain, chasing each other and the pigeons. Another park had a long swimming pool with many people splashing, swimming, and enjoying the cool water.

On the lengthy city blocks, a variety of businesses sat one after another, packed densely next to each other. They passed laundries, bakeries, bookstores, clothing stores, tobacco shops, and so many more. Such an assortment of shops were lined up on each block of the city.

Continuing, they rode near to the city office buildings which were built around a square. In the center of the square, stood a tall flagpole. On the top flew an American flag. Below it, the Ohio state flag flew, both fluttered in the breeze. The Ohio flag looked like a banner, a pointed swallowtail in red and white stripes. The blue on the flag surrounding the white circle had seventeen white stars. Looking up at the state flag, Aunt Alisa mentioned that the white circle with the red inside stood for the buckeye.

Betsy had to ask the question which every visitor asked, "What is a buckeye? Is it really a deer's eye?"

Her aunt laughed and said, "Folklore has various answers, but it refers to a dark brown nut with a big round tan spot on it. The nut comes from the buckeye tree, native around the Midwest. Carrying the nut is supposed to bring you luck, but that's just a superstition. The tree grows in the wild and lives up to eighty to one-hundred years. The leaves are toxic, and the nuts are acid-tasting." Later, Betsy discovered that the buckeye name permeated throughout the state.

As they continued their ride on the yellow trolley, they passed a whole city block under construction with deafening sounds of workers hollering, diesel engines running, and dust and smoke coming from within the area. Passing another street, men were using noisy jackhammers, chipping away the pavement and the concrete sidewalk. It reminded Betsy of a dentist's drill. Her aunt told her that construction went on throughout the city.

They soon passed two of the historic hotels which her aunt pointed out to her. One of the hotels stood six stories high while the other rose a few stories higher. The Golden Lion had an elaborate entrance with shiny brass-lined glass doors. A few blocks away the Hotel Baudelaire rose up with shapely windows. She excitedly glanced closer at each of them as they rode past. They traveled farther away from the downtown area to an older part of town. Here, the Hotel du Toussant stood with manicured lawns, trees, and shrubs. They rode past a historic manor and another small park. Her aunt noticed that Betsy's excited eyes took in the city like a girl in a candy shop. She shook her head and thought that her niece had a lot to learn about living here. But she recalled how it felt to be young again with a bright future in front of her.

Finally, they came to the end of the trolley route. Her aunt then suggested that they take a walk around one of the parks before heading back. Betsy had appreciated that her aunt had taken her through the city. They found a bench under the shade of a big tree; sitting they continued talking. Her aunt wanted to know more about their move and her mom's condition. Betsy wanted to know more about getting a job. Back and forth, they talked, enjoying the time together. Soon, it was time to leave, and they walked back to the trolley station. Nearby, a parked street vendor sold hot dogs and drinks. Aunt Alisa stopped and bought them each a drink. They sat on a bench and waited for the next trolley.

While they sat drinking, her aunt delicately said, "Once you get a job at one of the hotels, they will have uniforms for the housekeepers to wear. But you should think about dressing up for your interviews. Your appearance will matter. I would be happy to lend you a few dresses to wear if you want. You'll want to dress up and even put on some make-up."

Glancing at her aunt, Betsy noticed that she wore a lovely yellow dress with little white heels. She also had on a pair of earrings and a necklace. With her make-up and lipstick, she realized that her aunt looked more dressed up than she did. Suddenly, she felt plain and unattractive. She had no make-up on her face. Embarrassed of her western-styled clothes, she glanced down at her denim skirt, her fringed brown leather vest over her plain white blouse. She then frowned. Her clothes seemed out of place here in the city.

But her aunt grinned and said, "Don't worry. I will help you." She paused and took out a pack of cigarettes from her purse. She offered one to Betsy who shook her head. "I buy this brand of cigarettes because each pack has a few coupons on the back. I've saved the coupons and got a hair dryer for free." She looked surprised at her aunt. Another means of collecting coupons, like the stamps. Her aunt smiled and took a long puff, "I smoke just to keep my nerves steady."

"Thank you for showing me the city," she said. Her aunt thought that her niece would do fine once she got familiar with the big city.

One of the trolleys arrived and they boarded it, heading back through the city to home. On the way back, Betsy noticed how the people were dressed: men in suits, women in dresses and suits. Earlier that morning, she recalled that her dad now wore a new suit to sell cars. After they had moved there, he even had cut his auburn hair into a flat top. His well-worn lumberjack clothes with his heavy boots were stuffed into a box stored in a closet. Now, her dad had never looked so handsome going to work.

At dinner that evening, she told her parents about her trip into the city. They listened quietly since they both had lived here and knew the city well. Her dad saw the excitement in his young daughter's innocent eyes.

Her mom spoke up and said, "I'm glad you're happy with our move here. I was worried that you would be sad leaving Riverside."

"No, I'm glad we moved here. But I'm anxious about getting a job," she replied.

"It may take a while and it won't be easy. This is not like Riverside where everyone knows you. I grew up here. There will be fierce competition for the jobs," said her dad.

She smiled, and said, "I can do it. Dad, I'm a big girl now. It may take a while to find one."

"Well, find yourself an upscale hotel with class, not a small motel. Your Uncle Jeb said you can work part-time at the dealership while you look for another job," responded her dad. She nodded, happy to hear that she would be making some money since she would need to buy some make-up and a few clothes. She wanted to fit into this big city.

After dinner, they watched the new television set. Her dad had purchased a black and white for her mom who spent her days watching the soap operas. They had an enjoyable evening listening to the news and laughing at the comedies. Soon, Betsy grew tired and headed for her bedroom.

In her room, she put on her nightgown and then, decided to write her friend Valerie and give her their address. Getting out a pen and her box of stationery, she sat on her bed, and wrote:

Dear Valerie, "How are you doing? Did you find summer work? We are settled in a nice house here in Crayton and I am doing fine. My mom is glad we moved here. I met my Uncle Jeb, Aunt Alisa, and my cousin Amy who is just 13. They live close to us, so we see them often. I am just starting to look for a job here. The ads are filled with housekeeping and waitressing jobs, so I hope I can find one soon. A couple of days a week I have been working for my aunt. I've been doing odd jobs as well as helping her with her bookkeeping. Crayton is a big city with lots of new things to see. I rode the trolley the other day into the downtown area. It is so exciting to be here. Are you going with anyone? How are all our friends doing? Here is my address: 3860 Kenington St., Crayton, Ohio. Please write and tell me how you are doing." Your friend, Betsy.

After finishing the letter, she scooted under her covers. Thinking of her long day, she closed her tired eyes. Since this morning, her mind had never stopped reeling at all the possibilities in her future. A new world had opened up to her with exciting experiences. With hope in her heart, she couldn't wait to get started. Her former life in the small town seemed so limiting and dismal. She looked forward to seeing the dresses her aunt would bring over. Betsy wanted to prove herself, showing her parents that she could be independent and resourceful. Yes, she wanted to work at a big hotel. As she dozed off to sleep, she heard the sounds of the city—a kind of hum that never stopped. She had experienced her first tour of living in the big city.

* * *

For the next few weeks, Betsy spent her days in a whirlwind of applying for the hotel jobs, interviewing, and waiting by the phone to hear the results of her efforts. She worked a few days a week at the dealership. At work, her aunt had a radio in her office, and they listened to many of the radio stations. With the sounds of music in her ears, Betsy cleaned up the break room and made fresh pots of coffee. The days slipped by slowly.

Before her interviews, her aunt brought over three cotton short-sleeved dresses. She told her niece that she could have them since the waist lines were too tight for her. Betsy quickly looked them over: one was a white dress with black polka dots, another was a light blue with a floral design, and the third one was a dark green dress. Each of them had a matching belt which she loved, especially the wide red one on the white dress. That became her favorite.

Her aunt also gave her one of her petticoats, saying that it needed mending. The white petticoat was a cancan with a few layers of netting around the lower part. The chic cancan would fill out the skirts. Her mom had seen them in the catalogues, but she had never ordered one. Betsy couldn't wait to try on one of her dresses with the slip. When she stepped out of her bedroom, they smiled, for they saw that her full chest had stretched the bodice too tight. The buttons would have to be moved over. That evening Betsy stayed up late sewing, moving over all the buttons and mending the ruffled slip. When she wore the dresses later, they looked much better on her. She struck quite a figure with her shapely body.

Betsy took her aunt's advice in dressing up for her interviews. She selected the white and black polka dotted dress with the wide red belt for one of them. She wore the blue floral dress for the other interview. Fortunately, her mom and Betsy had the same size shoe, so she borrowed a pair of white flats to wear. And for her make-up, she purchased some black mascara, an eyeliner, and a tube of red lipstick. A small compact of powder took care of her shining nose and rosy cheeks. For her hair-do, she gathered up her hair into a ponytail first, and then, twirled it into a fashionable bun on the back of her head. She looked older and more grown up. Borrowing a small pair of earrings from her mom, she clipped them on her small earlobes. After wearing them to her interviews, her ears throbbed. She had been glad to pull them off after reaching home. Later, she would buy her own earrings that didn't pinch her earlobes.

Her first two interviews did not go well. Figuring out the time to leave home and arrive at the hotels became her first concern. Luckily, her parents had given her a wristwatch for graduation. She had to ride the yellow trolley, timing the interviews with only minutes left. When riding the trolley, the crowded street car was filled with people hurrying to go to work. The crowding and the close timing made her uneasy. Rushing to the hotels and finding the right offices made her heart pound as she tried to remain calm and catch her breath.

At one of her first interviews, she laughed too loudly where she received looks of disapproval. She had been told that they hired only serious, hard-working housekeepers. She never heard from that hotel again. At another interview, she didn't smile, kept her excitement in check. She had been told there that they hired only happy, pleasant housekeepers. Again, no return call. *How do you strike an even balance at these interviews? When do you smile or laugh or remain serious?* The stress had been more than she had anticipated.

Betsy's interviews had gone badly, and none of them had called her back. She had been a complete failure, beaten down and discouraged. But her aunt encouraged her to keep looking in the newspaper and to apply for other jobs. She even applied for a waitressing job downtown, but that had turned out wrong for her. With no experience, she had no chance there at the restaurant. They were kind but told her to get some experience.

Every day, she snatched the daily newspaper and scanned the want ads. Every day, there were several motel jobs, but her dad had told her to apply for an "upscale" hotel. None of them were. She waited and worked, reading the ads. Besides her failed interviews, she felt bad working at the dealership.

One early morning, she finally saw two hotel housekeeping ads. One at the Hotel Baudelaire and one at the Golden Lion Hotel. Both were the downtown historic hotels which she had seen on her trolley tour with her aunt. Excitedly, she rode down to the hotels to get the applications.

Before leaving that morning, she dressed up in the blue floral dress with the cancan and white flats. She put on her make-up, clipped on a pair of earrings, and rolled her hair into a bun. Even though she was just picking up the applications, she wanted to make a good impression from the start. In the past, she had worn her typical western clothes with no make-up and her hair down. Perhaps, they had prejudged her when she had picked up the applications at the other hotels. That realization struck her as a possibility.

Overwhelmed with excitement, she walked towards the Hotel Baudelaire. A doorman opened the brass-lined door for her. Glancing around inside, she viewed the marbled floors and the gorgeous, lighted crystal chandelier. Outside, a brand new red Cadillac had stopped in front of the hotel. The doorman opened the door for the richly dressed couple with two children. They passed her in the lobby and moved to the historic desk to check in. Their footsteps clicked on the marble floor. The children whispered their excitement at being on their holiday in the city.

At the other hotel, the Golden Lion, a black limousine pulled up. In a rush of fury, two footmen came out from the hotel. Both occupants emerged from the sleek vehicle, one by one. The first was a gentleman dressed in a tailored, silky navy suit with golden cufflinks seen as he held out his hand to his companion. A white-gloved hand gripped the gentleman's hand. An elegant lady stepped out of the limousine, dressed in a purple gown with a short, white fur stroll wrapped around her shoulders. Their posh luggage had been loaded on a brass cart as the two quietly strolled into the hotel lobby. Outside, Betsy stood off to the side, waiting to enter the hotel. As they passed, a whiff of richly perfumed scent emanated from the couple. Betsy stood in awe.

Returning home later, she now knew what her dad had meant about choosing a classy hotel. She desperately wanted to work at one of them. She carefully filled the applications out, praying that one of these must be her destiny. Her parents made her feel good when they said that her past interviews would prepare her for these next interviews. Along with new hope, she would have to impress them with her past experiences and her bubbling personality, reined in a little. She must take on more of a professional manner, like the elegantly poised lady.

The next week kept Betsy on edge, waiting to hear whether she would get an interview at one or both of the historic hotels. Her first call came from the Hotel Baudelaire. The day of the interview went quickly by. The actual interview took less time than to get ready, to travel by the trolley, and to return home. Her interview went well, so she felt happy with her more focused answers to their questions.

Betsy went to work at the dealership the following day, telling her mom to call her if she received any calls at home. Her mom never called all day, so that night she felt let down. But her parents told her to keep a positive attitude. A call from the Golden Lion Hotel never came, and by the end of the week, she had not heard from the other hotel. At night in bed, she tossed and turned, going over every detail of the applications and of the interviews.

The week-end came with her cousin Amy wanting to go to the movies with her. To forget Betsy's anxious feelings, she decided to go with her. Her cousin enjoyed the evening, but her insides were in turmoil even though she smiled and chatted with her cousin. On Sunday, her mom had invited her aunt and uncle over for dinner. She spent that day helping her mom. She vacuumed their small house, set the table, and helped her in the kitchen. When her relatives came over, they questioned her about the job search. She had nothing to say except that she was waiting to hear. She enjoyed having family around that week-end.

That evening, Betsy took the time to look through the newspaper ads again. One ad caught her attention—an opening for a housekeeper at the Hotel du Toussant. She recalled that hotel had been the last one with the green lawns that she had seen on her trolly tour. The next days were spent in getting an application and waiting for an interview. No calls came in from the other hotels. Her fingers remained crossed every night in bed. Someday soon something would happen.

And then two calls came one day—a call from the Golden Lion Hotel and one from the Hotel du Toussant. Both wanted to interview her on the same day. Fortunately, one was scheduled in the morning and the other one was in the afternoon. The anticipation increased as the day approached. Everything had to be timed to reach both of the interviews. She rode the No. 22 yellow trolley in the early dawn to reach the Hotel du Toussant—her first

147

interview which went well. She liked the beautiful green grounds and the older part of the city. She had remained poised in her dark green dress.

Afterwards, she caught the trolley to the Golden Lion Hotel. Stepping off near to the hotel, she walked around and found a coffee shop to wait for the afternoon interview. While she drank a cup of coffee, she watched all the people in the coffee shop, coming and going. She noticed the busy streets with people and cars. Everyone had business to attend to. The time came for her to go to the interview at the hotel.

She went to the restroom to freshen up. In there, she looked at herself in the mirror. The bun on the back of her head was coming out with strands of hair slipping out. She didn't have much time, but she needed to do something. So, she took out the bobby pins, took out the rubber band, and brushed out her long, auburn hair. Lifting both sides up, she wrapped the rubber band around them, leaving the back of her hair to flow down her back. She decided then and there that she was going to get her hair cut shorter. Since moving here, she spent too much time fiddling with it. Glancing at her watch, she quickly powdered her face and then swept her red lipstick onto her soft lips. She hoped that she looked presentable. Crossing her fingers, she whispered to the mirror, "I'll be fine."

Rushing out of the coffee shop and walking down to the Golden Lion Hotel, she entered the lobby as the doorman dressed in a well-groomed uniform with a hat and white gloves opened the brass-lined door for her. He recognized her, smiled, and said "Hello." The lobby had a life-size statue of a golden lion positioned to one side. The tan marbled floors shimmered with the light from the three chandeliers. Hurrying to the second floor offices, Betsy made it with just minutes left. The interview went well and again, she felt that she did a good job of answering their questions. Before she knew it, she was on her way to catch the trolley to go home—and to wait, wait, wait.

The next day, Betsy talked to her aunt about getting a haircut. She gave her niece the name and phone number of her hairdresser. After calling for an appointment, she rode the trolley to the salon and had her long hair cut into a pixie cut which the hairdresser said would accentuate her hazel eyes and her cheekbones. With her hair off the back of her neck, she felt freer. In the mornings she could quickly fix her hair without the long drying time. She liked the fact that her earrings could be seen better. Glancing in the big mirror at the salon, she loved her new look.

While waiting to hear from her three interviews, she went to work at the dealership. Then, she received in the mail three long envelopes—each one of the hotels had answered her. All of their official letters said that they were pleased with her past experience. They would put her application on file for a year. Mystified at the meaning of the letters, She shook her head in disbelieve. The bottom line hit her soul hard; she hadn't gotten a job yet.

At dinner that evening, she showed the letters to her parents. Her dad read all three of them and frowned, shaking his head. While her mom read them, her dad thought silently about his daughter's dilemma. During this recession, landing a job in the city had been hard for her.

Her dad finally said, "I am surprised, but look on the bright side. They will call you if someone leaves or is fired. I'm sure you'll eventually get yourself a job."

"But what do I do? Should I look for another job or just wait?" she asked her dad.

"What do you want to do?" he asked.

"I don't know," responded Betsy, confused and disappointed.

Her dad added, "These are top-notch hotels. If you want to work at one of them, you'll have to wait. You know that we're in a recession nation-wide. That's the reason we moved here because the lumber mill was cutting back. In the meantime, you can work at the dealership."

"Yes, but they really don't need me. I worked the books for a while. Now, I sweep the showroom floor or straighten up the break room. Most times, I just sit and wait for an errand to run." They all realized that her uncle and aunt were trying to help their daughter out.

Changing the subject, her mom smiled and said, "I like your hair dear. It will be easier to take care of. Maybe, I will get my hair cut and styled someday."

Betsy replied, touching her hair above her ear, "Yes. Thanks mom. I like mine cut short."

After they finished dinner, her parents watched television while Betsy washed up the dishes. She headed to her bedroom, taking her three official envelopes with the letters inside. She placed them on her dresser, standing each envelope up against her mirror, lined up in a row. They stood as three potential doors. *Which one would open? How long would she have to wait to hear from one of them?*

This first month in the city had been exciting, but frustrating. Crawling into bed, she closed her eyes and stretched out her drained body. *What had she accomplished?* She replayed all the interviews and all her answers. Around and around like a merry-go-round they went in her head. That imaginary golden ring was out there for her to catch—she just couldn't see it yet. Eventually, she fell into a deep sleep, hoping for a better future.

* * *

One day Betsy received a letter from her friend Valerie who wrote:

Dear Betsy, "It was so good to hear from you. I have a summer job waitressing at the Saddle Horn Restaurant. Teri & I got a job there. It's a new one across the bridge down by the Cozy Motel. The wages are the same as cleaning rooms, but the tips are great. I'm saving my money for some new clothes. No, I am not going with anyone. There's been a party up at Skyline, but no one has asked me out. Teri & I have been going to the dances on Saturday nights. There are lots of dudes in town. I do meet some nice fellas at the café. One truck driver stops in each week & gives me good tips, but he's too old for me. Write & tell me of your exciting life in Crayton. I think I'd like to move to a big city. This place is the same old town with the same old people. There is nothing to do. If it weren't for the tourists, it would be dull all year long. I don't know what I want to do. I'm not going to school, so I guess I'll be working at the café." Your everlasting friend, Valerie.

* * *

Two weeks later, the call from the Golden Lion Hotel came. They had an opening and wanted to hire her. Betsy nearly dropped the phone when she heard the good news. Mrs. Troy, the Housekeeping Administrator, asked her if she could start right away--tomorrow. She told her that she'd be there. When her parents heard the news that night, they congratulated her. They both sighed a relief for they knew how long and hard she had worked at getting the job.

On the first day of work, she rode the No. 22 yellow trolley early before dawn to be there with time to spare. The hotel doorman Mr. Andrews said, "Good Morning." Betsy smiled, glad to be going to work. She followed the directions to the housekeeping floor in the basement. As the elevator opened, she heard the noisy chatter with the other housekeepers getting ready for the day.

Coming out of her office, Mrs. Troy smiled at her and said, "Welcome to the Golden Lion Hotel. I'm so pleased that you are here. I wanted to hire you two weeks ago. You seemed to be a caring, responsible person. Elizabeth, come with me to my office so we can fill out the paper work needed and get you started."

From then on, her first working day became a blur. After leaving the office, Betsy was given a black uniform with a golden lion embroidered on the left side. Mrs. Troy handed her a starched white apron that slipped over her head and tied around her waist. That day, she scrubbed, vacuumed, and cleaned eight hotel rooms until quitting time. After changing out of her uniform, she rode the trolley home, exhausted but excited.

Even though she was tired out, Betsy felt overjoyed to be working at the Golden Lion Hotel with its extravagant bedrooms and bathrooms. The first time that she walked into one of the hotel rooms, the beauty of it took her breath away. The large beds covered in golden bedspreads had tall ornate bedposts which reached high to the ornate ceilings. The tall windows were draped in thick, gold and black striped curtains. The room-size bathrooms had large bathtubs with marbled floors. Thick white bath robes hung in the bathrooms. Magnificently decorated from the first floor up, the entire hotel glowed with prosperity. She had been spellbound while she worked that day.

After coming home, her feet were hurting. With a fresh pot of coffee, her mom poured her a cup. Kicking off her white flats, she sat down. Over a cup of coffee, she told her mom about her busy day at the hotel. She began with Mrs. Troy who told her about how the historic hotel had to uphold its reputation and that to have an efficient staff of housekeepers was vital to that goal. Housekeeping took center stage in maintaining their notoriety. Their motto at the Golden Lion Hotel was TRRC—trustworthy, reliable, responsible, and caring.

"Mom, you know how it is to clean rooms. You did it for years. But this job is a little different. First, I'm in training for a week. I am teamed up with a girl named Darlene Overmann. She's really nice and we got along well. A floor manager checks over my work after I finish cleaning each room. Darlene told me that I got the job because the last girl lost her position. She had lifted a pair of diamond earrings from a guest. I guess it stirred quite a fiasco. They had the hotel's security officers search through their lockers. They didn't find them, but the girl finally admitted it and was fired. She turned out to be a kleptomaniac. Imagine that. I wouldn't dream of touching any of the guests' belongings. They do have gorgeous wardrobes and expensive jewelry. They often order room service. We have to clear away the carts of leftover food and drinks."

She stopped for a few minutes to sip her coffee which tasted so good after a long day. "Oh, I need to get a combination lock for my locker. And tomorrow, Darlene is taking me to Flow's Footwear, a shoe store downtown, to buy a pair of white support shoes which is part of our uniform. The housekeeping will take the cost of the shoes out of my first paycheck. And after a day of work, I know why. My feet are sore from wearing those flats."

"Why don't you wear your saddle shoes for one day? They have more support," replied her mom, sipping her coffee and listening to her daughter's job.

"Maybe. But I'll have to polish them up tonight."

"Tell me more," said her mom, thinking of how proud she was of her daughter.

"As you know, some of the rooms are vacant, while others still had guests staying in them. Generally, Darlene works on the sixth floor, so we rode the elevator up. The floor manager gave us the room numbers that needed to be cleaned. I have to follow a procedure for each room, going through the steps written down for me. After a week of working there, I know I will have those steps memorized. When I finish cleaning, I have to go through one of the blank sheets on my clipboard, checking off my work. If maintenance is needed, I indicate it on the paper. After finding the floor manager, I give her the check list for the room. She checked a couple of the rooms that I had finished. If all is good, she lets registration downstairs know that the room is ready for occupancy. If I follow the steps each time, I can't go wrong."

"That's sounds a lot different than when we cleaned rooms in Riverside. No one checked our work; we were on our own to do a good job. I am glad you got the position at the big hotel," commented her mom. "How long has Darlene worked there?"

"She's been there over a year. She really helped me today. Thank you for the coffee. It tasted good," she replied.

"Why don't you take a quick bath before dinner? Your dad will be home soon," said her mom.

"How is dad doing at the dealership?" she asked, wondering about his job during this recession.

"He's doing great. We did the right thing moving here," replied her mom, standing up and starting dinner.

Betsy took her mom's advice and walked down the hall to the bathroom where she took a hot bath. She soaked and rubbed her sore feet for a while in the tub. After finishing her bath, she slipped on her blue bathrobe and soft slippers. In her bedroom in the bottom of her closet, she found her scuffed up saddle shoes, polished them, and set them out for tomorrow.

Dinner time came and her dad asked her about her day. She told him the shortened version. He seemed happy that she was working at the Golden Lion Hotel. Her mom told her that she had to go grocery shopping tomorrow and that she would buy her a combination lock. Worn out, Betsy went to bed right after helping her mom with the dishes. Crawling under her covers, she stretched out her sore muscles. Shortly after her head hit the soft pillow, her eyes closed, and she slept knowing that she had a job. A great future lingered in front of her.

* * *

The next day came earlier than Betsy imagined. She wanted to sleep in, but her job called to her. At work, Mrs. Troy gave her a slip of paper that would get her a pair of shoes. She told Betsy that her floor manager had been pleased with her work yesterday. Her chest filled with pride that she had done an acceptable job on her first day.

After riding up to the sixth floor, Betsy glanced at Darlene in the elevator. She stood a little taller than her with a bright smile, sparkling blue eyes, and a pretty face. Her light blonde hair had been pulled up and held with a large clip near the top of her head. Her curls flowed down her head and back. Getting off the elevator, they began working. The two talked quietly in the rooms and became more acquainted.

Darlene had her eye on one of the maintenance guys, named Ray Orton. Over the last few months, they had a few conversations in the break room downstairs at lunch, but that had been it. He and his friend Slade Burler worked in the maintenance department, fixing leaking faucets, unplugging toilets, and replacing burned out light bulbs.

Darlene asked, "Do you have a boyfriend?"

"No, but I would like to meet someone. I haven't done much except to look for a job," replied Betsy, thinking she would like to meet some friends.

"Maybe, if Ray ever asks me out, I will suggest we double date with you and his friend Slade. What do you think?" asked Darlene.

"I would have to meet Slade first. We may not hit it off," commented Betsy.

"I think you two might like each other. We'll see. I have to get a date from Ray first," she said.

They worked until their break time, riding the elevator down. In the break room, Darlene bought a pack of cigarettes from the machine. Betsy had brought a sack lunch and bought a soda. Sitting down, the two talked. Betsy offered Darlene part of her sandwich, but she thanked her and said she had to watch her figure. She smoked while Betsy finished her lunch. Darlene offered her a cigarette and said, "Here have one."

"I've never smoked," she replied, not sure she wanted one, but took one any way.

"Well, don't inhale. Just keep the smoke in your mouth. It'll take a while before you can inhale," said Darlene as she lit her cigarette. Betsy followed her advice and smoked her first cigarette.

"Listen, I have a bad situation. I know that we've just met, but my roommate moved out of my apartment. Suddenly, she decided to get married two weeks ago. I can't afford the apartment on my own. I've been asking around here, but no one is interested. Would you consider moving in with me? I think we'd get along just fine," she said. Her eyes were filled with concern. She put out her cigarette butt in the ash tray sitting on the table.

Betsy thought for a moment and asked, "Where is your apartment?"

"It's down third street on the corner of Drake and Kirby. Of course, you don't know where that is. It's just four blocks from here. Where do you live now?" she asked, striking a match as she started smoking another cigarette.

"I live with my folks. Dad calls it the Hill District. It's far from here and I ride the trolley," she answered.

Darlene said she knew the district and that it certainly was farther out than her apartment. They talked some more about her small apartment which had a kitchenette, a living room, a tiny bathroom, and one bedroom. She said that they'd be sharing the bedroom, and her friend had left her bed.

Betsy thought about it and said, "I like the idea."

"Give me your answer soon, because the rent is coming due in two weeks," she said.

"Sure. I'll let you know. Let me talk to my folks. I'm sure they would be fine with it," replied Betsy.

Just then, the two maintenance guys Ray and Slade came down the hall to the break room, laughing and kidding with each other as they walked. The two were in high spirits.

"Tell me what happened on that third floor room. The floor manager said the lady was all upset about her faucet," said Ray.

"There was nothing wrong with that faucet. She just wanted some attention. She was hanging all over me. But her husband came in and that stopped her flirting really quickly. What a piece of ass on her though," said Slade, smiling at his buddy Ray.

The two continued on into the break room, stopping in front of the soda machine. While Slade was getting his drink, Ray looked around and saw the two girls.

"Hi, Darlene," he said smiling at her. He then got his soda from the machine. They both walked over to the table and sat down opposite the two girls.

"And who is this red-headed beauty? I haven't seen you before," said Slade, eyeing Betsy. His light brown eyes held a curiosity behind them.

"She's our new housekeeper. Elizabeth, this is Ray and Slade," she said, drawing on her cigarette.

"Oh. Please call me 'Betsy,'" she replied, noticing how friendly they both were.

She had glanced at the two when they came into the break room. Both were of medium height, wearing the hotel's uniformed black shirts with the golden lion logo and slacks. Ray had a thin body with dark brown flat top haircut and big brown eyes. His wide-smile filled his face. Slade had a broad-chest, a narrow waistline, with his blonde hair slicked back. When the girls had heard their conversation coming from the hall, Darlene rolled her eyes and laughed. They both were typical guys looking at the lady guests staying in the hotel.

After their introductions, Darlene commented, "We've just finished our break. We have to run."

"Wait. Can't you stay another minute? I'd like to talk to you," said Ray, standing up. He moved over and stood in front of her and said, "We should get together. I'd like to take you out," looking into Darlene's blue eyes.

She smiled and sweetly said, "Call me. Maybe we could go on a double-date. My friend Betsy just moved here."

"Sure. Give me your phone number," said Ray, handing her a little tablet and pen from the front pocket of his shirt. She smiled, wrote down her number, and handed back the tablet and pen. "Thanks, I'll call you," he said, obviously happy.

When the two girls left, they heard the guys talking. Betsy heard Slade say, "You *bet* I'll take her out. She's a looker. Did you see that front rack on her?"

Their words faded as they reached the elevator. Betsy blushed at his words. Usually, she wore her leather vest or a sweater to cover her large bustline. But here with her tight black uniform and a white apron, she had nothing covering it.

Darlene smiled at Betsy, "You certainly impressed Slade. What do you think of him?"

"I don't know yet. He is good-looking. He seems nice," she replied as they stepped into the elevator and rode up to the sixth floor to clean their rooms.

After work that day, Darlene took Betsy to the Flow's Footwear where she bought herself a pair of the white shoes. She handed the sales lady the slip of paper. The new shoes were so comfortable.

That evening, she talked with her parents about moving into Darlene's apartment closer to her work and the hotel. Her dad knew the street names, mentioning that he agreed that it would be easier for her to get to work. Her mom worried about her being alone, but Betsy reminded her that she wouldn't be alone. They talked back and forth about the apartment and about living there. Her parents decided to help her move. Her dad mentioned that the apartment was several blocks from a run-down area with street people living. He warned her to be careful.

In addition, he said, "I want you to set up a bank account to deposit your hotel wages. Keeping cash in an apartment is not a good idea." Betsy agreed. Her mind had been turning over the idea of moving out all afternoon. She had been thrilled to hear that her parents hadn't objected.

Her mom asked, "What if you two can't get along?"

"If it doesn't work out, I'll move back here. I think I'll leave most of my stuff here and just take some of my clothes, not a lot. I'll be working most of the time with only a couple of days off. I'll come and visit," she replied.

"We'd like to meet Darlene. What about her family?" her dad asked.

"Dad, you can meet her when I move in. But she told me all about herself and her family. She grew up here and graduated last year. Her family are workers, like us. Her dad Casey and her older brother Daren are both construction workers. Her mom Edith works in the kitchen at one of the hospitals. Darlene is one year older than I am," explained Betsy. Her parents nodded and understood, but they had their doubts about her living away from them. However, they knew that she needed to start her own life, just like they had when they were young.

That night in her bed, Betsy thought about how eager she wanted to move. She didn't mind living with her folks up until now, but the idea of being independent had sparked her imagination. Now that she had a good paying job, she wanted to be on her own and make her own decisions.

Her thoughts shifted to meeting Ray and Slade at the hotel. She would like to go out. In her past years in high school, she had dated a couple of her boyfriends. But she never became serious with anyone. Now, she wouldn't mind going out with Slade. He certainly was handsome even though his comments seemed a little crass and bold. She thought that he looked a little older than she was. But she wanted to know more about him. With all the new experiences that had happened recently, her mind slowly tired out. She finally dozed off and fell asleep with the hum of the city.

* * *

The next days of her training at the hotel went by quickly. Darlene had been delighted to hear that Betsy would be moving in that week-end. In addition, Ray had called and wanted to go out. He said that Slade would like to go with Betsy. The two girls talked about it excitedly.

On her day off, early Saturday morning, Betsy began getting ready to move to the apartment. Her mom Clara helped her go through her closet and her dresser drawers. She had washed her bedding—the blankets and a bedspread. Her mom gave her an extra pair of sheets and bath towels to take with her. She also set aside a few dishes, silverware, and cups. Without noticing, her mom packed two extra cooking pans that she didn't use. She gave her one of her empty stamp books, telling her to save the green stamps from the grocery store. Finally, with a few small boxes and two suitcases ready to go, she noticed that her mom had a worried look on her face.

In total silence, her parents drove her to the five-story apartment building on Drake and Kirby. Her friend's apartment was on the second floor, number 203. Darlene opened the door and welcome them in. Betsy introduced her parents. She noticed that in the bedroom that there wasn't a dresser. Darlene told her that her girlfriend took it, but her parents were bringing over her dresser from their home today.

Shortly after all of Betsy's belongings were carried up the stairs, Darlene's parents (Casey and Edith) showed up at the apartment with the dresser. After coming upstairs, Darlene introduced her parents to Betsy's. Casey asked Gordan to help bring up his daughter's dresser. After setting it down in the bedroom, their parents visited with each other. Their dads hit it off immediately. Both growing up in the city, they talked about their livelihoods, getting into construction and about selling cars. Their moms also shared stories about their daughters. Edith talked about her work in the hospital kitchen. Everyone had a friendly visit.

When it was time to leave, Betsy's dad gave her a quick hug and her mom struggled to keep her tears in check. The two sets of parents walked down the stairs to their cars and drove away.

After they had left, the two girls finished unpacking Betsy's belongings. Darlene was happy to see the few dishes, silverware, and cups added to her kitchenette, saying that her girlfriend had taken most of the dishes with her. Both were surprised with the cooking pans. In the bedroom, Betsy made up her bed, filled her side of the closet with her few dresses, and slipped her underwear into two dresser drawers. She realized that she needed to add to her wardrobe—new dresses and a few heels to match. Breathing a sigh of relief, she flopped down on her new bed, smiling. Her heart thumped in her chest as the excitement of being on her own had become a reality.

While Darlene took a bath for her date tonight, Betsy opened the apartment window in their bedroom, looked out across the city and felt a warm summer breeze against her face. Scanning the horizon, she saw the numerous tall city buildings—offices, hotels, and apartments. The hot summer sun had sunk behind the buildings, leaving the sky a dull orange color.

Lying down on her bed again, she listened to the noises surrounding her. Muffled voices could be heard, doors opening and closing, footsteps on the stairs, and the buzz of cars, stopping and starting on the streets below. Being on a corner put them with four streets converging. An occasional honk of a car horn pierced the air. Unusual smells came from the other apartment—aromas of food cooking. Yes, this would take a while to adjust. But it felt invigorating. Everything pulsed with life around her.

Betsy then took a warm bath, shifting her thoughts to her date with Slade. Darlene hollered at her to hurry that she needed to put her make-up on. They rushed around getting ready.

Grabbing her favorite white dress with black polka dots out of the closet, Betsy slipped it over the cancan. She slipped the wide red belt around her small waist and buckled it. Going into the bathroom, she patted her face with powder, put on her mascara, and covered her lips in red. She brushed her short auburn hair quickly. On the dresser, she picked up a pair of her earrings out of her small jewelry box. With a bottle of perfume, she dabbed a little behind her ears, thinking she would like to buy another bottle. Slipping on her white sweater and grabbing her purse, she was ready.

A knock at the door sent Darlene dashing to open it. There in the hallway stood Ray, dressed in a brown suit, ready to go out. Seeing her in a light green dress he said, "Wow. You look great." He came into the living room as Betsy came in from the bedroom. "Hi, Betsy. Hey, Slade is downstairs in the car. We're going to a night club with live music. Let's go," he explained.

They took the stairwell down and out of the apartment building. Walking along the sidewalk, Betsy saw Slade, leaning against his shiny, white and black car, a '56 Oldsmobile, smoking a cigarette. In a nice black suit, he straightened up, tossed his cigarette butt to the curb, and stood with a cocky smile on his lips. With his arms outstretched, he walked towards them.

"Well, well, well. What do we have here? Look at you," he said, not taking his eyes off Betsy. His interest made her heart beat with anticipation. He grabbed her hand and twirled her around, watching her skirt flare as she turned. She laughed as she spun around, taking his hand in hers. After she faced him again, he pulled her up close to him, smelling her sweet perfume.

"Mmmm. Nice," he whispered to her.

"Hi, Slade. How are you?" she asked, catching her breath and smiling.

"I'm better now that you're here. Let's go, beautiful," replied Slade, swinging open the car door with a flare. He moved with class and a smoothness that Betsy had not seen in a guy before.

Darlene and Ray crawled into the back seat. Driving through the downtown streets to the night club took quite a while. Slade talked about the club and the band. The crowded streets around the club frustrated him, for he couldn't find a parking place. He drove around a couple of times, looking. Finally, he told Ray that he'd

160

drop everyone off and that he'd have to park over a block.
Stopping in front of the club, the three of them stepped out of the
car. With a full moon shining, the summer night air thumped with
the music coming from inside. The red sign of Back Street Club
glowed brightly against the dark, grey building.

"I'll grab us a table," said Ray as he closed the car door. Slade
revved his big V-8 engine a couple of times and waved at them. As
he drove away, Betsy glanced at the shiny polished car.

Walking into the loud noisy club, the three pushed through the
dark, smoke-filled crowded room. Leading the way, Ray found a
small table on the left side of the band who had just finished a
song. Over the microphone, the lead guitarist announced a short
break as the band members all headed towards the bar.

Ray asked, "What do you girls want to drink?"

"I'd like a gin n' tonic," replied Darlene.

He looked over at Betsy, "The same," she replied.

By the time he came back with the drinks, Slade had walked
into the night club. As he moved through the crowds, people
nodded at him or talked to him briefly. He kept his eyes scanning
the tables for Betsy. Finally, their eyes met. He smiled and nodded
at her. She noticed how casually he talked and moved slowly
among the couples. When he stopped at the bar to order, Ray stood
up and walked over to him. They talked together, ordered a shot of
whiskey, smiled, and gulped down the amber liquor. The bartender
then handed them each a bottle of beer.

Meanwhile, at the table, Darlene and Betsy sipped their drinks
and waited. The band members had returned, getting ready to play.
Ray and Slade walked over to their small table. Slade slipped his
hand on Betsy's shoulder and brought it down her arm as he sat
down. His touch sent chills down her spine. He smiled. Scooting
his chair closer to hers, he took a long drink of his beer. The rock
n' roll band began to play a hit song by Bill Haley & the Comets.
Excited, couples moved to the dance floor.

Slade leaned closer to Betsy, "Do you want to dance, Bets?"
Nodding, he stood up and looked at her white sweater, "Let's lose
this." She took it off and he slipped it on the back of her chair.
Grabbing her hand, he swung her onto the dance floor, dancing
several songs. The lead singer sang, filling the room with his voice.
Another song by Gene Vincent kept them dancing fast. When they

tired, they returned to their table and ordered another round of drinks. Then, the band played a slower song by the Platters.

Standing up, Slade wrapped Betsy into his strong arms as they moved to the dance floor. They danced slowly. He held her tightly to him. She felt his firm body grind against hers. She smelled his spicey cologne and felt his warm hand on her waist. Her heart beat fast in her chest. Her mind told her that this was only their first date and that she needed to take this slow. She didn't even know him. They continued to dance. More drinks came until late into the night. The club became more crowded and rowdier by midnight.

Ray turned out to be the dancer. His fast footwork spun Darlene all over the dance floor. On a few of the songs, the other couples would move over and give Ray and Darlene the dance floor, clapping when they finished. Betsy watched in amazement. After several dances, Darlene told him she needed a break, so he turned to Betsy and asked her to dance. Without thinking, she jumped up and they moved to the dance floor. She didn't notice that Slade looked at them in shock and then, frowned.

Betsy felt Ray's strong arms slip around her and the other couples turned into a blur while he swept her onto the dance floor. Moving around, she stepped lightly, spinning at a slight pressure to her back, and twirling with his hand in hers. Her skirt flared; the motion brushed a slight breeze around her legs. His smiling eyes were on her face, pleased with her ability to dance with him. When the song ended, she laughed, delighted at the experience of dancing with him. They walked back to their table.

However, Slade looked displeased, and his anger had risen slowly as he watched them dance. Steaming with jealousy, he stepped up to Ray and shoved him away from Betsy. Shocked, Ray stumbled back, nearly falling down.

"What the shit? Why did you punch me? I know she's your date. Hey, I'm sorry. I'm sorry," said Ray, apologizing. Slade advanced towards him, getting into his face.

"Keep your hands off Bets. She's mine," replied Slade, shoving his finger into Ray's chest.

"I got it, buddy. I said I was sorry. I didn't mean a thing by it. Lighten up," complained Ray.

Slade finally backed off. The tension stayed for a few more minutes until the band started another song. Ray took Darlene's hand and said, "Come on, let's dance." He wanted to get away from Slade and let him cool down.

After Betsy and Slade sat down, she stared at him and couldn't believe his anger. She didn't understand and asked, "What was that all about?"

"Like I said. You're with me. When I take a gal on a date, she's mine for the night. No one messes with her," he replied. His harsh attitude struck her unbelievable.

"But I *am* with you. I had one dance with Ray. Besides, this is just our first date. I went out with you to have some fun. Are you saying I can't dance with anyone else?" asked Betsy.

"That's right. I don't want any one stepping in between us. I get jealous. Listen, I like you," he explained, reaching for her hands and holding them tightly in his. "That's how it is Bets."

She nodded while her heart beat faster hearing his affectionate words. But that scene of jealousy stayed with her. Slade had turned against his friend so quickly, punching him. His friend seemed to take it in stride as if he knew about Slade's reaction. Such violence like that she had never seen before.

"Forget about it. Ray knows how I feel. Let's dance," he said, rising up from his chair. She rose and he pulled her close to him. They danced slowly. He lowered his head against her cheek and whispered sweet, sexy words to her. She flushed red in the dark club. They continued dancing until the song ended. While they walked back to their small table, Betsy saw Darlene and Ray finishing their drinks.

Ray looked up at Slade, "We're ready to leave. How about you?"

"Sure. Let's go," he replied.

Their little disagreement had been forgotten. They all stood up and moved through the crowded club to the door. The city's midnight air chilled Betsy as she pulled her white sweater around her. Slade slipped his arm around her as they walked over a block to his car. While they drove back towards the apartment, Ray and Darlene made out in the back seat. Slade glanced up at them in his rear-view mirror, smiling.

Betsy felt awkward listening to the two of them in the back seat. Slade looked over at her and said, "Tell me about yourself."

Along with a few groans from the back seat, she told him that she was born here in Crayton but grew up in Riverside. He asked where that was. She told him. She mentioned how hard she worked at getting her job at the Golden Lion.

She said, "I really like living here with so much going on. It's definitely a big adjustment."

"There's a lot more I can show you. The greater metropolitan area has around 500,000 people. In fact, there's a music festival with popular singers and bands coming soon. I saw a poster the other day. I could get tickets. There's also baseball games at the Duey Stadium if you like baseball. Or we can go to the Holladay Amusement Park where we can ride the roller coaster and other fun rides. Like I said, there's lots to do."

"Wow. That's all here in the city? That's amazing. I'd like to see everything," she replied, thrilled with the idea of going to all those exciting places.

After parking near the apartment, he turned to her, "I'll get tickets for the festival. Come here and give me a kiss goodnight," smiling at her and begging her to come closer to him.

She slid over next to him. His arm reached around her shoulder, and he leaned in close, looking into her hazel eyes. He waited. His eyes moved to her lips. His attractive glance made her move to kiss his lips, softly. "Good bye. Thanks for a great night," she whispered.

That wasn't enough for him. Her coy and soft words incited his desires. With his arm around her shoulder, he embraced her closer to him. While his hand caressed her breast, his soft lips covered her mouth in a forceful kiss. He kissed her again and again. She gasped at his touches. His kisses moved to her neck, below her ear. When he smelled her sweet perfume, he groaned. She then pushed him gently back with her hands on his broad chest and whispered, "I need to go." Her head spun not only from his kisses, but her desires were swirling inside of her.

Breathing hard, he released her, frustrated that he had to stop. "Damn it, girl," he said under his breath. "I'll call you or see you at the hotel." Betsy picked up her purse, opened the car door, and stepped out of the car. After the two in the back seat said "goodbye," Darlene crawled out from the back. The two girls walked to their apartment door while Ray jumped into the front

164

seat. Slade revved his engine, pulled out of the parking place, and drove away.

The two took the stairs to their second-floor apartment. Inside, Darlene spoke excitedly about Ray and about how much she liked him. Betsy didn't say much about Slade. Her emotions were all tangled up. Darlene mentioned the argument between the two men. Betsy told her that Slade didn't want her to dance with anyone but him. That upset her, for the restriction seemed silly, ridiculous, and unreasonable.

Darlene concluded, "That's not so bad. He must really like you to be so possessive." Betsy recalled that he had said that he liked her.

After getting ready for bed, Betsy went to the window, pulled aside the curtains, and looked out over the sparkling, night lights of the city. The tall buildings reached into the sky like windowed towers. Overall, the evening had been thrilling with the live music and dancing. Recalling Slade's kisses and touches, she fingered her lips. Though he seemed domineering, she looked forward to going out again with him.

Over in her bed, Darlene had fallen asleep quickly. Despite the fact that she was tired, Betsy decided to write her friend Valerie before going to sleep since her life seemed so thrilling now. She wrote:

Dear Valerie, "I have a job at the Golden Lion Hotel. It's downtown. Plus, I just moved to an apartment with a friend I met at work. Her name is Darlene & is really nice. Her place is closer to the hotel, so I don't have to ride the trolley into work. I'm not doing much, just working. I have to wear a black uniform & a fancy white apron to work in. You would laugh seeing me dressed in them. Cleaning the elegant rooms is a lot of work but I like it so far. I met a guy at work. He seems really nice. We went out to a fancy night club & danced. Tell me more about who is going to the dances. Have you been dating anyone I know? I'm tired & will write more next time." Your best friend, Betsy.

Afterwards, she snuggled down under her covers, thinking of Slade's passionate kisses, of their dances together, and of the exciting places that he was going to take her. The big city had so much to offer, not like her small town. Her Saturday had started out with a move and ended with a date. *Could her life get any better?*

* * *

During the next couple of months, Betsy worked at the Golden Lion Hotel with Darlene, spent time dating Slade, and deposited most of her wages into a banking account. While working at the hotel, the two girls enjoyed cleaning the hotel rooms together. The time with Darlene went fast for her. During lunch breaks, Slade and Ray would sometimes meet them. Slade would talk about his work at the hotel. For him, his maintenance job had been the best paying job that he ever had. Flirting with Betsy, he would hold her hands or touch her slightly on the neck or shoulder. To go with her sandwiches, he'd buy her different flavors of sodas from the machine. She also had started to smoke, just to settle her nerves. Everyone around her smoked—Darlene, Slade, and Ray.

Betsy found out more about Slade growing up here in the city. As a young boy, he had joined the Boy Scouts, earned his badges, and went to the scouting camp with his troop in the summer time. That's where he and Ray had met one summer. Slade said he had liked getting out into the woods during those trips. She had told him about Riverside and the big Rockies out west.

Later that autumn, the four of them went to the big music festival with three top hit singers and four rock n' roll bands. They performed popular songs one after another from seven pm to two am. The blaring music thundered in their ears while they drank a pint of gin and one of whiskey. The crowded arena grew into a wild and crazy party. Dancing elbow to elbow and singing with the performers, Betsy held on to Slade thrilled with excitement.

After it was over, they staggered out of the arena with the crowd and headed home. The two girls stumbled up the stairs to their apartment and fell into their beds without undressing that night. The next morning both of them had hangovers from their drinking, sending them to the medicine cabinet for aspirin. Betsy had a terrible headache and went back to bed with a wet cold washcloth over her eyes and head. Darlene managed to make them coffee.

A few weeks later, Slade took Betsy to the Holladay Amusement Park. They rode the lengthy roller coaster with its speeding force pushing their bodies this way while the tracks turned and twisted up and down. The ride delighted her so much that she couldn't stop laughing. On the Ferris wheel, he kissed her as they went up and around. Later, they ate hot dogs and cotton candy. After returning to the apartment, she told him that she wanted to go on the rides again. He told her that he'd take her, but he never did.

Many Saturday nights, the four of them went to the several night clubs around the city—the Marigold Club, St. Jack's Club, the Stock League, and the Back Street Club. She noted that that's what Slade and his friends did for entertainment in the city. That glitzy night life started to get old. The crowds knew the two guys, and they seemed to take pleasure in meeting everyone. Slade and Betsy danced, drank, and smoked. They were becoming quite well-known as a couple. In fact, many nodded and smiled at her when she looked their way. She wore her new dresses and heels that made her feel part of the city life.

Naturally, Betsy never danced with Ray again; he kept his fancy dancing for Darlene. And no one else danced with her, only Slade. Even though a few guys would look at her, they'd turn away when they saw him. They knew better than to tangle with him. She didn't like his possessive attitude and felt caged, not free to do what she wanted. He controlled her on their nights out together. The excitement of the night clubs slowly dimmed for her.

Working at the hotel or shopping downtown gave Betsy a chance to be herself again. With Darlene, she laughed and talked. She enjoyed the time with her friend in the apartment, listening to the radio or cooking meals. Darlene helped her shop for the stylish dresses which showed off her shapely figure. She kept her hair short while Darlene let her hair grow. They shared their dreams of finding a guy and settling down.

As the months past, Darlene and Ray's relationship became more serious. She spent several nights at his apartment, sleeping with him. Even though Slade pressured her for more intimacy, Betsy kept him at arm's length. Despite his obvious frustrations, she had avoided sleeping with him.

One evening, parked near the apartment, they had heated words in his car. After kissing and making out for a while, she pushed him gently back and told him she had to go. Turning from her, he grew angry and struck the steering wheel. Frightened at his outburst, she slid over and grabbed the door handle. If he was going to act like this, she wanted no part of it.

He asked, "What are we doing here? You keep pushing me away. You keep teasing me, but you won't put out?" His cold, serious look took her by surprise.

Shocked at the sexual suggestion, she turned, looked at him, and replied, "No. Of course not. I'm just not ready. We've just met."

"I've taken you everywhere, to the park and to all of the parties. I've showed you a fun time. Do you even like me?" he said in his cool way.

"Yes, I do," she admitted quietly.

"Well then, what's the problem? Why can't we be together?" he asked, sliding over to her. He had her up against her door. Taking her in his arms, he covered her lips with a passionate kiss.

She struggled against his arms for a second, but his forceful kiss set her desires racing. She did like him. After another kiss, she took a breath and whispered, "I'm not ready for anything more than this. Please." Glancing in her hazel eyes, his fingers brushed down her face, stopping at her lips. His fingertips crossed her lips back and forth, feeling the softness. His eyes told her that he was weighing his options with her.

"Well, I'll be waiting," he whispered back. She nodded, opened the car door, and stepped out of his car.

"Good night," she said as she closed the door. Turning, she headed to their apartment building, ran up the stairs, and unlocked the door. Stepping into the apartment, she thought of his harsh words and his persuasive kisses. He wanted her. But something had stopped her. Although she had been attracted to him, she disliked his jealousy and how he controlled her. He would have to change if he wanted to have any relationship with her. He might be waiting a long time.

In between her busy days of her working at the hotel and her nights of dating Slade, she managed to ride the No. 22 yellow trolley home to visit her parents a couple of times. Her mom Clara had been curious about her job and her roommate. She told her parents that she had been dating. Her dad Gordan wanted to meet this guy, so she said she'd bring him home.

However, when she asked Slade to come with her to meet her parents, he said that he had to go to a party and meet up with his friends. After that, she had asked him several times with the same excuse. One time, he told her that he had to work overtime at the hotel. Suspicious, she had checked, and it turned out that he did have to work. But the other times that he made excuses had puzzled her. *Why not meet her folks? Was she a fool to be with him?*

* * *

With the snowy cold winter months came the holiday seasons of Thanksgiving, Christmas, and New Year's Day. Dazzling colored lights, large pine wreaths, red and green ribbons decorated the downtown streets. The shops filled with shoppers, buying goods and gifts for the holidays. Darlene's dad Casey brought them a small Christmas tree with a box of decorations. Their apartment looked bright and cheery after decorating the pine tree with a string of lights, a few green and red bulbs, and an angel on top.

The Golden Lion's hotel business increased with more holiday guests and more rooms to clean. The glamorous ballroom on the main floor had been booked for several holiday events. Mrs. Troy announced that housekeeping staff would get overtime pay for volunteers who worked those events scheduled in the evenings. Betsy wanted the experience of doing something new plus the added money would help buy Christmas gifts for her family. She gladly volunteered, but her roommate wasn't interested since she wanted to be with Ray, spending the nights at his apartment.

When Slade heard that Betsy would be working at the holiday events, he frowned at her. "The best parties are during the holidays. The clubs have special nights with singers and bands," he complained to her.

"I'll keep the New Year's Eve free," she said.

"Well, I like to show my little red-head a good time. You know how much fun we have," he said.

With cleaning the rooms and volunteering at the special events, her scheduled filled up with little time for dating. They saw each other in the break room once in a while. Ray and Slade made arrangements to go to the Marigold Night Club for New Year's Eve. They had bought special tickets for a dinner there which included a full evening of music and dancing.

Darlene and Betsy found time to go shopping for new outfits to wear. The clothing stores were filled with holiday dresses and gowns. Betsy didn't want to spend that much on a gown but chose a simple black dress. Darlene swooned over a long satin red gown and tried it on. She hoped that Ray would ask her to marry him. Betsy cringed at the thought of marriage. Darlene might be ready, but she wasn't.

"How can you think of marriage? You've known him for only five months," asked Betsy.

"He's the one. I know it," she replied as she took off the red gown. Betsy just shook her head. They left with their holiday dresses, planning the evening at the Marigold.

The two girls had to work that day before New Year's Eve, so they had to rush home from the hotel to get ready for their dates. Betsy had bought herself a new bottle of perfume and a pair of dangling earrings and necklace that dressed up her black dress. As she primped in front of the bathroom mirror, she put on her red lipstick. Smiling, she thought about the night ahead. After weeks of working, she looked forward to a night out. She even thought that maybe she was ready to be with Slade tonight. Her roommate crowded into the bathroom, trying to put the finishing touches to her make-up and long blonde hair.

A knock at the door and Darlene opened it. Ray, in a dark navy suit, stood gazing at her. "You look gorgeous," he commented. Handing her a wrist corsage of white roses, he added, "These should match your red dress." She smiled and thanked him, showing Betsy her white roses and then, she sniffed the corsage before he slipped it on her left wrist. He leaned down and gave her a quick kiss. This touching moment between the two made Betsy turn away. She heard him whisper to her, "We're going to have some real fun tonight."

Down in the car, Slade waited for the three of them to come down. He had the car running, anxious to get to the club and find a parking place. Darlene and Ray crawled into the back seat. When

Betsy slid in, Slade smiled at her and handed her a wrist corsage of red roses.

He said, "I hope you like red," and slipped the corsage on her wrist. She thanked him as the sweet blossoms filled her nose. They drove to the Marigold Club and found a good parking place. With a crescent moon, the night's winter air froze their breaths as they hurried down the street to the club. As Darlene and Betsy checked in their coats, Ray and Slade went to locate their table. Everyone sounded in a festive mood, dressed in elegant gowns and suits. Betsy noticed that the two guys were stopping and talking at different tables, smiling and nodding at their friends.

Finally, they motioned to them to come to their table. Ray met Darlene half way there, putting his arm around her. They looked adorable together; many turned to look at Darlene and her lovely red gown. Betsy followed them, and Slade pulled out the chair for her to sit. He leaned down and gave a quick kiss on her cheek and said, "You look nice." He breathed in her new perfume. His hand touched her shoulder and squeezed. She felt happy that he liked her new black dress. The touch of his hand sent warm feelings throughout her body.

The evening of dining and drinking went by fast. They ordered their drinks, and the band began to play as couples moved to the dance floor. Slade excused himself for a while as he walked around, meeting the new couples coming in for the dancing. He mingled among them and then came back.

As soon as the band began to play, Ray and Darlene were dancing on the crowded dance floor. She had been in high spirits from the beginning. Betsy sat, smoked a cigarette, and sipped her gin n' tonic. Then, Slade rose and took her hand. They danced to a slow song. He held her tight against his broad chest with his strong arm. His hand on her back kept caressing her as his hips moved into her. She smelled his spicey cologne and closed her eyes as they danced closely, her body swaying and moving. They danced several more songs until the band said they were taking a short break. He kissed her lips softly when they stopped dancing. She felt his strong desires as she relaxed against him.

The four of them returned to their table. Sitting down, they ordered more drinks as a barmaid walked around. Opening his wallet, Ray slid under his hand a few folded dollars towards Slade.

Nodding, he picked up the bills. From inside his suit's breast pocket, Slade slid over two pills under his hand to Ray.

Glancing at Darlene, Ray asked, "Do you really want to have some fun tonight? Take these little angels and you will see stars tonight."

She laughed and picked them up, glanced at him and asked, "Are these like the ones we've taken before?"

He smiled at her with a meaningful grin and whispered, "Oh no. These are much better."

She took the two pills, popped them in her mouth, swallowed them with her gin n' tonic, and said, "I can't wait." The two held hands, looking at each other.

Reaching again into his breast pocket, Slade slid two pills over to Betsy, "Here's two for you Bets. It's time for you to relax and have some fun."

Betsy glanced down at his hand covering the pills on the table. Shocked, she kept her eyes lowered. She wanted no part of those pills. Shaking her head, "No, no. I'm good. Just another cocktail will be fine."

Just then, the barmaid brought their drinks, and he slid the two pills back into his breast pocket. He glared at her with irritated eyes, disappointed that she didn't take the pills. But she ignored his sour looks and took out a cigarette. He struck a match for her as she drew in the smoke from her cigarette to settle her nerves. She hid the shock of seeing the exchange by drinking and smoking.

The band returned and started playing. Ray and Darlene move to the dance floor. In fact, the crowd at the club had been getting unruly and wilder. Betsy heard Darlene's high excited voice laughing as Ray spun and twirled her on the dance floor. She sounded giddy and happy. They went on like this for several songs, never stopping to drink or to sit down.

Slade stood and asked her to dance, but she said "No, it's too crowded. Let's wait." Shrugging his shoulders, he left her sitting. He moved around the room, talking to people. She knew that he had been upset with her for not taking the pills, but she didn't care what he thought. With a strong conviction, she sat disheartened at this evening's turn of events.

Suddenly, a piercing scream came from the dance floor. Betsy glanced over and saw a flash of red falling to the floor in the crowd of dancers. Confusion erupted. People were yelling, pushing, and shouting. The band stopped playing. Someone hollered, "Call an ambulance."

Quickly from across the room, Slade came over to her and grabbed her arm, "We have to go." He pulled her towards the coat checkout room up front. While they waited, she tried to see what was going on, and asked, "Was that Darlene?"

"Yes. She fainted and fell down. The club called an ambulance. They'll take care of her. It'll get crazy around here. Trust me. We've got to go," he replied, eager to leave.

"But I should go with her. She might need me," said Betsy while he helped her put on her coat.

"No. Ray is with her. You'll be in the way. Come on," he said. Into the cold night, they hurried out and down the street to his car.

While driving her home, she started to worry about her roommate, "I hope she'll be all right."

"Listen, she'll be fine. Okay. I'll call you. Now stop fussing," he said. While he drove to the apartment, he seemed pre-occupied. With her head buzzing from the drinks, she held onto his arm while he walked her up the stairs to the apartment. Giving her a long kiss, he told her not to worry and get some rest.

Stepping into her apartment and taking off her coat, she sat down on their small couch in the dark. From the window, the dim glow of the city shone onto the floor. In the gloomy apartment, the steady noise of the cars and the steady hum of the city reminded her of the celebrations going on. She turned on the lights, changed out of her dress, and slipped on her blue robe and slippers. Her rose corsage had wilted. She tossed it into the garbage. She warmed up the left-over coffee on the stove, poured herself a cup, sat down and waited for Slade to call.

RING. RING. She rushed to the phone, "Hello, Slade?"

"Hello, no. This is Mrs. Troy at the Golden Lion Hotel. Is this Elizabeth?" she asked.

"Yes…yes," she replied.

"Oh I'm so glad you're home. I've been calling around. I have a serious situation. We are going to be short a housekeeper tomorrow. One called in sick tonight. I know it is your day off, but could you come in tomorrow?" asked Mrs. Troy.

Betsy thought for a minute and said, "Yes. I can." She would rather be working than sitting here.

"Thank you so much. See you in the morning. Good bye," she said.

After hanging up the phone, she reached for her purse with her address book and phone numbers. She called Slade—no answer. She called Ray—no answer. Finally, she called Darlene's parents—no answer. She had no idea which hospital to call. She didn't want to call her parents until she knew more. They would just worry about her unnecessarily. Frustrated, she didn't know who else to call. Putting her face into her hands, she felt alone and helpless in this big city.

Her mind shifted. She needed to get some rest. Turning off the lights and crawling into bed, she worried about Darlene's condition and the terrible night that she had experienced at the Marigold. *Why didn't Slade call?* She fell into a restless sleep with the New Year's Eve's distant celebration going on in the city.

* * *

Her alarm clock rang too early for Betsy the next morning. Rubbing her eyes, she wanted to stay in bed but crawled out of her covers. While she ate breakfast, the apartment felt empty and lonely without Darlene. No call from Slade. He had the day off, so he wouldn't be at the hotel. Hurrying, she dressed, slipped on her coat, and left the apartment. A cold morning wind blew through the streets and whistled around the tall buildings, chilling her. The remains of the night parties could be seen on the sidewalks and in the gutters—empty beer cans, tossed liquor bottles, and discarded paper New Year's Eve hats. She recalled her miserable evening again as she walked to the hotel.

Approaching the brass-lined doors, the doorman Mr. Andrews greeted her with "Happy New Year." Betsy smiled and wished him the same. She rode the elevator down. After changing into her black uniform and white apron, she walked down to Mrs. Troy's office who sat at her desk. She smiled seeing her.

"Good morning, Elizabeth. Right on time as usual. I'm assigning you to the seventh floor with Dee Rupherd. She's in the break room," said Mrs. Troy. "Oh, you'll be getting overtime pay today. Thank you so much for coming in on such a short notice."

"I am happy to help out. I'll go and find Dee," she said.

Leaving the office, she went down to the break room. A middle-aged woman with dark brown hair sat drinking a cup of coffee. Smiling, Dee was pleased to see Betsy. Talking, the two left, rode the elevator up to the seventh floor, and began cleaning the hotel rooms. Betsy's exhausted body slowed her down today. Later, the floor manager came into one of the rooms that they were cleaning and told Betsy that Mrs. Troy wanted to see her downstairs.

She rode the elevator down, concerned. Walking down the hall, she saw a dark suited man sitting in Mrs. Troy's office. He stood up when she came in.

Mrs. Troy looked at her and said, "Please close the door." She did and sat down. Mrs. Troy then introduced her to Detective Jordan from the Crayton Police Department.

"Miss Crocket, I'm doing an investigation. I'd like to ask you a few questions," said Jordan.

With a frown on her face, Betsy nodded and said, "Of course." The detective took out a small notebook and pen.

He started with, "Do you know Darlene Overmann?"

"Yes, she's my roommate. Is she okay?" asked Betsy, worried.

"Why do you ask?" he looked at her.

"We're on a double date last night at the Marigold Night Club. She fainted and they took her to the hospital," she responded.

"Were you with her all evening?" asked the detective.

"Yes. I was with her all evening until she fainted," replied Betsy.

"You said you were on a date. Who were you with?" he asked.

"I was with Slade who I met here at the hotel. He works in maintenance," she replied.

"What's Slade's last name?" the detective asked.

"It's Burler," she replied.

"How long have you known him?"

"I've been dating him for about five months," she replied.

"Who was Darlene with?"

"She was with Ray Orton who also works here in maintenance," Betsy answered.

"Are Slade and Ray close friends?" he asked.

"Yes," she replied.

"Tell me a little about them," he added.

"They are a lot of fun. We've gone to a music festival and several of the night clubs. They seem to know everyone," she explained.

"Have you ever suspected that Darlene might be taking drugs?" he asked.

"No, but last night she took a couple of pills," she replied.

"Was that before she fainted?"

"Yes."

"Where did she get the pills?" he asked.

"Ray gave them to her."

"Where did Ray get the pills?"

"He gave Slade some money and he handed him the pills," she replied.

Jordan nodded, closing his notebook and slipping it and his pen into the breast pocket of his suit jacket. After a thoughtful pause, he said, "Thank you, Miss Crocket. That's all the questions I have for today. I may need to speak to you later."

Standing up, he glanced at the housekeeping manager and said, "Thank you. I'm headed back to the station." He left the office as he closed the door behind him.

Betsy looked at Mrs. Troy, "What's going on?"

Mrs. Troy sighed and said, "Darlene is in the hospital with a suspected drug overdose. And Slade Burler and Ray Orton have been arrested and charged with selling drugs."

"What happens now?" asked Betsy shocked at the news. She glanced down at her hands tightly clasped in her lap. Suddenly, everything shifted into place at the clubs with Slade and Ray.

"I don't know. We'll have to wait and see how this works out. I need you to go back to work. Your teammate Dee needs your help."

She nodded and rose, leaving the office more worried than before. She worked with Dee until break time. Since she hadn't brought a lunch with her, she bought a soda and sat down to smoke. Dee chatted on, asking her all about her life. But Betsy didn't feel like talking. She avoided saying much and replied, "I just come here, work, and go home. My life is pretty simple."

Those words rang false in her head. Actually, her life had gotten terribly complicated.

Afterwards, they went back up to the seventh floor and worked the rest of the afternoon. Dee was still in a friendly mood in contrast to her own worried, dark mood. With a false smile, she moved through her afternoon cleaning the beautiful hotel rooms.

After work and back at the empty apartment, Betsy fixed a bite to eat and brewed a pot of coffee. She decided to call Darlene's parents. Concerned, she dialed their number. Her dad Casey answered the phone. Betsy asked about Darlene. He said she had been discharged from the hospital and was home. When she asked if she could talk to her friend, he said to "keep it short." He sounded unhappy, distraught, and upset.

"Hi, Betsy," Darlene said. Her weak voice sounded flat.

"Hi. How are you feeling?" she asked.

"I'm doing okay," she replied.

"What happened last night?" she asked.

"I am really upset with Ray. Stay away from Slade, Ray, and their friends. Don't talk to anyone about what happened last night," warned Darlene, annoyed. Betsy thought: *too late. She already had.*

Changing the subject, she asked, "Are you coming back to work?"

"Yes. I'll be there tomorrow. See you then. Bye," she said. The two hung up.

Sitting down to drink a cup of coffee, she felt all alone in this small apartment. She looked around and saw the decorated Christmas tree standing in the corner of the living room. Thinking of the holiday, she had bought everyone special presents this year with her extra wages. She had enjoyed the holiday with her parents and her aunt and uncle. She had bought her cousin Amy a special gift of various colors of nail polish. Her family had eaten a delicious meal and celebrated their first Christmas here in Crayton.

The happy memory faded as the troubling reality of the recent events settled in. Standing up, she walked over to the tree. While mulling over everything that had happened, she took down the decorations. She picked off the round shining bulbs, and she reached up and grabbed the angel at the top. Finally, she slipped off the string of lights and stared at the drab, unadorned tree. The pine needles were dry and falling off. Slipping on her coat and gloves, she took the dead tree down the stairs and back around to the alley where the garbage cans stood. Leaning it against one of the cans, she hurried back upstairs to pack up the decorations and to sweep up the needles.

Afterwards, sitting down with another cup of coffee, she took out a cigarette. She lit it and drew in the smoke. Her nerves were frayed. Everything that she thought fun and exciting here in the city had turned ugly. The handsome Slade had smooth talked her into thinking he was a nice guy. But he had a double life, one at the hotel and one at the parties. No wonder he didn't want to meet her parents. His phony life hurt her deep inside her heart. He turned out to be the worst mistake in her life.

* * *

The next morning she went in to work, hoping to see her roommate. While she changed into her uniform, Darlene came in. Heavy make-up covered her tired face. Mrs. Troy came in and asked Darlene to come with her to her office. They were gone for some time. Betsy waited for her in the break room, smoking a cigarette with Dee and a few others.

As she sat there waiting, she saw Darlene, a security guard, and Mrs. Troy walk by in the hall. Suddenly, the break room filled with whispers and heads were shaking.

Betsy turned to Dee and asked, "What's going on?"

"Well, it looks like Darlene's been fired. They're going to clean out her locker," she replied. "I bet you'll be teaming with me today."

Shocked, she sat thinking of her roommate. Later, Mrs. Troy came in and told her to work with Dee. The two of them left.

Betsy's day of cleaning seemed like the longest day. The news about Darlene shot through the hotel like a wild fire. Concerned and stunned again, she finished cleaning the hotel rooms that afternoon.

Rushing home to the apartment, she ran up the stairs to see and talk to her roommate who had been lying down in the bedroom. Darlene got up when she heard Betsy come in. Sitting on their beds, the two looked at each other with saddened eyes. Her roommates eyes were red from crying.

Darlene said, "Oh dear. What a mess. Since I lost my job, I'm going to have to move out of the apartment. Maybe, you can find another roommate before the end of the month."

"Oh, I'm so sorry, but I don't want another roommate. Can't you find another job?" she asked.

"No. My parents insist that I move back with them. I need to let this thing blow over before I start looking for another job. The hotel won't give me a reference, so I'm starting out on my own. I don't know what I'm going to do. Look how long it took you. With the recession, it'll be hard," she explained.

Sadly, Betsy asked, "What about Ray?"

"Oh, I'm finished with him. He seemed nice and we had fun, but he never intended to marry me. He just used me. This is serious trouble. You stay away from Slade and his friends. I'm sorry about the apartment," said Darlene, a tear falling down her cheek.

"Don't worry. I'm done with Slade. I can move back with my folks. I'll be fine. Say, we better fix something to eat," she said, standing and heading towards the kitchenette. She needed to keep busy and not get tangled up emotionally with Darlene's life.

"I see you took down the tree," Darlene said, following her and looking around.

"Yes, the celebrations are over. Let's eat something," replied Betsy, opening the fridge.

Later that night in bed, Betsy's thoughts of moving out depressed her. This whole situation reminded her of something she saw in the city. As she walked to work one day, she saw workers standing around an opened manhole in the street. As she passed by, she stopped and glanced down into the large dark hole. A step ladder descended into the black. That's where she stood now –in a dark hole with the big ugly city above her. The weight of the city sat on her shoulders. Instead of climbing up the ladder, she had been forced to climb down into that dark hole like a failure she was. Her freedom and independence had been stripped away. She would have to move back home. Even though she had her hotel job, she wondered about staying here in Crayton. The lure of the big city life had been shattered along with her dream of finding a guy and settling down. *Should she be considering moving back to*

Riverside, a place where she knew everyone, a small town without all the strangers? Those thoughts chased each other in her head as she dozed off to sleep.

* * *

Early the next morning before going to work, Betsy wrote a quick letter to her friend Valerie. In the letter, she wrote:

Dear Valerie, "Don't move to a big city. It's not that exciting. Things have gotten rotten here. I don't like it here anymore. I'm tired of being around so many strangers & not knowing anyone. When I go to work, I don't even look up at the tall buildings. The hotel is so beautiful, but after a while, even it has lost its glamour. The winter has set in. It's cold, windy & messy walking to work in the snow. The guy who I dated turned out to be a jerk. I'll tell you more about him later. I'm so mad at him. Oh, I have to move back in with my folks. So much for being on my own." Your sad, miserable friend, Betsy.

* * *

During the cold, wintery January, the two girls moved out of their small apartment on the corner of Drake and Kirby. While Betsy had been at work one day, Darlene had moved out first, taking the dresser and one of the beds. She left a note saying "*Goodbye. Sorry it didn't work out.—D*"

Coming back to the lonely, empty apartment spurred Betsy on to call her parents and arrange for them to come on her day off. In the meantime, she went to the Golden Lion Hotel each day and continued to work and save her wages. She teamed up with Dee permanently who chatted on and on. But Betsy didn't mind. She kept her mouth shut and worked cleaning the hotel rooms, one by one each day.

On her day off, she packed her belongings, boxed up the kitchen things, folded up her bedding and her bath towels. By noon, her parents were there. While her dad loaded the car, she swept and mopped the floors, leaving the apartment clean and ready for the next renter.

The move home meant that she would have to rise earlier each morning to make it into her job on time. She had to ride the crowded No. 22 yellow trolley every day and every afternoon. The winter months slipped by, and spring was in the air.

Betsy thought about leaving the big city and moving back to Riverside. Her parents did not know of her plans. She had kept it to herself and continued to work at the hotel. Sometime later, she found out from Dee that Slade and Ray had been convicted and sentenced for four years for selling illegal drugs. Everyone at the hotel had heard the news. Knowing a little of the situation, she kept quiet and didn't say anything to Dee while she talked on about it.

One morning at the hotel, she had just come down the elevator to go to work. Detective Jordan walked out of Mrs. Troy's office. Seeing her, he motioned to her to come over and said, "Hello, Miss Crocket. Do you remember me? I'm Detective Jordan."

"Yes. Hello," she said, walking up to him.

"I am here on a different matter. Listen, I need to tell you something. We've heard rumors on the street that Slade and his friends blame you for his conviction. He wants revenge. His friends are bad people. I'm worried and concerned about bodily harm. If there is any way you can leave the city, I suggest you do it," he said.

Stunned by the information, she answered, "I have already moved out of my downtown apartment and I'm living with my folks."

The detective stared into her eyes for a moment and said, "Be careful." He turned and walked away. Her heart beat fast in her chest as she thought of the detective's words. She headed upstairs to the elevators to work with Dee on the seventh floor.

That dire warning echoed in her mind for a long time. His words made her look over her shoulder every day. Episodes of fear gripped her soul when she rode to work and back home. She trusted no one. The city had become a grey, dismal dangerous place.

* * *

Shortly after her meeting with the detective, Betsy decided to write her friend Valerie. She wrote:

Dear Valerie, "How are you doing? Are you still dating? I moved back in with my folks. My job at the hotel is going well. I even had to train a new hire one week this month. But the reason I am writing is that I am thinking of moving back to Riverside. Is there some way I could stay with you for a short while if I do? Just until I find a job there. Knowing that I would have a place to stay would help make my decision. I don't know how soon I can move back." Your friend, Betsy.

After writing to her friend Valerie, Betsy kept thinking about moving. But she had good wages and she enjoyed working at the hotel. The Golden Lion Hotel provided her with a safe place. She knew everyone there: Mr. Andrews, Mrs. Troy, Dee, and all of the other housekeepers.

Then one day, Valerie wrote back:

Dear Betsy, "Are you really moving back? I hope so. Yes, you can stay with me as long as you like. I talked to my parents & they said okay. Teri & I are still going to the Saturday nite dances. The truck driver has been stopping in each week. He's seems nice. Sorry this letter is so short, but I have to get some sleep. Call me if you decide to come." Your friend, Valerie.

Reading her letter gave Betsy a plan if she decided to move back to Riverside. But she needed to build up enough money to leave on her own. She didn't want to borrow from her parents. Thus, she stayed, worked, and planned.

Whenever the holidays came around at the Golden Lion Hotel, Betsy worked the special events in the ballroom. With the extra pay, she enjoyed preparing and serving at those events. Those nights working kept her busy and her mind off the dreadful past. Mrs. Troy had been so pleased with her that she eventually became a floor manager. That position gave her a raise and made her proud of her accomplishments at the hotel.

A few guys that she had met wanted to date her, but she feared getting involved with another guy like Slade. She couldn't trust anyone yet. Avoiding the night clubs that Slade had taken her to, she dated a few times and decided on no second dates. The guys in the city all were about the same. They dressed up in suits, partied, and even, took drugs. She now noticed all the nonsense going on. There were all kinds of drugs available, from the ink blot to angel dust to speedballs to pot. She avoided it all, drinking her cocktails and smoking. Her hope of a sensational life in the big city darkened.

Fearing for her safety, her mom and dad were happy to see her home each evening. Once a month on Sundays, her aunt and uncle with Amy came over for dinner. Her cousin Amy yet admired her. They became closer and went together to movies and other events. She took Amy to the Holladay Amusement Park on her birthday.

Eventually, she lost the excitement of living in the big city with all its strangers. Her panic attacks bothered her when she rode the yellow trolley or went shopping. She never lost the fear of running into Slade's friends from the parties. She stayed home most evenings, watching television or listening to her radio. In her bedroom at night, she thought often about going back to Riverside. The comfort of living at home kept her in a dilemma. But she felt the tug of wanting to be on her own and to live independently of her parents.

* * *

It was in 1961 when Betsy finally decided to move back to Riverside. Calling her friend Valerie, she surprised her friend and told her she'd see her soon. Against her mom's advice, Betsy quit her good paying job at the hotel. She had saved enough money to start her life over. At the dealership, her Uncle Jeb had a grey jeep pickup that he sold her at cost. With new tires on the pickup, she prepared to leave Crayton. Her mom didn't want her to leave, but her dad understood. He knew that she would be returning to a small town where she had grown up. She packed her belongings in her pickup and left Crayton—the big city. Finally, she had crawled out of the dark manhole of the city, regaining her freedom. The three days of driving back through the four states gave her time to shake free of her past. She left behind the fiasco with Slade and with Darlene, the tangled mess of her city life. She drove away from the disappointed metropolitan city of Crayton with its thousands of strangers. With the weight of the big city left behind her, she thought of the small mountain town where she knew everyone, and they knew her.

The people of Riverside welcomed her back. She stayed with her friend Valerie a few days while she looked for a job and a place to live. At the Dark Horse Tavern, Dick and Arlene Knudsen gave her a part-time job and she rented one of their upstairs apartments.

She wrote to her parents in Crayton and told them that she had arrived at Riverside and had a good start at getting settled here. They missed her but understood why she had left. Betsy wanted them to say thanks to her Aunt Alisa and Uncle Jeb for their support. Her cousin Amy had been a senior in high school, and she wished her well. With her aunt's help, she could now do books for the tavern. On several occasions, she worked as a barmaid, making good tips serving drinks in the evenings. With her past hotel experience, she could handle the job with ease.

Betsy cleared away anything that reminded her of the city. Her wardrobe was the first to go. Even though she kept her black dress, she got rid of all of the other dresses and heels. Taking on her western look again, she wore a pair of jeans with a fancy leather belt, a black leather vest with a western shirt, and a pair of cowboy boots. A silver turquoise buckle cinched her small waistline. She kept her auburn hair short and wore a pair of dangling silver-turquoise earrings. Betsy stopped smoking. She had the start of a new life.

Her anxiety about dating men developed from the city continued. When approached, she became frosty, defensive, and suspicious. She concentrated on keeping busy at work. Her past experience made her cautious about dating. No man would take away her independence again.

At the tavern one evening, she served beer to an old timer named Mitch who reminded her of Uncle Jeb. While he drank a few beers, she overheard him tell another guy that he needed someone to ride his horse Dynamite. She wanted to learn how to ride, so she told Mitch that she'd be interested. He asked her if she knew how to ride. She said no but she could learn if he would help her. He agreed and they got together.

The first time that she mounted the horse, Betsy's heart beat fast, sitting high in the saddle. Mitch adjusted the stirrups to fit her legs. After a few days of instructions, she began riding Dynamite, giving him the exercise that he needed. She learned how to groom the buckskin, who loved the treats that she brought him. He'd muzzle her hand until she gave him a carrot or an apple each time. She laughed and stroked his neck, feeling his warm body against her. Mitch kept his horse stabled there in town, so she rode when she could get away and groomed him throughout the year.

Then one Friday afternoon, she attended one of the rodeos held at the Double D Ranch. She watched the wranglers ride the broncs and loved the exciting barrel racing. Down at the corrals, she practiced racing Dynamite around a few barrels. Finally, she raced him at one of the rodeos. Betsy and the buckskin didn't come in first, but that didn't matter to her. The thrill of riding him gave her pleasure. But after another rodeo, Dynamite came up lame, so she had to stop racing him for a while.

Her experience with Dynamite gave her time to build up her confidence again. Not only did she enjoy riding, but also the horse had been the perfect listener. During her rides, she had told him of her troubled past. The buckskin's ears would swivel back and forth as he listened. As she brushed his beautiful coat, the gloom that she had acquired in the city lifted. She had her freedom and that filled her with joy.

Eventually, she landed a permanent job at the Mercantile, but still worked part-time at the tavern. She kept herself busy. Her friends wanted to know how it was to live in a city. She told them the big city wasn't what it appeared to be and that behind all the excitement there was an ugly side to it. Her friends asked about her ex-boyfriend, and she told them that it was over, avoiding talking about her past.

A year after moving back, she started dating again. She wanted to find a guy and settle down. At the Dark Horse Tavern at a wedding reception, she met a handsome rancher named Chet Fletcher who had an easy smile and a caring nature. She danced with his Uncle Fred who showed off his quick dancing steps. She loved dancing again. Chet took her up to a nighttime party at Skyline afterwards with several of her friends. They had a great time together; he talked about his family and the Battle Axe Ranch. As the evening grew to a close, she invited him up to her apartment for a final drink. They spent the night together with both of them seeking to erase a relationship that had gone wrong. They both had past demons to forget. Her heart soared at the chance to be with someone whom she could trust.

Soon after that, she met another guy Craig Webster. He had returned from the Army and worked at the Johnson Ranch. He rented the other upstairs apartment down the hall from Betsy. Just getting back to civilian life, Craig drove a turquoise Bel-Air and parked it behind the tavern. They dated and enjoyed each other's company while he told her of his military experiences and of his travels around Europe. Even though he wanted to know of her past, she avoided talking about herself for she didn't want her present situation to be clouded with her dreadful past. Before long, they had slept together after a few dates. He had kind eyes, no-nonsense attitude toward life. She hoped that he would ask her out again. At last, her life had turned around and her future looked bright.

* * *

Betsy was making change for a customer when over his shoulder through the front window of the Mercantile, she saw a dark gray pickup. The driver of the pickup was staring intently at her, and she recognized him as Slade Burler. She dropped her head in concern. Anxiety gripped her heart. Her hands shook and her mind shifted into a panic.

She didn't want to have a scene in the Mercantile. Calling out to the owner, she said that she was going out for her lunch break. She walked out of the store, opened the passenger side door of the pickup, and stepped in and asked, "What are you doing here?"

"Well, that's not very friendly of you. I spent a great deal of time finding out where you were. I've come a long way to see you Bets. Let's go for a ride," replied Slade in his smooth voice, starting up the pickup and backing up. He headed north out of town.

"I don't have anything to say to you. You can just turn around and go back to Ohio," said Betsy, upset and nervous.

"Settle down. I just want to talk," he said, turning off the highway onto a dirt road. He drove up to a parking lot at one of the trailheads. "Let's take a walk."

They got out of the truck. Betsy headed towards the trail that took them into the mountains. Still wearing her white apron from work, she said, "I'm on lunch break. I don't have a lot of time."

"Keep walking," he replied. As she continued walking in front of him, she thought: *Why did Slade show up here?*

As they walked, she heard the crunch of his footsteps behind her on the dirt trail. He asked her to stop, and they walked over to a big log. Before she sat down, she turned towards him. Shocked, she saw a knife, but she did not see the fist that knocked her unconscious. Her body suddenly went limp, and Betsy's world went black.

When her parents contacted the sheriff concerned about their daughter, Sheriff Tom Lindon with a search team went looking for her. After a long search the next day, Chet Fletcher, a member of the sheriff's search team, found Betsy's dead body lying under an old log near the trail leading into the wilderness. Slade had gotten his revenge.

Gigi's Path

Georgia (Gigi) had stopped at the Riverside Post Office before heading back to her sister's house after work. The crowded post office had many town's people picking up their mail. They were greeting each other, smiling, and talking with each other. Gigi spun the tiny dial this way and then back again and opened the small post office box. Up on her tiptoes, she looked into the little box and saw a long official envelope. Eagerly sliding it out, she saw it addressed to "Mrs. Georgia Marder." Glancing at the return address on the envelope, it indicated that these were the final papers in her divorce.

Gigi had the urge to tear open the envelope and read it right there in the post office, but instead she slipped the envelope into her purse, waiting for the privacy of home to read it. Hurrying out of the post office, she walked down the sidewalk, past the few businesses that lined the small mountain town's main street. Her sister Gina's home stood three blocks away. She had been staying with her sister, waiting for the divorced from Hank to be finalized.

The two sisters, Gina and Gigi, were alone in this world. Their dad had died in a roll-over on a mountain road one winter when Gina was a senior and Gigi was in junior high. Their mom had survived the wreck, but her injuries kept her in pain for years. After struggling with the grief and pain, their mom took to drinking for a long time. Eventually, she spent her days and nights drowning in a liquor bottle. She died at forty-seven. Now, both of their parents were buried in the Riverside Cemetery with a tombstone etched with their names: *Logan and Mary Sutton.* The epitaph etched in stone read *In Loving Memory.*

After her sister Gina graduated, she had met and married Tod Gourdy who worked at the hardware store. They had been married for five years with two brown-haired daughters—Harriet and Theresa. Gigi had become part of her sister's married life. She helped her with the newborn babies and watched each girl grow. Her sister developed into a loving wife and mother, caring for her husband and daughters. Their happy marriage stood as a model for Gigi who had dreams of following in her sister's footsteps. She imagined finding a man to love and to raise a family.

However, Gigi's marriage to Hank Marder had been a miserable one.

Her older sister had encouraged her to petition for this divorce. Along with Gina and Tod's help, she had filed her petition to divorce Hank months ago. Her divorce attorney told her that this was a no-fault state so no court hearing would be needed unless her husband Hank opposed her petition. He didn't. The cost of filing and the court fees astounded Gigi since she made only a minimum wage at the General Store in Riverside. Fortunately, the judge ruled that her husband Hank would have to pay for those fees. He had been angry with that ruling, but he would have to pay.

Her husband had delayed the divorce over these six months, using the pretext that he had to work in order to pay the fees. Those months had been an ugly time for her. After he received the papers, he had called and hounded her, saying that she should pay for some of the court fees. She told him no and hung up on him. Undeniably, he didn't want to pay. Finally, he had succumbed to her petition for divorce. She would be free of him and would reclaim her maiden name of "Sutton."

As Gigi walked down the dirt road to her sister's home, her dreary, miserable married life came flooding back. Her sister had told her that she didn't know how to pick a good man. That was a joke between them about her marriage to Hank Marder. She had married him five months after her high school graduation. At the time, she had been young and foolish, taken in by his false promises.

Gigi had met Hank at one of the Saturday night dances held every summer during the tourist season. He had been a thin, nice-looking man with black curly hair and brown eyes. Besides being a few years older, he had a rough side to his looks. When he had asked her to dance, she had been so excited to catch the attention of this strange guy.

Hank had stood out from the rest of the crowd that evening. He hadn't been a wrangler like all the other guys with their blue jeans and scuffed up cowboy boots. No. Hank had worn a pair of black jeans with a black leather vest over a blue shirt. His black boots had been polished and he had known how to dance. Gigi had been attracted to him. His looks had sent warm feelings through her.

After a night of dancing, he had asked for her phone number and had said that he'd call her when he came back into town. And he had called her for a date each time that he had returned to Riverside. They would dance most of the night and then, he'd walk her home holding her hand and later with his arm around her. His attention had put romantic ideas into her head. She had thought that this had to be love. She had been a moth to a flame, a deadly match.

She recalled those summer evenings with the moon shining above them and the warm night air. While they slowly had walked home, he had told her that he owned his own semi-truck. That first night that they had met, he had hauled a load of supplies to the lumber mill. The next day he hauled a trailer of finished lumber from the lumber mill to Idaho. He had explained that he had a permanent contract with the lumber company to haul their finished lumber to numerous states. Then, when he'd dropped off the load, he'd call around for another load somewhere else. This continuous cycle had given him a way to make a living. He had hated an empty run, for he would suffer a loss when he would drive back without a load. Gigi had been impressed by his line of work that night.

After the summer months, Hank finally had made his move. He had talked her into going to his motel room after one of the dances. He had a pint of whiskey which he had poured each of them a glass. While she sipped the strong liquor, he had downed his quickly and had followed it with another.

Looking at her, he had said, "Hey, drink down that whiskey like a good gal." She had smiled and had gulped it down, choking as it slid down her throat. Moving towards her, he had pushed her towards the bed, kissing her. He whispered, "Let's take this a little further tonight. What do you say, Gigi?"

Glancing into his intense brown eyes, she had felt herself pushed back onto the bed. He had slipped down beside her. His warm body had pressed against hers. He eagerly had kissed her again and again. Their kisses had been laced with whiskey. She had gasped as the chills went through her body. As her arms surrounded his neck, she had whispered shyly, "Hank, slow down."

Her shyness had seemed to excite him, and he said, "Don't you like me? Gigi, you're the sweetest gal I've ever met. Come on. I can't think of anything else but you. All night, you've been dancing with those long legs and flirting at me with those beautiful eyes." His hand had moved under her skirt, and he had caressed her hip and thigh. He had deepened his kisses to her neck.

"But...but I can't. It's not right," she said, feeling awkward at his advancing hand.

"What are you worried about? I've got protection. Come on," he murmured, kissing her.

She whispered back, "I've never done this. I'm not sure." She had hesitated to go any further.

"Oh, come on. I'm crazy about you. I'll be your first. We'll go slow," he replied, breathing hard while he moved against her.

Gigi had a small shapely body and long, slender legs. With a charming smile and a soft voice, she had light hazel eyes and short brown hair. He had muttered in her ear that he adored her looks and that she had been the "cutest gal" that he had ever met.

Her shy innocence had put a challenging glint into his brown eyes. Hank had fumbled with her buttons and opened her blouse. She had tried to cover herself, but he had slapped her hands away. His rough hands had brushed against her soft skin on her side. He had dug his fingers into the small of her back, sending warm feelings throughout her body. Moving them up, he roughly had squeezed her breasts, kissing them. His intense moves against her body had taken her breath away. His obsessive kisses, his fervent touches, and his begging words in her ear eventually had sent her desires soaring. His love making had been intense and rough that night in his motel room.

Looking back on that evening, he had taken advantage of her innocence. She had been daft, silly, and foolish.

The next morning, Gigi had woken just after dawn to an empty bed. Rubbing her eyes and looking around, she had wondered where Hank was. Realizing that she was alone, she suddenly felt let down. She had recalled his large, rough hands that had sent her crying and moaning into the night. They had made love more than once. He had told her he couldn't live without her and wanted to marry her. Those words had seemed so sudden, but after sleeping with him, marriage had appeared to be the next step in their relationship. She had imagined a happy future with Hank.

Slowly, she had slipped out of the bed, picked up her clothes from the floor, and walked into the bathroom. While she dressed, her heart beat fast thinking of his powerful, rough ways that he had treated her. Hank had overwhelmed her, leaving her with deep scratches, sore, and bruised. No one ever would know; she would never tell anyone, even her sister. A single tear had slid down her cheek as she thought of that innocent girl who had vanished in the night. Before leaving the motel room, she had found his short note: *See you on the next trip. I'll call you. –Hank*

She had been crazy to sleep with him without really knowing him.

On his next trip, he had presented her with a small diamond engagement ring, asking her to marry him. At the time, Gigi had thought it romantic. That fall they were married in a small church ceremony in Riverside. Her sister Gina had tried to talk her out of marrying him for she didn't think that she knew him well enough. She also did not like how the truck driver had treated her sister. There had been something about Hank that she didn't like, but she couldn't convince her sister to wait. Gigi had been eighteen, young, and smitten with the man. She had imagined a happy life with him.

For their honeymoon, Hank had taken her on one of his hauls. She had recalled how unusual it felt to be riding high above the other vehicles in his huge, green semi-truck with its sloped hood. She had discovered that a different culture existed among the truck drivers. He had told her about the weigh stations and had shown her his log book. Mounted in the cab, he had a CB radio and would speak into the mic on their trip, clicking the button to respond to other truck drivers. As soon as Hank sat behind the wheel, he had taken on a different way of talking—a CB slang. His handle was the 'Green Viper.' Painted on the truck's doors under the company name of "Marder Trucking" was a black snake with long fangs, piercing yellow eyes, and a forked tongue. The phrase "*Quick Service*" had been his business slogan.

Her curiosity had peaked at the distinctive words that he used. The CB lingo gave the truckers tips and warnings about accidents or about patrol cars, bad drivers, or the weather. There had been all kinds of CB 10 codes: 10-4, 10-10, 10-20, 10-28. She had lost track of them. The patrol cars had a couple of code words—the Bear and Smokey. He had told her that her name even had a special meaning — the "Georgia overdrive" which meant putting the gear into neutral. He had chuckled when he said that a southern trucker had told him that one. With all the CB chatter from the other truckers on the road, Hank didn't talk to her much. His eyes had been on the road, and he had paid little attention to her.

During those days on the road, there had not much for her to do sitting in the passenger side. She had gazed with little interest at the countryside passing by. She had picked up his pack of cigarettes and had started smoking. When they did stop for fuel, she had bought a few magazines and tabloids to read on the trip. His cab had been a sleeper with only a single bed. So they had to check into motels. She hadn't notice that they weren't the best motels and had sleazy, drab looking rooms. His intense love making had continued on their honeymoon trip. She had become familiar with his rough ways and thought she had gotten to know him.

She should have paid more attention to his renegade truck driver attitude. His handle should have been a clue.

* * *

Coming into her sister's house, Gigi hung up her coat on one of the hooks by the front door. She opened her purse and pulled out her important envelope. She heard her sister in the kitchen fixing dinner. Gigi called out to her sister that she'd be right there to help. Her nieces Harriet, five-years-old, and Theresa, three, were in their bedroom playing with their dolls. She walked down the hall to their bedroom and greeted them, giving each of them a hug.

Wanting to change out of her clothes, she grabbed a pullover shirt and a pair of jeans from a dresser drawer. She then walked down the hall and into the bathroom where she opened her purse and lifted out the long envelope. Quickly scanning the official letter, she glanced down at Hank's sloppy signature, now her ex-husband. Yes, there on the bottom of the page were both of their signatures. What a relief she felt, but the happiness that she had expected to feel didn't happen. Her empty life and a failed marriage now rose all around her. Without Gina and her loving family, she would have been helpless and homeless.

Before helping her sister with dinner, she changed her clothes, washed her face, and brushed her hair. Looking into the mirror, she told herself that her life would be much better without Hank. The divorce was final.

But then, she recalled the three grueling years of her troubled marriage. After the honeymoon trip, she had expected him to take her on other trips and that they would be together. But that didn't happen. When she asked about going, he had looked at her with surprise, and said, "What? Shit, gal, I can't afford to take you. I have payments on this rig every month. Sorry, you'll have to stay here."

Naturally, she had waited eagerly for him to return to their small, rented house. His time away each month would be days. He'd call during his long hauls from the cities far from Riverside. Unfortunately, she could never reach him since he would be on the road, and he would call from a pay phone. When he did call, they would talk for just a short time.

Trying to occupy her time while he was away, she had spent many days visiting with her sister and nieces and getting involved with them. She had gone to the local library with them and had checked out books to read. At night, she would be by herself in the small house. The loneliness permeated her life, night after night.

At the library one time, she had noticed a United States map on one of the walls. Walking over to it, she had glanced at the different cities that Hank had called from. They were cities all around the West—from Idaho, Utah, Nevada, and Colorado. After looking over that map, she realized how far he must drive for one haul. The distances had astounded her. No wonder that he had been away so long.

When Hank did come home after a long haul, he'd bring home a bag of dirty clothes and an empty stomach. He had expected home cooked meals and cleaned clothes. He'd drink a six-pack of beer and shots of whiskey, sleep all day, and make love at night. He'd stay a few days and be off again on the road.

Hank's visits home had become more unsettling each time. They had argued about the smallest things. She had lashed out at him, upset and angry for his long absences. Her loneliness had become unbearable.

Money had become another issue in their marriage. He had a business account at the local bank. When they married, he had set up her own account where he would transfer money in, just enough to pay the rent, the utility bills, and a little for food.

He proudly said, "I will provide for you."

She asked him, "Shouldn't I get a job?"

"Absolutely not. No wife of mine is going to work. Besides, when I come home, I want you here. You're my gal," he responded.

Despite those plans, she would get down to just a few dollars left during some months; she had to budget the money carefully.

She had always wanted to have a family. For months, she had waited, hoping that she'd get pregnant. She even had visited the doctor, who after a check-up had told her everything seemed fine and advised her to give it time. But with Hank's visits being so sporadic, nothing had become of their intimacy.

During his visits home, she had spoken to Hank about wanting to have a child. Many times, he had ignored her until she pressed him further. Finally, he claimed that he didn't want a family until he could settle down and raise them. He had started using protection. Thus, her life became empty with no chance of ever having a child with him. Their marriage life slowly had begun to unravel.

Alone and miserable, she had spoken to her sister Gina who became worried about her sister's marriage. She had listened to her sister's complaints about Hank. Gina thought about how much she hated seeing her sister married to him. She had kept quiet, afraid to get involved. Her sister had made the choice to marry him, and she would have to work it out for herself.

Gigi should have realized that marrying Hank had been reckless.

By the time he had returned home, Gigi's resentment had increased. His absence became more agonizing, and he'd only call to let her know where he was. When he did call, he'd tell her that he had to wait several days for a load to haul home. That waiting period had gotten longer and longer. When he'd return for a period of time, he had made the demands of a cruel, ruthless, and heartless husband. Then, after getting a call, off he'd go, hauling another load.

One time later after he'd returned home, she had been washing his clothes and had found a newspaper ad in his back pocket of his jeans. Unfolding the ad, she had read: *Wanted: CDL Experienced Truck Drivers for Short Hauls.* The address and phone number given at the bottom had been the city of Dover, California. *Had he been looking for another job?*

Coming into the kitchen after a long afternoon nap, he had walked over to the fridge and asked, "Do you want a beer?" Glancing over at her, she had shaken her head. He had pulled one out and popped off the top. After taking a long drink, he had sat down at the table.

She placed the ad on the table. "I found this in your pocket. Are you looking for another job?"

"Yeah, so what? You're always bitchin' at me because I'm gone all the time. If I took that short haul job, I'd be home every night," he explained. This news had shocked her.

"That means we'd have to move to California. Why don't you look for another line of work here in town? We could stay here, and you could start over. Look at Tod, my brother-in-law. He started at the hardware store and worked his way up. You could give up being a truck driver," she said.

While she talked, he had become angrier and angrier until he finally had walked over to her.

WHACK! He had struck her with the back of his hand. Her head had snapped to the side with a sting that had brought tears to her eyes.

"You have no right to talk to me like that. I'm a truck driver," he shouted.

With her hand covering her stinging cheek, she had jumped up from her chair and ran from him into their bedroom, slamming the door. His violence had frightened her. He had followed her, even madder than before, throwing open their bedroom door.

"Don't you dare slam a door on me. And don't talk to me about gettin' another job. Do you hear me? Do you?" he shouted at her. She knew that she had crossed a line.

Through her tears, she whispered, "Yes, okay, okay. I'm sorry I suggested it."

"What do you expect of me? Quit complaining. You need to be more grateful, gal. I spend long hours on the road while you're sitting here at home. Son of a bitch. Get over here," he ordered her. He then wanted to assert his dominance over her—just like a bully.

Afraid, she had moved slowly to him. Grabbing her, she had struggled against him while he had yanked her into his strong arms, kissed her, and cursed at her, demanding that she please him. He then had pushed her onto the bed and had pressed his body against hers. She had let him have his way with her, fearful to resist him. During his stay, his nights of rough treatment had melted into one after another with bruises and scratches. She cooked, washed his clothes, sat smoking while he ate, slept, and drank his beer. Soon, he received a call from the lumber company and out the door he went, eager to get on the road.

After he left, she had gone into the kitchen, taken a glass from the cupboard, and grabbed the bottle of whiskey under the sink. She had poured herself a little of it, sitting down at their kitchen table with the bottle in front of her. While she downed the amber liquor, her thoughts had whirled with fear and sorrow for their future. *What had this all meant?*

She once had believed that a wife should support her husband, but somehow, her situation had seemed impossible. She had endured the rough nights with him only by closing off her mind and separating herself from her body, fearing his anger if she resisted. His slap had brought the cold, hard truth of her terrible marriage. This had frightened her so much that she knew he would never give up truck driving as she had suggested. She had known that he loved the highway. Driving a truck had been all he had known, and he wouldn't change. But she had never planned on ever leaving Riverside with her sister and her family living here. This had been her home.

Suspended in shock, she had poured herself another drink, gulping it down. While the liquor ran through her battered body, sorrow filled her heart. She wasn't going to leave Riverside and live somewhere in California, isolated from those who loved her. Moving there wouldn't change anything between them.

Later that evening, she had gone to bed, crying herself to sleep, scared, exhausted, and worn out. During the night, she dreamt of Hank's violence against her. She had woken in a panic, shaking in fear. Sweat poured out from her body. Those bad memories would be with her for a long time.

* * *

Another year went by and nothing in their married life had changed except that their financial situation became dire. Hank had been making only two runs a month from the lumber company. He would call and talk about how difficult it had been to find a return load home. Sometimes it would be a couple of weeks before he would come home.

One time, he had returned in a sour mood. Leaving her home, he had gone down town to a local bar. While she had waited for him to return, she had realized that he hadn't brought in his dirty clothes. She rose and headed out to the green truck. She had found his bag behind the driver seat where it usually was stored.

She had glanced around the cab and had seen a woman's purse behind the passenger seat. Curious, she had opened the purse and had found several pictures of Hank and a blonde, smiling together with his arm around her. One had a picture of her standing in a red bikini near a swimming pool. Scrolled on the back were the words: *To Hank, Love, Dottie.* Another picture had the two of them at some bar with drinks in front of them. The blonde was kissing him on the cheek as he smiled. Gigi had gasped as she looked through them. She had grabbed the pictures and his bag of clothes and had gone into the house. Now *he* had crossed a line in their marriage.

When he returned home, it had been after midnight. He had stumbled into the house, mumbling to himself. She had been waiting for him. The pictures had been arranged on the table as she drank a glass of whiskey and smoked her cigarettes. Along with the liquor, her resentment slowly had grown as the time past. She had resolved to face him, no matter what.

"What are you doing still up?" he slurred in his drunken state.

"I went out to your truck to get your dirty clothes. I found a woman's purse with these pictures inside. What's going on?" she asked him, pointing to the pictures.

He had glanced at the pictures and then, had stared at her for a moment and admitted, "That's Dottie my girlfriend. I stay with her in Dover while I'm looking for a load. By the way, I'm moving out there." She had glared at her husband in shock. The tense silence had hung in the air. He lashed out at her, "She treats me much better than you, and she pleases me. She's pregnant and I'm going to live with her." His barbed words had struck a finality to their relationship.

"So, it's over," she said, slowly rising. She had waited for him to say something, but he didn't. She had walked back to the bedroom and shut the door. He hadn't followed her; she had sighed, relieved as she heard him leave.

That night he had slept in his green truck. Gigi had realized that his long absences were more than just waiting for a load. He'd been fooling around with the blonde, so there were probably other women in other cities. Throughout the night, she couldn't sleep. *What was she going to do now?*

She was tougher than Hank knew. He obviously had no affection for her, and their marriage had finally failed. Each time he came home, her soreness and bruises had healed while she had kept her mind closed, stiffening, strengthening, and reinforcing her survival. Yes, she had been trapped, but she could work it out.

After a long night, the early dawn came. She had heard Hank start his diesel engine, rumbling loudly in the quiet dawn. She had risen out of bed, slipped on her robe, and walked to the front door. He had driven off, headed for the lumber company to get a load. That had been the last time she had laid eyes on him.

Gigi had spent the next few days in an emotionless, bewildered, and dazed state, not sure of what to do. But his leaving had only begun her misery. The day after he had left, she received a long official envelope addressed to her husband. Opening it at home, she had read the foreclosure notice on the truck loan. Later that day, the landlord had dropped by and had told her he was sorry, but she would have to pay the three months back rent by the first of the month, or he would be forced to evict her. Then she had checked and found out that the bank accounts had been emptied, and she could not afford even groceries. She finally had to call her sister, worried, anxious, and worn out.

When she told her sister of Hank's pregnant girlfriend and that he had left her, Gina couldn't believe it. "You should never have married him. He never treated you right," her sister said, recalling their past conversations about him. She had always suspiciously thought that he wasn't who he appeared to be, a loving man. He had worn a mask. She now had recognized his falsehood.

Obviously, his sly, cold, cruel character had remained hidden until now.

"I know," replied Gigi, looking tired with dark circles under her eyes.

"You look terrible. Have you been getting any sleep?" asked her sister, concerned.

"No. I can't sleep. He's gone and I have no money. Now, what do I do?" she asked, anxious and upset.

"If you don't love him, I would leave him. I suggest that you divorce him," replied Gina. She hoped that her sister would take her advice.

"I don't love him, but I don't know anything about divorce. Do you?" she asked.

"No, not exactly. I'll ask Tod. He might be able to advise you," said her sister.

"Oh, I don't want to get him involved with my problem," she groaned.

"He already knows," said her sister.

Gina had kept her husband informed for she had been so worried about her sister. Tod had been furious when she told him of Gigi's troubled marriage and of how Hank had struck her. Her husband had no respect for a man who would hit a woman. He agreed that her sister deserved better, and that Hank was a "two-bit sidewinder."

Later when her sister told her what Tod had said, Gigi had nodded. There it was again—the image of the snake. Hank had been a viper, striking and putting fear into her heart.

That day, the two sisters had talked more about getting a lawyer and taking it one step at a time. When Tod came home that evening from work and after her young nieces were in bed, the three of them had talked. Tod got out a pencil and paper and the telephone book. Together they had made a plan for her to divorce Hank.

* * *

Walking in the kitchen to help her sister, Gigi set the table, poured the girls their milk, and helped her sister set the food on the table. Tod came home and they all sat down to dinner. Her niece Harriet had only a few weeks of school before the Easter vacation and talked about her day. Theresa had played with her dolls and had made cookies with her mom.

Tod asked Gigi, "How is your job going at the General Store?"

"I've been busy. With summer coming, we'll soon be in the tourist season. We're stocking the racks and shelves," she replied, thinking of her busy day at the store.

"Us too. We've had a steady business with the ranchers," he said. He had worked his way up for the past years to an Assistant Manager at the Riverside Hardware Store.

After Hank had left her, Gigi had to move out of their small rental house. Tod and Gina had insisted that she move in with them until she could get her life figured out. Fortunately, she had hired on at the General Store, the oldest one in Riverside. The store sold western clothes for men and women, sporting equipment for fishing and hunting, groceries with a meat counter. She worked wherever they needed her, either in the office, in the store, or at the cash register.

Her work in the office allowed her to meet most of the ranchers, their foremen, and their wranglers. She took the ranch orders and wrote out fishing and hunting licenses. Along with her wages, the store had kept her busy and she loved the variety. After finding her job, she had started saving for her own place. She had paid her sister a little money each month which helped with the groceries. Living these months with her sister's family had been difficult for her, but they had always been close. They took each day, each week, each month at a time.

Smiling at Tod and her sister, she thought how happy they were in their marriage. With two growing daughters, they were going to try for another baby. Thinking of herself, she had wanted the same—a happy marriage and children. But her marriage had fallen apart with Hank. She would have to start over.

After dinner, Gigi helped her sister wash up the dishes and clean up the kitchen. Once they had finished and sat down at the little kitchen table to talk, she took out a cigarette to smoke and offered her sister one. They usually took a little time and talked before putting the girls to bed.

Her sister looked at her and said, "The doctor told me not to smoke when I get pregnant."

"Oh, I won't smoke either. I started this nasty habit with Hank, but I should stop," she said, putting her pack of cigarettes on the table. "Listen, I have good news. I received the papers today. Hank finally signed."

"Thank goodness. But you know that your divorce has been final without his signature," said her sister.

"Yes, I know. I feared that he would never pay those court fees. With his temper, I just didn't know. But with his signature, I know it's really over," she said.

Tod walked into the kitchen and said, "I'll get the girls ready for bed if you two want to talk."

"Oh, Tod. Gigi got the final papers," said Gina.

"Did he finally sign?" Gigi nodded at him. "Good. You've had it rough," he commented.

"Listen, thank you both for helping me get through this. Now that it's final, I want to look for an apartment as soon as I can," said Gigi, thinking ahead to getting her life started again.

"You don't have to rush. Take your time. We were glad to help you out," he replied. The two girls came running in the kitchen, chasing each other. "Okay, that's enough running in the house. Let's get ready for bed." He left with Theresa in his arms and Harriet hanging on his leg as he walked them down the hall, laughing with the girls giggling.

"You're so lucky, Gina," she said, living with them had been the only thing that kept her from going crazy over these months waiting for the divorce to be finalized.

"You can start over now. You'll find someone. I'm sure of it," said her sister.

"I'm not so sure. What about the rumors in town? No one will want to date me—I'm divorced," said Gigi. She worried about what the future held for her. She hated the thought of dating again.

"Listen, we've been through this before. Remember how the town gossiped about our mom's drinking. Yes, it was harsh on us, but people in a small town talk. So what? We ignored it and rose above it, and now, you'll do it again. The town gossips don't know all the details about your horrible marriage. You're better off without him," continued her sister.

"Yes, I know. But already, at the store today, a few of the ladies came in and were whispering about me. I could tell by their looks. I feel such a failure. How did I go so wrong," she admitted to her sister.

"Now, that's enough. Put your past behind you. You made a mistake. But you're still young and beautiful. And you're a good person. There's plenty of men who would date you. You'll meet someone. I'm sure of it," repeated her sister.

Tod came in the kitchen and told Gina that the girls were waiting for her to read a bedtime story. She rose and left.

With her sister gone, Gigi lit a cigarette, drawing in the smoke. Glancing at Tod, she said, "If you hear of a place, let me know. I'm serious about getting out on my own."

"Sure. I understand. Let us know if we can help," he said.

"Oh, you've done more than enough already. Again, thank you. I've saved a little to get me settled," she commented.

"Okay. Good night," he said, heading for their bedroom down the hall.

She finished her cigarette, got up, and moved to the living room and made up her bed on the couch. Earlier, her sister had brought out the bedding for her tonight, placing the sheets, a pillow, and the blankets on the couch. Gigi tiptoed into the girl's bedroom to get her nightgown and robe. Her nieces were snuggled in their beds. She went over and gave them each a kiss.

Quietly, she said "Good night."

With sleepy voices, they replied, "Good nite, Auntie."

Her heart swelled with love for her two nieces. Out of this divorce, something good had come of her living with her sister and her family. They all had become closer, and she thrilled at being part of their life and seeing them each day. Her sister's family had given her strength to keep going despite her feelings of defeat at her own marriage.

In the bathroom, she slipped on her nightgown and robe and headed to the living room. Walking down the hall, she moved towards the couch. *RING. RING.* The phone rang loudly in the quiet house. This late at night she knew that it had to be Hank. No one else would call this late.

She lifted the receiver, "Hello."

"Is that you Gigi? It's me," said Hank. Her heart quickened at the sound of his harsh voice. She would rather not talk to him.

"Yes. What did you want?" she asked, quietly.

"I paid those damn court fees. Aren't you a piece of work. I've found a gal who doesn't whine about my job. You were such a sour puss. Damn you," he growled in the phone. His cynical words sounded angry.

"Hank. Stop it. It's over. Did you ever love me? I'd like to know."

"Love? Are you serious? You're nothing but a damn--," she held the phone away from her ear as he called her a string of vicious names. She wasn't going to listen to him anymore and hung up the phone. She was finished with this rough renegade who had made her life miserable.

Her sister came down the hall, wondering who had called.

"It was him," she told her.

"What did he want?" her sister asked.

"Just to tell me off. I hung up on him. Listen, if he calls here again, don't talk to him," she said.

"Sure, I don't want to talk to him anyway. Well, good night," she said, turning and heading back to bed.

She slipped off her robe, adjusted her pillow on the couch, and crawled under her blankets. Hank's call threw her emotions into a whirlwind of hurt. Around and around the images of the years with him had gone through her mind—his green truck, her dashed hopes of motherhood, his slap on her cheek, the fanged viper on his truck, his empty love, his cheating, and his rough handling of her in bed. Three years of living with a man who didn't love her—a husband who had abused his wife. No children. An empty marriage. She had been a failure. *Would she be able to start over?* Tears filled her eyes while the wounds went deep into her soul. The darkness surrounded her as she turned off the lamp by the couch. She had to forget her past with him, but it would not be easy.

* * *

Finding a place to rent with her wages in Riverside hadn't been simple. It had taken longer than she had planned. However, one day on the bulletin board at the Mercantile, one of Knudson's apartments had been advertised. After contacting Dick Knudson about the apartment, she had moved into the one-room apartment which had a bed on one side with a small brown couch and chair on the other side. A small kitchenette stood opposite the door with a small bathroom to the left of the kitchenette. For her, it had been perfect with a lower rent than any small house in town.

When she moved out of her sister's house, her nieces had been the ones who said they would miss her. Their words had struck a loving chord in her heart. Keeping her family in her life had been the right decision. A move away from them would have alienated and destroyed her. Her resolve to stay in Riverside had been the best decision. Cutting the string that bound her to him had taken its toll on her emotionally. The long months of waiting for her divorce had kept her anxious and moody.

She had been careful not to talk about her divorce or her ex-husband to anyone in detail. The town knew about the divorce and that she was on her own. Once in a while when she would walk down main street to her apartment, she felt the stares and heard the whispers. She recalled her sister's advice and ignored them. The people in the town certainly wouldn't have condemned her if they knew how dreadful her marriage had been. Time would be on her side. They would soon find something else to talk about.

Smiling, she had kept quiet, and her head held high, trying to regain her reputation. Her job at Riverside's General Store had kept her busy in the day. She had interacted with customers and gained confidence while she worked. At night, her sister Gina would call, and they would talk. During one of her calls, her sister had suggested that she should go out to the bars on Friday or Saturday night, just to meet guys.

"Oh, I can't go alone. I don't want to appear that desperate," said Gigi.

"No, you aren't. But you know a lot of ranchers and the wranglers after working at the store. Just go for an hour, have a beer, and leave," said her sister.

"Would you and Tod come with me? That would make it seem less obvious," she asked.

"We would have to get a babysitter. But I'll ask Tod. He might like to go out," replied her sister. Gina called the next day, and they planned a night out.

That next week-end, she met her sister and Tod down stairs at the Dark Horse Tavern. She relaxed when they came in and sat down with her at the little table. Tod bought two draft beers and a soda for Gina. When the jukebox played a country song, Tod and Gina danced. She watched them, noticing how in love they were. She sat drinking her beer and smoking a cigarette.

After another song or two, a couple of the wranglers danced with her. Her sister had been right. Jim McDob from the Double D asked her first to dance. After that, several others danced with her. When Brody Johnson from their family's ranch danced with her, he pulled her close to him. She had not felt a man's body against hers for so long that she stepped back from him and started to talk. Even though she wanted to be friendly, she didn't trust herself. She did notice a few curious stares from others in the tavern when she danced. Their eyes made her nervous and jittery.

Earlier that evening before going out, Gigi became over anxious and worried about going out, called her sister, and told her she didn't want to go. Her sister said, "Sis, you can't back out. I've arranged for a babysitter. Tod and I are both looking forward to a night out."

"You two go out. Maybe, next time I'll go with you," she replied, reluctant to go.

"Absolutely not. You're going. Get dressed and we'll meet you in about an hour. I've got to go. The girls need a bath tonight. Bye," said her sister with the girls' voices in the background.

Gigi hung up. With no more excuses, she took a quick bath and thought about tonight. She realized that she was making too much of a fuss. Her nervousness surprised her. It was just an evening out of her lonely apartment. She recalled her long nights of crying into her pillow and making her sore eyes puff shut. Most of her nights alone were exhausting and intolerable. The dark ugly images of Hank and her marriage haunted her. She wanted to forget about him and maybe, this night out would help her.

After her warm bath, she went through her closet, looking for the right outfit to wear. She finally settled on her black short mini-skirt with a cream-colored blouse and a light green sweater. She wore her only pair of black heels. After putting on her make-up and brushing her hair, she was ready. As she walked out of her apartment and down the stairs, she thought that she could always leave earlier if it went bad. She'd let her sister and husband enjoy their evening together.

However, later in the tavern and as the evening went on, Gigi danced and began to feel like herself again. With her soft voice, she laughed and talked with the guys who danced with her. She kept her heart guarded and emotions subdued. She would not let herself be taken in again. Nothing serious came of that evening, but Gigi had made the first steps in starting her life over.

* * *

That evening at the tavern had given her a new beginning. The spring months brought a change in the weather with warmer days and rain. At the General Store, she worked, keeping busy helping customers. Many of them were local ranchers and her acquaintances grew.

A few weeks later, Gigi wanted to go out again, but Tod told her sister that he didn't. He wanted to spend time with his daughters, so the two sisters went out together. They went to the Pole Cat Bar, just for a few drinks.

For some reason that night, Gigi yearned for some affection. She had watched an older cowboy come in. As he glanced around the bar, he had a lonely look in his eyes that she instantly recognized. Something in his appearance and eyes sparked an interest in him. She wanted to know more about him. When she went up to the bar to get another beer, Gigi directly introduced herself. He was Clyde Fletcher, a recent widower. She then asked him to come sit with her and her sister. After introducing her sister, he talked a little about the Battle Axe Ranch and his family. Her sister made her excuses and left, thinking that her sister would have an enjoyable evening with this widower.

Clyde asked her to dance, and they had some close, affectionate moments. When he drove her back to her apartment, she asked him up for another beer. But he reluctantly refused, leaving her standing empty handed. The reality of his refusal slammed into her as she walked up to her apartment. *Why did she do that? No one was going to want her.*

After that refusal, she felt disheartened. She knew that she had overstepped the situation with Clyde. She had been ready and willing, but he had not. She knew that she had to be more cautious.

Tonight showed her that finding a man would take longer than she thought.

A week later, Jim McDob called and asked her out to the movies one Saturday night. Afterwards, they went to the Pole Cat Bar and had a few drinks. He talked about his work at the Double D Ranch and the many guests they had coming to stay in the summer. He also told her about the local rodeos that they held on Friday afternoons and suggested that she should come a watch. Then, he drove her back to her apartment, walked her up the stairs, and stopped in front of her door. With her keys in her hand, she waited. He seemed hesitant, so she thanked him for the evening. Giving him a big smile, she said in her soft voice "good bye." He smiled and left.

The next week, Brody Johnson took her out to dinner at the new restaurant, the Saddle Horn. He talked about their ranching plans for the summer. They had finished branding and the next week, they would be driving their cattle to their summer camp. Again, they stopped at the Pole Cat Bar and had a few drinks before he took her back to her apartment.

Both dates had been pleasant evenings out, but she kept her emotions guarded and kept their dates on a friendly basis. She had been mildly interested in their ranch work—not overly excited. Both Jim and Brody had sensed that from her. They all parted as friends.

Every morning, Gigi rose and walked down main street to the General Store. She kept busy at work, meeting people and keeping her thoughts hopeful. Fortunately, her ex-husband lived in California, so the details of his other life was never revealed here in Riverside. One day Anna Severson from the Norseman Ranch came in to buy clothes for her son.

Another time, Clyde Fletcher and his new wife Lettie came in and set up an account for the Battle Axe Ranch. Gigi carefully kept quiet as Clyde stood there in the back office. She and Lettie had been in school together. They talked and she congratulated Lettie on her marriage. Somehow, seeing them married gave her hope. If anyone had odds against her, Lettie did. Everyone thought she would be a spinster her whole life.

Gigi talked to other local ranchers as they made special orders of food supplies for their ranches. These many contacts gave her a chance to see life outside of her narrow life that she had experienced with Hank.

One night out at the Dark Horse Tavern, she met another man, Jack East, the helicopter pilot. Noticing her sitting at a small table, he asked if he could join her. She smiled at him and nodded "yes." They both recognized each other. Over the last few months, she recalled seeing him in the store. Jack appeared to be middle age with close cropped brown hair and clear blue eyes. He had high cheekbones with a chiseled jawline and his full lips were enticing. He wore a leather flight jacket with several patches and khaki pants. Before sitting down, he slipped off his jacket and hung it on the back of his chair. With a grey pullover shirt, he had an ex-military look in his appearance. That attracted her immediately; he wasn't a part of the ranching world.

Jack ordered them drinks and they talked. While they chatted, the jukebox had been playing and many couples were dancing. Finally, he asked her to dance. She rose, placing her hand in his. Every nerve in her body responded to his touch. An unusual feeling shot through her. His blue eyes were intense and piercing as they glanced down and up again at her small, shapely body to her long, slender legs. She blushed. That night she had dressed up in a red sweater over her black mini-skirt with her little black heels.

They moved onto the dance floor where he pulled her into his strong, firm body. They danced closely on the first dance, moving together across the floor. His hand on her lower back pressed her close against him. She felt his firm, warm body against her. She breathed in a distinct whiff of his aromatic cologne. When the song ended, she reluctantly stepped back, wanting to feel his closeness. A fast song began to play on the jukebox, so he kept a hold of her hand, and smiling, he swung her around in a twirl.

"Come on, let's dance," he said in his deep voice. His enthusiasm was catching, and she moved to match his steps. She couldn't believe how excited and relaxed she was with him. Jack knew how to have fun with his wide-opened smile that made her knees go weak.

After a few more dances, they sat down at their small table. He ordered them another round of drinks. He then spoke of his helicopter business and how he combined his agricultural degree with his piloting. He finally mentioned that she should come out to his place and see his chopper. She couldn't help but think about Hank and his trucking business. But Jack sounded more confident and self-assured where her ex-husband sounded smug and cocky.

"And what about you? Tell me about yourself," he inquired.

For some reason, she let down her guard with him and told him that she had been divorced recently. Hearing about her divorce didn't seem to bother him. His impassive eyes showed her that he understood. With his world-wide perspective, he told her that he had known one of his military buddies who had married and then had divorced.

"Oh. You were in the military?" she asked.

"Yes, I was drafted during the Korean War. But what about your ex-husband," he quickly changed the topic back to her, avoiding talking about his military experience.

"Hank? He doesn't live here and left me for someone else," she responded. He looked at her for a moment, noticing that there was much more to her story which she wasn't saying.

To comfort her, he said, "Hey, some marriages don't work out." They each took a sip of their drinks. He glanced at her and continued, "Forget him. Let's have some fun." They rose together and moved to the dance floor. He held her close to him; as she danced, she shook her mind free of Hank. She had to forget him if she ever wanted to move on.

When he drove her home, he followed her up to her apartment and she offered him another beer. Sitting together on her brown couch, she kept her distance from him as they chatted and drank a beer. He told her more about being a pilot and how he loved flying his chopper. Finally, he finished his beer and said he needed to leave. After slipping on his flight jacket, he leaned down, gave a brief kiss on her cheek, and left.

Afterwards, she crawled into her bed, thinking of her time with Jack. She felt herself falling for him, sending warm feelings through her. She recalled his warm firm body against hers, his wide smile, his military appearance, and his strong, fun-loving personality. She hoped that he would call her again. Closing her eyes, she fell into a deep sleep.

* * *

The summer months came gradually upon the mountain town, bringing warm days and cool nights with the moon, passing from full to crescent. Tourists filled the motels, the cafes, the stores; visitors came to stay at the dude ranches, to ride horseback into the mountains, or to fish the multiple streams and lakes. The gas stations filled the vehicles heading to the Wyoming mountains and national parks. All businesses were thriving, including Jack East's Helicopter Service.

Gigi's life turned around after meeting Jack that night at the tavern. She had an optimistic outlook that gave her hope in her heart. During the day, she kept busy at work, focusing on the many customers who came in to buy western clothes, purchase fishing licenses, and buy groceries. At night in her apartment, she would imagine the possibilities with Jack in her life. But she didn't hear from him for quite a while. She knew that his business kept him busy, for she recalled that he said that his flights picked up in the summer and fall months.

Unexpectedly, Jack came into the General Store one day to purchase a fishing license. After they both walked back to the office, she filled out the blanks on the fishing license while he told her that his best friend Dennis Carter and he were going on an overnight fishing trip. Nervous, she had to keep her hands steady as she wrote. Being so close to him in the small office made her jittery. She could smell his aromatic cologne and saw his white teeth as he grinned. Recording his details from his driver's license, she noticed that he was thirty, nearly nine years older than she was. Lowering her eyes down, her mind whirled with excitement. Jack's authoritative deep voice and handsome face made her insides turn with anticipation. After he signed his name on the license, she looked at the bold strokes of his signature. She tore the slip of paper from the pad, handing it to him. Their fingers brushed against each other's. They both glanced up. A brief flash of fascination came to them.

Folding the fishing license and putting it in his wallet, he smiled, glancing at her and said, "Thanks. I'd like to see you again. Would you like to go out with me?"

She hesitated a minute. His sharp blue eyes seemed interested in her. She quietly replied, "Yes, I'd like that." Her heart beat fast.

They rose and left the office. He said, "My scheduled has filled up, keeping me in the pilot's seat. I don't know exactly when, but I'll call you. Okay? Maybe, we can get together on one of your days off."

"Yes. Good bye. Enjoy your fishing trip," she said.

"Oh, I'm looking forward to getting away for a few days," he said as he left.

She watched him leave the store. Back to work, she counted down the hours until the end of the day. That evening her sister had asked her over for dinner. She hurried over there after work, bringing her nieces each a pair of new slippers from the store. Their little bare feet at night and in the morning could use them.

When she came into her sister's house, the smell of dinner made her stomach rumble. She seldom fixed much for herself at the apartment—a can of soup or a sandwich at night. Her nieces were surprised with the new slippers, quickly trying them on. The two girls were growing up so fast. Her heart swelled at being so lucky to be around her family.

She smiled at her sister and said, "Hi, sis. How are you doing? Any news?"

Gina shrugged her shoulders. but asked her, "How are you doing?"

She smiled, "I'm doing fine. Hope you don't mind me buying the girls the slippers."

"Of course not. That was so thoughtful of you. Now tell me. You look as if you have some good news," looking at her sister who seemed so happy tonight.

"Yes well, I saw Jack today. He bought a fishing license," she said.

"And?"

"He said he'd call me. Oh, sis. Maybe, he's the one," she replied.

"Now wait. Get to know him first. Remember, you need to take it slow and really get to know a guy before you get seriously involved," warned her sister.

"I know, sis. But he's so different than Hank. I'm older and smarter now. I know what I'm doing," she insisted. As they talked, the two set the table and waited for Tod to come home.

Theresa came into the kitchen to show her aunt a picture that she had drawn with crayons. Sitting down at the little kitchen table, Gigi lifted Theresa into her lap while she hugged the little girl. She looked at the little red and green stick people that her niece had drawn. Kissing her, she breathed in the fresh smell of the child's hair. She wanted to be a mother someday. Harriet had followed her sister into the kitchen, wanting some attention too.

"Auntie, see my new picture book from the library," said Harriet, showing her the book.

"Come here, sweetie. Tell me about the story," replied Gigi, slipping her into her lap. Now she had both girls balanced, clutched in her arms.

Harriet then opened her beautiful picture book, and said, "The story is about a little fairy getting lost in an enchanted forest. See? Here is Alette. Isn't she beautiful." They all looked for a long time at the page that showed the little blue fairy with gossamer wings surrounded by a dark green forest.

"Does she find her way out?" she asked.

"Yes, but she meets some mean spirits who play tricks on her," said her niece. Turning the pages slowly, she pointed to the little yellow creatures who were hiding behind a thorn bush. Harriet spoke more about Alette's story as she turned the pages. Her little fingers touched the pictures as she told the rest of the story. Theresa listened with opened-eyes and glared at the picture book. Gigi loved hearing the story and having her nieces in her arms.

Just as Harriet finished the story, their dad Tod opened the front door and came into the house. Both girls jumped down from her lap and ran to meet him, shouting "Daddy. Daddy."

"Hi, my little angels," he said, going down on one knee to hug them. He rose, walked over, and gave her sister an affectionate kiss on the cheek. Turning, he saw Gigi, smiled and said "Hi. Good to see you. Dinner smells good, dear."

They all then sat down for dinner, talking and eating. After a few minutes into their dinner, her sister suddenly excused herself and headed for the bathroom. When Gina returned holding her hand over her mouth, Tod looked concerned at her. She said, "I must have eaten something that didn't agree with me." But her eyes made a knowing glance at her husband and then at her sister.

Smiling, Gigi knew what she meant. Tod dropped his fork while his face looked surprised and shocked.

Both girls glanced at their dad and said, "Daddy, what's wrong?" They sensed something going on with the adults. Little children are smart, but innocent.

"Oh, nothing. Everything is fine. Daddy's just clumsy tonight." He could barely contain his excitement while they all went back to eating.

After dinner and the girls were in bed, her sister told them that she had felt odd all day, a little dizzy and queasy. She wasn't sure, but she thought she might finally be pregnant. Gigi thought about how thrilled she was for her sister. She left early that evening to give them their privacy.

Back in her apartment, she sat on her brown couch after pouring herself a little whiskey to celebrate her sister's good news. She recalled how excited they were. If it were true, with a new baby on the way, she would have another niece or nephew to hold and cuddle. *Would she ever have her own baby?*

Later that night, she had another dream—a bad one. Somehow her niece's story of the enchanting tale of the lost fairy, the mean spirits, and Hank coming into her apartment all melted into a horrible nightmare. Fear gripped her heart as she woke in a panic. She had imagined her ex-husband making his harsh demands on her while she struggled against his roughness. She felt trapped like the little fairy in the dark forest. With her body shaking and cold with sweat, she rose, went into the kitchenette, and drank a glass of water.

She looked out into the dark night from the window over the sink. *Would Hank ever show up at her apartment?* She would fight him off if he did. Determined to protect herself, she moved over to the door with one of her kitchen chairs. Bracing the chair under the door knob, she stepped back to her bed and slipped under the covers. She had to keep him out of her life. *Would she ever be free of his horrible memory?*

* * *

The weeks seemed to pass by slowly for her. She counted each day since she had last seen Jack at the store. Her sister's morning sickness increased, and their conversations centered around her pregnancy. Gigi started to worry that Jack would never call.

Then one night, the phone rang, and it was Jack calling.

"When do you have a day off?" he asked in his deep voice.

"On Monday, next. Why?" she replied. *What did he want to do?*

"Good. I'll come pick you up," he replied.

"Where are we going?" she asked.

"Let's leave it as a surprise. See you on Monday," he responded with a 'goodbye.'

Anticipation filled her days and nights, waiting until Monday. Yes, here she was waiting again, but this was different. She reminded herself that she was just getting to know Jack and that she should not get too involved too soon.

On Monday early in the morning, the phone rang about seven o'clock. She crawled out of her bed and answered the phone. Jack had to cancel their date. He had an unexpected call and needed to fly to Winston that day. Her voice filled with disappointment. However, he explained, "I will be back before dark though. Would you still want to go out? Maybe, to dinner instead?"

She brightened up and replied, "Of course. I'll be ready."

"Great. I'll call you when I get back. Bye," he said.

She had the full day in front of her. She dressed quickly, had a bite to eat, and called her sister to see how she was feeling. Her sister then asked her to come over to help with Theresa. She had been feeling bad.

Happy to help, Gigi spent the morning with her niece, watching and playing with her while her sister rested. After fixing Theresa a sandwich for lunch, she read her one of her story books while her niece laid down for an afternoon nap. Later, her sister Gina felt better, so the two sat drinking tea and chatted. She thought that she'd see the doctor to make sure. Her sickness might be just her stomach acting up. False alarms did happen.

Her youngest niece woke up from her nap and Harriet came home from her day at school. Gigi noticed that her sister still looked pale, so she told her to go rest and that she would fix something for dinner. She sent the girls to play in their bedroom, telling them to be quiet while their mom took a nap. Walking back to the kitchen, she went about fixing a casserole. She also baked a pan of brownies for dessert. She put the casserole in the oven, set the table, and waited for Tod to come home. When he returned, he asked her to stay and eat, but she said that she had a date with Jack that night. Tod thanked her for helping and she left.

Just as Gigi opened the door of her apartment, the phone rang. Rushing to pick up the receiver, she panted, "Hello."

"Hi, Gigi. You sound out of breath," said Jack.

"Yes, I just stepped in the door. I've been over at my sister Gina's today," she explained.

"I'd like to meet her. Is she as pretty as you?" he said kidding with her.

"She's married and has two little daughters," she replied.

"Oh, I guess you're stuck with me then. Listen, I'll come by and pick you up, if you still want to go to dinner. I know it's a little late," he said, apologizing.

"No. I mean yes; I like to go to dinner. It's fine," she said, fumbling with her words. She sounded like an idiot. Her nerves seemed on edge, anxious to see him again.

He replied, "I'll see you soon. Bye."

When his dark green pickup drove up and parked behind the tavern, she left her apartment and met him coming up the stairs. He looked great in his leather flight jacket, smiling at her as she came down the stairs. They drove out to the Saddle Horn Restaurant. He asked about her sister and her family. She sat politely and chatted a little about them and about her day with her nieces.

Walking into the restaurant, they were escorted to a table. He helped her with her light jacket and pulled out her chair. The dimmed-lighted room had a quiet atmosphere on this Monday night—not many people were there. A pretty barmaid came up, batting her eyelashes at Jack. He seemed to take the attention in stride as if it happened all the time. He asked Gigi what she wanted; she ordered a whiskey sour, and he, a double scotch. The barmaid never looked at Gigi—her eyes were on Jack.

While they looked over the menu, a young waitress came and took their order. Again, the waitress eyeballed Jack with interest. She stood close to him on the other side of the table. Gigi ordered first and while he ordered, she took a long sip of her cocktail.

Jealousy sprang up unexpectedly. He must get this all the time. After the waitress left, he gulped down his scotch. He raised his glass and the barmaid returned quickly. Grinning at the pretty girl, he joked with her while he ordered another double and a bottle of beer. Afterwards, he relaxed, leaning back in his chair.

"I'm sorry about today. When I get a call, I go," he explained. The barmaid returned, he paid and tipped her as she set down his drinks. He nodded at her and said, "Thanks."

"I understand. You have a business to run," she said, trying to keep control of her pang of jealousy from telling off that barmaid. She had to remain calm because she recalled his open, fun-loving personality.

"Yes, one that I love. I'm making another run to Winston tomorrow. Would you like to go with me?" he wondered, taking a sip of his whiskey.

"Oh, I'd like to, but I have to work," she replied, disappointed.

"Okay. Maybe, another time," he said while he finished his whiskey and chased it down with a swallow or two of his beer.

The waitress brought out their meals, and they settled in and ate quietly. She had noticed how his face lit up when he talked about flying. She had never flown anywhere, even on an airplane, so the thought of flying in a helicopter intrigued her. She wondered if she would like to fly in one.

When they had finished their meal, he ordered another round of drinks. They talked quietly more about each of their lives. Jack talked about his fishing trip with his buddy Carter up into the mountains. He laughed as he recalled how stiff he was from riding a horse all day. She noticed again his fun-loving attitude. He asked more about her. She told him more about how she stayed with her sister while waiting for her divorce.

After a while, she realized they were the only ones in the restaurant. He noticed that too, and together they rose to leave. He left a big tip on the table while she slipped on her jacket. He grabbed his flight jacket and they left.

"Let's take a drive," he said walking out to his pickup. Gigi leaned on his arm with her head dizzy from the cocktails. After getting in, he drove down main street, turned at the bridge, and followed Sheep Creek up until he turned left to a side road. He drove along the Skyline road and parked, looking over the small town below with its sparkling lights. He slipped his arm around her shoulders, pulling her towards him. She tensed up, not sure about him. She guarded her emotions.

Glancing at her, he said, "I've been looking at those soft lips all night wondering how they would taste. Come here." She closed her eyes as she leaned closer to him. His lips sought hers and his gentle kiss sent her heart beating fast. She wanted to relax, but her past experiences flooded her mind with fear. She stiffened as he kissed her again.

Sensing her reluctance, he whispered, "What's wrong?"

"It's nothing," she replied in her soft voice.

"It doesn't feel like nothing. I'm getting a disturbing message here," he murmured back as he kissed her neck, smelling her perfume behind her ear. He gently held her as he kissed her again. Then, he leaned back and said, "Tell me. What is it? Are you not interested?"

She shook her head, "No, it's not you. It's me." She slightly turned from him, glancing out the windshield of his pickup into the dark night with a crescent moon. *Should she tell him of her past?* She might lose him. He might think badly of her, not worthy of his love. *Could she be honest with him?*

"What do you mean?" he asked, pressing her for an answer.

"It's hard for me to talk about," she said quietly.

He frowned at her, "Talk to me, nothing can be that bad."

She took a long breath in. He waited. Then, she opened up, encouraged by his gentleness. She told him of her marriage, of her husband cheating on her, and his rough demands of her when he came home from his long hauls. She couldn't tell him everything; Hank's abuse of her remained a secret. But she ended by telling him that she had experienced a dreadful relationship, one that left her fearing intimacy.

Silence filled the car, with only the sounds of the night surrounding them. He thought for a moment, and then, pulled her into his firm chest. Her cheek rested on the front of his leather jacket. "Did he hit you?"

She didn't respond for another moment, but whispered, "He hurt me."

"That bastard." He put his finger under her chin and raised her face. "Listen, you're with me now. Forget about him." She gazed into his kind, blue eyes.

He seemed to understand without condemning, blaming, or accusing her. She relaxed against him, feeling relieved while he surrounded her with his firm arms. He held her tightly for a moment.

Then, he whispered, "Hey, come on. Let's take a look at the stars." He opened the pickup door and stepped out, helping her out. Closing the door, they raised their heads and gazed above at the canopy of brightly twinkling stars against the black sky. She leaned against him as he wrapped her in his arms. She felt safe in his arms, and his genuine gentleness made her feel comfortable.

They stared at the vast scenery in front of them, the dark mountain peaks and the glowing lights of the small town below the mesa. Their eyes rested on the distant horizon where the outline of the mountains met the night sky.

"You can't imagine what it feels like to fly," he whispered. Turning to her, he gently pushed her back up against the pickup. He pressed his body into hers, looking into her eyes and down to her lips. His fingers came up and he put his hand behind her neck, caressing her cheek. His clear blue eyes caringly roamed her face, looking deep into hers.

"You know, you're the first one I've taken out since I came here three years ago. When I saw you in the tavern that night, sitting all alone, I thought 'What is this pretty lady doing, sitting by herself?' I just had to meet you," he leaned down and touched her lips gently with his.

His tongue pressed her lips to open. Her knees felt weak as she opened her mouth and his tongue sought out her warm mouth. He groaned as they kissed. She felt her desires stirring as she lifted her arms and her fingers slipped around the back of his neck. Drawing him closer to her, she returned his passionate kiss. His body moved against her while her heart beat fast. She felt herself melting. They were both breathing hard.

Bringing her hand down to the front of his flight jacket, she leaned her head back. She fingered his patches and felt the soft leather under her hands. Glancing up into his eyes, she whispered, "It's late. We should go."

Sighing, he pulled her into his chest holding her tightly. He nodded and murmured back, "Okay, maybe next time we'll..." he left the words unspoken, for they both knew they wanted to see each other again. This evening out had further sparked the attraction they had felt weeks ago.

He opened the door, and they slipped into the front seat. He held her close to him as they drove off of the mesa and down the dirt road back into town. Behind the tavern, he parked and walked her up the stairs to her apartment. While she searched for her keys in her purse, he waited. She smiled, moved closer and kissed him, "Good night, Jack." He embraced her and kissed her again, begging for more. She whispered, "I have to go." He took another deep breath and stepped back, nodding.

Before she turned, he said, "Good night. I'll call you." Giving her a soft kiss on the cheek, he turned and walked down the hall to the stairwell.

Stepping into her dark apartment, her body throbbed with warm desires. Turning on a light, she slipped off her jacket. He had wanted her; she had stopped him. She worried that they were moving too fast. Yes, she wanted him, but she didn't want to make the same mistake as before—rushing too quickly without really knowing him. Her hesitation gave her time to rethink about who he was. *Was there room in his heart to love her?* His love of being a pilot seem to come first. *Would he cheat on her?* She wanted a different relationship this time—one of love and caring, not of demands. She had to be sure before she gave her heart to him.

* * *

The hours at work seemed to drag slowly by for Gigi the next few days. At night, she waited for a call from Jack. When she first moved into the small apartment, she thought about saving up for a black and white television, something to occupy her lonely nights. But she had never purchased one, only settling on a radio. She had a library book that she had been reading, but her interest swayed. She sometimes sat for minutes on one page, not reading but just gazing at the words and thinking of him.

She discovered after her first week in the apartment, the sounds of the tavern below made their way upstairs. The thumping of a musical beat coming from the jukebox echoed up through the walls. On Friday and Saturday nights, the murmuring sound of voices grew louder than on other nights.

She phoned her sister often to hear about how she was feeling and how the girls were doing. Sitting on her couch, she smoked, read, and waited. The loneliness had started to take its toll on her. In bed, she spent sleepless nights, thinking of Jack.

At work one day, she overheard two ranchers mention the name 'Jack East.' Her head quickly turned towards the two men. They were coming up to the counter to pay for their purchases.

As the two approached the counter, Gigi smiled at the first man, "Did you find what you needed?'

"Yes, I've got a new pair of boots," he replied. While she rang up the amount, the two ranchers kept talking.

"Yeah, East flew up to the Battle Axe Ranch's summer camp and picked up Dave Knox and flew him to the hospital," said the rancher.

The other one asked, "What happened to Knox?"

"Don't know. We'll have to wait to find out. I don't know how East flies that whirlybird around here. He's got guts to get into that old military bird," said the rancher.

The first one added, "Well, you know two years ago, he flew up into those mountains and saved that hunter's life. We're lucky he's here." He handed Gigi the cash for his boots. She counted out his change and handed it back to him. He picked up his big shoe box, stepping aside for his friend.

The next rancher had a pair of jeans. She rang up the sale, he gave her the money, and she counted out his change. She bagged his jeans in a paper sack.

"Thanks for shopping here. Come back again," said Gigi to the two ranchers. They each touched the rim of their hats to say 'goodbye' and left.

Afterwards, she took a break and went into the restroom. Her mind spun, thinking about Jack and about what the two ranchers had said. Remarkably, Jack had flown his chopper to help not only the hunter but now, Dave Knox. He had never spoke of his rescue flights here in Riverside. But she recalled that he had been in the military. Washing her hands and splashing a little water on her face, she gathered her thoughts and focused on going back to work.

* * *

Some days later, Jack called and wanted her to fly with him to Hadley on Sunday—the next day. He told her he'd pick her up before dawn and to wear jeans and a warm sweater. Eager to go with him, she had waited for him at the bottom of the stairs, inside the door. When she walked out to his dark green pickup in the early morning, she felt the cool air from the night against her face. He smiled at her when she slipped into the warm truck and scooted next to him.

"Hi, Gigi. Ready?" he asked.

"Why are we flying to Hadley?" she asked as he headed south out of town towards his place.

"It's a courier run for the lumber company. We'll fly there and come right back. It'll be fun having you with me," he replied, smiling at her.

With a short drive out of town, they passed the lumber company and he turned left towards the Rock River with a line of tall cottonwood trees. This was her first time out at Jack's place. At the end of the graveled road, an old military helicopter sat in front of a Quonset hut, larger than life. The odd-looking chopper had a clear bubble surrounding two inside seats. The long overhead rotor blades stretched over the bubble with a small set of circular blades on the tail. Unbelievable to her, she wondered if the scant-looking machine would fly.

In the hut, he handed her his spare leather flight jacket and said, "Here, wear this. It'll keep you warm. The weather is clear this morning. I'll start the preflight first before we take off." He helped her slip on the jacket over her yellow sweater. "You look great. Let's go." The oversized jacket covered her small body down to her thighs. Pushing the sleeves up to her elbows, her hands felt the softness and smelled the scent of leather.

Outside, she watched him walk around his chopper, touching certain parts resembling a routine. He was all business, with a stern look on his face. He then waved her over. When she came up to the helicopter, he said, "Climb into this side and I will fasten your seat belt. After landing, we will have to wait until I cut the engine and the rotors come to a full stop. Only then will we unbuckle and exit the craft. This is important. Go ahead and get in."

When she had settled in the seat, he reached into the cab, fastened the seat belt around her, pulled it snug, and latched it. The closeness of his body, the warmth of his arm, and the scent of his aromatic cologne reminded her of their night up at Skyline. He handed her a pair of headphones to cover her ears.

He said, "Put these on. I hung the doors just for you. Keep your hands away from the controls." She noted that there was a duplicate set of controls on her side.

He walked to the other side of the craft and climbed in. After he tightened his seat belt and slipped on his set of headphones, he looked at her and said, "There will be some strong vibrations. But don't worry. Are you ready?" She smiled and nodded.

"Good – hang on and remember what I have said."

Hang on to what? There was nothing to hang on to except her seat which she grabbed with both hands.

He started up the engine and the blades began to whirl. She heard the loud engine and saw the blades turn-- *'whaump'* *'whaump' 'whaump.'* As the blades gained speed, they blurred, spinning like a top. She became dizzy looking up at them. Glancing down in front, she still could see them above in her peripheral vision on the whole flight.

As Jack pushed on the controls, the chopper rose and lurched forward, rising above the ground. He looked at her and flashed a 'thumbs up.' When the chopper broke free of the ground, she felt the pull of gravity as the chopper lifted and her stomach made a flip. The chopper floated on a cushion of air, hanging there a foot or so above the ground. Suddenly the tail pitched up and the chopper started moving across the ground picking up speed and altitude as it moved along. Her body felt the strong vibrations, just like he said.

After they were higher above the ground, the vibrations ceased. She glanced down at her feet and saw the tiny hut and the cottonwood trees lining the river. With the loud high-pitched scream of the engine, she was glad that she had on a pair of headphones to filter out the noise. Any conversation had to be through their headsets.

"How do you like it, so far?" he asked.

"It's beautiful up here," she replied.

The hut, the river, the trees, the town, the houses, and the people were miniature pieces of a toy world. Here in this bird's eye view, she realized that her existence was merely a tiny spot in this gigantic world. Suddenly, her past life with Hank vanished as she physically and mentally rose above it all. The breathless vision left her understanding what Jack meant when he told her about how it felt to fly. The buoyancy gave her a sense of wonderment. Smiling to herself, she felt giddy, excited, and free again.

Jack piloted the chopper towards a distant notch in the mountains looming in front of them. The chopper traveled straight for Tepee Pass. Rivers below looked like blue twisted ribbons. They moved over the dark green forests with the barbed tips of the tall pines pointing up at them. Riding so high above the earth, she gasped at the striking moving scenery below.

Sitting in the clear bubble created an open view on all sides of her—like a front row seat. She glanced at Jack who kept his eyes looking around. He sat engaged confidently in his seat using his arms and feet. He had a control bar between them, another stick in front of him, and two pedals on the floor. Once in a while, he would look at the gauges in front of him. She saw the lighted dials and the needles, but she couldn't make out what they were. While his whole body was involved in piloting, he kept the helicopter moving steadily along.

Soon, the chopper flew over the rugged Tepee Pass. As she looked around, they seemed to be on top of the world. On the other side of the pass, she viewed the distant sharp pointed snow-capped peaks and the town of Hadley nestled in the basin below the mountains.

Jack made radio contact with those at the airport. His radio buzzed back and forth with responses. She couldn't understand most of what was said. Some of it reminded her of the trucker's CB codes. Flying over the flat ground covered with sagebrush, he headed towards an open airstrip after another radio contact. She saw a landing pad marked with an "H" out in front of them. He slowed the chopper as he approached the helipad.

Gradually, they descended, and the helicopter hovered above the ground and the vibrations started again. He eased the chopper to the ground. When the skids touched, Gigi took a breath of relief. They were on the ground again. After he cut the engine and the blades slowly came to a stop, he slipped off his headphones and hung them up.

He turned to her and said, "How was that for your first flight?"

She flashed him 'a thumbs up' and smiled. He grinned at her.

"Stay right there. I will come around and help you out." He soon appeared at her door and opened it. Reaching over, he unbuckled her belt. She felt the thrill of his warm touch, remembering his gentle hugs.

He offered his hand while she stepped out and stood, a little wobbly. She leaned against him for a minute to steady herself, and said, "Thanks. It was amazing." His strong arm went around her, and he gave her a little hug. He seemed pleased to have her beside him. The excitement of being with him went through her.

"Let's walk over to that service office," he said to her. With his long strides, she had to skip along to keep up with him.

"Jack, please slow down. I can't keep up with you," she said in her quiet voice.

"Sorry, I wasn't thinking," he replied slowing his pace. They walked along the paved road over to the small building. She liked walking beside him. Dressed in his spare flight jacket, she felt part of his world as a pilot. She could tell that he loved flying. *But why a helicopter?*

A guy named Pete stood up when they walked in. Jack greeted him. Pete looked over at her and said, "I see that you have a co-pilot with you today Jack."

He grinned and said, "No, she's my girlfriend." Looking over at her, he added, "ahh, I *think* she's my girlfriend. This is Gigi Sutton. This is her first flight in a chopper." Pete greeted her as she smiled and blushed at the introduction. *Yes, she'd be his girlfriend and maybe, more.*

Pete walked over to a desk and handed Jack a small box. "Here's the part. It came in last night."

She glanced at the box, "Is that what we came for? That little box."

Pete laughed, "Yes. This part has the whole lumber mill shut down until Jack flies back with it."

Pete had an invoice for the part which Jack initialed. Afterwards, he spoke up, "Hey, Jack. There's a commercial company—Chopper Solutions—inquiring about moving into the area. That company is planning to bring in three big helicopters and they have signed contracts with the forest service and the power company. They would be stiff competition for you. They want to hire a flight operations manager. I gave them your name Jack. You might want to consider it."

"Okay, thanks. I'll think about it," he replied, frowning with unease.

Afterwards, the two shook hands and Pete called out, "Nice meetin' you ma'am. Glad Jack has a pretty lady to fly with." The friendliness surprised her, for she had become part of his pilot's world.

Hand in hand, the two of them left and headed back over to his chopper. She had heard Pete's words of concern and asked, "What did Pete mean about that company?"

"It's something I need to seriously think about. But right now, let's get this part back," he replied.

The two walked back to the chopper. He placed the small box behind the pilot's seat. She shook her head, amazed at the whole flight for one part.

Then, he focused on his routine preflight check around the chopper. When he finished, he motioned for her to get in and he came around to her side of the chopper. Reaching across her again, he strapped her in and gave her the pair of headphones. She was now use to the routine and smiled at him, glad again for the close contact.

Stepping into the pilot's seat, he buckled up, placed his headphones on, and glanced over at her. "Hang on." He flipped the switches to start the engine, glancing at the gauges in front of him. The rotors whirled with a *'whaump' 'whaump' 'whaump'* as the blades overhead gathered momentum. Waiting until they were spinning at full speed, he pushed on the controls and the chopper lifted, hovering above the helipad for a few minutes before lurching forward. The chopper ran along the airstrip for a while gathering speed and then gained altitude.

He piloted the chopper again towards the pass—the distant notch in the mountains. By now, she knew what to expect and relaxed more on the return trip. She had confidence in his ability to fly this helicopter. Over the pass they went and down the other side, above the forested mountains and valleys, and across the small town, heading for Jack's place. As they approached his landing spot, she saw another vehicle parked next to the Quonset hut. He eased the chopper down and when the skids touched the ground, he cut the engines. While they waited for the blades to stop rotating, they gave each other a 'thumbs up,' slipping off their headphones. This flight had made a deep impression on her.

Jack looked at her, "Wait here. I'll be right back to help you out." A man wearing a hard hat waited by a pickup from the lumber company.

Stepping out of the chopper, he grabbed the small box from behind his seat, and walked over and handed it to the man. Speaking for a few minutes, they then shook hands and the man crawled into his pickup and drove off. Jack returned to the chopper and helped her out. She again leaned against him as she got her balance after the ride.

"Let's go in. I have some paper work to do. Maybe, you could fix us some lunch in the back," he glanced down at her and slipped his arm around her.

They entered his small office in the front side of the Quonset hut, taking off their flight jackets and hanging them up. He walked her through a door to his place in the back.

"Do you live here?" she asked, seeing the small kitchenette and bed.

"Yes. I like to be here next to my chopper. The lumber company leased the hut and land to me when I started up my business. Make yourself at home. Oh, there are some fixings in the fridge. I won't be long," he said as he turned and left.

Gigi glanced around at his small place. First, going into the kitchenette, she made a pot of coffee, put a can of soup on the stove, and fixed them a couple of sandwiches. She then went into the tiny bathroom and looked at the messy image of herself. She washed up and brushed out her hair, fluffing it up. The headphones had flattened it. She thought how easy it felt to be with Jack. They fell into a comfortable closeness, being together today. She heard him come back and quickly added red lipstick to her pale lips. Coming out of the bathroom, she saw that he stood by the coffee pot, waiting. She walked towards him as he reached out to her.

"Come here. I loved having you beside me today," he said. She felt his firm hands go to her small waist. He leaned down and gave her a kiss on the cheek. "You're the prettiest co-pilot I've ever flown with." His wide-grinned showed his friendly, teasing manner.

She laughed and softly said, "I've never flown before, so that was quite an experience."

"Really? Well, I'm going to have to fix that," he replied. Moving from her, he added, "I'm hungry. Let's eat."

They both sat down after she poured each of them a cup of coffee. Silently, they ate their lunch and drank. They chatted about their morning flight. Afterwards, she cleared the table and took the dishes over to the sink. He came up behind her. She felt his arms go around her.

He brushed his head against the side of her hair, seeking out her neck and kissing her. He whispered, "Leave them." A chill went down her spine.

She turned and stared into his eager eyes, "What?"

"How about we finish what we started on our last date. I am not sure how far you want to take this, but I promise not to hurt you. Just tell me to stop," he said, leaning down to kiss her soft lips. She felt his wet tongue, begging her to open her mouth. Lifting her arms around his neck, she breathed in his masculine scent. She opened her mouth and sought out his tongue. Mixed with the taste of coffee, they passionately kissed.

She laughed softly when he lifted her up onto the kitchen countertop. Adjusting her legs around his small waist, her heart beat fast. He gently lifted her yellow sweater, seeking her soft skin with his firm hand. She gave a little gasp. He murmured to her, "Should I stop?" She shook her head. He caressed her slowly, "I'll take it slow."

His hands moved to her lower back, pulling her body into his. He moved and kissed her neck. He whispered sweet words that sent wild thoughts through her mind. For a brief moment, she recalled Hank's rough treatment of her, but quickly, she freed her mind, giving Jack her full attention.

Calming down with a deep breath, she returned kisses to his neck where she slid her tongue out and teased the sensitive spot below his ear. Pulling his white shirt up from his khakis, he slipped his shirt off. She glared at his naked chest. Her hands ran along his bare broad chest and down to his slim waist, feeling the firm soft skin of his warm body. He moved her closer to him, looking deeply into her eyes and seeking her consent. "Should I go on?"

She whispered, "Yes, yes." He leaned slowly towards her lips and gently kissed her, tasting her sweet lips. His tongue sought out her mouth again, making her mind whirl with anticipation.

He then lifted her up, holding her close to him. They both breathed hard while he moved over to his bed, setting her down. He moved on top of her, slipping his knee between her legs. She again gasped. He whispered, "It's all right. I'll be gentle." She nodded slowly while he pulled her closer to him. He slowly kissed her, caressing and feeling her soft, smooth skin. He groaned, "Oh, my. You're too much." As he kissed her and affectionately touched her, he desired more of her.

Under her sweater, his hands caressed her breasts and she arched her back against him. His gentle love making was intense. The two lovers continued to seek out their intimate desires, nestled in his bed that late afternoon. She had forgotten all about her ex-husband, giving her full attention and body to Jack who did not disappoint. As he promised, his love was intense but gentle.

As twilight approached, the two hadn't left the bed. Outside, the chopper sat next the Quonset hut, waiting for its next flight. *RING. RING*. His phone rang several times before he reluctantly left to answer it, slipping on his pants. She rose and dressed, going into the tiny bathroom to brush her tangled hair and freshen up. She noticed her flushed face.

When he returned, she asked, "Is that another job?" stepping out of the bathroom. He nodded while he finished dressing, she added, "I need to get back to town. Do you have time to take me home?" Suddenly, she felt awkward, uneasy and unsure while she gripped her hands in front of her. *How does she move on from here? Will she see him again?*

"Yes. Hey, come here. Are you all right?" he said, seeing her hands and sensing her uneasiness.

She blushed and in a soft voice whispered, "Yes, of course. I am more than okay."

Moving closer to her, he took her in his arms and hugged her tightly, "I love being with you. You have such a sweet, loving, and calming nature about you. I want to see you again." She leaned against him, recalling his gentleness and tenderness.

"Sorry, but I have to go," he whispered, apologizing.

Together they walked into the front office. He lifted the spare flight jacket off of the coat rack. "Here. I want to give you this." Surprised, she looked up at him, thinking to refuse the jacket. But he slipped it over her shoulders and kissed her. "No. Keep it. It looks terrific on you."

He drove her into town with the two of them snuggled closely together. He told her that they might get together again on her day off.

"I'll call you," whispered Jack as he kissed her goodbye. She stepped out of his pickup and went up to her apartment, clutching the leather jacket. Her heart beat fast thinking of their morning flight and their afternoon together. She definitely looked forward to being with him again.

* * *

Gigi now lived in a dream world with her heart devoted to Jack. Her thoughts were all focused on him so much so that it was hard for her to go to work. She wanted to be with him as much as she could. He would call her whenever he had time. They talked sometimes at the end of the day. He had daily flights to make, and she had to work.

Her sister's nausea still plagued her, so Gigi started going over to her house after work instead of returning to her apartment. She helped fix dinner, took care of her nieces, and did a little housekeeping. After Tod returned home, she would eat with them and then head home.

Jack would call late and would talk about his various flights. He worked tirelessly on his chopper, maintaining it when he wasn't in the air. One night, he called unexpectantly and said to meet him at the tavern, and they'd go out to eat. He had to come into town for a few supplies. He told her that he wanted to take her flying on her day off. She said she looked forward to seeing him.

She hurried to her sister's, planning to meet Jack later. But she noticed that her nieces' dirty clothes were piling up in their hamper. With her sister not feeling well, she decided to wash a few loads. Her sister wanted to hear about Jack, so they sat and talked. After Tod came home and they had eaten, she finished folding the clean clothes. When she had finished, she left her sister's later than she had planned.

She hurried to the Dark Horse Tavern down on main street, hoping Jack would still be there. Coming into the crowded, smoke-filled bar, she saw him sitting on a stool, drinking. She worked her way through the crowd up to the bar and slipped onto a barstool next to him.

"Hi, Jack. Sorry, I'm late," she said, feeling bad.

"Hi. Where have you been? I thought that my little lady had stood me up," he said, teasing her.

"I've been at my sister's," she replied.

"How's she doing?" he asked.

"She's coming along. Have you eaten?" she replied.

"Yes, I just got back," he said. "Do you want a drink?"

"Yes, a draft beer," she replied. He ordered her a beer while he had a shot of whiskey. She added, "What did you do today?"

"I had a busload of school kids come to see my chopper. They were sure excited. I let them sit in the pilot's seat," he replied. "I hope at least one of them was inspired to be a pilot, but you never know about kids." He continued to talk about his day. He seemed to be in high spirits.

She drank her cold beer, smoked a cigarette, and asked, "Do you like children?"

"Of course. Those school kids were impressed with my chopper," he repeated.

"Do you ever want a family?" she asked, wanting to know his view.

"Yes, any man wants a family once he's settled down," he answered.

Her heart skipped a beat at his answer. He ordered another shot of whiskey. After another beer, she wanted to leave, but he wanted to stay and dance. While the jukebox played, he held her close while their bodies swayed together. He ordered more shots until he started to slur his words. The hours slipped by until it was getting late, close to midnight.

"I need to go," she finally said with her head buzzing.

"I'm too drunk to drive back. Will you let me crash at your place tonight?" he asked, standing up and holding onto the bar.

She hesitated for a second, "Yes. Let's go," she said, slipping her arm around his waist and he leaned against her. They left the bar and shuffled up the back stairs. After she opened the door, he stumbled into her apartment and plopped down on her small couch.

"Come here, my little lady. Wrap those long legs around me. I want to kiss you," he said. She sat down while his arms pulled her into a drunken kiss. He smelled like a whiskey bottle.

"You're drunk. Relax. It's late," she said, pushing him gently away.

"That's right, love. I'm too drunk to be of any use to you tonight," he sounded apologetic. He leaned back and closed his eyes. She smiled at the thought.

"Come on. Let's get you ready for bed," she said.

Slowly rising, he stumbled towards her bed across the room. She helped him take off his flight jacket as he managed to kick off his shoes, slip out of his khakis, and pull off his shirt. He crawled under the covers, rolling to the far side of the bed against the wall. He mumbled how much he liked her. Within minutes, he had fallen asleep.

She stood looking down at the blanketed-form of his body in her bed. He had called her 'love.' *Did he mean it?* She had never seen him this drunk before. At least, he was a teddy bear and not like her ex-husband. She shuddered at the dark image of how a drunk Hank had treated her.

Shaking off those bad memories, she undressed, slipped on her robe, and went into the bathroom to take a warm bath. She had experienced a busy day and now, the exhaustion had hit her. Slipping into the warm bath water, she leaned back, submerging herself up to her chin. The liquor from the beer had made her head spin. She relaxed, soaking in the warmth. She heard Jack call her name.

"I'm taking a bath. I'll be out in a little while," she said, raising her voice, but she didn't think he could hear her. After scrubbing, she rose, dried off, and slipped on her robe. Coming out of the bathroom, she went over to her dresser, lifted out a nightgown, and slipped it on. Moving towards the narrow bed, she noticed that there was only a little room left on the bed, but she slipped under the covers, instantly feeling his warm body under the sheets. His heavy arm came around her and he pulled her into him, curling himself around her. With her back to him, she snuggled closely up to him.

"Mmmmm, there you are, Gigi. Good night, love," he muttered, half asleep.

She rested next to him but couldn't sleep. There it was again—he called her 'love.' His breath tickled her neck. Her body throbbed with his firm, warm arm around her waist. The clock in the kitchenette ticked away the minutes. Finally an hour later, she relaxed enough that she fell into a deep sleep.

* * *

In the early dawn, she woke up and felt him crawling over her slowly. She murmured 'oh' and he whispered that he'd fix breakfast. She had the day off, so she covered her head with the covers, complaining that she wanted to sleep. As she laid there half asleep and half awake, she heard Jack taking a shower. He was humming, making a lot of noise. Her mouth was so dry that her tongue stuck to her lips. She rose, slipped on her robe, went over to the sink, and drank a glass of water. The coffee had finished brewing, so she poured herself a cup and sat down at the table, trying to shake off the grogginess.

Jack came out of the bathroom, dressed quickly, and said, "Good morning. Thanks for letting me crash here last night. Like I said, I'll make breakfast."

He sounded in good spirits despite his drunken state last night. While he made breakfast, she glanced at him with his slightly wet hair. He looked handsome with his slim build and full chest. She sipped her coffee. Soon, breakfast was spread out in front of her. She thanked him for cooking while they quietly ate their meal.

"You said that today is your day off, right?" he asked. She nodded. He added, "Come spend the day with me. I'll take you flying. I'll even buy some steaks for dinner tonight at my place. What do you say?"

"Sounds great. I'll give my sister a call and let her know. She's going in today to see the doctor. I hope he gives her something for her nausea," she said.

"I'll be back here in half of an hour. I have to make a stop at the hardware store. I need a few supplies," he said. Slipping on his flight jacket, he left.

Gigi got ready, made the bed, washed the dishes, and called Gina. She told her sister that she'd be at Jack's and to let her know about her doctor's visit. When Jack pulled up into the back parking lot, she slipped on her flight jacket, smelling the leather, and left her apartment. She came down the stairs and met him coming into the back door.

"Are you ready?" he said as they walked out to his dark green pickup. He looked up at the sky, "It looks a little grey. I'll have to check with the weather service anyway." After driving to his place and parking next to his Quonset hut, they went into the small front office.

Jack said, "I'm going to call in for the weather." He picked up the phone while she took the paper sack back to his kitchenette, slipping the steaks into the fridge.

Moving back to the office, she heard him hang up on the phone and said, "Well, there's no flying today. They say there are severe thunder storms on the way and it's likely all aircraft will be grounded. We'll have to just hang out around here." He smiled with a knowing glint in his eyes.

A few minutes later, the office door swung opened, and Dr. Carter walked in and said, "Jack, do you know the location of the Wilks' summer cabin?"

"Yes. I do. What about it?" he replied.

"I've been treating their young boy for a chronic condition for a number of years. I received a message that the boy passed out for almost an hour. I need you to fly me up there, so I can examine him," said Carter.

"The weather guys say we have a severe thunderstorm on the way. Hell, by now they probably have grounded all aircraft." He paused, "But I am going to get that sick kid."

"I'm going with you," replied Carter.

"You and I flew together in Korea, and you know better than that. We can't have you isolated if I have to set that chopper down in the middle of nowhere due to weather. I'll bring the kid here," he said.

"It's a plan. I'll be waiting here," agreed Carter.

Gigi stood up, looking puzzled and noticed the direct exchange of words between the two men. Jack grabbed a small flight bag and purposefully strode out the door.

Dr. Carter turned towards her and greeted her, "Oh, hi Gigi."

They both moved over to the little window watching Jack get ready to take off. Neither spoke, waiting. Soon they heard the *'whaump' 'whaump' 'whaump'* of the blades. The helicopter made a slow climb as it headed towards the mountains. They watched it disappear until it was only a small dot. Her heart fluttered and she gave a sigh of concern.

After a moment of silence, she heard Carter ask, "Is there any hot coffee?"

She nodded and replied, "I'll make us some."

A short time later, the telephone rang. Carter pointed and said in an abrupt commanding loud voice, "Don't touch that phone. They can see him on radar now, and they probably want to know what's going on. Whatever you do, do not answer the telephone."

"Why not?" she asked.

"Because Jack's going to be in a world of trouble for making this flight," he responded.

About forty-five minutes later, they heard the approaching helicopter with its *'whaump' 'whaump' 'whaump'* of the blades. Jack eased the chopper down on the ground just as the thunder storm broke over Riverside. Carter hurried out to his car, grabbed his black medical bag, and ran out bent low to the pad, checking on the young boy before the rotors had even stopped. He and Jack worked as a team to get the young blanket-wrapped boy into the doctor's car. They gave each other a 'thumps up' and Dr. Carter drove off.

Jack came into the office with a wide-grin on his face. She ran to him, throwing her arms around his waist and hugging him.

"You had me so scared. Why did you do it?" she asked with tears spilling from her eyes.

He glanced down at her, "Hey, hey. Are those tears for me?" He wiped them from her cheeks with his thumbs as he held her head between his hands. "It's all right. I'm fine. The boy is really sick, but Doc says he's going to be okay."

The telephone started ringing. She said, "Doc said not to answer it."

He chuckled and picked up the phone, "Jack East here. Not in this weather. No... no... I've been having lunch with my little lady. Okay, whatever you say. Bye."

"What's that all about?" she asked.

"Well, he says they saw me on radar. But I am not admitting to it. He threatened that if I ever pulled a stunt like that again, he'd see to it that my pilot's license is revoked." He paused, "Looks like I'm going to get away with it this time. I think they know about the sick kid."

He didn't seem upset about it. "Aren't you concerned?" she asked, realizing the risk that he had taken.

"Not really. I've contacted Chopper Solutions last week and told them that I would take that position of flight operations manager. They're bringing in three big choppers. We've been negotiating with the lumber company for them to take over this lease. It's all working out perfectly. It'll mean a more stable and secure income year round," he explained.

He glanced into her surprised eyes, and she asked, "What about your old chopper?"

"Oh, I'm going to keep it. We can make you the permanent co-pilot and we can enjoy it together," he replied with a sparkle in his blue eyes.

"What do you mean?" she asked.

He rose and moved close to her. With a longing look on his face and a desirous glint in his eyes, he held her hands. "Let's get married," he replied, eagerly waiting and squeezing her hands tightly.

His unexpected words took her breath away, and for a moment, she thought: a life with Jack would be exciting and intense, and his passionate love would be strong and gentle. She whispered an inaudible 'yes' in her soft voice.

He leaned down, "Is that a 'yes' you whispered?" he said in his deep voice. Speechless, she nodded. Embracing her with his strong arms, he gave her a fierce kiss, sealing their future.

Anna's Path

The predawn grey eastern sky turned a bright pink tinged with orange. North of the mountain town of Riverside, the Norsemen Ranch sat in a long valley with the blue, forested mountains surrounding it. The early summer song birds were chirping and tweeting their musical sounds. They were the day's alarm clock to the world, announcing another day for those who slept.

The widow Anna (Hartman) Severson rose from her bed, slipped on her clothes, and walked down the hall to her sons' bedroom. Cade, Jr stood in his crib, wet and crying for her to get him up. "Momma," he cried. Lifting him up out of the crib, she wrapped an arm around him. On the other side of the small bedroom, her oldest son Andy turned over in his bed and covered up his head with his pillow. The baby was too noisy for him. Since they had moved into the old ranch house, the two boys had bunked together. Andy still hadn't adjusted to having his baby brother sleeping in the same room.

"Andy, you have to get up and get dressed. You have a big day ahead of you, helping with the cattle," said Anna while she took off the baby's wet pajamas, changed his diaper, and dressed him with a pair of bib overalls. Her other two children, the girls, Heidi, now seven-years-old and Bridget four, were getting up in the other small bedroom. Anna could hear the girls talking about what they wanted to do that day. The children were eager to explore the new ranch since they had moved there.

Her children had been her daily routine, taking care of them had occupied her mind. The loss of her husband still hung around the edges of her thoughts. But each day, each month, the love and care of her children had kept her from collapsing into the sorrowful dark world of grief. Only at night, alone in her bed, did her grief-stricken heart send her into tears.

For many months after her husband's tragic death, she had mourned. Night after night until she finally had cried herself out. Over a year had passed without her husband. She now only felt the emptiness of her bed, controlling her thoughts towards her children until sleep overtook her. Like this morning, the children were there to pull her forward into each day.

From the kitchen, the sounds of her mother-in-law Ingrid getting breakfast ready for the family could be heard. The welcoming smells of food hurried everyone to get up and ready for the day. Anna came into the kitchen and took a bottle of milk from the fridge. As she warmed it up in a pan of water on the stove, she glanced at Ingrid and said, "Morn." Ingrid responded by coming over and giving the baby a kiss on the cheek, "Morning to you both."

Anna had lived with the Seversons for nearly nine years now. Her life with Caden had been short—just eight years. He had been mauled and killed by a grizzly up in the mountains. After his tragic death, Hans and Ingrid had supported her and the children. They had stepped in as loving and caring grandparents from the start.

Years ago, Anna's own parents Walter and Abigail Hartman had fled Germany in 1935. Her father had feared that his Jewish wife would be persecuted. After coming to America, they had traveled far into Wyoming where in 1937, Anna, their only child, had been born here in Riverside. Her father had found a job at the lumber mill. He worked hard and long hours, always volunteering for any overtime work. Her beautiful mother stayed at home, keeping the house and raising her.

Anna had been raised in a quiet, orderly home. They lived meagerly, but her parents taught her to be a proud individual. Growing up, her mother had given her chores and had expected much from her. At school, Anna had no problem with her school work, but socially she never found a close friend. She had been a gangly girl and had been teased by her grade school classmates.

Not until she became a junior in high school did she blossom into this young woman who would turn guys' heads. She herself had never felt beautiful for her nose was too long, and her ears were too small. In high school, the popular and handsome Caden had noticed her. Even though he had often spoken to her at school, they never dated until the night of their graduation. And both of them in a drunken state had made love; she became pregnant that night in the backseat of his car with the full moon lighting the sky. Her unexpected pregnancy had been an embarrassing situation for an unmarried young girl.

When she discovered her condition, her parents were shocked and astounded with the terrible news. Her mother wanted to send her away. But her father had resisted and had talked her mother into being more sensible and reasonable with their only daughter. They finally had invited Caden over one evening. Anna had been horrified at what the outcome would be. But when they confronted the surprised Caden, he had immediately taken responsibility. Sitting next to her on their couch, he had turned to her and had said, "Will you marry me Anna?" She nodded and quietly said, "Yes." *What else could she say being pregnant and unmarried?*

Both parents on both sides had been happy for them. They were married that fall in a quiet church wedding. She then had moved into their big log house at the Battle Axe Ranch and had started her life as a wife and an expectant mother.

For a brief period of time, she had faced the wrath of the town's people when she married into the Severson's well-established ranching family. The rumor circulated that she had trapped the popular, good-looking Caden into marriage.

Caring deeply for her and their children, Caden had been a good husband. They were fond of each other, but not in love. The children had kept them together. Like his father, Caden worked hard every day, shouldering the responsibility of the ranch.

Finally, after Anna had married and had the three children, her parents had returned to Germany. In the late '50's, her parents began communicating with their relatives in Europe. They became aware of several elderly family members who needed assistance. So, in 1960, they returned to take care of the old family members.

A year later, Anna had the difficult task of calling them overseas and informing them about her husband's death. They were both shocked and wondered how she and the children were doing. Before her husband's death she had written them regularly. But afterwards, she didn't write them for a long time. *What would she say to them?* She had been consumed by his death that she would sound like a wailing widow. No, but she had sent them pictures of the children.

She missed her parents but knew that they had responsibilities back in their homeland. They had never seen her fourth child. Her mother would have called him her *liebes kindlein* (sweet baby), like she did when each of the other grandchildren were born. Her children had known their grandparents—their Oma and Opa, and after they had moved away, they eagerly waited for their letters

239

from Germany. Andy and Heidi remembered them more than little Bridget.

Her baby Cade squirmed, reaching out for his bottle and said, "Ba, ba." His baby words prompted her to check the milk which was ready.

"Here is your bottle," she said, sitting down at the kitchen table. She held him in her arms while he drank. Her nearly nine-month old baby had grown so big. He had been a happy baby with golden locks and bright blue eyes. Fate had taken her husband away before he knew of her pregnancy. Widowed, she now faced raising her four children without a father. Sadness struck her sitting at the table, glancing around at the children while they came in for breakfast.

Her children were growing up so fast. Andy, nearly nine-years-old, planned on working alongside his grandfather Hans this summer who had hired their foreman Chuck Nubbin and a summer hand Tom Fletcher. Her son had latched onto Hans after his father had been killed. For over a year now, his grandfather had been happy to have his grandson beside him, teaching him the ranching world that he knew so well.

Hans, the silver-headed nearly seventy-year-old grandfather, came into the kitchen with a bucket of milk after milking their new dairy cow Magic. Her daughter Heidi had named the cow. Heidi lived in the world of fantasy with fairies and magical spirits, consuming library books about them.

Hans then walked around giving each of his grandchildren a morning hug and a kiss, and a little tickle. He caressed Cade's golden locks, smiling and laughing. He called them his little 'cowpunchers.' Looking around, he said, "Andy I want you to start gettin' up and milkin' Magic. It's goin' to be your job for the summer."

Andy looked surprised at his grandfather, "Sure I'll do it."

Heidi spoke up, "Grandpa can I held milk Magic too? I want to learn."

"Okay. But this isn't make-believe, Heidi. It's serious. The cow has to be milked every mornin'. And, just as a reminder, you both are responsible for takin' care of your fillies. Andy, start trainin' Jewels in the corral a little each day. Heidi, Moonbeam needs to be fed her grain each day. Don't forget to groom your horses, checkin' them for any problems. Get to know your horses well. Pay attention to their mannerisms," said Hans. Andy and Heidi smiled at each other, pleased that they had important responsibilities for the summer. Heidi followed her brother around since she was a young child. What he did, she followed.

Little Bridget spoke up, "And I'm going to get a puppy to take care of, aren't I Grandpa?" Hans nodded at her, knowing that she didn't want to be left out.

"Yes, the puppy will be a good addition to our ranch," he replied, thinking of the border collie. He would like to train the collie to work with the cattle.

While Hans drank another cup of coffee, he talked more to the children about their chores and their important responsibilities to their ranch.

Coming through the back door, Chuck, their foreman, walked into the kitchen for breakfast. He greeted everyone "Good mornin'." He sat down, quietly and ate his breakfast, listening to Hans and his plans for the day.

Chuck had joined Hans in running their new Norsemen Ranch. Hans had depended heavily on Chuck. A tall, slender man with black curly hair and dark brown eyes, had a quiet, confident nature about him. Anna had admired him, and they had gone out together on a few casual lunch dates. They had a common past that bound them close as friends.

Before coming here, he had worked for Hans for four years before at the Battle Axe Ranch and had worked beside Anna's husband. When Caden had been mauled, Chuck had brought him down from the mountains, torn and bleeding. He had been beside the Severson's during that tragic day.

Clearing her thoughts, she rose and filled their cups with more coffee. The men continued to talk about the cattle. Hans had a particular way of doing things. He had always been a difficult man to work for, demanding the best, and sometimes, unreasonable perfection from everyone on the ranch. Anna had recently been worried that starting this new ranch would be too much for her in-laws. They were both approaching their seventies. Recently, she had suggested that Ingrid take a nap with the children in the afternoon for her mother-in-law seemed to wear out as each day progressed.

Sitting her son into his high chair and slipping on a bib, Anna fed him his morning cereal while the men talked about the work ahead of them. Hans had purchased their twenty-five head of cattle and needed to get them all settled in. He had also bought ten heifers from Brad Johnson which were arriving today. She hoped that Andy wouldn't be in the way. He still was too young to be much help. But Hans and Chuck had been giving the boy small tasks in helping them. Hans was happy to see his grandson eager and willing to help wherever he could on the ranch.

The men finally rose from the kitchen table and left with Andy following behind them. Anna said to her son, "Be careful. Don't get hurt. Follow your grandpa's instructions."

Although Hans had been cautious about Andy's safety around the horses and cattle, she still worried. A broken leg or arm. A blow to the head. Anything could happen when working on a ranch. She could imagine all kinds of injuries for her oldest son.

After breakfast, her two girls, Heidi and Bridget, wanted to play in the backyard of the ranch house on the swing that Hans had hung up on the old tree. After eating a baby jar of bananas, Cade wanted to get down and play. The girls wanted him to come out with them and play with his toy truck, his little pail, and shovel in a patch of dirt. Anna carried him out to his toys, set him down, and watched him eagerly start to play. She left Heidi in charge of keeping an eye on him, for the baby tended to curiously crawl away, exploring his new little world.

Coming back into the kitchen, she sat down drinking a second cup of morning tea. Ingrid had been telling her of their visit to Hadley where their fourth daughter Sonja just had their thirteenth grandchild—another grandson. Their visit had been short, but Ingrid had been able to help her daughter for a few days. Their new grandson looked like Sonja's husband Jake.

Suddenly, a scream split the quiet morning air. Then with a bang of the back door, little Bridget came running in, hollering and crying, "Mommy, mommy. Cade fell down and he's got blood all over him."

Anna's heart jumped into her mouth when she first heard the scream. Hurrying out the back door, she rushed towards her baby. Heidi held the sobbing and bleeding Cade, trying to comfort him. They sat on the ground next to his toy truck.

"What happened" asked Anna, picking up little Cade and looking desperately to find his injury. Under his chin, an ugly cut with blood gushing out took her breath away. Her head swooned a little, seeing the blood and her little son crying and injured. She needed to get him into the house and stop the bleeding. Her mind raced ahead: this was Wednesday, so Dr. Carter would be in town at his medical office.

"Oh, mommy. He fell on his truck," replied Heidi, starting to cry. "I'm sorry mommy. I'm sorry. I was pushing Bridget on the swing."

"Heidi, it's not your fault. Okay? Be a brave little girl and give mommy a hand. Come on. Quickly," she said, comforting her daughter with her words.

Holding Cade close to her, she headed towards the back door. Inside, Ingrid helped stop the bleeding and cleaned the wound while Anna called the doctor's office. His nurse Alice said to bring her son right in and Dr. Carter would work her in between his appointments.

Together with Ingrid's help, they manage to quiet Cade down and to pack his diaper bag with a bottle of juice. Ingrid noticed that Bridget was still upset, so she picked her up and held her in her lap at the kitchen table.

While holding the baby in her arms, Anna dug in the cookie jar for a few cookies for the children. Giving one to Bridget, she gave her a quick hug, and said, "Be a good girl for Grandma. I'm taking your brother to the doctor's." She gave the baby and Heidi each a cookie.

"Did Cade get a bad ouchie?" asked little Bridget.

"Yes, but he'll be all right," she said. Turning, she grabbed Heidi's hand. "Let's go. You can hold the baby in the car. Keep his hands away from his chin. Keep this gauze on his cut. Let's hurry."

"Wait," said Ingrid, pulling a piece of paper from her apron pocket. "After you're finished at the doctor's office, stop by the General Store and pick up this list of groceries."

"What? I can't," said Anna, desperately wanting to leave.

"Yes you can. Listen, we're short of supplies in the pantry. I've called this order in and it's ready. I was planning on going in tomorrow, but you can stop on your way back. Of course, take care of Cade first. The doc will stitch up that little cut and he'll be fine," explained Ingrid.

"Are you sure the order is ready?" she asked.

"Yes. With us living farther out from town, we can't waste a trip," she replied. Anna nodded, quickly took the list from Ingrid, and left with Cade and Heidi. Her mother-in-law had always been a strong ranch woman—a model for her to follow. A caring, sturdy woman organized, steadfast, and dedicated.

The long drive into town had been torturous for Anna. She shook inside and her heart beat fast while she drove. Parking in front of the doctor's office, she hurriedly walked around and opened the car door, lifting Cade into her arms. He had munched on his cookie and seemed fine, except for the gauze under his chin. Heidi followed her into the doctor's office, carrying the diaper bag. They had to wait for a short time.

In the little examining room, Dr. Carter (Denny), dressed in a white lab jacket with a stethoscope around his neck and wearing his jeans and cowboy boots, came in. Here stood the good-looking man who was interested in her. But today, as a doctor, he took only a moment to nod and smile at her but turned and focused on the baby Cade whose shirt had dried blood down the front. Anna was so thankful to see him while she quickly explained how the baby had fallen on his metal truck and cut his chin.

Slipping off the gauze, Dr. Carter examined the jagged cut under the chin and said, "Hi little buddy. Looks like a bad cut there. We need to stitch that up."

While he slipped on some surgical gloves, he indicated for Anna to put the baby on the examining table. His nurse Alice came in with a tray of medical instruments. Cade suddenly became frightened at seeing all the strangers and started to cry, calling out to her. "Momma...momma," he sobbed while she placed him on the table.

"Shhhhhh," she said to her son. "You'll be fine."

Anna held her son while the doctor quickly numbed his chin with a needle. Cade cried out more, and she had to hold his little arms down, softly talking to him. "It'll be all right son. Mommy's here."

While Dr. Carter carefully stitched the jagged cut, he concentrated on her son's little chin. Finally, he said, "There.

We're all done. Now, I have a sucker for a brave little guy like you."

He turned and selected a red sucker from a drawer. Unwrapping it, he gave him the sucker, and her son quickly grabbed it with his little chubby fingers and popped it into his mouth with tears streaking down his little red cheeks.

Anna smoothed his son's tousled blonde hair, affectionately touching his head. She noticed the tiny black stitches under her son's chin. The doctor then placed a bandage across the cut. Little Cade sat up, sucking on the sweet candy.

Anna sighed a breath of relief that the frightening ordeal was over. Smiling at him, she said, "Thank you."

While the baby sat quietly there, Anna slipped off his bloody shirt. Heidi pulled out a clean shirt from his diaper bag, handing it to her mom. She carefully, between keeping his sucker in his hand and avoiding his injured chin, slipped on a clean shirt.

"He'll be fine. Just to be safe, we need to give him a tetanus shot," he said. He noticed Heidi who had helped her mom. She sat wide-eyed and concerned. "Would you like a sucker too?" She nodded and he handed her a green one from the drawer.

"What do you say?" said Anna.

"Thank you, Dr. Carter," replied Heidi, now smiling at him.

The nurse had returned with a prepared needle for his tetanus shot. Her son screamed the loudest as the nurse gave him the shot in his thigh. The sucker fell from his fingers onto the table. Tears again streamed down his face as Anna picked him up and held him close to her, quieting him. She handed him his sucker, but he turned his head away, crying loudly against her shoulder. She rubbed his back and quietly said, "Shhhhh. It's all right."

"How are you doing?" asked Dr. Carter, turning his attention to her.

"I'm okay. A little frazzled. Thank you again for seeing us today."

"I'm glad I was here. Take care of the cut and keep a bandage on it. The stitches need to be kept clean and dry. Give him a baby aspirin if he's fussy or has a fever from the shot. Call us if he has any serious reactions," he said. "I'll take out the stitches next week when I come up." After he rose, they moved out of the examining room. "By the way, I'm driving out to your ranch tomorrow," he added.

"Why?" she asked, surprised.

He said quietly to her, "Hans said I could pasture my stallion there. He's too young to be corralled downtown. While I'm there, I can check on Cade." He paused, glancing at her, "I'd like to see you, too."

"Oh," she replied quietly to him. She felt his warm hand on her lower back while they walked out of the room. He affectionately caressed her back. Hearing his calm voice and feeling his tender touch, she wanted to collapse into his arms, seeking comfort, but not here in his office. She had to remain strong.

Standing in the hall, Jack East looked at both of them and said, "Hi Doc. Hi Anna." He recalled meeting the widow. Jack was the next patient.

Dr. Carter motioned for Jack to come into the examining room. "What seems to be the problem?" he asked his old military buddy.

"I have a rash on my arm. Thought you might have something for it," replied Jack, rolling up his sleeve.

The doctor looked over the arm and nodded, "I'll write a prescription for some lotion that will clear that up." Taking out his prescription tablet, he scribbled on it and handed a slip of paper to Jack.

"I'm looking forward to our fishing trip," said his friend.

"Me too. I need a little break," he said. They had planned an overnight fishing trip into the mountains.

"By the way, why are you pasturing your horse at the Norsemen Ranch instead of at your family's ranch?" asked Jack with a puzzled look.

Lowering his head and smiling to himself, he replied, "Hans suggested that I pasture my horse at his ranch so it would be easier to go horseback riding with Anna." Raising his eyebrows, he gave his buddy a look that told him the real reason—his interest in the widow.

Jack nodded, rolled down his sleeve, rose to leave and said, "Thanks, Doc. I'll get this filled at the drug store." He turned at the door with his wide grin and signaled him with his thumbs up, "That's a good decision to pasture your horse there." Jack walked into the small waiting room as the widow with her two children were leaving.

Anna left the doctor's office, put the children in the car, and drove down to the General Store. She left Heidi in the car, holding and feeding the baby. With his little red cheeks, the baby eagerly sucked on his bottle. Exhausted after the ordeal, he had settled down into his sister's arms and closed his eyes, drinking down his juice.

Her daughter seemed so young to be holding her baby brother, but Heidi had developed a motherly mindset toward the baby right from the start. Even though she was so young, she seemed much older.

Anna hurried into the store and swiftly walked down the grocery aisles, picking up the items on Ingrid's list. After a short time, she returned to the car with two sacks of groceries and a young boy who was bringing out their five cases of canned goods on a utility dolly. She had returned to open up the car's trunk as the boy filled it up. She gave him a quarter and thanked him for his help.

While Anna drove out of town, she glanced once at her youngest son. This little accident with him had frighten her to the core. An accident like this reminded her that her children's lives could be taken away from her just like her husband's. As a widow of four children, she suddenly felt fearful of her future. She couldn't imagine losing one of them.

Making the turn to the Norsemen Ranch, she recalled the words that Denny said to her as she left the office today. Her mind whirled with anticipation at the thought of seeing him tomorrow.

Thinking about their past, the two had known each other for a long time, going to the same school but different classes. Older, Denny Carter had grown up on the Double D Ranch but had left to pursue a different life than ranching—the Army and later, medical school. After many years, he had returned to Winston, setting up a medical practice there. Once a week, he traveled to the small office here in Riverside. He also made occasional visits to the nearby Indian reservation from time to time.

As her physician, he had treated her dying husband at the hospital in Winston, and he had delivered her baby. Today, he had stitched up her baby's chin. Denny had been there at critical times of her life and had been a definite comfort to her.

She thought of his touch today which reminded her of their recent dates together. Even though they had known each other for a long time, they had just started dating after the Grady's spring wedding reception at the Dark Horse Tavern. Denny, a nice-looking doctor with brown eyes, light brown hair with greying temples, had been drawn to her. They had danced and talked. He had a calm, tender attraction towards her. After a few dates though, she realized that he had been captivated by her. After an afternoon ride up to Skyline, he had even declared his love: *"I love you, Anna. You're in my thoughts when I wake and when I go to bed. I dream about us. We could build a life together with the children."* His declaration of love took her by surprise. Those tender words filled her heart with hope for the future. But she hadn't been ready to have a relationship just yet; she needed time. She would see Denny tomorrow, but right now, she had to focus on getting back to her daily ranch chores and her children.

* * *

After getting back to the ranch, both grandparents and the other children were concerned about Cade's accident. The baby soaked up all the attention, clinging tightly to her. But after eating his lunch, he fell asleep, snuggled in his crib wrapped in his blue blanket and holding his little ragged teddy bear.

Unpacking the canned goods, Ingrid restocked the pantry and suggested mixing a batch of cookies with the girls. Anna decided to plant some of their vegetable garden. Soon after they had moved there, Hans had plowed a large garden plot. She had taken charge of planting the garden while Ingrid watched the children. Earlier that month, she had planted potatoes, but that afternoon, she decided to plant another row or two of beets, carrots, onions, and squash.

She badly needed the time to herself. Coming back from the barn with a hoe, she stood for a moment, scanning the dark, forested blue mountains. The stunning view of the green valley and the Norsemen Ranch refreshed, strengthened, and invigorated her. She breathed in the fresh air, smelling the faint scent of rain and noticed that there were dark clouds coming from the north. Rain would be here later. Glancing at the ranch house, she saw in the kitchen window, her two daughters with their grandma making cookies.

She started working the plowed ground to form a couple of rows. Her lower back muscles felt the strain of hoeing. She then bent down and started to plant the seeds, slowly covering them with the dark soil.

Anna hoped that this move here to the Norseman Ranch would be her last move. Nothing had been easy these last three months. It had been unsettling for all of them. Those few months living in Riverside were disappointing. After applying for several jobs, she had come up with nothing. She didn't understand why no one would hire her. She thought that the businesses must felt that being a mother with four children didn't qualify her for a job. *How ridiculous.*

While living in the little rental house, she had slept on a rollaway bed which had been lumpy and uncomfortable; thus, she had lost sleep. She could not stand the ever-sounding noises with the main highway coming right through town, and the smell and noise of the vehicles had filled the air. At night, the gagging smell of the burning garbage barrels in the alleys had risen up with the smoke. She gladly had packed her belongings and with her children had moved out to their new Norsemen Ranch. She and the children liked living on a ranch much more than living in town.

In this old ranch house, she now slept in her own bed and in her own bedroom. She had separated the children—the boys and the girls each in their own rooms. The quiet nights were filled with the sounds of the croaking frogs and an occasional hoot of a night owl. In the dark black sky, the stars twinkled more brightly here on the ranch away from the town's lights. A fresh, cool breeze floated through her opened window at night.

While she planted the vegetable seeds, the wind picked up ahead of the dark rain clouds descending into the valley. Anna felt the gusts against her face, sending a few loose tendrils of hair into her eyes. She glanced up at the old windmill beside the barn spinning fast. She finished planting, picked up the garden hoe, and headed toward the old barn.

Stepping into the barn, she noticed that Heidi was bringing her filly Moonbeam in to groom her. The filly was young and frisky, giving her daughter some trouble. After years at the Battle Axe Ranch, her husband had taught Anna how to handle the horses. She headed over to the filly, taking hold of the rope halter, placing her hand on the young filly's muzzle.

Murmuring to the filly, she said, "Hey, Moonbeam. Quiet down while Heidi brushes you. Quiet down." Working together, the filly settled down while Heidi brushed her neck, her mane, and her body. A bright sudden flash followed by the thunder overhead made Moonbeam stepped back, neighing with her little ears moving back and forth hearing the thunder. Her big brown eyes rolled in fright.

"Let's put her in one of the stalls until the storm passes," suggested Anna.

"Okay. I'll get her some grain," replied Heidi.

Anna led the filly into the stall, closing the half-door, all the while talking to her. Heidi brought over a bucket with the grain. Moonbeam eagerly put her muzzle into the bucket and munched on the grain. Another flash and thunder clapped overhead. The filly's head rose, and her ears twitched. Snorting, she tossed her mane.

"Let's make a dash for the house," said Anna.

They ran together, holding each other's hand while the big rain drops started to fall all around them. The rain pelted their heads, faces, and bodies. Slightly drenched with rain, they came into the back door, breathing hard. They kicked off their muddy shoes to dry and to clean them later. Ingrid had watched them running from the barn and met them with towels from the linen closet in the hall to dry the two of them off.

"My word. You both got wet," she said, rubbing her granddaughter's hair with a towel.

"Thanks Grandma," said Heidi. "I brushed Moonbeam and gave her some grain. She doesn't like the storm."

"We left her in the barn until the rain passes," added Anna, drying her face and arms. She shivered a little. "I planted another two rows in the garden. I will finish tomorrow." Bridget came into the kitchen, carrying her doll that she had been playing with in her bedroom.

"Come. Let's have a cup of tea Anna. I'll fix you girls a cup of hot chocolate. We can have a few of our cookies," said Ingrid, moving toward the stove to put the kettle on.

The rain storm continued overhead with lightning and thunder. Anna went down the hall to check on the baby. Tiptoeing quietly into the boys' bedroom, she looked down at him while he slept in his crib. He looked flushed to her. When he woke, she would check his temperature. She returned to the kitchen.

After Ingrid had prepared their tea and hot chocolate, all of them sat down at the kitchen table, listening to the rain hitting the roof above them. After finishing their snack, the girls' droopy eyes told her that they were ready for their naps. She also encouraged Ingrid to take one. Walking down the hall to their bedroom, they laid down. Anna slipped a knitted cover over each of them, giving them a quick kiss. The girls usually took their naps right after lunch, but today had been an unusual day.

Anna walked over to the boys' room, glancing into the crib where she saw that Cade was sitting up in his crib. She headed to the bathroom, opened the medicine cabinet, and picked up their thermometer. Going back to the crib, she spoke soothing words of comfort to Cade, who needed to be changed. She took time to check his temperature. He didn't like it, but she tickled his tummy. Afterwards, she noted that he had a slight temperature. His thigh was red, inflamed, and swollen a little. He wanted up, holding out his chubby fingers to her. After changing his diaper and slipping on his bib overalls, she lifted him into her arms. Walking back to the bathroom, she got the bottle of baby aspirin out.

In the kitchen, she set him down into his highchair and gave him a graham cracker for him to nibble on. Fixing him a cup of juice with a crushed baby aspirin in it, she handed him a covered cup. He eagerly drank his juice. She opened a baby jar of peaches and fed him the snack. He babbled away with his baby talk while she spoke to him about their trip to town and his doctor's visit. She noticed that the bandage was still there. She carefully washed his face and hands with a cloth, cleaning away the crumbs and peaches.

Cade then wanted down to play. When they first moved to the ranch, Grandma Ingrid had emptied a bottom drawer in the kitchen for the baby to play with some of his toys and an old wooden spoon. He would spend hours playing there where they could keep an eye on him. She lifted him up and put him down while he eagerly crawled to the bottom drawer and began to play, smiling and giggling.

While he played, Anna busied herself with getting dinner started. Walking into the pantry, she checked on the seed packets left to plant tomorrow-- cucumbers, peas, and green beans. She had a pack of sunflower seeds that her daughters could plant. This fall, Ingrid would want to put up jars of pickles and of beets. Her mother-in-law had taught her so much about running the ranch house that she said a small prayer thanking her for the good fortune.

Thinking of the freezer and their meat supply, Hans had always hunted elk every fall. They had butchered their old milk cow, so they had half of a beef left.

Anna fixed a meat loaf, washed and wrapped the potatoes in foil, and turned on the oven. Ingrid came into the kitchen wanting to help, but she told her to sit down and have another cup of tea. She slipped the dinner into the oven. Glancing out the window, she noticed that the rain storm had passed, leaving the dark ground soaking wet with puddles in the low spots.

"Are you feeling all right?" asked Anna. Her mother-in-law had looked worn out and she worried about her.

"I'm just tired," replied Ingrid, fixing herself a cup of tea.

"Maybe, you should go see the doctor," she suggested.

"Oh, nothing is wrong with me that sleep won't fix," replied Ingrid, shrugging off the suggestion. "But, perhaps, I should go in."

"Yes, that's right. We've made an appointment for the baby next week. Come with us and talk to the doctor. He can take a few minutes to check you over," she said.

"Okay, but don't make a fuss. Do you hear? Don't fuss over me," warned Ingrid sipping her tea.

Anna glanced at her mother-in-law while she drank her tea. Ingrid's light brown hair had turned grey over the years. Her worn-out face had deep wrinkles around the corners of her eyes and mouth. Anna knew below the surface was a determined, resilient, and strong woman who raised her four daughters and one son. The loss of her son had saddened her, and she had kept a picture of him on their dresser in their bedroom. Anna had noticed that she sometimes stopped in front of the picture, sadly touching the beautiful smiling photo.

Ingrid had grieved silently while Hans had been devastated. He had lost his will to ranch and that had led to the selling off of the Battle Axe Ranch. The bad memories had haunted him. But here he was again, back at ranching. Just like Anna, they had not liked living in town. Ranching ran through their veins.

Anna left the kitchen, collected her sewing bag and the material she had recently purchased, and came back into the kitchen. "I'm going to cut out a couple of bib overalls for Cade. He's growing out of the old ones so fast. And later, I plan to sew the girls a few jumpers and skirts for school next year."

"I'll help. I really love the brown corduroy and the blue denim cloth you picked out," said Ingrid.

The two worked together, spreading out the corduroy on the kitchen table, pinning the pattern onto the cloth, and cutting the bib overalls out. Anna folded up the cloth and pulled out the denim. Again, they worked at cutting out another bib overall, only in the blue denim. After they had finished, they cleared the table.

"I'll sew them tomorrow after I plant the garden," said Anna.

While she left the kitchen, Ingrid started to set the table for dinner. The two women had worked as a team for nearly nine years now. Both felt at ease working with each other.

Anna loved to sew. Her mother Abigail had taught her to knit, so now, Anna always had something to knit in her sewing bag. Her mom had given her several patterns that she still used. She had finished a blue sweater for Cade. With the left over blue yarn, she wanted to knit a baby blanket for her sister-in-law Sonja's new baby boy. She also would have to order more yarn for she wanted to knit each of the girls a sweater by Christmas. She usually sat in the evening and knitted.

Close to dinner time, Hans, Andy, and Chuck came into the back porch, slipping off their rain slickers and hanging up their hats and coats. They had knocked off the mud from their cowboy boots on the steps coming up to the back door. Washing up in the kitchen sink, they were hungry after a day of working. To Anna, Andy seemed really tired, rubbing his eyes.

Anna glanced out the kitchen window and saw Tom Fletcher's red pickup leave the ranch, after he had put in a full day working with the men. While she went down the hall to wake up the girls, the baby Cade crawled over to Grandpa, pulled himself up, and stood behind Hans.

Laughing, Hans felt the little guy behind him, reached around and lifted him up into his arms, "Hi litl' cowboy. How's that chin-chinny doin'?" he said tickling his grandson.

"Grappa," cooed Cade, grabbing his grandpa's big nose. The baby pushed his nose and Hans made a honking noise. Then, they both laughed. He placed his grandson into his highchair.

Going down the hall, Anna woke up the girls and told them to wash up for dinner. They came in excited to see Grandpa back. They were anxious to tell him of their day. Their young happy voices filled the air.

Everyone sat down at the table while Ingrid and Anna set out the meal. They all passed the food around, talked about their day as they filled their hungry stomachs. Anna settled down in her seat, glancing around the table at her children and her in-laws. She felt so thankful to have such a loving family around her.

* * *

Later, after everyone had gone to bed, Anna took a quick bath, soaking up the heat into her tired muscles and body. After washing up, she shampooed her long, blonde hair. She thought about getting her hair cut after seeing how easy it was to maintain the girls' hair after they had their hair cut. But she shrugged her shoulders, knowing that she would probably not find the time. Their new ranch was farther from town as Ingrid had mentioned today.

Stepping out of the bathtub, she wrapped herself in a towel. Holding her head down, she wrapped her long, wet hair into another towel. She took her lotion and rubbed her face, her arms, and her legs with the soothing creamy lotion.

After dinner tonight, Andy had taken a quick bath and crawled into bed. Then, she had given the girls and Cade their baths. The baby had played with his little duckies, splashing water all over. She had to change the wet bandage under his chin. He squirmed and fussed when she pulled it off but settled down after she put a new bandage on the cut. He took his bottle and quickly went to sleep. She hoped that he would sleep through the night.

Walking down to her bedroom, she slipped on a nightgown, sat down at her dressing table, and brushed her long blonde hair until it was dry. She moved back into the bathroom, hanging up the wet towels, and brushed her teeth. She noticed that the clothes hamper was filled with dirty clothes, and the diaper pail was filled with dirty ones. With four children, keeping them in clean clothes had been a weekly laundry routine.

In her bedroom, she opened her window a little, feeling the fresh, cool mountain breeze coming through it. Standing and looking out at the ranch, she saw the dark shadows of the night with the twinkling stars above. Her thoughts turned to the long day.

The yoke of responsibility around her neck and shoulders felt heavy. The load she carried daily tugged at her. Like an ox, she plowed forward pulling the weight of her children behind her. She had to be strong for them. Fate had handed her a challenging destiny, alone without a husband. Crawling into bed under her covers, she craved a connection to someone whom she could touch and feel again. A loving face of someone who would occupy the empty pillow beside her. Someone who could reach her soul and love her.

Several months ago, there had been one handsome man who had awakened her desires as a woman. After Hans had sold the Battle Axe Ranch, Chet Fletcher, alone, had started her thinking when he had taken her by surprise; he had reminded her of her husband. Even Hans and Ingrid had noticed the similarities. But Chet, after a secret quiet, intimate moment in the stable, didn't want to raise her four children. That didn't surprise her since most men wouldn't. He had been a very gentle, compassionate, and caring man who had encouraged her to date, saying that she was young and beautiful, deserving to be loved. Afterwards, he had become a close friend.

In fact, all of the Fletchers had become close friends of her family: Fred, Matt, Tom, and Clyde. They were a distinctive family who had faced a tragic death like they had; Clyde had lost his wife and the sons had lost a mother. They had a bond that connected them, mourning the loss of a loved family member.

As a widow, she had no models to follow; she had known only old women, not young like herself. She didn't want to seem too desperate like a wolf on the prowl. She hoped that she had more sense than a wild animal. Half of herself had been lost with her husband's death. With Chet's words ringing in her ears, she knew that she had to regain that buried passion that she had felt with him. *How did a widow move forward and love again?*

She thought of Denny whom she would see tomorrow. Her heart beat fast at the thought of his tender touch. However, every time she tried to think of her future, Caden's blurred face would emerge, reminding her of the excruciating sorrow she had experienced. Even after a year, his memory was still there. *Would she ever be free of him?* To love again. She had to try, for Denny Carter had wanted her to move towards a relationship with him. *Would the children accept him?* His main practice was in Winston. *How would that work out?* She became afraid of being disappointed, rejected again. The worrisome questions kept her mind whirling. However, as her tired eyes closed against the darkness, her final thought came to her: living alone without a companion for the rest of her life would be unthinkable.

* * *

Anna woke to an early grey morning light while the morning birds chirped and tweeted outside her window. She heard the cattle bellowing in the pastures, calling to each other. A morning fog hung above the river and a moist mist hung in the dark forests after the rain the day before. She stretched and opened her eyes to the grey light coming from her window. Rising slowly, she dressed and began her day.

In the middle of the night, Andy had awakened her, bringing sobbing Cade with him. She had changed his wet diaper, checked his temperature, and had given him another baby aspirin in a bottle of juice. She comforted him, holding him and walking around until he finally fell asleep in her arms. Putting him slowly down into his crib, she covered him and slipped back to bed.

That morning, she headed down to the boys' bedroom and saw that the baby still slept while Andy was getting out of bed to milk the cow. She put her finger to her lips to shush Andy who rubbed his eyes and nodded, looking over at his brother asleep in his crib. As Andy went down the hall to get his sister, she heard their whispers.

"Hurry up slow poke. We've got to milk Magic," said Andy.

"I'm coming. You're not the boss of me," replied Heidi.

Shaking her head, Anna left and went on down the hall to the kitchen where Ingrid had just started to fix breakfast. By the time Andy and Heidi had returned, everyone had risen and eaten breakfast. The clouds had moved beyond the mountains and the valley to let the sun brighten the morning's intense blue sky.

Coming down the dirt road to the ranch, they heard a couple of pickups approaching the house and barn. Hans and Chuck, with Andy following, headed out to greet the Carter's from the Double D Ranch. Mark (known as old man Carter) with his wife Eloise rode in the first pickup truck pulling a horse trailer. Their son Denny followed in another truck, bringing his stallion. Hans and Ingrid welcomed them.

Greeting Eloise Carter, Ingrid invited her in for a cup of coffee. The two had known each other for years and were anxious to visit and catch up on each other's lives.

When the two women came into the kitchen, Cade sat in his highchair while he munched on a graham cracker. Her daughters had gone back into their bedrooms to dress for the day. As Eloise sat down, Ingrid poured her a cup of coffee, setting out a plate of sugar cookies on the table. She cleared the rest of the morning dishes from the table and put them in the kitchen sink to wash later. She then made another pot of coffee for the men.

"Hello, Anna," said Eloise, a tall elderly woman with short white hair and bright blue eyes. "My is that your baby? Last time I saw you, he was just a tiny one. And I saw Andy your oldest outside. He has really grown tall."

While she gave the baby another graham cracker, Anna replied, "Hi, Mrs. Carter. It's nice to see you again. Yes, the children have really grown." The girls shyly came into the kitchen. "And here are my two girls. Heidi and Bridget. Girls, what do you say to our guest?"

Both smiled and replied, "Hi, Miss."

"Why don't you two find something to do until the men finish with unloading the horses. I don't want you out there getting in their way," said Anna. The two girls left and went into the living room. Heidi sat down to read one of her books and Bridget got out her box of crayons and coloring book.

257

"Oh my. What lovely girls you have. They were so young when I last saw them. Do you like living here at your new ranch?" asked Mrs. Carter, sipping her coffee. Ingrid passed her the plate.

Cade saw the cookies and babbled away, holding out his chubby fingers for a cookie. Ingrid got up and gave him another graham cracker instead. He looked at the cracker and shook his head, pointing at the cookie. "ookie, ookie, momma," said Cade with his baby words. The women laughed as Eloise handed Anna the plate who took one and gave him a cookie. The baby quickly picked up the sugar cookie and munched on it, smiling at everyone.

"Yes. The children are very excited to be here. With summer ahead of them, they have a new place to explore," replied Ingrid as Anna and she smiled at each other.

The women continued to talk while Cade had finished his cookie and cracker. Anna washed his face and hands with a cloth and set him down to play in his kitchen drawer of toys. He quickly crawled over and opened it.

Outside, the men were unloading the two horse trailers. Hans had bought three older horses from Mark: a black gelding by the name of Gallo, a dark-brown quarter horse named Trotter, and a reddish-brown broodmare named Pippi. Looking over the three horses, Hans needed his own horse to ride. Gallo suited him, and with the broodmare Pippi, he also wanted to raise a few horses for the ranch. Andy stood back and watched as the horses were being unloaded. Hans had told him that he would be riding one of them until his filly Jewels was older.

Denny had brought his spirited white stallion Ghost to the ranch in one of his dad's horse trailers. After the ride in the horse trailer, his stallion stomped around and snorted. He touched the muzzle and spoke quietly to his horse. Anxious to see Anna, Denny looked towards the ranch house. Hans noticed and asked Mark and him in for coffee. Chuck said he would get to work on some of the ranch repairs. Andy wanted to spend time watching the three horses, wondering which one he would be riding.

The three men headed into the ranch house. By pasturing his horse at the Norsemen, Denny realized that Hans had been a matchmaker. He smiled to himself, for the old man had manipulated the situation. That was fine with him. He now had another reason to see Anna.

Coming in through the back door, Hans, Mark, and Denny walked into the kitchen. The women all greeted them, and Ingrid poured them a cup of freshly brewed coffee. Anna added more cookies to the plate. After the men had sat down, Anna sat beside Denny. She naturally wanted to see him. Hearing their grandpa come in, the girls came in from the living room. They ran over to see him sitting down as he called them his 'litl' cowpunchers.'

"Grandpa are we ever going to punch the cows?" asked curious Bridget. Everyone smiled when he replied that she needed to be a little older.

Then, Heidi said "hi" to Dr. Carter, remembering him from the doctor's visit. Bridget hid shyly behind her mom sitting at the table.

"Mom, can we go play outside?" whispered Bridget.

"Yes but stay away from the corrals and the new horses," answered Anna. "Now, go play and be careful," she added. The two girls left through the back door, eager to get outside in the fresh morning air. The bright sun had warmed the morning while a sharp blue spanned the sky. A perfect day for playing.

Denny smiled at Anna and said, "How's Cade doing? I see he's playing."

"He's fine now but had a little fever. There's a little redness and swelling around the shot," replied Anna.

She looked into his brown eyes, noticing that he looked so differently than yesterday at his office. Today, he had on a yellow plaid shirt with a light-brown denim vest with his jeans. He seemed so casual and natural sitting in their kitchen. Her strong attraction to him drew her into thinking how a relationship would be with him. Her heart skipped a beat and she looked down to keep her feelings hidden.

"I'd like to check out his stitches and his thigh. May I?" he asked.

"Yes, of course. Let's take him down to his room," she replied, rising, anxious to be with him alone.

"We'll be right back," said Denny to everyone, rising with Anna and moving over towards Cade on the floor, playing. He squatted down beside her son and said, "Hi, little guy. What do you have there?"

259

Her son looked at him with a wooden spoon in his hand, laughing he banged on the drawer. Anna reached down and picked him up. Together, they walked down to his bedroom.

When they left, the parents smiled at each other, noticing that the couple had left together. They all hoped that Denny and Anna had something special going on between them, for they had all noticed a kind of relaxed, casual intimacy between the two. The parents continued to talk, drink, and snack on the cookies. As ranchers, Mark and Hans had been in several situations where they had worked together. The men talked about their cattle, and the women chatted about their families.

In the boys' bedroom, Anna slipped off Cade's bib overalls to change him and let Denny take a look at his thigh. He took a few minutes to check the shot area, nodding. Then, he slowly took off the bandage and looked over the stitches.

"Yes, buddy, you're going to have a little white scar left," he said after Anna got another bandage. He put it on, "The cut looks fine, and his thigh looks okay."

"Good. By the way, is your stallion going to like it here?" she asked. She finished changing the baby's diaper and slipped on his overalls. Cade picked up his little ragged teddy bear, playing with him in the crib.

"Yes, how could he not like staying here next to someone as beautiful as you? Seriously though, he'll be much better here than in the corrals as you know. I'd like to take him out for a ride next week. If you're free, we could take a short ride together after I finish my appointments," said Denny, looking at Anna's lovely face and blonde hair. She took his breath away just looking at her. She had on a pair of tight jeans and a blue plaid shirt, tucked in at her small waist line. Turning towards him, she felt his hands on her waist. "I'd like to see you again. How long do I have to wait Anna?" he whispered as he stepped closer to her.

Her heart tightened at his tender touch. His warm body near her sent her emotions stirring. Smiling up at him, she spoke quietly, "I'm not sure but I'd like to see you, too." He leaned down and she felt his lips kiss her temple as she leaned against him. He caressed and squeezed her sides as they leaned against each other for a brief intimate moment.

Cade looked up and babbled, "Kissy, kissy momma." The two stepped apart, smiling. Anna's face blushed red at the situation. She reached down and gathered her son in her arms as her son smushed his lips against her cheek, giving her his slobbering, open-mouthed baby kiss.

"Hey, sweetie. Give Denny a kiss too," said Anna, teasingly.

The baby leaned way over and reached out to Denny who lifted him into his arms. Cade quickly gave him his wet baby kiss. Laughing loudly, Denny delighted in the baby's kiss and then, his chubby fingers grabbed his nose.

"Watch out. He loves to pinch noses," she said, watching her son interact with Denny. Yes, Cade would accept him easily if she married him.

"Wow, what an energetic little guy you are," he said. Glancing at Anna, he said reluctantly, "Sorry, I'd like to stay but I have to get going. I have to drive back to Winston today."

"Thanks for checking on him," she said. The two of them walked down the hall. She asked, "Doesn't that get tiresome, driving back and forth?"

"Yes, a little. But I'm used to it. There are so many patients in both towns that have appointments," he said as they came into the kitchen. He sat down, still holding the baby who seemed happy to be sitting at the table.

Grandpa saw his grandson and said, "Hi, litl' cowboy. How's the cut?"

Denny smiled, "It looks good." The baby then wanted down, so he lowered him carefully to the floor. He quickly crawled back to his toys and the kitchen drawer.

Everyone had finished their coffee, so the Carter's rose to leave.

"Thanks for the coffee and cookies. It's been nice visiting with you, and seeing your growing family," said Eloise.

Mark glanced at Hans, "Let me know how the horses work out for you. They should be a good addition to your ranch." Hans nodded in thanks.

Denny reached into his vest pocket of his shirt and handed Hans a check, "Here's a little something for pasturing my horse," he said.

"But I don't need anything for doing this," answered Hans, surprised at the amount as he glanced at the check.

"Yes, you'll need to buy grain for him. Take it. Thanks for letting me pasture him here," said Denny, finishing his coffee and a cookie. He rose and followed his parents out the back door. Anna followed him out, reluctant to see him go. She wanted more time with him.

As they all came outside, Bridget came rushing up to Anna, and excitedly hollering, "Come quick mom. Heidi's stuck."

"What? Where?" Concerned, Anna looked around desperately for her little daughter. She didn't see her anywhere around the ranch.

Denny sensed the concern in Bridget's voice, and asked, "Where exactly is she?"

"She's up on top of the windmill. Andy is trying to talk her down, but she's too scared to come down the ladder. She's crying," gasped Bridget, nearly in tears.

Denny didn't wait another second, but quickly hurried to the windmill standing next to the old barn. Glancing up he saw the little girl up at the top, holding on to the ladder. He turned his head quickly and said, "I've got this. Don't worry Anna. I'll get her down." He stepped up on the first rung of the ladder and started up.

"Denny, be careful," his mom hollered at her son.

A little crowd formed at the base of the windmill, looking up. They saw Denny scale up the ladder. He stopped just below Heidi, talked to her for a minute. Anna covered her eyes from the brightness of the sun to watch them. Her heart beat fast at the thought that her daughter had gone up that old windmill. *Why was she up there?*

The others said nothing, just waiting for Denny to come down with the little girl. The silence of the moment terrified Anna as she gasped, seeing her daughter so far up on the old windmill. Denny moved down the ladder with her daughter in front of him. He guided each foot down to the next rung. With him behind her, they slowly came down, rung after rung. Reaching the ground, he looked at Heidi and commented, "Wow, you had quite an adventure, but you're safe now."

Anna came up to her, desperately seeking her daughter, "Oh, Heidi. Why did you go up there?"

"Andy told me that it was easy climbing up the windmill, and he could see all the world from up there. The rungs were far apart, but I made it up. But when I started down, I couldn't see the rungs and got too scared and froze," she responded.

Holding her close to her, she said, "Don't go up there again." Turning to Andy, she asked, "Why did you go up the windmill?"

"Hans sent me up to repair the ladder. I pounded the nails in on the rungs and secured the top. I didn't think Heidi would go up there," he replied.

Little Bridget asked Heidi, "Andy wouldn't tell us, sis. Did you see the dwarves holding up the sky at the top of the world?"

"No, I was too dizzy and scared to look around," replied her sister.

Anna recalled the story that Grandpa had told the children of the dwarves a month ago. Little Bridget didn't understand that those incredible stories were only folktales and not real. Hans had explained that, but Bridget was too young to understand.

"Thank you, Denny for getting Heidi down," said Anna.

He just nodded, and said, "No problem. Listen, I should be going. Dad, I'll swing by and drop off your horse trailer. Sorry, mom, I have to run. Can't stop," he said, apologizing. The time was getting late. Even though he missed spending time with them at their ranch, at least, he had visited with them once in a while coming up to Riverside.

Getting into his blue pickup, he headed out of the Norsemen Ranch. Anna waved to him as he waved back at everyone. Hans and Mark shook hands before they left. Anna took Heidi's hand and with Bridget in her arms headed into the ranch house. Ingrid had carried the baby out when she had heard the excitement. Now, she too headed back into the house. Hans and Andy went back to the corrals to work with the horses.

The morning with all its excitement had slipped by fast. After lunch, along with the girls and the baby, Ingrid laid down for a nap. Getting the hoe from the barn, Anna worked in the garden, forming the rows and planting the vegetable seeds. She thought of the windmill incident. *Would there ever be a day when her children didn't get into trouble?* And she thought of Denny and how quickly he responded. His training as a doctor, and perhaps, his military background had kicked in. She would never be able to thank him enough for his quick action. She was glad that Andy had not tried to climb up that windmill to get her daughter down. *Oh, mercy.*

That evening after dinner, Hans sat down at his old grandfather's desk set up in a corner of the living room. He was bringing the ranch records up-to-date. Anna had been knitting, starting on the little blue blanket. She remembered that she had the charges from the General Store still in her purse along with the doctor's bill. Rising, she came back and approached Hans working at his desk.

"Here are a few more charges," she said, handing him the slips of paper.

"Oh, thanks," he said.

"Are we doing okay? I mean all the expenses of the ranch," she asked.

"Yes, we're fine. Why do you ask?"

"I thought, perhaps, I could help with the record keeping. You and Ingrid have been so supportive of me and the children. I want to do my part to help. I think I should know how things are running. You could show me," she explained.

"You can do your part by raising our grandchildren. This ranch is for their future," he said. Hans had always looked forward, planning ahead. She liked that about her father-in-law. He was a kind, but hard, demanding man. "Well okay, bring over a chair. I could use the help. Sit beside me and I can show you how I keep the records. If something happens to me or Ingrid, I expect you to take over."

Anna lowered her eyes to keep the shock of his words sink in. *This would be her ranch to run!* She recalled that she had wanted to stay at the Battle Axe Ranch and run it, but he had told her no then. Something had changed his mind since then. His change of heart gave her a thrill.

She sat down next to him while they worked for about an hour on the books. He had a simple method, so Anna could see how the columns and numbers were kept. When they had finished, he rubbed his tired eyes and said it was time for bed.

"One last thing, Hans," said Anna. "I know that Heidi was so excited to get Moonbeam for her birthday, but I don't think she is handling the young filly very well. She is so small, and the filly is too jittery."

"Oh? I hadn't noticed. I thought that she could feed him his grain each day. What is happenin'?" he seemed puzzled.

"I'm worried that she'll get kicked by that frisky little filly. Heidi hasn't been around horses like Andy has. He's taller and knows how to handle his filly. He's been with you working with the horses and the cattle for a number of years. Heidi hasn't," she said with a frowned concern on her face.

"Listen. She needs to bond with her horse, no matter what. She has to learn, and the best way is by doin'. But I'll talk to Chuck, and he could spend a little time with her and the filly. He's really good with horses," explained Hans.

"All right, but I don't want her to get hurt learning how to handle Moonbeam," she added. "Good night. Oh, I forgot to tell you. Ingrid has agreed to see the doctor next week."

"She has? Good, I'm worried about her. Let me know if the doctor finds anythin'. Good night," he said, turning off the lamp on the desk.

Anna walked down to check on the children. Stopping at the boys' room and peaking in, she saw that they both were sleeping soundly. Stepping next at the girls' room, Bridget was sound asleep, but Heidi was wide awake.

"Mom, I'm sorry about going up that ladder. Andy had gone up and down so easily. I thought I could too," she whispered. Anna sat down on the bed beside her.

"Listen, you can't follow your brother around. He's older and more experienced than you. Now, about Moonbeam. She needs to get to know you. That's all. Just feed her the grain and Grandpa said that Chuck will show you how to handle her. You know that she is only three or four months old. She isn't like Jewels who is nearly two years old," explained Anna, hoping her daughter would understand. She went on, "Remember when I grabbed her halter and put my hand on her muzzle to settle her down. That's how you should lead her. She needs to get use to your touch and what you want her to do. Talk to her and touch her muzzle once in a while. Giving her a treat like a carrot or an apple helps too. Just holding on to the lead rope doesn't get you close enough to her."

"Okay. Mom you were so good with her," said Heidi, yawning.

"Yes. Your dad taught me a lot," said Anna.

"I miss daddy," she said sadly, thinking of him.

"Yes, we all do. Say a little prayer to him in heaven. Good night, sweetie," she said softly, giving her daughter a kiss and tucking the blankets around her.

She left and walked down to her bedroom. Remembering her husband, he had helped her become the confident ranch woman she was now. But after his death, he lay in that cold, dark grave at the cemetery. He would probably encourage her to go on being that ranch woman and to raise their children. He most likely would not want her to cut her love life short either at such a young age. Somehow, she knew that he would want her to marry again. But that had been the part that had been difficult for her to do. She would have to come to terms with it someday.

While she undressed, she thought about her long day and all the events that had happened. She realized as the children had gotten older, her life had become more complicated and worrisome. They were getting into more serious situations than when they were just babies.

Going down to the bathroom, she washed up for the night. She had only met Denny's parents a couple of times over the years. Visiting with them today, reminded her that he had been raised on a ranch. Early in their dating, she again remembered their ride to Skyline. He had implied that she was playing a game with him. She had been hurt by those words, but more recently, he seemed to understand that she needed more time. The hurt of being left a widow stung deeply into her soul.

Opening her bedroom window again, she looked out into the dark shadows. The stillness surrounded her except for the natural sounds of the mountains, a distant call or howl in the wilderness. In her bed, she thought of Denny, his tender kiss, and his warm hands caressing her. She wanted to get to know him more. Next week, he asked her to go riding. As she closed her sleepy eyes, a week seemed like a long time away.

* * *

Even though Anna had a busy week with cooking, sewing, and gardening, time slowed to a snail's pace. The girls were excited about planting the sunflowers. Bridget went out to the garden each day, waiting to see the little seedlings pop up from under the dirt.

Their foreman Chuck spent an afternoon with Heidi, showing her how to handle her young filly Moonbeam. Anna watched from the porch, making sure that her daughter wouldn't get hurt with the unpredictable filly.

After training and grooming his own filly, her son had been practicing his lassoing skills. Anna smiled at his attempts to use the long rope. Hans encouraged him to keep handling the rope until it became an extension of his arm and body. Slung over his shoulder, Andy carried that rope everywhere with him, to meals and to bed.

The day came when they needed to drive the herd to the summer grazing lands. Andy rode the quarter horse Trotter, and after a long discussion with Ingrid, Anna decided to go along and ride her mare Rhapsody. She hated to leave the children all day, but her mother-in-law said she could manage just fine. Anna slipped on her jeans, her blue-plaid shirt, and her worn cowboy boots. After braiding her hair tightly, she dug into a box in her closet for her brown cowgirl hat which she hadn't worn for a long time.

After brushing the dusty, faded hat, she slipped it on her head. Memories of working with Caden came back. Her life had been filled with living on the ranch, not only cooking and cleaning, but also with branding, haying, and rounding up their cattle. In-between her pregnancies, she had helped wherever she was needed with her husband guiding her. But today, she set those old memories aside. She was making new memories with their new ranch and anxiously wanted to get an overview of their land. Becoming knowledgeable seemed important to her since she had been keeping the records.

The long day of riding on her mare gave Anna a respite from the routine duties of the ranch house. Plus, the ride had rekindled and reawakened her love of the ranch life. Throughout the morning and into the afternoon, they drove the herd up into the forested, blue mountains and to the lush, green meadows. She had been pleased to see that her son Andy handle himself well on the drive. Hans had kept close to him, watching and instructing him. A satisfied pride sprung up inside of her seeing her oldest son driving the cattle. Yes, he would make a great wrangler.

When they returned late that evening, Anna's whole dusty-caked body screamed exhaustion and fatigue. Riding all day on her mare made it nearly impossible for her to crawl into a warm bath before bedtime. Snuggled under her covers, her tired mind thought about the added burden of the Norsemen Ranch and its success. With sore muscles, sleep came quickly as she closed her eyes to a long, dusty day of riding.

On Wednesday morning, Anna, Ingrid, with the girls and the baby, drove into town to see the doctor. The sitting room was filled with waiting patients. When the nurse called out her name, they all walked back into the small examining room, anxious to get the little stitches out. These last few days Cade had kept pulling the bandage off, so she had finally left it off.

With a smile and an affectionate glint in his eyes, Dr. Carter came into the room. After they greeted, he turned to the business at hand. Pulling on his surgical gloves and with a few quick, precise snips of a tiny pair of scissors, he quickly picked out the black stitches. Cade cried at being on the table again, but Anna held him, whispering for him to be quiet. The little red sucker made the baby smile while Anna suggested that the doctor take a look at Ingrid.

"Sure. What seems to be the problem?" he asked, turning to Ingrid.

"Come on, girls. We'll wait until Grandma's done talking to the doctor," she said. Holding the baby, she grabbed Bridget's hand and left with Heidi following. They sat in the waiting room. After a while, Ingrid came out.

"Let's go," she said, gathering the children and ready to leave. Anna wanted to question her, but she obviously didn't want to talk.

Glancing at Denny, Anna asked, "Are you still planning to come out to the ranch and ride tonight?"

"Yes, I'm looking forward to it. I'll see you later," he said, smiling. He headed back to his examination room, occupied with the next waiting patient.

In her purse, Anna had another list of supplies from Hans and Ingrid had her own list to pick up from town. They made their stops before driving back to the ranch. With more charges to the ranch, Anna thought about their costs. They needed salt blocks for the herd and more grain for the additional horses, and fresh produce and groceries. The children seemed to eat more as they grew older. Andy had a bottomless stomach at meal time.

The other night while she worked on the records, she had added Denny's check to the books. She liked keeping the records which gave her a sense of responsibility and an overview of their costs.

While they drove back to the ranch, Anna asked, "What did the doctor say?"

"He took some blood. He'll let me know if the tests show anything. I'm fine Anna. Don't fuss," insisted Ingrid. But she couldn't help but worry.

The afternoon came and went. Evening approached; dinner ended. No Dr. Carter. A phone call came late that evening while she sat knitting in the living room. Hans answered it and said it was for her.

"Anna, sorry I didn't make it there today. An emergency came up. Can we make it for next week?" asked Denny, apologizing.

"Yes," she replied, disappointed but she understood.

"Great. By the way, you're welcome to ride my stallion if you want. He needs some exercise. He's a little high strung, but I'm sure you can handle him. I'll see you next week. Good bye," said Denny, as she said "Good bye."

Anna listened to the phone's dead silence. She realized that his role as a doctor would always make demands on him. *Could she live with that? An emergency just a phone call away?* She admired and respected his work, recalling how he had been there in her dire situations. Denny was a strong man with an impressive calling, devoted in helping others. This part of his life she would need to accept, sharing him with the public. The pang of jealousy rose inside of her, making her regret that she had those feelings.

The next day when everyone was taking a nap, Anna decided to go for a ride on Denny's white stallion Ghost. Walking down to the pasture, she stood looking over the horses. The white stallion had taken over as the dominating horse. He had already humped Pippi several times since he had been brought to the ranch. Hans would get another horse plus Rhapsody was already carrying his foal. A month ago while the two horses were corralled together in town, the stallion had mounted Rhapsody and gotten her pregnant.

Moonbeam, the orphan filly, stayed close to Rhapsody while Jewels ran around the pasture, kicking up her back legs and showing off. The personalities of the horses amazed her. Rhapsody expected her to go for a ride when she came down to the pasture. Her mare snorted, tossed her mane, and muzzled for a treat.

"Sorry Rhapsody. I'm riding the stallion today. Don't get jealous," she whispered to her mare, giving her a carrot.

Curiosity drove the big white stallion over to her. Stroking his long neck, she touched his wet muzzle first before giving him a carrot. With a bridle, she slipped it over his head after he crunched the carrot. She had decided to ride bareback just around the pasture.

After mounting the big horse, he stomped around, snorting anxious to run. She sat firmly on him with her knees clutched against his wide body. As she gave him her heel in the side, she leaned forward and felt his powerful body move beneath her as he took off running. The wind brushed her cheeks and her braid bounced behind her. With one of her hands clutching onto his mane, she rode him around while the other horses scattered. The white stallion raced around the pasture from one end along the side to the other end. Twice around until he finally settled down.

She moved him into a walk, holding firmly on the reins. He responded quickly to her commands. Yes, he certainly was spirited like Denny had said. The horse reminded her of Denny's fiery, powerful advances towards her. His love for her had been constant, every time he came out to the ranch. She missed seeing him, in fact, his absence had become a great frustration to her. It drove her crazy waiting to see him drive down the dirt road to their ranch and spend time with him.

After a while, she dismounted, slipping to the ground and leading him over to the gate. While she stroked his long neck and mane, she whispered to him as she leaned against his beautiful white body. Rhapsody and Pippi would have good foals from this stallion. Refreshed after her ride, she headed back to the ranch house.

As promised, Denny came to ride the next week. They had a short ride for he had arrived later than planned. Anna set out to show him their ranch and the surrounding mountains north of their land. They rode silently across the long valley. Dismounting at a small creek, she noticed how easy he swung down off his horse. They watched their horses drink the cool water. Denny squatted down by the stream and cupped his hand for a sip. Anna occupied herself with her mare, who moved to the fresh grass growing along the banks. She tied the reins loosely to a small aspen tree.

Following her, he tied Ghost near her mare, and moved through the tall pine trees further into the forest. After coming to a tree, he stopped, pulled out a pocket knife, and started carving on the bark.

Curious, she followed him and came up to him, "What are you doing?"

"I'm carving our initials into this tree. It'll remind us of our time here," he replied. He had finished her initial *A* and started on his *D*. Then, he carved a lopsided heart around them. She smiled, delighted with an amusing feeling inside. He was such a romantic, and she loved his attention. Hoping that she would move to a closer relationship, he continued to pursue her.

Glancing at each other, he held out his arm for her to come to him. His alluring glint in his brown eyes called to her. She smiled and slowly stepped closer. Folding her into a tight, comforting hug, the two came together. With her cheek against his jacket, she breathed in his male scent. Keeping his arm around her, they walked over towards an old log and sat down.

"I'm truly sorry about last week," he said, holding her hand while he rubbed the back of her rough hand.

"Don't worry. You're here now," she replied. "Did everything turn out okay with the emergency?"

"Yes, it did. You know that this will happen from time to time. It'll take a strong woman like yourself to put up with my heavy schedule," he said.

"I understand," said Anna, thinking of their initials and of his persistent desire for her. She glanced around at the horses who were busy munching the grass, swishing their tails against the flies, and snorting their satisfaction.

"I've been thinking a lot about my two offices, the one in Winston and the one here in town," he said with a serious look in his eyes.

"What do you mean?" she asked, curious.

"Perhaps, I should relocate here in Riverside and drive to Winston. I would have to move, but it appeals to me. I need to consider it though. I'm not sure about anything right now," he said, with a candid look in his eyes as he glanced at her. His look told her he wanted to see her reaction.

"That's interesting. What's your plan?" she asked.

She felt him move closer to her and his arms went around her as he leaned down to seek her lips. He whispered, "I don't know, but I'd like to see more of you, Anna. Once a week is not enough for me." Setting aside his thoughts of moving, he turned his eager desires towards her.

His large soft hand closed around the back of her head, and he moved her closer to him, and she felt his warm lips descended on hers as he gently kissed her—just a brush of his lips. She closed her eyes while she raised her arms around his neck, pulling him closer to her; he kissed her again and again. Desire took hold and sent them into a whirlwind of emotions. He embraced her tightly, feeling her small body against his. Every one of her nerves responded to his powerful touches. Breathing hard, his hand caressed her. She let herself relax against him. Finally, he leaned back, knowing they should stop, for time had passed too quickly for them.

"It's getting late. We better head back," he murmured against her ear.

She heard the reluctance in his deep, low voice and sensed his desires, as her own emotions had risen in anticipation of his kisses and touches. Yes, their lives had called them away from their private moment.

While they rode back to the ranch, his face showed that he was seriously mulling over his proposal. Her thoughts were back at the tree with their precious carved initials captured in a heart. Without much talk, they unsaddled their horses, groomed them, and fed them grain in the barn.

"Why don't you stay for dinner?" she asked while they walked their horses down to the pasture. Opening the gate, they released them. His white stallion took off running while her mare sought out Moonbeam.

"No, but thanks. I have to drive back to Winston," he replied.

"Tonight? You should stay overnight," she added.

"I have early appointments in the morning. Can't stay. I'll grab something to eat later. It's only a couple of hours to Winston," he answered, taking the idea of driving back in his stride. Anna recalled that he had been doing this for years. Back and forth.

Standing next to his blue pickup, he said, "I'll see you next week, barring no emergencies. Oh, I almost forgot. When you brought Cade in for his stitches, your children may have been exposed to chicken pox. It's going around town. Have they had any signs—tired, out of sorts or blisters?"

She frowned, "No, not so far. But I'll watched them closely. Drive carefully."

He gave her a slow kiss on her lips, and then, stepped into his pickup. He waved his hand out of his window as his blue truck disappeared down the road to the highway. She waved back and sighed, thinking that she wouldn't see him again for another week. She worried about him driving back so late.

Going back into the ranch house, the family was getting ready for dinner. She told Ingrid about the outbreak of chicken pox. The children seemed fine with no signs. They had a quiet evening until bed time came.

After getting the children ready and into bed, Anna relaxed, knitting her blue baby blanket and thinking of Denny and his thoughts of moving to Riverside. *Would he move?* The thought filled her heart with hope. She enjoyed the fact that he had spoken to her in confidence. She held the possibility close to her heart.

* * *

A few days later, the three children came down with the chicken pox. They were miserable and stayed in bed for several days. Then Andy got it from the girls. He seemed to get the worst of it with a high fever. Ingrid took care of the girls while Anna took care of Andy and the baby. Denny called the next week and said he'd be there too late to ride but wanted to drive out to see her.

"Oh, Denny. The kids came down with the chicken pox. You better not come," she told him.

"What? No, I'll be there and check them over. Do any of them have a fever?" he asked concerned.

"Yes, Andy has. The others seem to have a mild case. A few blisters. It's been hard on the girls. They've been complaining about the blisters itching," she explained.

"Listen, I'm almost done here at the office. I'll leave in a few minutes," he said, hanging up the phone.

Anna closed her eyes, exhausted after trying to keep Andy's fever down. She had given him aspirin and had bathed his hot body with a cool washcloth. The baby also lay sickly in his crib holding his ragged teddy bear. She had given him a baby aspirin in a juice bottle, but he didn't have a fever.

Earlier that morning, Ingrid decided to make chicken noodles for the sick children. She cut up a chicken and put the pieces in a pot of water to cook and make the broth. Anna mixed up her mother's homemade egg noodles, rolling them out to dry. Later, she cut the dried dough into the slim noodles.

She now walked into the kitchen, to drop the dried noodles into the hot chicken broth. Ingrid and she worked together preparing the dinner for everyone. While the noodles simmered on the stove, Anna fixed a cup of tea for Ingrid and her. The day had been long for both of them.

Soon they heard the doctor's pickup coming down the road to the ranch. Anna waited at the door. He came out of his blue pickup carrying his black medical bag. She opened the door, "Hi, Denny. I'm glad you could come and see the kids."

"Hi, Anna," he stepped into the kitchen. "Hello, Ingrid. Let me see the children." He moved down the hall, following Anna. He checked over the girls who seemed fine. Then, he walked into the boys' bedroom with Andy and Cade. Examining the baby, he noticed that he seemed fine with only a few blisters, like the girls. But turning his attention to Andy, he frowned.

"Would you leave while I examine him?" he asked Anna. She nodded and waited in the hall, listening to him who seemed so calm and direct.

Curious the girls came out of their room, "What's happening to Andy?" asked Heidi, knowing that he was worse than she was.

"I'm hungry," complained Bridget, holding her stomach.

"Okay, now girls. Go back into your room. Andy will be fine. As soon as the doctor is done, we'll have dinner," she said, pushing them back into their room.

She leaned up against the wall with her folded arms, waiting for Denny to finish with her son. Coming out of the bedroom, he said, "He'll be all right. I gave him a shot. Give him lots of water to drink. He'll feel better after a few days. I brought some lotion for their blisters. Rub this on them. It'll help with the itching."

She held the bottle in her hand while they walked into the kitchen.

"Something smells delicious," he said.

"Can you stay for some chicken noodles?" asked Ingrid.

"No. I have another stop to make. One of the McClure kids has the blisters near his eye. I want to look him over," replied Denny.

"Is that their son Roger by any chance?" asked Anna.

"Yes it is," he replied. "But I will take some of those noodles in a cup," he smiled as Anna quickly went to the stove and dished out some broth and noodles into a coffee cup.

"You really should sit down and eat," she complained, handing him the steaming cup.

"This will hold me until I get back to town. Oh, I'll bring your cup back. Call my nurse if Andy doesn't get better. Okay?" he said, heading out the door to his pickup. He held the cup carefully, while he drove out of the ranch.

Hans, Chuck, and Tom all watched the doctor drive off. They waved at him. Hans and Chuck headed into the ranch house for dinner while Tom left in his red pickup for home. Ingrid had set the table as everyone came in for dinner. Anna walked down to the boys' bedroom, picked up the baby, put him in his high chair, and slipped a bib around his neck. Ingrid told her she'd feed him. So, Anna fixed a bowl for Andy and left to give him some noodles in his room.

"Mom, I can feed myself," said Andy pushing himself up to sit against his headboard. She noticed that he had blisters in his short hair and his arms.

"I know. I'll get you a glass of water," she replied, handing him the bowl.

Hans came down, peaked in, and asked, "How are you doin' Andy?"

"I'm fine. The Doc gave me a shot. I don't think I'll be milking Magic," replied Andy, smiling weakly.

"Don't worry. We'll milk her. You eat, rest, and get better," said Grandpa. He turned and left to eat his dinner. Anna came in with a glass of water and set it down on the little table beside his bed. Her son had finished the warm broth and was spooning out the noodles.

"These are like Oma's. She made this when we were sick," said Andy, chewing and swallowing.

"Yes, that's her recipe. She brought us chicken noodles that time we were all sick with colds. Now, here drink a little water," she said.

After he finished eating and drinking, Andy scooted down under his covers, exhausted and tired.

"Now, if you get to feeling worse, come in and tell me," she said, tucking his covers around him.

"Thanks, mom," he said, closing his eyes.

"Good night," she whispered.

Moving down the hall and into the kitchen, she sat down at the kitchen table to eat. The girls had finished their meal and Ingrid was going to put them in bed.

"Rub some of that lotion on those blisters," reminded Anna.

Ingrid nodded, picked up the bottle from the kitchen counter, and took the girls down to their bedroom. They wanted her to read them a story. The baby reached out with his chubby hands as Anna lifted him out of the highchair and held him close to her as she ate her meal. After dinner, everyone decided to go to bed early for it had been a long day for all of them.

Anna slipped under her covers, but she laid there with her eyes opened, listening to the children and hoping they all would sleep through the night. When Denny drove out to see the children, he had put her worries to rest, especially concerning Andy. Denny said that this would take about a week before the children were better. She thought of the other families in Riverside who were dealing with this outbreak of chicken pox and the demands they would make on him. It had been a real comfort to have him here. She finally closed her eyes and fell into a deep sleep.

In the middle of the night, she woke up, worried about how the children were doing. She stepped lightly into the children's bedrooms to check on them. Andy felt very hot, so she woke him, gave him an aspirin, and made him drink a glass of water. When the baby heard her, he woke up in his crib, crying. Anna fixed him a bottle of juice to put him back to sleep. Satisfied that they were all right, she tiptoed back to her bedroom, crawling under her covers and falling back to sleep.

* * *

The rest of the summer was much calmer than the first month with the stitches and the chicken pox. The children seemed to settle down more except for a few scrapes on the knees. The girls and the baby's little legs and arms became covered in bug bites until Anna had them wear long sleeves and jeans.

In the middle of summer one day, Lettie Fletcher called about Bridget's puppy. Anna and her daughter had driven over and picked up the puppy that she named Dwarfy. The little border collie became a delightful addition to the ranch. Bridget chased her all over, playing and taking care of her. Hans took to the dog and started training her with his whistles and hand gestures just around the barnyard. Dwarfy was a quick learner, so Hans saw a great potential in her helping with the herd.

Grandma Ingrid came up with a great idea for the girls—a unique playhouse. On days when they had no washing on the clotheslines, she slung an old bedcover over one of the lines, creating a tent for the girls to play in. They would spread out the cover and place rocks to hold down the sides. Ingrid would throw an old rug inside. The tent became a perfect place for Heidi to read and for Bridget to play with her doll. Dwarfy loved being around the girls. A few times, Cade would crawl in and play with his toys. Anna took the metal truck away and hid it in the top of her closet. No more accidents on that dangerous truck. The best time of all for the children is when Ingrid and Anna would fix them lunch and bring out the little sandwiches and lemonade for them to have a picnic in their makeshift tent. The shaded area kept the children from the overhead sun beating down on them.

During the hot summer days, the vegetable garden grew, the sunflowers reached up with their large brown heads fringed with yellow petals to the sky, and the large fields grew tall, waving hay to be cut for the cattle. Hans worked long hours getting the fields irrigated. He also worked on the repairs needed on the old ranch house, the big barn, and the bunk house. Roofs had to be fixed and every building needed a coat of paint or stain. Chuck and Tom worked beside Hans who pushed to get the repairs done before winter.

Their foreman Chuck rode up to check on their small herd once a month—bringing the cattle a new salt block to lick. When he rode up one time, he found one of their steers had got trapped in a bog and died. The scavengers had a feast over the dead steer. He couldn't do anything but report back to Hans that time. Another time when he rode up to check on the herd, he saved a young bull caught in a roll of barbwire. Afterwards, he led the young bull back to the ranch. Hans called the veterinarian Steve Kullens from Midler who drove up and took care of the young bull who ended up losing one of his eyes, but he healed and survived. Andy helped feed him until he got better and named him Winkum after the blind eye. The bull went on to sire many young calves.

Their survival on this ranch depended on raising and selling their livestock. Anna found out that they were lucky to lose only one steer that summer while other ranchers in the area lost more. When she did the books, she had to put the lost steer in the negative column. She didn't like the loss.

Denny's trips out to the ranch were fewer than he had planned, for his practice kept him late into the afternoons. When he did show up, they both enjoyed their time together. He told Anna that he loved coming to the ranch more each time.

On one of his visits, Denny asked Andy to ride with them. Evidently, the two of them had talked more about roping than chicken pox the month before. Riding out into an area that had been cleared by the lumber company, they stopped and dismounted. There were left over stumps which became great targets for him to practice roping. Denny showed him how the hold the rope, make a lasso, and toss it around a stump.

After he had practiced for some time, Denny told him to try it from his horse. Her son worked tirelessly at lassoing a stump that afternoon. She watched her son who eagerly wanted to learn and with Denny's calm manner and instructions, he succeeded. As the afternoon moved closer to twilight, they all rode back to the ranch. Andy thanked Denny for his help as the doctor stepped over to his blue pickup. Her son excitedly took off, wanting to show his grandpa how he could throw a lasso.

She stood next to him as he was getting ready to leave. He smiled at her, embracing her into a tight hug. She leaned against his warm body, wishing that they had more time. But she was happy about seeing him and her son together. She said, "Thanks for working with Andy. I didn't know if he would ever learn to throw a lasso."

"Well, I've had a lot of experience growing up on a ranch," he replied, recalling his years on his dad's ranch. "Listen, I'll see you next week."

"Yes. Stay for dinner next time," she said, as he leaned down waiting to kiss her. She felt his warm breath on her face.

"Sure. Can I get a kiss goodbye?" he whispered as his lips touched hers. They held that kiss for a long time. She did not want him to go, but he stepped back, "Good bye." He crawled into his blue pickup, and reaching out the window, he handed her the cup that had held the chicken noodles. "Here, I keep forgetting to return this."

She took the cup, "Plan to come for dinner next week." He nodded and drove away, waving good bye.

However, the next time he came was two weeks later. His appointments had run over, so he had called with an apology. When he finally drove out, Anna and he rode to their tree with the carved heart. After they had dismounted and sat on the old log, he excitedly told her about his buddy Jack. "He is getting married and I'm his best man. Look for an invitation to the wedding. I'd like you to come."

Interested, she asked, "Sure. Who is he marrying and when?"

"He's marrying Gigi Sutton who works at the General Store. You should know her. They're setting the date. Will you come?" he asked.

"Yes, I do know her. I'll be there," she replied.

He smiled and embraced her, "I'd like us to be moving towards something like that. When are you going to say 'yes'?"

She leaned against him, thinking of how she had thought about his proposal but still wasn't ready. Quietly she said, "Denny, I haven't said 'no.' I just need some more time."

He whispered, "I know. I'm not pressuring you. But I want to be with you every day, not just once in a while. Can you understand how I feel?"

Instead of waiting for an answer, he covered her lips with a desperate kiss. His lips moved down to her neck, just below her ear and kissed her again. Goosebumps went down her body and she imagined him by her side. Yes, she would love to move forward—someday. But then, she remembered dinner, "Denny, it's getting late. Everyone will be waiting for us to get back to have dinner."

He murmured, unwillingly, "Oh, Anna. You're impossible."

She smiled up at him, "I'll race you back," slipping out of his arms.

Laughing, they sprang to their horses. He mounted quickly on his white stallion while she stumbled to get her boot into the stirrup. "You know that my stallion can out run your mare by a mile," he said, teasing and taunting her. While she mounted her mare, Denny and his stallion moved in a circle around her. His stallion snorted and tossed his mane at the excitement in the air.

"Don't be such a braggart," she hollered at him while a heel into her mare's side gave Rhapsody the command to take off. He followed, laughing and enjoying this playful side of Anna as they rode through the pine trees. On the home stretch, Denny's white stallion raced past Anna's mare to win the challenge. They, then, slowly walked the horses back to the barn, cooling them down.

After taking care of their horses, they walked together into the ranch house. He stayed and had dinner with the family. Hans and he talked about the herd and the ranch. The girls sat quietly and watched the doctor sitting at their table. They didn't often have a visitor who stayed for dinner. Andy and Denny seemed to have a quiet connection after the lasso lessons. The baby sat in his highchair and babbled, ate, and made everyone laugh. He left late that night and drove to Winston. She again watched him drive down the dirt road, leaving her standing there, waving. Watching him leave, her heart felt like a deflated balloon each time he left.

* * *

The next time she saw him was at Jack and Gigi's wedding in town. Anna came in late to the little church ceremony. When she arrived, she slipped quietly into the last wooden pew. The church had only a small group sitting at the front—the smallest that she had ever seen at a wedding. Gigi's only family members was her sister Gina who was her matron of honor and her husband Tod with their two daughters Harriet and Theresa.

Jack's parents didn't come, but they were excited to hear that their only son was finally getting married. They had nearly given up on him. Jack's two sisters and their husbands had driven all the way from Illinois to see their baby brother walk down that aisle.

One of the pews was taken up with the Carter's—the parents, the two brothers Ted and Ken with their wives, and a sister Melanie. They knew Jack when he and Denny were in the Korean War together.

After the ceremony, numerous photos were taken of the couple with Gina and Denny standing next to them. Other family photos were taken. Anna smiled at how handsome and distinguished Denny looked in his black tuxedo. Their eyes met as they both anxiously waited to see each other. When all of the photos were finished, Denny walked towards her. She felt his hand pull her into a hug. Smelling his distinct, aromatic cologne, she felt the rich cloth of the tuxedo against her cheek. Her heart warmed with his strong arms wrapped around her.

"I'm so glad you came. I thought that you decided not to come," he said.

"I'm sorry I was late. It took me longer than I thought to drive into town from the ranch," she said apologizing.

The married couple came up to the two of them. Anna congratulated both of them. Jack's wide-grin looked at Denny and said, "I did it buddy. I married her. I found me the prettiest co-pilot who loves to fly with me." They had a long, mutual friendship between them as they gave each other a quick hug.

The bride Gigi, in a beautiful crème colored brocade gown, smiled quietly beside Jack. She looked gorgeous with her shapely figure and her full breasts. She had a small tiara atop her short brown hair. Jack couldn't keep his eyes off of her. Her hazel eyes sparkled while Jack's eyes traveled up and down her body. Anna saw her tug at Jack's arm several times, trying to get him to leave. They needed to go to the reception at the tavern.

Anna turned to Denny and said, "I'll see you at the reception."

He looked at her, "Okay. Let's go Jack. We have to cut the cake before you two take off for your honeymoon."

"Where are you going?" asked Anna.

"We're flying to Hadley in Jack's chopper and staying at one of the mountain resorts," replied Gigi, excited, thinking of the helicopter ride they would be taking.

They all left the church and headed towards the tavern. Even though the church had only a small group, the tavern had filled up with the town folks. Everyone clapped when the young couple came in. Jack's new position as a flight operations manager had brought three big helicopters to the town. The Chopper Solutions had hired three pilots with their families to fly them. Jack's old business sign came down and a new commercial sign went up. Gigi had moved out of her apartment above the tavern and had moved into Jack's place.

Anna had driven down to the tavern and sat in her car while she waited a few minutes. Arriving by herself, she had been anxious about coming to this wedding since she hadn't been to a big event all summer. Usually Hans and Ingrid would be with her. They were her umbrella that shielded her from public scrutiny. As a widow, she still felt exposed, bare, and naked before the town's eyes. Today's wedding and reception left her without the protection she needed since they both had encouraged her to go.

Knowing that Denny would be expecting her, she walked down the street to the tavern door. Stepping inside the noisy bar, she stood glancing around for him. Every eye scanned her while she looked for one pair of brown eyes that sought hers out. The flash of recognition came when she saw him standing within a crowd all greeting each other and drinking. She felt the heads turn towards her as she moved through the crowd. Her beauty turned everyone's head as she slowly made her way to Denny.

The town had been gossiping about the doctor and her. They had noticed that after his appointments that Dr. Carter drove north out of town, not south to Winston. He had been spending time at the Norsemen Ranch. The town wondered if the young widow would marry. Their gossip and speculations were coupled with Jack and Gigi's courtship and final marriage. The town needed a wedding to talk about.

Denny took Anna's hand and walked her to his place at the wedding party's table—right in front with the three-tiered wedding cake. The couple had cut the cake with photos taken. After which, everyone came for a piece of the tasty white cake and sweet frosting. Denny pulled her chair out and asked what she wanted to drink.

Anna had an empty stomach for she had taken too long to get ready to eat before she left. After a frustrating time of deciding what to wear to the wedding, she had tried on several dresses until she finally ended with her blue floral dress that had a flared skirt. She asked for a punch. He brought her a glass after he got another drink from the bar.

The wedding couple sat down for the few congratulatory speeches. Gigi's brother-in-law Tod toasted the couple and praised them in finding each other. Denny toasted his old military buddy with the happiness of finding a woman who would put up with him and his crazy pilot's life. The couple then danced while the jukebox played a special Elvis Presley love song. Jack motioned for others to join Gigi and him. Denny took Anna's hand and then moved to the dance floor while other couples followed.

As Anna leaned against Denny in his fancy tuxedo, memories of her own wedding and reception with Caden came rushing back to her. She had been so miserable with morning sickness that she had counted every minute until they left. She didn't want to repeat a wedding like that. But then, she felt Denny's warm lips kissing her near her ear and told her she looked beautiful with her hair up. His breath tickled her as he pulled her closer against him. That was another reason she had been late to the wedding. She had trouble keeping the braid on top of her head and thus, she ended up sticking a dozen hairpins all around it to keep it in place.

When the song ended, the wedding couple wanted to leave saying that they needed to get off the ground before the weather changed. Jack and Denny hugged each other again, and he said, "Thanks for being here. You're next." Anna noticed that they smiled knowingly at each other. After they left, the crowd continue to drink and dance, celebrating the couple's wedding.

Denny wanted another drink. All the town's people seemed to want to talk to him, so Anna moved further from him as a crowd surrounded him. She slipped back to her seat and watched the couples dance. Glancing at Denny from time to time, she nibbled on the last of her piece of cake. Finally, he came back with another drink in his hand.

"You disappeared on me. Listen, I want to talk to you, alone. Would you come with me? I'm moving into Gigi's apartment upstairs," he asked, while he downed his amber drink.

Surprised flooded across her face, she asked, "When did you move?"

"Come on. I'll explain," he replied, pulling her up from her chair. They moved through the crowd to the back of the tavern and took the back staircase where he followed her upstairs with his hand on her waist. Stopping in front of his apartment, he dragged his keys out of his pocket and unlocked the door. "Welcome to my mess."

Inside, boxes were piled around the small one room apartment. "Do you want a beer, a shot of whiskey, or maybe, a cup of tea?" he asked, slipping off his black tuxedo's jacket, loosening the bowtie, and unbuttoning the top button of his white shirt. He stood waiting to hear what she wanted. He looked so handsome that her heart warmed.

"I'll take a beer," she replied, glancing around for a place to sit. He cleared away some of his clothes on the small brown couch.

"Sorry, I'm still getting settled in," he apologized. He moved over to the small fridge in the kitchenette and pulled out two bottles of beer. After popping off the tops, he walked over and handed her one. "Let's drink to my new place." They clinked their bottles together and he took a long drink. She took a sip and waited for him to sit down so that they could talk. She was anxious to hear what he had to say to her.

"Thanks for the beer. So, you moved here," she said, glancing around at the small one-room apartment.

Finally, he took a breath and sat down next to her on the small couch. "It's been quite a busy time for me. I am relocating here like I said and commuting to my Winston office," he said taking another long drink from his beer. There was not a coffee table, so he set the bottle on the floor next to his feet.

"Wow, you have been busy," she replied realizing that he now lived in town. "How lucky that you were able to get this apartment."

"Yes. Gigi moved out a few days ago. I'm still getting settled. My brothers are bringing a few furnishings from our ranch, my dresser and a wardrobe. I'm sure my mom has thrown in some other things for me," he said.

He leaned back and closed his eyes for a few minutes, a little tired from all the planning and his head buzzed from the liquor. They sat silently next to each other. In the tavern below, they could hear the sounds of a musical beat and the muffled hum of a crowd. Anna listened intently and they smiled at each other. She noticed that he looked tired around the eyes. She took a sip of her beer, setting it down next to her feet. He reached out for her free hand and squeezed it. "I've been thinking of us, of you." He slid closer to her, wrapping his arms around her. She felt his warm body next to hers, sending wild thoughts into her heart.

"I'm happy you are here, in town. I mean, in this apartment," her thoughts seemed to tumble out. She could see that he had been planning for them to be together. And sitting here, alone, in his apartment warmed her deep inside. It would be so easy to let him in.

"Is it possible you are ready to be with me? I'll continue to come and see you, but I want more," he whispered still holding her tight in his arms.

"I know you do. But..." she replied.

"But what?" he asked.

"I have reasons to be cautious," she replied. He leaned back and looked into her blue eyes, trying to understand.

"Do those reasons have names? Your children by any chance?"

"Those and more..." she answered, glancing into his brown eyes and scanning his greying temples and his strong jawline.

"What other reasons are there? Tell me. I want to understand completely, no hidden thoughts. We need to be open with each other," he said, again searching her eyes, her beautiful face, and the large braid on top of her head. He reached for the braid, started to pull at it but stopped.

"Let me. It's full of hairpins," she said as she raised her arms and started sliding out the pins. The braid fell free, and she felt his warm hand untangle the band and took apart her braid until her golden hair fell down in wild, tangled curls to her shoulders. His eyes widened as his heart tightened in his chest.

"My word, you're gorgeous Anna. I've never met anyone like you. You're an incredibly strong, compassionate woman," he whispered, threading his fingers through her golden silky hair and spreading it out. He lowered his eyes to her soft pink lips. She licked her lips, feeling his warm touches and smelling a whiff of his aromatic cologne. His lips descended on her mouth and were impassioned with his love. His caresses had every nerve in her body come alive.

He murmured, "I love you, Anna. Why can't you say 'yes'?"

Continuing to kiss her, she caught her breath and leaned back, "Do you know that I come with four children. Four. I'm a package of five. What about them? My life has been devoted to them. I have lived day by day, trying to keep going. How would it work with us?"

"I don't have all the answers, but I do know that I love you. I'm willing to take a chance. The children will adjust. Think of us together," he replied.

"I have thought about it. I do have strong feelings towards you. But I don't think that this is that easy. Listen, I'm really a mess inside. I'm still not ready," she rushed through her thoughts, trying to be honest with him. She didn't want him to be disappointed when he got to really know her busy life and all her worries.

He noticed that she seemed troubled and apprehensive, and quietly said, "Relax Anna. I know all this. We don't have to decide anything right now. Let me ask you. Is your sorrow still holding you back from loving me?" he glanced deeply into her eyes.

She closed her eyes and said, "He is still there, but not as much. I'm honestly trying to put him aside." She lowered her head and wrung her hands together.

He took her hands in his, glancing down at them. He noticed her rough hands. The skin was chapped, and the knuckles of her fingers were cracked and red. They were working hands not smooth like his. She felt embarrassed of her hands and whispered, "I didn't get a chance to polish my nails."

He smiled, brought one of her hands up to his lips, opened it, and kissed the palm. "Just remember that I love you," he murmured. Her heart swelled at his words again. When she sat beside him like this and felt his arms around her, she knew they would be good together. He had more intelligence, ambition, and compassion than any man she had known.

Suddenly, *KNOCK, KNOCK*. Her eyes-opened wide and she reached up to fix her hair and moved away from him.

A loud voice came through the closed door. "Hey, brother. Are you in there? Where did you go?"

Caught in an awkward situation, she whispered, "Where's your bathroom. I need to fix my hair?" She panicked. "Oh, I need to braid my hair." Denny helped her find the pins scattered around on the couch. Rising, she headed for the small bathroom, closing the door. She didn't want anyone to see her in such a mess.

Looking into the mirror above the sink, she quickly pulled her hair back and braided it behind her. There was not time to put it up on top. She just hoped that no one would notice. Splashing water on her face, she tried to calm down. Glancing around for a towel, she had to shake the excess water from her hands. A few boxes sat on the floor. She opened the top one and found his towels. She took one out, finished drying her face and hands, and hung it on the towel bar. Pausing at the closed door, she listened to the voices in the apartment.

"Hi, brother. We've got your furniture downstairs in my pickup. Let's go down and get them," one voice said.

"Okay. Go on down. I'll be there in a minute, Ken," said Denny.

She waited until there was a knock at the bathroom door. "Are you done, Anna?" he whispered to her. Opening the door, she came out.

"I have to go. It's getting late," she said hurrying towards the open door.

"Wait, don't leave. Stay until after my family leaves. Don't run away," he urged.

"No. Come see me when you're settled," she replied. "We'll talk later."

Just then, his brothers Ken and Ted were carrying in a dresser. Behind them came his dad Mark and his mom Eloise each carrying two empty drawers.

"Where do you want this?" asked Ken, setting it down and looking around. Seeing Anna, he added, "Oh, hello, Anna." She greeted everyone while they all stepped into the small apartment.

Turning to Denny, she again said, "Sorry, I need to get back to the ranch. Good bye." She glanced around at his family. They all nodded.

"Okay, I'll call you," he said. He wanted to say more. Denny took a deep breath as he watched the blue floral dress with the beautiful blonde braid pass out of his apartment. Gone again. He desperately wanted to follow her, but his family drew his attention back.

Anna walked down the hall, stopped at the top of the stairs, and listened. His family was talking about her and Denny.

"What's happenin' Denny? Sneakin' off to cuddle with the widow?" said one of his brothers.

"Is she still playin' hard to get?" said the other one, joking.

"It's none of your frekking business. Don't talk about her like that," replied Denny, outraged. She had never before heard him speak this way.

"Listen, boys knock it off. Leave your younger brother alone. Let's get the rest of the furniture," came his dad's response to the jabbing.

Their words had tumbled down the hall, loud enough for Anna to hear. Embarrassed, her cheeks blushed red. Tears flooded her eyes as she hurried down the stairs. Wiping the few tears with her hand, she entered the tavern from the back door. She put on a fake smile as she bravely made her way through the crowded, smoke-filled room. A few noticed her but didn't stop her. Out of the tavern door and into her car, she headed back to the ranch. Her emotions whirled inside while she thought of Denny, his confident voice, his tender words, and finally, his brothers' cutting insinuations. Yes, she was running away from the complications.

Over a year ago, the death of her husband had made her feel that she had tumbled over a steep water fall, sending her deep into a pool of churning water below, tossing her around. Her sorrow had kept her down. She struggled to get above this darkness, drowning in the indecisions surrounding her widowhood and her desires to love again. There had to be a surface where she could breathe and feel completely confident in her love for the man who loved her. She desperately wanted to be with Denny.

* * *

At the Norsemen Ranch, the final days of the hot summer were on them. After the East's wedding and reception, Anna settled back into her daily routine, taking care of the children and her chores. Every once in a while, the vulgar comments of his brothers came back to her, reminding her that people were gossiping about them. To keep herself busy, she weeded the vegetable garden and then, she sewed. While the children and Ingrid took their naps, she spent her afternoons sewing a few skirts and jumpers for the girls. School was approaching and they needed clothes, shoes, and coats. She ordered a few items for the children's wardrobes and skeins of yarn out of a catalogue. When the children had gone to bed, she started to knit a vest and two sweaters for Christmas—a dark green vest for Andy, a soft lavender sweater for Heidi, and a pale yellow one for Bridget. She wanted to knit Denny a warm neck scarf for him, choosing a deep maroon that would set off his distinguished looks.

Anna waited to hear from him and to go riding again, but they never went again that year, nor did they finish their serious talk. After he moved to town, he called her and apologized for not coming out, but he had too many appointments. He told her to ride and exercise his white stallion as much as she wanted. When he called, they would talk longer each time. He wanted to know how she was doing, and he often asked about the children. When she asked about his practice, he sounded happy. The nightly phone calls, however, never satisfied her. They had no more private, intimate moments together. She craved his presence, not just his deep, low voice on the phone.

Denny concentrated on his office in Riverside. The town's people were pleased to have a full-time doctor. But he still had to travel down to his Winston office and the hospital. After a month, he had worked out a manageable schedule where he balanced his appointments, split between two offices. He kept notes on each of his patients, spending many hours using a Dictaphone recording them. The next year, he bought a small cassette recorder into which he dictated the details of his cases while he traveled, saving him a great deal of time. The nurses then would transcribe them for his records.

Late at night, Anna spent time going over the ranching books, watching the money go out. Hans had kept her abreast of his ranching plans when he spoke to her about rounding up their cattle from the grazing lands, driving the herd down, cutting and baling their hay for winter, and selling a few steers in the fall. Chuck worked the horses and helped Andy and Heidi with theirs. Bridget's puppy grew and Hans' patiently had trained her. Anna rode her mare and Denny's stallion.

She kept Denny's words about his love close to her heart. Those words filled her with joy, reminding her that he was waiting for her to say yes. Her nights were filled with imagining them together. She longed again to feel his tender kisses, his passionate touches, and his warm body against her. With him in town, his closeness made her feel reassured. *But would he wait?*

Picking up their mail one day that late summer, Anna received one of her mom's letters from Germany. She anxiously read it; they were doing fine but missed them. The children loved hearing from their other grandparents—Oma and Opa. Oma always wrote a few of her German phrases in her letters. Heidi had become interested in other languages and would scan Oma's letters for them and write them down in a small notebook, asking her mom to translate the words.

Naturally, Anna had grown up hearing various German words and phrases. She sometimes shared them with Andy and Heidi who remembered her parents the most. Little Bridget, who barely knew them, laughed at such odd sounding words. As young children, Opa had taught Andy and Heidi to count to three since he would point to each of them and count: *eins, zwei, drei* (one, two, three), and then told them they were *meine Enkelkinder* (my grandchildren). They all laughed, loving the heavy accent in his voice.

When Anna decided to write back to her parents, Heidi wanted to add a little note to Oma and Opa, only in German. That night at the kitchen table, Heidi sat with a pencil in hand as Anna showed her what to write. She wrote down a sweet, tender phrase that said, "*Ich bin klein und mein Herz ist rein*" (I am small, and my heart is pure.). The children signed the note and she slipped it in the envelope to her parents. She told her children that their grandparents would be very happy to read a note in German.

During the first week of September, the three children started their school year. Anna had taken them all in for haircuts, making a day of shopping. Ingrid came with her and together they all had lunch before heading back to the ranch. The children again had to ride the bus to school, so getting them ready became Anna's morning routine. Excited little Bridget would be going only a half day, for kindergarten had been scheduled for the afternoon. A special bus for those ranch children going to kindergarten came a little after lunch, so Bridget rode the bus home with Andy and Heidi. After the first day of school, Bridget loved being a big girl going to school. Andy and Heidi were all happy to meet up with their classmates after the long summer.

Cade, however, missed his brother and sisters. He crawled around looking for them and going into the girls' bedroom. His legs were getting stronger as he stood up holding onto whatever was close for him. Anna held his little arms as he took step after step, but when she let him go, he sank down to his bottom and took off crawling. She guessed he would be walking nearer to his first birthday.

Their hired hand Tom Fletcher quit his job with them and returned to high school, so Chuck and Hans had their days filled with only the two of them to work the ranch. The hay had been cut and left to dry for about three days.

Early one morning, Ingrid rose and made breakfast. Taking care of the baby, Anna rose and woke up the children for school. Hans crawled out of bed, dressed, and had breakfast. Chuck came in and ate while the men planned to bale the dried hay. Hans talked about how anxious he wanted to get it done so the cattle would have feed for the long winter months. The two men sat, drank a second cup of coffee, and talked. Andy and Heidi had left that morning for school. Bridget sat at the kitchen table after breakfast and colored with her crayons. Cade crawled to his kitchen drawer to play with his toys.

For the last two weeks, Ingrid and Anna had been putting up pickles, beets, and beans. The canning in the hot fall days made both of them sweat in the kitchen while the huge kettle boiled, and the pressure cooker sputtered. The pantry shelves slowly filled up. Anna found a patch of black currants down by the river, so she had been taking a bucket down, fighting and swatting the bugs, to collect the dark berries. After cleaning them, she made the berries mixed with apple juice into a batch of jam. When other fruit came to the General Store, Ingrid and Anna made peach preserves, apple butter, and orange marmalade. The potatoes were dug up and stored in the root cellar along with their squash, carrots, and onions.

Ingrid and Anna were having a cup of tea after a long morning of canning. Bridget had caught the school bus for the afternoon kindergarten. Cade had laid down for his nap, sucked his bottle of milk and had fallen asleep. Suddenly, Chuck came rushing into the kitchen and catching his breath announced, "Hans collapsed in the field. Call the doctor," he ordered.

Ingrid jumped up, slipped on her coat, and followed Chuck out. Anna stood stunned and shocked for a second before she rushed to the phone and made the call. Outside, Chuck harnessed the buckboard to Trotter while Ingrid headed out towards the hay field, walking fast. When she got there, Hans whispered a few quiet words to her as she held his head in her lap and gripped his hand in hers before he closed his eyes and left this world.

Pulling up with the buckboard, Chuck jumped down and stood respectfully by the two. He whispered, "Ma'am. We better go. I'll come back for him."

"No, we'll take him with us," she insisted. Brushing aside her tears streaming down her cheeks, she rose and helped Chuck who struggled to pick up Hans' heavy body and place him on the buckboard. She climbed up beside the body, held his hand, and stroked her dead husband's face, crying silently. Chuck went to cover his body and face with his jacket, but she shoved it away. "No, just drive us back." While the horse slowly pulled the buckboard back to the ranch, Ingrid sat, straightening his silver hair, combing through it with her fingers. As she moved her lips, she talked to Hans in a silent conversation all the way back to the ranch house.

Anna saw them coming down the dirt road and hurried out to meet them, "I've called Dr. Carter. He's on his way. Ingrid, how is he?" From the way they both looked at her, she realized the worst. Chuck had climbed down just in time to catch Anna as she collapsed into his arms. When the world around her went black, he swept her into his arms and took her into the ranch house, putting her on the couch in the living room.

In the back of the buckboard, Ingrid gave her husband Hans a final kiss, took off her coat, and covered his body. Giving him a final glance, she moved into the ranch house, checking on Anna. Ingrid glanced at Chuck, "She fainted like this before when my son got hurt. Can you take care of her? I need to call my daughters." He nodded. She turned, went to the phone, and started to make the phone calls.

Anna opened her eyes with Chuck sitting beside her on the couch. She started to get up, but he said, "Stay put. You've had a shock." She laid back down, closing her eyes. He held her hand and squeezed it. Glancing at him, she sat up and he leaned towards her as her arms went around his neck.

"Oh, Chuck," she cried as he held her close, rubbing her back.

"It'll be all right Anna. We've been here before," he whispered, trying to keep his voice steady. Sadness flooded their hearts.

"I can't believe it," she murmured through her tears. "What happened?"

"He was complainin' about feeling bad this mornin'. I decided to stop early, thinkin' we could finish tomorrow. That's when he collapsed. I wanted to bring him back to the ranch, but he said to let him lie there and go get Ingrid. He wanted to look at the sky."

"What's Ingrid doing?" she asked.

"She's callin' her daughters," he replied, rising. "I need to go out and wait for the doctor." She nodded, rose from the couch, and went to find Ingrid who had just finished calling her four daughters.

Seeing Anna, Ingrid asked, "Are you all right?"

"Yes. What about you?" she replied. Anna gathered the old woman into her arms and held her tightly. Ingrid relaxed against her for a moment, taking in the comfort of her daughter-in-law. Anna felt the anguish flowing through her.

"We said our 'good byes.' I'm going to my bedroom," said Ingrid. Together, arm in arm, they walked down the hall. "I'll be all right. Come get me if you need something."

She walked into her bedroom and shut the door. Anna stood in the hall with a thousand thoughts going through her head. Ingrid seemed so decisive, collected, and calm unlike her own reaction of collapsing and falling apart. Glancing at her wristwatch, her thoughts tumbled to the children who would be coming home soon.

Dinner had to be started. What other calls did she need to make? Her folks in Germany—another tragic overseas call to them. *Would Fate ever stopped bringing her misery?*

She heard Denny's voice as he stepped into the ranch house. Rushing to him, he quickly embraced her and comforted her. No words were spoken for he wanted to protect her from the sorrow he saw etched across her face.

Finally, he asked, "Are you all right?"

"I am now. I fainted like a fool. I'm shaking inside," she replied.

"It's been a shock. Be strong. I'm here beside you," he whispered. He held her tighter. Then, he asked, "Where is Ingrid? I should check on her." They moved down the hall to her bedroom.

Quietly tapping on her bedroom door, she said, "Ingrid? The doctor's here. He wants to see you."

After a few minutes, Ingrid opened the door, "Hello, Dr. Carter. I already know that Hans is dead. Here's his best suit to dress him out. I want to be left alone. Do you understand?"

She handed Anna a navy blue suit with a white shirt and bolo tie. Ingrid then closed the door. Anna looked worried.

"She wants to be alone. I do have to make some calls. We'll check on her in a little while," he said.

Just then, Anna heard Cade crying, waking up from his nap, wet, and hungry. Frustrated, she said, "I'll take care of him and be with you in a minute. You know where the phone is."

Anna handed him the suit of clothes and went into her son's room. He babbled and smiled at her, "Momma." Her tears wouldn't stop while she changed his diaper and put on a pair of dry bib overalls. His delightful chubby face made her wipe her cheeks dry. She needed to get a hold of herself.

Sorrow and grief again flooded her heart. Happiness had been an imaginary empty illusion. Her recent happiness had disappeared like the iridescent pearly clouds across the horizon. Facing Hans' death, she realized that Ingrid followed her as a widow. Their future darkened around her as she gathered her baby in her arms, smelling his innocent youth and hugging him closely to her.

* * *

The early Saturday morning brought the bright eastern skies lighting up the dark forested mountains. Shadows streaked across the long valley as the orange orb rose higher, warming the cool fall air. The newly stained and painted old buildings of the ranch colored with the golden sunlight.

Last night, the Severson family all managed to get through the tragic realization of Hans' death. Between Denny and Chuck, everything had been arranged. The funeral would be in a few days. The four daughters would be coming from all around the country to their dad's funeral: Karalee and Russell, Annette and Ian, Nysa and Stuart, and Sonja and Jake. All of their families would be here with the total of Ingrid's thirteen grandchildren including Anna's four. They were all shocked by the news. Growing up on the Battle Axe Ranch, they had fond memories of their father Hans. Now, they were interested in visiting the new Norsemen Ranch. Anna didn't know where everyone was going to stay, but Ingrid called around and reserved rooms at one of the local motels.

This morning, Anna rose wanting to get to the kitchen before Ingrid, but as she walked drowsily down the hall, she heard her mother-in-law already up. Ingrid had slipped on her apron after taking a quick morning bath. She looked rested with a frown between her brows, and Anna met a determined set of eyes.

"Morn," whispered Anna.

Silently, Ingrid nodded at her. The two set to work on getting breakfast for their family. Ingrid mixed up her biscuits using the cream from the day before. The two children left to milk the cow Magic. The baby woke, needing to be changed and fed. A little later, Bridget came into the kitchen and wanted to be held as she crawled up into her mom's lap while she fed the baby in his highchair. Cade smiled at his sister, and mumbled, "Sissy, Sissy" in his baby words.

"Mom, who's going to sit in Grandpa's chair now?" asked Bridget, sadly looking at the empty chair at the head of the table.

Anna kissed her daughter's cheek and whispered, "Don't worry. It'll be all right dear."

Last evening, the children were devastated to hear the sad news. The girls piled around her on the couch, tears streaming down their young cheeks while she hugged them. Denny had a few private words with Andy who had taken the news like a young man that he was growing up to be. The baby was oblivious to all the unhappiness, playing in his kitchen drawer with his toys.

When Andy left, Anna followed him. He closed his bedroom door. And when she tapped on it, he said he didn't want to talk. But she went in. He turned away, hiding his tears, quickly wiping them from his cheeks.

"Oh Andy. Come here," she said, embracing her oldest son.

"Why dad? And now Grandpa?" he asked. She noticed that her son was holding in his sorrow, trying to be brave despite the hurt.

"That's the big mystery—why. Let it out, son. There's no shame in crying," she whispered. "Tears are the price we pay for loving someone deeply, like you did with your dad and now your Grandpa." She held him tight against her while he sobbed into her shoulder, feeling overwhelmed with sorrow. But after a while, he settled down and she said, "It'll hurt for a long time, but eventually, you must go on. Make your dad and Grandpa proud." He nodded and she left him alone, closing the door.

Ingrid spent all night in her bedroom. Anna had taken her a dinner plate, and the girls made their grandma a cup of tea. Thanking them and embracing them, Ingrid hugged and kissed her granddaughters. Then, she closed her bedroom door, leaving them all standing in the hall.

This morning, Ingrid looked at Anna after they had eaten breakfast, "You're going to be in charge of the ranch now."

Anna took a deep breath, "Do you think we should stay? How will we manage?" She had her doubts, despite all of Hans' words and plans.

"Like we always have. We get up and go to work day after day. You know everything about ranching. Hans gave you the reins long before this all happened. There's no selling or moving away. Do you hear?" emphasized Ingrid. "I'm going to live the rest of my life right here, beside you and the children. No more fussing."

She saw a determined old widow sitting across from her. Then, Andy and Heidi came in from milking, sat down for breakfast, and began eating.

A knock at the back door broke their silence. Chuck walked in with Fred, Clyde, and Lettie Fletcher. They had arrived a few minutes ago after hearing the news last night. By now, everyone in town had heard and their hearts were saddened to hear that the old

Norwegian had died. His long-time notoriety in the community left an enormous empty hole in the ranching world.

Clyde carried a chocolate sheet cake and Lettie, a large casserole dish for the grieving family, and Fred, a basket of rolls. They greeted the new widow along with their sympathy. With a brave face, Ingrid slipped the casserole into the fridge, and Lettie said, "I hope your family likes lasagna."

"Thank you. We do," replied Ingrid.

Everyone sat down at the kitchen table while Anna made a pot of coffee.

"We came to help. My son Tom is on his way," said Clyde, looking at Chuck who quickly looked at Ingrid. The old woman smiled and gave Fred, Clyde, and Lettie a warm glance. Their kindness overwhelmed her as she swept a tear from her eye.

"Thank you. We could use the help," replied Ingrid. Pointing to Anna, "She's in charge now. Chuck, I'm depending on you to stay on. Now, eat your breakfast before it gets too cold."

"Yes, ma'am. I'm here to stay," said Chuck. Glancing at Anna, he continued, "The hay needs to be bailed today. There's another field to be cut," he replied, talking between bites as he quickly ate his breakfast.

Another knock at the back door. With his hat in his hand, Tom came into the kitchen. The children all brightened up to see him. He had been working the ranch all summer. Everyone greeted him.

The little kitchen was getting crowded, so Anna suggested that the girls go play in their rooms. She wiped the baby's face and hands, lifted him from his highchair, and set him down to crawl off and play.

"Ma'am, I'm really sorry about Hans. I'm here to help on week-ends for a few weeks," said Tom. He apologized for not being able to help after school, but he had basketball practice.

"Thank you, son. Sit and have something to eat," replied Ingrid. Anna rose and poured the coffee. Homemade biscuits with sausages were passed around.

Andy piped up and said, "I can help, too."

"Well, there's plenty to do," replied Chuck. Wiping his mouth with a napkin, he had finished eating and took a sip of his coffee.

The men sat around and talked more about the work for the day. Finally Clyde rose. "Shall we get busy?" he asked in his take charge manner. They all gulped down the last of their coffee, said their good byes, and left the kitchen.

Clyde and Fred ran the baler while Chuck and Tom cut the next field of hay. Andy was sent to feed the horses. When he finished, he joined the men out in the fields, helping where he could.

The women worked in the house. The laundry baskets were full of dirty clothes, and Anna started the washer and hung three loads out to dry on the clotheslines. The children would need clean clothes for school. Lettie helped in the kitchen and with the washing.

Anna wanted Ingrid to sit and relax, but she said she needed to keep busy. Yesterday, Anna had picked another bucket full of cucumbers and Ingrid wanted to make another batch of pickles. With the three women working together, the boiling water in a pot was soon filled with jars of pickles to process. The children stayed in the house and played or read. After lunch, they took their naps.

The women took a break after lunch and talked.

"When you have the round-up Anna, I'll have Clyde bring our border collie Maggie along to help. She'll be a great help," said Lettie, thinking ahead to next week's round-up.

"That's a good idea. That will help little Dwarfy follow Maggie's lead," she replied. Anna had considered all the ranch work that Chuck had mentioned.

Ingrid sat considering the funeral and said, "I told my daughters not to wear black at the funeral. Yesterday, I saw you pressing your black wool suit Anna. Just put that back in that bag and zip it up. Wear something colorful. We're celebrating Hans' life, not his death. Besides, Hans never liked the color black."

Both Anna and Lettie looked surprised. "Won't the town think we are being disrespectful?" commented Anna, fearing the gossip of such a showing.

"I don't care what they think. It's my husband's funeral. I'm respecting Hans," insisted Ingrid, satisfied with her decision.

"Are you taking the children to the funeral?" asked Lettie.

"I'm not sure. I think Andy and Heidi will go. But it's better that Bridget and the baby stay," replied Anna. She recalled that they had left the children at home with Abigail Johnson when they had her husband's funeral.

Ingrid considered the question, "I think we should all go. It may help them to grieve. Children need to be part of our life. We can't shield them forever. Bridget should go. The baby will be okay."

That settled it. The children would go. She noticed how decisive her mother-in-law had become. Thinking on it, she knew that she would have to follow her example in running the ranch in the future.

When the day ended, the hay had been baled and stacked in the barn. The other field had been cut to dry for a few days. Dinner came with everyone hungry and tired. Filling their empty stomachs, they ate the delicious food that the Fletchers had brought. Fred, Clyde and Lettie with Tom left with thanks from the Seversons for their help.

Anna had noticed the emptiness that surrounded them without Hans' silver head and his sparkling blue eyes. They would miss his loving words, his knowledge, and his wise guidance. The children would miss his old folktales and his laughter when he teased or tickled them. He had dominated their lives and they would suffer the loss for years to come. As little Bridget had noted—his chair sat empty at the kitchen table.

The yellow glowing lights at the Norsemen Ranch darkened as bedtime came early for Ingrid, Anna, and the children. In her bed, Anna closed her tired eyes and thought of the coming funeral, recalling Caden's. The sorrow lay deep in her soul. Now, Hans would be joining his only son in the cemetery. Her heart felt as if it had been torn apart again in these last few days. Tears filled her eyes and she silently wept into her pillow.

If she had felt a heavy yoke on her shoulders before, now it had grown even heavier with the responsibility of the Norsemen Ranch. She reached deep inside to gather strength that she was going to need. Yes, Hans, and her husband, had given her the means to do this, but the weight frightened her, hoping that she could maintain their livelihood.

* * *

On the day of the funeral, the town and all the ranches had been drenched the night before with a heavy rain storm which raged with flashes of lightning and of deafening thunder. In the morning, heavy darkened clouds filled the sky, making it a grey day. The

299

blue mountains and peaks were soaked, and the dark forests dripped with the dew. The river ran muddy water against its banks. The sun never found the earth that day, so a cold, chill air surrounded the people who had ventured out to the little church.

Like Ingrid had instructed, the Severson's large family members all wore colorful clothes. Filling the wooden pews on the right side of the church, they stood out against the black town mourners. The people filled not only the church but the grounds around the outside. Standing against the chilly day, town's people paid their respects to Ingrid and her large family.

All of the grandchildren sitting in the wooden pews wiggled and shifted through the long minister's words. A baby's loud cry broke the stillness in the church. It was Sonja's newborn. She needed to nurse him, so she sat down, covered herself with a baby blanket, and nursed him. Silence again descended on the mourners.

In Anna's arms, Cade fussed and wanted down to crawl, tired of being held. Denny had managed to sit a few pews behind her. He slowly moved up to her row and reached over and took Cade into his arms. Somehow that settled the baby for a while until they all left for the cemetery. Denny and Anna stood tightly beside each other in the crowded row. She grabbed his free hand and squeezed it. His warm firm hand gave her comfort.

He stayed with her, carrying Cade when they walked over to the cemetery. She had a hold of the girls' hands as they walked together with Denny. The town's people all murmured their sympathies to Ingrid as she walked slowly with her family. Many noticed the bright colors, but no one dared to speak a word to the widow as she stared ahead with her chin held up.

Chuck, Clyde, Fred, Tom, Chet, and Brad Johnson carried Hans' casket over to the cemetery. Many people left after the minister said a few gravesite words. The Severson's stayed at the cemetery while thanking the Johnson's and the Fletcher's. They lowered Hans' casket into the dark grave while Anna stared at the ghastly hole in the dark earth. Fred walked over to Ingrid, giving her his sympathies. Turning to Anna, she felt his arms surround her and he held her tightly to him, just like he did that night on the mountain when Hans torched the grizzly hide. Fred whispered that if she needed any help, he would be there. They parted and he stepped back.

Anna glanced at the Caden's tombstone next to his grave. She picked up one of the smaller arrangements of red and white carnations adorning Hans' grave. With her two daughters and son, she told them to follow her over to their dad's grave. She realized that none of the children had been to his grave, nor had they ever seen his grey marble tombstone. The four of them stood together looking at the inscription: *Hans Caden Severson, Jr. 1937 – 1961, A loving son and father.*

"Do you mean that daddy's been here all the time? I thought he was up in the mountains," said little Bridget.

"Yes, my dear. I probably should have brought you all here to his grave sooner. We can come here and put flowers on your dad's and your grandpa's graves, if you want," she said to her children.

"My dad's first name was 'Hans'," stated Andy, reading the inscription. Heidi looked curiously at her mom.

"Yes, that's right. We called him by his middle name," she explained. They stood together as the chilled air seeped in through their clothes.

Little Bridget finally said, "I'm cold."

"Yes. Let's go. I am cold too," replied Anna.

Cade had started to fuss while Denny held him, so Anna walked over and took him into her arms. "Come with us, Denny. We're having a luncheon over at the Saddle Horn Restaurant," she said.

"Sure, but I have appointments starting at two," he said, looking at his wristwatch. He had thirty minutes before he had to be at the office. Together they left with the children and headed toward the restaurant.

The Saddle Horn had set up a buffet in their banquet room reserved for the Severson's family. When Anna, Denny, and the children came into the room, the family had started filling up their plates. Ingrid told Anna that they were all leaving for home after the luncheon. The tables quickly filled up with their family members who had not seen each other for a long time. This was the first time they had all been together in one room since Caden's funeral. The noise level had gotten so loud that Anna and Denny couldn't hear each other talk. Ingrid with her daughters were all talking about their children who ate quickly. The younger ones were running around chasing each other until their parents stopped them.

Anna made her children stay in their seats until they finished their lunch. Then, they joined their cousins. Anna went around and talked to each of her sisters-in-law and husbands. All of them were anxious to get on the road; they had checked out of their motel rooms and wanted to get back to their homes. While they were getting ready to leave, Ingrid hugged them, holding tightly to her grandchildren and giving them a kiss. The banquet room finally emptied out except for Anna, Ingrid, and her children.

Denny had left shortly after they had arrived, grabbing a sandwich to take with him to the office. "Sorry I've got to go," he said. She had started to stand up, but with his hand on her shoulder, he had told her to stay.

She had looked up at him, "Thanks for being here today."

"I'll call you. Maybe, we can get together soon," he had whispered, giving her a kiss on the cheek as she sat with Cade in her lap. He lingered there for a moment. She had breathed in his familiar scent and then he left. She had watched him leave the banquet room, suddenly feeling lonely.

Finally, back at the Norsemen Ranch, Anna put Cade down for a nap with a bottle. Ingrid wanted the girls to take a nap with her, so they all cuddled down and slept with their grandma who wanted the company.

While everyone was sleeping, Anna decided to find Chuck and talk in more detail about the ranch. Changing, she slipped out of her dress and pulled on her jeans and her blue flannel shirt. Grabbing her jacket, she left the ranch house. She found Chuck in the old barn. He had been at the funeral but had left after the gravesite ceremony. Before he left, he told her that he wanted to get back to the ranch and would see her later.

In the barn, he had been moving some of the hay bales around. He stopped when he saw Anna stepping through the wide opened doors.

"Hi, Anna. Sit," he said, pointing to one of the bales. He waited for her to sit, and then, he sat down on another one. He brushed the hay off his jeans and took off his leather gloves from working.

"Thanks. I came here to talk more about the ranch," she said. "I must admit that I know a little about it, but you know so much more. I'm depending on you to help me. How do you see it?"

"One thing is on our side," he replied.

"What is that?" she asked.

"We have a much smaller ranch than we did over at the Battle Axe. I can handle our herd. After that rain last night, we need to wait to bale the hay that we cut. Later, the cattle need to be rounded up and driven down here. Clyde said he and one of his sons would ride with us. We just have to give him a call to set it up," he explained.

"Are we going to have to hire anyone permanently?" she asked.

"I don't think so. We can hire a wrangler in the spring before brandin' just like we did with Tom and let him go after the round-up," he replied.

They sat silently in the old barn. She had so many questions, but she didn't want to overwhelm him, for some of her questions were really just worries. She didn't want to shift her burden over to him.

"You know that I have been keeping the books for the ranch. So that is taking care of. And we have a good cushion to fall back on. But we will have to sell some of the steers each year," she said.

"Good. I have somethin' I need to tell you. Do you remember when Hans helped the Fletcher's rebuild their damaged log house? And then, he helped Fred move that old cabin from town?" he asked.

She nodded, "Yes, what about them?"

"Well, seein' that old cabin rekindled the woodsman in Hans. Come here to the back room. Let me show you," he said, rising off the hay bale and pointing to a back door. She followed him into a small room with a tall bench table against the wall and a few wooden stools. On this long rough table, he spread out a sketch of the ranch and it's buildings. He laid a large drawing of a log cabin down next to the layout of the ranch.

"Hans had been plannin' to build a log cabin about here," said Chuck pointing to a place next to the old ranch house. "He told me not to say anythin', but he's been cuttin' down pine trees, strippin' them of the branches and bark, and preparin' them for a log cabin."

Anna stood glancing down at the plans. Her eyes widen as she realized what Hans had been doing. Surprise crossed her face.

"My word. He's worked himself into that grave," she whispered.

"He wanted to build a cabin for Ingrid and him, givin' you the ranch house. He hoped that you'd get married before too long," he said.

She slowly sat down on one of the wooden stools, still in shock. Her voice found no words to express the wonder of Hans and his resourceful ways of thinking of others.

"I've been with him a few times when he worked on those logs. They are still up there in the mountains, stacked up. He planned to build the cabin in the spring. He's notched all of them. I could bring 'em down next spring and get it built. What do you think?" he said, sitting down on the other wooden stool. He glanced at the plans, studying them closely. Hans had taught him a lot about how to build a log cabin.

"I have no idea what to do. Did Ingrid know about this?" she asked.

"No, Hans kept his plans close to his chest. I'm the only one who knew," he replied. He noticed that she looked so stunned, startled, and bewildered. He added, "Listen, let's not focus on this. I just wanted you to know about it." He folded up the plans and the sketch. The two sat for a few minutes in silence. She considered the idea of a log cabin, but her mind shifted back to the ranch.

"Did we get enough hay for the winter?" she asked.

"We might need more. Let's sit down and talk after the round-up," he replied. "Can I ask you somethin' personal?"

"What?" she asked.

"Are you goin' to get married? I've seen you and the doc together here at the ranch. When we were saddlin' the horses, Carter talked a lot about how he missed ranchin'. He'd be a good asset Anna," he said. He stood up and walked out of the back room.

She quickly looked down and blushed at his question. She had been mulling that over for a long time. They would be well-matched. Rising, she headed back to the ranch house.

The afternoon slipped into twilight and then into evening. Hans' death hung around everyone's mind. They had a quiet evening by the wood stove, reading, sewing, and playing until bedtime.

After the children were in bed, Anna sat in the kitchen for a final cup of tea before going to bed herself. The ranch was foremost on her mind. Chuck's revelation about the log cabin gave her pause. And then, the consideration about her and Denny's future. Waving away those thoughts, she had to focus on the children and on the ranch. That decision about Denny would have to wait. Finishing her tea, she left the kitchen, turning off the lights and headed towards her bedroom.

With Hans' death, her life suddenly felt even more complicated than before. Compounded with the responsibilities of the ranch, she recalled how within just a year and a half that her life had been turned upside down. Nothing seemed normal. The future's uncertainty would have to be confronted. Alone, she thought about the need for a shoulder to lean on. She needed reassuring. Touching the empty pillow beside her, she would have to do it alone, by herself. She would have to be strong for her children and for Ingrid. *How long would Denny wait for her now?* Another delay. She desperately wanted to see him. Closing her eyes, she turned over and curled up under the covers. Sleep slowly took her into the dreamworld. The dark shadows of the night surrounded the exhausted young widow.

* * *

The fall months around the Norsemen Ranch were busy getting ready for the long cold winter months. Anna rose each morning, facing every day with doubts. *What could happen today?* Andy, Heidi, and Bridget were busy with school work, excited about what they were learning. Cade had his first birthday and took his first steps along with his two front teeth finally breaking through the gums. When the men rode up to get the cattle, Anna rode along. The border collie Maggie and little Dwarfy turned out to be so helpful that Anna thought she'd like to get another collie.

And she did call around and got another young pup for the kids to raise during the winter months. By spring, the collie would be old enough to run with Dwarfy and herd the cattle. Heidi named the male collie Loki, keeping with their ancestral tradition at the Norsemen Ranch.

Chuck kept his promise and worked every day to manage the herd and finish the repairs that Hans had wanted completed. Tom Fletcher showed up on the weekends for a month after the funeral. The two men worked from dawn to dusk. Tom told her that he didn't want to be paid, but Anna insisted that he should be paid. She didn't want to live off of charity any longer than necessary. Besides, Tom had put in a full working day alongside Chuck.

Hunting season came and Chuck with his friend Jim McDobb took their horses up for a week of elk hunting. He cleaned his .30-30 Winchester loaded the pack saddle and headed for the mountains. They came back down on the fourth day, loaded with eight quarters of meat. Jim took his meat and Chuck hung his in a shed to cure. With Ingrid and Anna wrapping, he butchered the quarters one night. After they filled their deep freezer along with packages of scraps for the collies, Anna felt pleased.

Denny called often, but he was swamped with appointments. He rarely made it out to visit her, and he only came for dinner. The children were happy to have him at their kitchen table, for they had much to talk about. He listened to what they were learning in school, and he questioned them about their studies.

Anna listened all the while thinking about him and her together. She watched his hands hold his knife or fork, imagining them caressing her. When he laughed in his deep, low voice, she recalled his whispers into her ear. As he drank his coffee, she saw his soft lips which had kissed her, sending chills down her spine. Yes, their evening dinners kept his image alive for her. But then, he left, driving away, waving 'goodbye,' and leaving her wanting him.

During those months before the holidays, they both understood that they lived in two demanding worlds. When Denny stayed for dinner, they managed to catch a few private moments when the children were busy. Ingrid helped by shuffling the children away so they could have some quiet, cozy, intimate time together.

On a Thursday before their holiday vacation, Heidi asked, "Are we going to light the Menorah like Oma did with the candles?" The children had recalled the mystery of the Jewish traditions of lighting the candles which Oma called the Festival of Lights. They didn't know much more than that, but they loved the candelabra with its glowing candles.

Anna smiled, "Of course. This will be our first Christmas at our new ranch, and we should celebrate it like we always have. I'll unpack the Menorah and set it on a table next to the Christmas tree."

"Oh, mom. Can we make a popcorn string for the tree?" asked Bridget. She liked eating the popcorn more than stringing it.

"Yes. We can also make popcorn balls for the holidays," said Ingrid, getting into the mood of the holidays.

"And speaking about your Oma and Opa, I received a Christmas gift from Germany from them today. I'll put it under our tree, but she wrote a short letter saying that they loved your German note to them. They taped it on their fridge and look at it every day," said Anna, pulling the letter from her apron pocket. They spent time reading the letter, and afterwards Heidi looked for the German phrases, again writing them down.

As the holidays approached, the children got excited about putting up a Christmas tree and decorating it. Chuck and Andy rode into the mountains and cut a tree the week-end before Christmas. After the green pine tree stood in the corner of the living room, the baby couldn't leave it alone, pulling off the bulbs or crawling under to get the gifts. Anna finally piled the gifts on a table with the Menorah and took off the decorations from the lower branches. To Cade, the tree was a new toy for him to play with.

Ingrid and the girls made sugar cookies with cutters shaped like bells, candy canes, stars, and stockings. They frosted them, sprinkling them with green and red sprinkles. Anna made her mom's fruit cake soaked in brandy.

Leaving before Christmas, Chuck traveled to Midler where he celebrated the holidays with his mom, dad, and his sister Emma and her family. Surprised, Anna had given him his gift before he left, saying she hoped that he enjoyed the visit with his family. She had knitted him a bed cover made from the left over yarn. The warm cover had turned out to be a colorful addition to his bed in the bunkhouse.

Anna asked Denny to spend Christmas Eve with them. Ingrid wanted her to make her mom's Matzah ball soup for their dinner. The dumplings were made with matzah meal and after they were cooked, the large dumplings were put in a chicken soup with a few vegetables. The children loved them.

For the Severson's, opening their presents on Christmas Eve had been their tradition. After dinner, they gathered in the living room while Andy and Heidi passed out their gifts. Denny loved his knitted neck scarf, and the children tried on their knitted gifts. Oma and Opa had send them a box of special chocolates which were passed around. Ingrid and Anna had gone Christmas shopping for the children when they were at school. They had picked out a pocket knife for Andy, a little jewelry box for Heidi, a doll for Bridget, and set of plastic tools for Cade. Anna bought them all a new pair of gloves, and for Ingrid, she bought a lovely head scarf to wear.

Cuddled around the warm wood stove, the children sang a few Christmas songs. Then, going into the kitchen, they had a cup of hot chocolate and a few of their sugar cookies. Denny slipped his arm around Anna as they sat on the couch watching the orange and red fire flicker in the wood stove.

"I'd like to take you out to celebrate New Year's Eve," said Denny. "I'll fix us a little dinner and then we can go out dancing."

"Sounds fun. Maybe, I can bring something for dessert," she said.

"Sure," he added. Glancing at his watch, he continued, "I should go. It's late and it's going to snow tonight." He leaned down and kissed her. She put her arms around his neck and leaned into his body. "I look forward to our night out. I miss being with you," he whispered in her ear as he kissed her soft neck.

She murmured back, "Yes, me too."

He slowly stood up, held out his soft hand to her as she slipped her hand into his. She rose up from the couch into his arms again. He embraced her one last time before he left. Walking together into the kitchen, he said 'goodbye' to the children, slipped on his new neck scarf, and pulled on his coat. Anna walked to the door as he opened it. They looked up at the dark sky with a heavy snow starting to fall.

"Be careful driving back. Give me a call when you get there," she said. He nodded as she watched him walk to his blue pickup. With his wipers clearing the snow off his windshield, he left the ranch. Anna watched his red taillights disappear down the dirt road to the highway. She thought of him going back to that empty apartment, alone. Closing the door, she moved back into the kitchen and joined the children while they had their hot chocolate and cookies. Ingrid poured her a cup of tea while she took one of the children's sugar cookies.

Later the phone rang, and she spoke to him for a few minutes. They all went to bed with the white snow blanketing the ranch, the livestock, the wide valley, and the forested mountains.

* * *

The next day, a cold morning, Anna, Ingrid, and the children rose early. While Chuck was gone, she and Andy had planned to feed the herd. After eating a quick bowl of warm oatmeal, they bundled up and headed out. Andy and Heidi quickly milked Magic. The cattle were bellowing with their warm breaths floating into the cold air. Anna hitched up Gallo to the buckboard and helped Andy load the bales of hay. She drove out and into the pasture while Andy broke up the bales and tossed the hay out for the hungry cattle. Both of them were shivering when they finished. Riding back to the old barn, Anna unhitched Gallo, brushed him down, and fed him his grain. Andy went to feed the other horses in the other pasture.

Coming into the kitchen, they all had a hot drink to warm them inside. The next few days were exhausting, but they had worked together to keep their livestock fed until Chuck came back.

The heavy snow had left deep snow around the ranch. One day with the sun shining, Anna suggested that they go sledding. She knew they would be headed back to school soon, so she wanted to be with them as much as she could. They bundled up again and headed towards a small hill behind the old barn where they could sled. With Cade in Anna's lap, they rode down the hill several times. She could tell that he was thrilled with the ride.

The children's laughter filled the cold winter air. The border collies Dwarfy and Loki leaped through the snow, chasing each other and the children. The girls and Andy started a snowball fight. Finally, chilled to the bone, they went back into the warm ranch house where Ingrid had baked cinnamon rolls. They warmed up with a hot chocolate and a roll. Their red cheeks were chapped from the cold when they laid down for naps.

New Year's Day was soon approaching, and Ingrid planned to bake a ham for dinner. Anna could think only of the evening that Denny planned for them. She baked an apple pie, dressed up in a warm, red sweater, and black slacks. Recalling that he liked her hair up, she fixed her braid on top of her head. On icy roads, Denny drove out to the ranch to pick her up. Before she left, Ingrid privately told her to stay in town tonight. She didn't want to worry about them coming back to the ranch on treacherous roads. She also told her to invite him to their ham dinner. Anna nodded and gave her a hug.

While he drove back to town, she sat quietly next to him, not speaking since he needed to focus on driving the icy roads. Her mind had been spinning with eagerness to be with him. Parking behind the tavern, they walked upstairs to his apartment. Warming in the oven, he had made a simple beef stew which he dished out and lit a candle on his little table. He opened a bottle of wine, pouring them each a glass. She thought that it was so romantic and so like him.

After they had eaten, she glanced at Denny. Since the holidays, she had mulled over his desires for her. She had made her decision and didn't want to delay it any longer. "I want to get married," she announced.

He quickly glanced up from his glass of wine and sputtered red liquid over the table as he gasped. Setting it down, "Did you just say 'yes'?" amazed at her proposal.

"Yes… yes… yes. I am ready to take that step. I know there's much for us to work through—the kids and the ranch, but …" she stopped as he rose and came over to her side of the table. He took her hands in his and lifted her up into his arms.

"Don't talk," he whispered as his lips descended on her soft lips. He kissed her passionately while he slowly walked her over to his bed. They fell on the bed, madly kissing each other. She tasted the wine in his kiss as his warm hands slipped under her red sweater to feel her velvet soft skin.

His fierce, fiery desire had been set loose and in a whirlwind of emotions; he soon had taken off his shirt and had lifted off her sweater as they kissed each other. Her braided hair tumbled down while his fingers sought out the feel of her silky hair, freeing it of its twisted braid and sending her hair in a wildly tangle mess of curls. His bare chest brushed up against her breasts as he caressed them. Her body responded to his firm loving touches. She melted into his body.

Yes, she had made the right choice. No thoughts of her husband, only of this man who was ravishing her. A burning desire rose deep within her, more than she had ever felt before. Her hands moved across his bare chest. She softly kissed him as her wet lips followed her hands. He groaned at her loving caresses. He moved between her legs, pulling her into him. He murmured in her ear, "I love you so much Anna."

She whispered back, "I love you."

While the glowing candle on the small table melted down and finally burned out, the two lovers discovered their sensual attraction for each other could not be satisfied with one loveable moment, but they made love several times. Afterwards falling into a luring sleep, they dragged the covers over them, wrapped in each other's arms.

Down below in the noisy, crowded tavern, the New Year's Eve party was in full swing. Hearing the beat of a song and the buzzing hum of a crowd below them, Denny woke, rubbed his eyes opened, glanced at Anna lying in his arms, and groaned, "Oh no, living here has its disadvantage."

She opened her eyes, moved above him, and leaning against him, she gave him a kiss, "Forget about them. You're like a wild tiger."

"I should be. I've had my feelings locked down for over ten months. I've counted every day and every night waiting for you. Cold showers helped," he smiled, flipping her over, moving on top, and pulling her under him as he kissed the soft spot below her ear. "And I don't want to let you go. But I told Jack we'd hook up with him tonight. Do you want to go down? I know you like to dance."

Snuggling against him, "I love it here, but sure, let's go down."

He smiled, "But first, I have a little something to give you." He leaned over on his elbow, opened a little drawer on the side table, and handed her a small, box wrapped in red. "Open this."

She scooted out from under him and slowly unwrapped the ribbon, and then the beautiful red paper. A small black box looked at her from inside the bigger box. Opening it, Anna saw a dazzling round diamond with smaller sparkling diamonds surrounding it. She gasped and glanced at him amazed. "Oh, how gorgeous." Her heart beat fast.

"I had planned on asking you tonight, but you got the jump on me. I hope you like it," he scooted up next to her. "Try it on."

She slipped it onto her fourth finger. "It fits perfectly. How did you know?" she asked. "But it's too exquisite to wear."

"Nothing is too good for you. I asked Ingrid to help me," he replied.

"She knew?" she recalled that Ingrid had told her to stay with him tonight—it wasn't just the icy roads that she was talking about.

"Of course. I planned on giving it to you on Christmas eve, but I had to send it away to get it sized. I told Ingrid that I was serious about making you my wife. She blessed and hugged me, saying that I would make a good husband and father," he explained, smiling at the tender memory. "She's one remarkable woman, just like you Anna." He leaned down and looked seriously into her blue eyes while his fingers pushed her silky hair behind her ears. "With you and your children, we'll make a great family together."

"Let's not talk about them tonight. But I do want to get one promise from you," she said, looking up into his handsome face, and into his intense brown eyes.

"What?"

"I don't want to have another child until Cade is out of diapers," she said seriously looking for his response.

He leaned back on his pillow, laughing in his deep low voice. "Oh Anna. Of course. I understand. Anything else?"

"No. Let this night be about you and me," she said, turning towards him and with her arms around his neck, she pulled him into a heated kiss. Her kiss sent him wanting her again, and he slipped her under him, touching her with his roaming hands. But she gently pushed him back and whispered, "What about your buddy Jack? And the party? Let's go down. We can finish this later."

He sighed, "Okay," and fell back again on his pillow.

They quickly dressed. She combed and fixed her wild, tangled hair, braiding it tightly, but leaving it down. She noticed that they had not eaten her pie, but she knew that they would be coming back up after midnight.

Going down the stairs and into the tavern, the two moved through the crowds to join Jack and Gigi who had a small table at the back of the tavern. Denny announced his engagement to the couple, and she had to show them her sparkling diamond ring. He asked Jack to be his best man. Jack waved down the barmaid and ordered a bottle of whiskey with four shot glasses to celebrate. Anna limited herself to three shots and finally turned her shot glass upside down. She couldn't help but look at her engagement ring, shining in the smoke-filled tavern.

Many of the ranchers were there along with the town people. Jack's excited words about his military buddy getting married circulated around the tavern. Soon everyone had heard, and the news ran through the bar like a wild fire, and before long, everyone felt happy for the Severson widow and their local doctor. They shouted "Anna and Denny" several times, congratulating them. Every time someone congratulated them, Denny and Jack gulped down a shot. Gigi and Anna both tried to slow the men down, but they were in a party mood, kidding and joking. Then, Chuck with his date came over and wished them the best. The two men shook hands; Chuck gave Anna a knowing nod. She lowered her head and blushed, recalling his words about Denny.

Even though Denny got terribly drunk, Anna pulled him onto the dance floor where they danced close together. The midnight hour came, and they counted down the last ten seconds until the hour struck twelve o'clock. Kissing in the new year, the couples came together. Denny invited his buddy Jack and Gigi up for coffee and a piece of pie.

Finally, holding on to each other, the two couples stumbled upstairs to his apartment. Coming into his place, Anna put on a pot of coffee and Gigi cut the apple pie. The two men sat at the small table, talking about their work—helicopters, flying, medicine, and ranching. They enjoyed each other's company while they all drank the coffee and ate the apple pie and sobered up. Both men had a second piece, and Gigi complimented Anna on her delicious pie.

Ultimately, Jack and Gigi left, leaving Denny and Anna alone. He smiled at her, embracing her into his arms. Together, they turned out the lights and moved into his bed.

"Come here, my love. My head may be spinning, but I want to finish what we started earlier." They came together, folded in each other's arms.

A crescent moon hung in the cold night sky. The freezing winter night frosted up the apartment windows while inside their burning desires kept them warm.

* * *

A month later, in February, they were married. Anna had called her parents overseas but this time with good news. The couple chose to have a small ceremony at the Carter's ranch—the Double D. She asked Gigi to be her matron of honor along with Jack as the best man. Anna wore a light blue chiffon dress; the two men rented tuxedos with white jackets and light blue cummerbunds. In the Carter's large living room and with a short ceremony, the minister wedded them with their loving families surrounding them. The guests included their closest ranching friends: the Fletcher's and the Johnson's. Denny invited his nurse Alice and his receptionist with their husbands.

Eloise and Ingrid planned the wedding, the dinner following, and baked a special wedding cake. Denny's dad Mark bought the champagne to celebrate his youngest son's marriage.

When they exchanged rings, Denny had chosen a simple gold band for her to wear with her diamond engagement ring. She slipped a matching gold band on his fourth finger. After the minister announced them as husband and wife, the children all gathered around the couple.

Denny and Anna didn't go on a honeymoon; they returned that evening to the Norsemen Ranch beginning their life together. When they were alone in their bedroom, he gave her a special wedding gift—a golden heart necklace with their names engraved on it. Romantically, she recalled the tree that he had carved their initials *A & D.*

After the wedding, Anna couldn't believe how the children easily welcomed Denny into their lives, for he didn't push himself onto them. Slowly, the children adjusted to his presence. He added so much to their lives and with his intelligence and his world-wide experiences, he knew so much about everything. He showed an honest interest in who they were as individuals.

On the week-ends, he along with Chuck helped with the ranch which he said he had missed. He groomed the horses, helped feed the cattle, and took a look at the ranch's books. Yes, his medical practice kept him busy during the week, but he managed to balance a full life with Anna by his side.

She knew that there would be clashes, even maybe some arguments or disagreements. Not every day would be easy, but with Denny by her side, she knew that she had found a deep love that she had so desired. She no longer slept alone at night. With his head on his pillow and his warm body next to her in the night, he had carried away the darkness that had drowned her for nearly two years as a widow. Being Anna Carter helped put the pieces of her love life together. Happiness floated back into her life. She had a deep caring love for him who showered her with his constant, persistent love almost every night.

After a week of sitting together and eating their meals at their kitchen table, little Bridget asked her grandma, "Can Denny sit in Grandpa's chair?"

Everyone waited as the old widow nodded her grey head and said, "He certainly may."

Lettie's Path

While Lettie (Violet) Fletcher sat at her dressing table in the bedroom, she fingered liquid make-up to her face. She then opened her compact and took out the powder puff, brushing a light beige over her shining nose and cheeks. In her early seventies, her aged face had the usual sun spots on the side of her cheeks, a few wrinkles around her mouth, and deeper wrinkles in the corners of her eyes. Brushing a little mascara over her eyelashes, she looked into her two colored eyes—one blue and one grey. Her brown eyebrow pencil gave her an arched eyebrow over each of her most hated feature—her eyes. Even after all the many years, Lettie still cautiously lowered her eyelids. She had so many experiences from people who were shocked at her dual-colored eyes that she avoided looking straight at those who were unacquainted with her. Around her family, her friends, and most of the folks in town, she felt comfortable; it was the travelers who knew nothing of her unusual colored eyes. They had been appalled. Clyde would often protect her by moving in front of her, leading her as they walked.

Lettie normally didn't wear make-up, but this was an especially important day for her and Clyde. She pulled out the curlers from her white hair, brushed her short hair until it laid curling around her face, and fluffed her bangs with the comb. She then applied the dark rose lipstick to her pale lips. Pressing them together, she smiled at herself in the mirror. She did look better with a little make-up and color on, not so faded and old. Lastly, she sprayed a little perfume on her wrists and each side of her neck.

Clyde came into their bedroom, looking for a handkerchief in his dresser drawer. "Are you ready, Lettie? We need to go. I'll bring the car around front," he said glancing at her. "You look nice."

Her heart swelled with happiness at her adorable, devoted husband. They had been married now for forty years. When Clyde retired from the Battle Axe Ranch, they had moved out of the big two-story log house and settled into this small house in Riverside, where they continue to love and take care of each other.

"Yes, I'm ready," said Lettie, rising from the small bench. She thought of seeing her two lady friends whom she had met at the senior center, Charlene and Allie. They had been meeting for tea once a week.

"You don't even have your shoes on," he noticed as he glanced at her stocking feet.

"I know. I'll meet you out in front," she replied, walking to the closet and pulling out her brown shoes. With her old stiff body, she had found it difficult to lean down and tie the laces; thus, sitting on the bed, she slipped her feet into the shoes on the floor, raised each foot up on the bed, and tied the laces.

She heard Clyde, now in his eighties, leave their small house, closing the front door. Her handsome husband's hair had turned all grey, his face had a weathered-look with deep wrinkles around his sparkling dark brown eyes and around his mouth. His once tall frame now bent a little around his broad shoulders. She never failed to appreciate the man who gave her such a full, exciting life. She silently prayed that they would have many more years together.

Lettie walked over to her dresser, opened one of her drawers, and selected her rose-colored sweater to wear over her white blouse and blue slacks today. Even though it was summer, she chilled easily in the air-cooled rooms at the Riverside Senior Citizen Center downtown. Later, they were driving out to the Johnson Ranch for a barbeque. The mountain air would be cool, for it never got to warm here in the summer months.

Leaving the house, she stepped into the car, smiling at Clyde, "Let's go." She closed the door and slid over next to her husband. They smiled at each other.

He drove down to the front door of the senior center, parking, he turned to her, "I'll pick you up after coffee."

"Yes, don't forget to pick up the sweet bread wrapped up in the fridge at the house before you pick me up. Or we can stop before we leave town," said Lettie.

"I'll take care of it. Enjoy your tea with the ladies," he said, leaning over to give her a kiss.

Kissing Clyde on his soft lips, she whispered, "See you after coffee." She opened the door to leave.

"You even smell good. Maybe, we should drive back home and forget about goin' anywhere," he whispered. She could tell he was joking, but he had often let her know that he still desired her.

"No, dear. We're running a little late. I'll see you later," she replied.

"Don't forget your photo album. It's on the back seat," he reminded her.

"Oh, yes," she said, closing the front car door and opening the back door. She picked up her old album to show her friends a few photographs of her family today. Weeks before they had shared their family photos with her. Her friends had so many interesting stories to tell that she told Clyde many of them when she returned home. Now, today was her turn. She had started this album soon after she had married Clyde which held all her precious memories.

With the many years upon her, her thin tall body moved slowly towards the front door, stiffened by arthritis in her knees and ankles. She turned and glanced at Clyde who drove away, headed down the main street to Bert's Café to meet with a few old ranchers who had coffee from time to time.

Clutching the old album, she recalled their happy but eventful life together at their ranch. It seemed like yesterday that they had gotten married at the court house in Midler. Before meeting Clyde, she had been headed towards spinsterhood with her dual colored eyes and no prospects of marriage. But he had proposed. Yes, she laughed to herself—a business deal. And with a whirlwind of passionate love, his business idea quickly turned into a forty-year love affair that hadn't dimmed. In their old age, time seemed to move so much faster now. A day and then a week disappeared in a flash.

Smiling at her two friends, she moved slowly toward the table which held three cups, with tea bags, and a plate of cookies.

"Morning, ladies," said Lettie, smiling as she placed the album on the table, pulled out a chair, and sat down. Both ladies greeted her.

Charlene, a large eighty-year-old woman with grey hair and a warm smile, said, "I baked us some peanut butter cookies. I hope you like them." She had been widowed nearly five years ago and came to the center to meet others and participate in some of their activities, particularly bingo.

"Oh, that's so nice of you. I love cookies," replied Lettie.

"I'll get us some hot water for tea," said Allie, a thin, but sad widow of seventy. Her husband Stan had passed away last year. It had been heartbreaking for Allie, living without her husband. She had a daughter Joyce who lived on a nearby ranch with her husband and family. They would come to town as often as they could and visit with her. But it was the senior center that had provided many services to help her deal with her sorrowful situation. She came for the activities. Meeting Lettie and Charlene had eased her loneliness, for each week they had shared past stories and future plans.

Rising, Allie took the three cups and went over to the little kitchen area that had a pot of hot water. After coming back, the ladies all put a tea bag into each of their cups, letting it brew while they talked about their week.

"Umm. These are really a treat. I haven't baked for some time. Maybe, next week, I'll bake something for our tea," said Allie, smiled with a toothless grin, dipping her cookie into the tea before eating it.

"Let's look at your pictures," said Charlene, pointing to Lettie's old album.

Lettie had finished a cookie and said, "Okay. But, first, I need to tell you that I started as a housekeeper for the Battle Axe Ranch and now, forty years later, I'm still with the man that I worked for."

The other two laughed and nodded while they sipped their tea. Lettie rose and moved into a position where her friends could view the photos. Opening the book to the first page, she showed them her and Clyde's wedding photograph at the court house in Midler.

"We were married by the justice of the peace," she said.

"My you both look so young," commented Charlene, glancing at the picture.

"Yes, don't we. My, how time flies," replied Lettie, thinking of that day and recalling her navy wool suit that she wore. Turning the page of the album, she pointed to another wedding photo.

"This is Clyde's oldest son's wedding picture with Chet and Sophie. She was from Scottsville and had a college degree but knew absolutely nothing about ranching. We got along well with each other, and I helped her adjust to her new ranch life. Chet adored her and soon, they raised three sons and a daughter. But what's really amazing is that Sophie loved quarter horses. She convinced Chet, Clyde, and Fred to raise them. They did and it turned out a great addition to the ranch. They sold many to the ranchers around here. Their quarter horses became known state-wide."

Charlene spoke up, "I think my husband Val bought a couple of their horses when he ran one of the ranches. They were good cutting horses." Lettie nodded, surprised. Charlene explained that her husband had worked for several ranchers while they were married. She had worked cleaning rooms at the various motels until they retired.

"I wasn't involved with that side of the ranch, but Clyde may remember your husband. We had so many guests coming and going during the summer and fall that I didn't keep track of the horse business. But I'll ask him. Oh, there's my border collie Maggie sitting in front of everyone," replied Lettie. She then pointed to another picture in the album.

She continued, "And here is Fred, Clyde's older brother who was a rodeo man, following the circuit around the country from here to Texas to California. When he came home after weeks away, he would boast of the broncs he rode, the steers he roped, and at nighttime, bragging about the cowgirls he danced and partied with. His nickname at the rodeos was 'Lucky' since he won so many events. The last time he went rodeoing, he got kicked in the head by a steer, and ended up in a hospital with stitches. It nearly put him in the ground, but Fred came home saying that he met a really nice nurse but couldn't remember her name. A year later, that nurse Lucinda showed up in Riverside, looking for him. They were married shortly after. She's standing next to him," pointing to the photo.

"Oh my, what a wild story," said Allie, smiling her toothless grin again.

"She looks awfully young. How old was she?" asked Charlene.

"Yes, she was about five years younger. They raised two sons and one was in an accident. That was so sad," whispered Lettie, thinking of how busted up Fred's son Joe was. He had been returning from a rodeo late at night, fell asleep at the wheel, and crashed. They had to put down his horse who was in the trailer behind his pickup. The family took the loss of the horse hard, but thankfully, Joe had only sustained a few broken ribs and a concussion.

"Wait. I clipped that article in the newspaper years ago. Did he crash near Grady's ranch?" said Allie, frowning with her brows.

"Yes, that was Fred's boy Joe," replied Lettie, nodding her head.

"My, there was the McClure boy killed in a crash," added Charlene, sadly shaking her head.

"Yes, and I recalled that Henry Hudson and his wife crashed and died, too," said Allie, recalling the tragic and sudden deaths.

Wanting to change the topic, Lettie continued with, "Now, Fred was the one who hired me as housekeeper. Later, he took over the guide business at the ranch, making the contacts and scheduling the fishing and hunting trips. Those three small cabins at our ranch were seldom empty in the summer and fall. I cleaned and kept fresh linens on the beds ready for guests who stayed with us. I never saw such resourceful men as those Fletcher's," said Lettie, thinking of her busy life at the ranch.

She also recalled Fred's kindness that he had shown her over the years. He had taken care of his younger brother Clyde when they lost their parents. The two brothers were very close. Fred was devoted and dedicated to keeping the two of them together and continued supporting the family when Clyde married his first wife Beth (who died) and when Clyde married her. In fact, Lettie realized that Fred had set them up.

Tapping her finger at another photo of a tall younger man, Lettie continued, "Here is Clyde's youngest son Tom who was a great basketball player in high school. He continued to play with a scholarship to the state university. He married Carter's youngest daughter Melanie and they raised a son and a daughter. He took over the guide business at the ranch after Fred retired. Fred's son Everett works with him."

Lettie took a sip of her tea while Charlene and Allie looked at the photo.

"My, he's so handsome. I know the Carter's at the Double D Ranch. Old Mr. Carter was always calling the sheriff on those young kids dragging their cars by his ranch along the highway," said Allie, adding to their conversation. Picking up another cookie, she dunked it into her tea and munched on the soften cookie with her toothless gums.

"Yes, when he was young, Matt here, raced his fast cars. He had a red Corvette, and later a blue Chevy. I heard that he got a ticket once for drag racing out there," said Lettie, laughing and pointing to a photo of another wedding picture. "Here's his wedding picture. He married Torrie McClure. You know the McClure's who run the gas station and garage here in town. Well, they raised two sons and a daughter. But he and Torri left the ranch and went to the university. Matt became a teacher and is now living in Montana."

While the ladies looked over the picture, Lettie picked up a peanut butter cookie and took a bite. She had only a few more pictures to show them. Turning the next couple of pages, she stopped at a big photo.

"Now, here. Look at this one of the Severson's family at the Norsemen Ranch," said Lettie. Feeling a chill in the room, she pulled her sweater around her neck and buttoned it. There was a blower cooling the room.

"Oh, there's Dr. Carter who married Anna," said Charlene. "We were sure lucky to have him here. He was a good doctor." Everyone knew the doctor with his small office downtown and his other office in Winston, providing essential medical services to many people. They also recalled the widow Anna with her four children.

"I remember when Anna's husband was mauled by that grizzly bear. We were scared out of our wits until Wyatt Gordon finally killed it. I read it in the papers. The ladies at our church cooked a couple of dinners to take out to their ranch during their tragedy. The town couldn't believe it," said Allie, recalling sad incident.

"Yes, here's their eight children, four from her first marriage and four with the doctor. Their sons are running the Norsemen Ranch now. Here's Bridget who raised one of my border collie's pups. She named her pup Dwarfy and then later raised another collie name Loki. The two sisters Bridget and Heidi were such cute little girls. They've grown up and married. Their grandfather Hans died the year that they bought the Norsemen Ranch, but Ingrid lived six years after he passed away. Anna took over the ranch and after marrying Doc Carter, they ran the ranch together. He certainly was a busy man with doctoring and ranching at the same time." The two ladies leaned closer to see the picture.

Lettie continued, "Now, Hans' ancestors were the ones who first built and developed our Battle Axe Ranch. His ancestors came from Norway and Sweden. I heard the stories about their Scandinavian skills with the broad-head axe who came to cut down the big pine trees and make ties for the railroad when it first came across the country. The men were known as tie hacks and lived in camps in the mountains provided by the lumber companies. There's quite a long history about them. You've seen the monument on the bluff above Rock River. Most of them returned home, but some stayed and settled, like Hans' relatives. And I found out later, that my ancestor Liam Olsson came here and knew them," She paused, "With his skills, Hans along with others from town helped repair our log house at the Battle Axe Ranch when that fire nearly destroyed it," added Lettie.

"My husband was part of the town's volunteer fire department. Of course, just about every able-bodied man in the area was a volunteer," said Charlene as she bit down on one of her cookies. She thought how much she missed her husband Val who had worked hard wrangling at various ranches and had devoted himself to volunteering on the side. She had worried about him each time when he would get a call, jump in his pickup, and take off. The fire at the Battle Axe Ranch had been late at night and they were lucky to save the log house with only one side damaged. The Fletcher's came later to find the house saved. Clyde Fletcher himself shook her husband's hand and thanked him. Val never tired of volunteering until he died.

Lettie turned to the last few pages of her old album. Here were the pictures of her and Clyde's family. Pointing to a single photo of three, she said, "Here's my oldest son Erik named after my father. This is his brother Freddie who we named after Clyde's brother. They are both married and have each two children. Standing in the middle is my lovely daughter Daisy. She is married and lives in Scottsville with her three children." Lettie's heart swelled at glancing at her three children. Clyde had granted her wish to become a mother, even though he had panicked each time she told him that she was pregnant. He had a deep-seeded fear and concern that something terrible would happen to her or the babies, but she only experienced morning sickness for a short time and the deliveries took place without incident.

"They are all so beautiful kids. How many grandkids do you have?" asked Charlene who had five.

"We have eleven," replied Lettie, counting them silently to herself before answering.

"I have just six and can barely keep up with them. How do you keep track of all of them?" asked Allie.

"That is quite a task for us, but I keep a birthday book along with an address book. My daughter and her husband have moved around. We don't call, but I do write," replied Lettie, closing her album and glancing at her wrist watch.

"I certainly am falling behind with my family," admitted Allie. "I should get organized like you are. That might help me."

The three sat for a few minutes, finishing their tea. Lettie rose and scooted her chair back in place. Charlene slid the old album over to Lettie.

"Do either of you have photos of your grandkids?" asked Lettie.

"Yes, but not in an album," replied Allie. "They're just in a drawer."

"I do," replied Charlene. "Should we plan to bring them next time?"

"Yes, let's. Bring your photos and I'll bring mine," said Lettie, thinking of the other photos of their grandchildren. Some were in another album, but many still needed to be added. They were stuffed in a shoe box in her closet. She should get them down before next week, sort them, and arrange them in that album that she had started some time ago.

Hearing someone open the center's door, they all turned to see Clyde step into the senior center and walk towards their table. Smiling, Lettie rose to meet him.

With his hand on his black cowboy hat, he said, "Hello, ladies." They both replied as he turned to Lettie, "Are you ready my dear?"

"Yes," she said, "Goodbye. See you next week," smiling to her friends.

Clyde again nodded at the two ladies, picked up the old album, and carried it as Lettie slipped her hand into his other arm as he guided her out the door.

Slowly, they came to the car, got in, and Clyde said with a glint of excitement in his eyes, "Let's go to the barbeque. Our family will be joining us there. Can't wait to talk to the boys about the ranch."

Lettie smiled as she slid next to her husband who drove them out of town towards the Johnson Ranch situated in a lush green pastured-valley surrounded by the wild blue, forested mountains.

About the Author

JMC North (Joanna) **author/ writer** / is a retired Assist. Prof. of English. Born in Wyoming and raised in small towns. Taught for 30 years in Colorado and Wyoming. Has been a drama director, a scriptwriter, and a pianist. Proud honorary member of Phi Kappa Phi and Wyoming Writers. With family, traveled America from coast to coast. Studied in Oslo, Norway, toured the other Scandinavian countries, and cruised the Mediterranean islands and countries. Taught composition, mythology, epic poems, gothic novels, dramatic literature, and folklore.

View all of my books: www.amazon.com/author/jmcnorth

A Note from the Author

Dear Reader:

Thank you for reading my book. I enjoyed writing about the six women's stories who were connected in some way to the *Battle Axe Ranch Trilogy*. The men also played a key role in their lives. This collection reveals the romance, betrayal, friendship, grief, and death that these women with their families faced in their lives.

Share: If you liked the book, please tell a friend or relative who might enjoy reading it.

Review: Please consider posting a short review. Honest reader reviews will help others to decide whether they would enjoy the book.

Contact: I love hearing from readers. Click on the FOLLOW button to keep in touch. See JMC North @ Goodreads, BookBub, Facebook, and Twitter.

Books by JMC North

Battle Axe Ranch Trilogy

Battle Axe Ranch: Book 1
An adventurous romance story of the Fletcher family caught up in a cultural clash of the '60's. Young Matt drives a red sports car-- the Red Devil--and attempts to escape his father's ranching demands. The family faces the hard challenge of running a Wyoming ranch with its predators set against the rugged Rockies. An emotional journey of the young seeking thrills, friendship, love, and acceptance.

Tempered by Fate: Book 2
A continuation of the *Battle Axe Ranch Trilogy* with the Fletchers struggling to improve their lives amid the backdrop of the wild and rugged Rockies. Set in the '60's, the family deals with new twists and turns of fate, new romances and love, friendships, rumors, and betrayal. Complicated conflicts continue and surprising experiences arise. Experiences that give readers insight to areas they may not have traveled themselves.

Fortified with Love: Book 3
The end of the *Battle Axe Ranch Trilogy* reveals the Fletchers in the'60's are faced with battles against the wildness and dangerous predators of the Rockies. The individuals confront real life challenges in their romances, loves, friendships, betrayals, deaths, and grief. Unexpected conflicts arise that are resolved with surprising outcomes.

Sisterhood of Hermia
Six women, each at various stages of life, encounter experiences that challenge them. This collection examines their vulnerabilities and their strengths as they face the joys and the heartbreaks of their circumstances. The characters come from the *Battle Axe Ranch Trilogy.* The *Sisterhood* expands their individual stories.

<u>*Frankenstein:*</u>
A Reader's Theater Script Adapted from the Novel

This gothic story is a psychological journey into a ghoulish world. The reader's theater script is adapted from Mary Shelley's *Frankenstein, or the Modern Prometheus*. It features the major themes, main characters, settings, and important events of the novel for a mature audience. Written for twelve main characters, the script portrays the infamous story of Victor Frankenstein and his Creature. The performance runs about an hour. Intermission would add to that time.

Made in the USA
Columbia, SC
23 December 2021

52262482R00180